P9-BYB-334

Praise for Linda O. Johnston

"In this exciting continuation of the Alpha Force story line, Quinn is a likable character, both sexy and strong, and Kristine's clever moves in crisis show an intelligence that will appeal to readers."
—*RT Book Reviews* on *Undercover Wolf*

"Ms. Johnston has a winner on her hands with this installment of the Alpha Force series."
—*Fresh Fiction* on *Undercover Wolf*

"*Back to Life* is a crafty tale, where the unseen paranormal element packs a powerful punch. Ms. Johnston gives readers a strong romantic suspense with life or death situations, and adds a sizzling dose of chemistry to heat up the pages."
—*Darque Reviews*

Praise for Linda Thomas-Sundstrom

"Linda Thomas-Sundstrom's well-written, action-packed novel will keep readers entertained from start to finish... A compelling page turner!"
—*RT Book Reviews* on *Guardian of the Night*

"Great vampire romance that will wrap you into a story that you will not want to put down. Tension and tragedy, pain, and unresolved emotions, are a part of this couple's soulful journey... Linda Thomas-Sundstrom has written a thrilling vampire novel."
—*www.NightOwlReviews.com* on *Golden Vampire*

"Thomas-Sundstrom combines strong characters and nonstop action for a terrific read."
—*RT Book Reviews* on *Red Wolf*

LINDA O. JOHNSTON

Linda O. Johnston loves to write. While honing her writing skills, she worked in advertising and public relations, then became a lawyer…and enjoyed writing contracts. Linda's first published fiction appeared in *Ellery Queen's Mystery Magazine* and won a Robert L. Fish Memorial Award for Best First Mystery Short Story of the Year. Linda now spends most of her time creating memorable tales of paranormal romance, romantic suspense and mystery. Visit www.lindaojohnston.com.

LOYAL WOLF

AND

IMMORTAL OBSESSION

Linda O. Johnston

and

Linda Thomas-Sundstrom

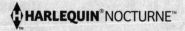

If you purchased this book without a cover you should be aware that this book is stolen property. It was reported as "unsold and destroyed" to the publisher, and neither the author nor the publisher has received any payment for this "stripped book."

Recycling programs
for this product may
not exist in your area.

ISBN-13: 978-0-373-60673-3

Loyal Wolf and Immortal Obsession

Copyright © 2014 by Harlequin Books S.A.

The publisher acknowledges the copyright holder
of the individual works as follows:

Loyal Wolf
Copyright © 2014 by Linda O. Johnston

Immortal Obsession
Copyright © 2014 by Linda Thomas-Sundstrom

All rights reserved. Except for use in any review, the reproduction or utilization of this work in whole or in part in any form by any electronic, mechanical or other means, now known or hereinafter invented, including xerography, photocopying and recording, or in any information storage or retrieval system, is forbidden without the written permission of the publisher, Harlequin Enterprises Limited, 225 Duncan Mill Road, Don Mills, Ontario, Canada, M3B 3K9.

This is a work of fiction. Names, characters, places and incidents are either the product of the author's imagination or are used fictitiously, and any resemblance to actual persons, living or dead, business establishments, events or locales is entirely coincidental.

This edition published by arrangement with Harlequin Books S.A.

For questions and comments about the quality of this book, please contact us at CustomerService@Harlequin.com.

® and TM are trademarks of the publisher. Trademarks indicated with ® are registered in the United States Patent and Trademark Office, the Canadian Intellectual Property Office and in other countries.

HARLEQUIN®
www.Harlequin.com

Printed in U.S.A.

CONTENTS

LOYAL WOLF
Linda O. Johnston

Loyal Wolf is dedicated to shape-shifters and the readers who love them!

And also to my husband, Fred, who, though not a writer, is an excellent sounding board for plot issues.

Chapter 1

Deputy Sheriff Kathlene Baylor steered down the narrow, tree-lined lane toward the entrance to Clifford Cabins, a rustic motel a few miles out of town. She was driving her personal car, a silver SUV, rather than an official Clifford County, Montana, Sheriff's Department vehicle, despite being in uniform. It was late afternoon, and she was off duty. If she'd had time to go home and change, she would have.

But she was too eager for the pending meeting to incur any further delay.

This outing was definitely not an official activity, though. In fact, it was just the opposite. Even though it should look, to anyone who might be paying attention to her, as if she was just dashing off to go meet up with an old friend.

Not quite.

Kathlene always considered herself a by-the-book, dedicated law-enforcement officer. But that was before.

Now she was too concerned about what was going on in Clifford County to do nothing, even though her boss, Sheriff Melton Frawley, was certain that she was wrong. That she was "worrying her pretty little head about nothing," was the way he put it.

She sniffed at the very thought of the way the whole department was encouraged by Melton to return to old, antiquated ways, when women weren't skilled and respected officers of the law, but handy cooks and cleaners who also entertained their men in bed.

She would have complained, claimed discrimination to the County Counsel, the City Attorney of Cliffordsville, or anyone else who would listen. Problem was, no one with any clout cared.

Well, maybe she had no clout, but she wasn't about to just sit there and let her county be overrun by anarchists.

She slowed down when she saw a small deer darting through the underbrush toward the road. Good move, she thought as the animal stopped, then leaped back into the woods. She wasn't a hunter but there were a lot of them around. Some legitimate.

The others were the ones who worried her.

At least their encampment was a few more miles down this road. And that deer—plus, much more important, the humans around here—might survive if what she believed was true, and the people she was going to see helped her do something about it.

There. She had reached the sign identifying the winding drive to the Clifford Cabins. She turned and headed toward them.

She'd received a call. Help had arrived.

She only hoped they would really figure out what was going on—and the situation was thereafter fixed appropriately.

* * *

A knock sounded on the cabin door. Right on time, Lieutenant Jock Larabey thought.

"Want me to get it?" His aide, Staff Sergeant Ralf Nunnoz, glanced toward Jock. Like his superior officer, he was dressed casually, with no indication that either one of them was in the military, let alone part of Alpha Force. Ralf had on well-worn jeans with a Seattle Seahawks T-shirt, since they were supposed to have driven from Washington State to drop in and see Jock's supposed long-term friend Kathlene Baylor before heading for Yellowstone National Park. Ralf's hair was short, of course, as was Jock's, but there was no other indication of their background.

"You're sure Click is hidden well?" Jock asked. He didn't want his cover dog seen, particularly this early in the assignment.

All Alpha Force shapeshifting members had cover dogs that resembled them in their changed forms, and Click looked a lot like a wolf, which was ideal. Jock was a werewolf.

"He's locked in the cabin next door with some beef jerky treats to keep him occupied for now." Even though Kathlene had reserved this cabin on their behalf, Jock had Ralf book another one next door in case they needed additional space. And cover. Like now.

"Good. Then let her in."

Ralf approached the wide wooden door attached to the cabin's fake log walls and opened it. "Jock?" said a woman's voice in a low, husky tone.

"You must be Jock's friend Kathlene," Ralf said more loudly, obviously in case there was anyone outside eavesdropping. "Come in. I'm his good friend Ralf Nunnoz."

"Good to meet you, Ralf." The female voice was louder now, too. Higher in tone, as well, in her apparent embarrassment.

The woman who had to be Kathlene Baylor, deputy sheriff of the local Montana county and seeker of Alpha Force help, walked in the door, looked around and approached Jock.

Not that she truly knew what Alpha Force was about. Jock was certain of that.

"Hi," she said, sounding relieved now as Ralf shut the door behind her. "Jock? I'm Kathlene."

"Good to see you, buddy," he said, donning their cover as if it was who they all truly were. He strode over to the woman and, ignoring her unappealing law-enforcement uniform, gave her a big hug.

She was tall, though not as tall as he was. She was slender. And those curves—his body reacted immediately as if their cover was that they were long-separated lovers instead of friends.

Hell, if he had known her in the past they would have been more than friends. He'd have had sex with her as fast as he could have seduced her.

Then.

But not now. They had a joint mission to accomplish. One that, if she was correct about what was going on around here, definitely needed Alpha Force's unique touch to straighten it out. And if Kathlene found out the truth about him, he felt sure that making love with him would be the last thing she would ever want.

Unless his seduction could convince her otherwise…

She backed up. Quickly. Her face was flushed. She was one good-looking woman, despite how severely her dark hair was pulled back from those reddened cheeks.

That face didn't need adornment. It was smooth, with sexy, full lips and sparkling eyes that peered out from beneath black brows that helped to frame them.

Her gray uniform wasn't the sexiest thing he had ever seen a woman wear—and yet Kathlene filled it out in all the right places. A definitely appealing bustline—as he had felt pressed against him. A small waist.

Of course the holster she wore at her hip didn't exactly turn him on, but it went with the rest of her gear. He wondered where her weapon was, figured she'd locked it up since she wasn't currently on duty, or so he assumed.

But admiring her—or not—wasn't why Ralf and he had come.

Right now he needed to get this woman's description of what was going on here.

And then Alpha Force could get to work.

Jock Larabey. Her old college buddy. Or so the rest of the world should believe.

The guy did look military, muscles bulging from beneath his snug University of Montana T-shirt. It appeared that he had indeed come here prepared to play the cover-story role they had decided on. They were supposed to have gone to the U of M, Missoula campus, at the same time and become friends there.

That was, in fact, the part of the state where she had grown up. And then had her life turned utterly upside down, when her parents—

No. She wouldn't think about that now. It was why she hadn't actually remained friends with people she had known back then, but she didn't tell anyone that.

And at the moment, she had something a lot more pressing to think about. But she hadn't expected someone as hot-looking as this man, with his wide shoulders, chiseled face and sexy hint of pale brown facial hair. His piercing hazel eyes surveyed her as if assessing whether she, too, was all she was cracked up to be. She forced herself to smile and was rewarded with a grin that suggested he had been assessing more than that about her.

And that hug? Appropriate for the situation, sure, but it had set her insides very inappropriately on fire.

She had to back away from those kinds of thoughts. Cool off. Or at least try to.

"We need to talk, Kathlene," Jock said.

She glanced toward the door. It was closed, and the other man, Ralf, stood nearby. They could, in fact, talk now.

"I know what the story is that you described to get Alpha Force's interest," Jock continued, "but I want to hear it directly from you."

"Of course."

This could take a while. She glanced around for someplace to sit. This cabin was as rustic in here as it was outside. Near one wall there were a couple of narrow beds with green plaid blankets, pale green sheets and pillows with matching covers.

Beds? Her mind again darted to that hug and the feel of his body against her. She quickly looked away.

In one corner was a kitchenette, and beside it a small table with two chairs. Should she sit there with Jock to go over the situation? Safer than anywhere near the beds, of course.

But what about Ralf?

Good thing he was still around. That also helped Kathlene focus on what was important, and not how her libido had been stoked.

Ralf stood near Jock, arms crossed, watching her. He
was shorter than Jock and not quite as muscular, but he,
too, looked strong. The gray in his black hair was surprising since he didn't look older than mid-thirties, only
a few years older than Kathlene. Ralf's facial features
were wide and suggested, like his last name, a Hispanic
background. Like Jock, his casual outfit didn't even hint
that he was currently in the military and on assignment.

Jock must have caught her indecision. He gestured
with one muscular arm toward the table. "You and I can
sit there, and Ralf will hang out near us."

Ralf strode toward the nearest wall and leaned against
it, arms crossed over his chest. It appeared that he was
used to taking orders from Jock. All Kathlene had been
told about them was that they were members of a covert
military unit called Alpha Force, her "friend" Jock was
a lieutenant and he would be accompanied by a noncom-
missioned officer.

She only hoped that the two of them could at least
provide whatever juice was needed to bring in more help
if needed.

And she expected it would be.

For now she, like Ralf, followed the sort-of instructions that Jock gave and sat at the table.

And decided how best to begin this conversation.

Jock sent Ralf to the kitchen area to grab bottles of
water for all of them. Until he rejoined them, this would
be a good time to learn Kathlene's background.

Like, did she believe in shapeshifters?

He laughed internally at the thought. That was a question that would never get asked.

As she spoke, she told him she had always lived in Montana, moving from Missoula after college.

Despite their cover story, Jock had never been in Montana before. He had grown up in Wisconsin, another state where there were more rural areas than city life. Where wilderness was the primary topography.

That was where his family had settled long ago. The remoteness helped to hide what they were. But what he was had made him gravitate toward the U.S. Military as soon as he first heard of Alpha Force.

Ralf returned and placed a bottle of water on the smooth but unpolished wooden table before each of them.

"Here's to our success in resolving the Clifford County situation," Jock said, raising his bottle.

"I'll drink to that," Kathlene said. Ralf joined them in their alcohol-free toast. The look on Kathlene's face nevertheless appeared strained, as if she doubted they in fact would be successful.

If so, he intended to surprise her. In many ways.

Right now it was time to really get down to business. And talk.

And make sure he ignored how much lust he felt for this lovely, obviously determined woman.

Kathlene started their conversation after downing a drink of water. "I chose this motel for you to stay in," she said, "because the former ranch where the people I believe are anarchists are gathering isn't far from here."

"Yes, the anarchists," Jock said. "Why we're here. I'd like you to tell us why you think that's who they are. I've looked at the file that was started on this matter before Alpha Force was called in, but as I said I want your version."

"Of course." She seemed to hesitate, but only for a second. And there was nothing at all hesitant in the strong, sure glare of her blue eyes. "I could be wrong about the whole thing but I don't think so. The number of people at the apparent conclave, all men as far as I can tell, keep increasing. They stay mostly to themselves but when I've headed in the direction of the formerly abandoned ranch where they live, I've sometimes heard gunshots."

"It's late summer," Ralf said from behind them. "Isn't it hunting season for something?"

"The season for large game like elk, moose and all tends to start in late September. But when any members of this group have come into town, they seem to make it a point of saying they've been holding target practice to be ready when the season starts."

"That target practice could also be with the intent of hunting more than wildlife," Jock said.

Like people?

That was the crux of their involvement here. They would find out about what these hunters, or whatever they were, were up to.

And stop them if necessary.

Perhaps in the form of an animal they otherwise would hunt.

A wolf.

Jock glanced at Ralf, who nodded. He undoubtedly knew exactly what Jock was thinking.

The sudden glance between Jock and Ralf stoked Kathlene's curiosity. This man wasn't a fan of hunting? His look of displeasure actually pleased Kathlene. She might have gone into law enforcement, but her intent was to save as many lives as possible, human and animal.

Especially human. That was the reason she had become a deputy sheriff. She knew more than most people what it was like to lose loved ones to unanticipated and unnecessary violence.

"What about wolves?" Ralf asked. "Are they fair game?"

"Yes, sometimes," Kathlene said. "I'm not sure what the season for them is this year."

"Oh," Jock said.

Kathlene couldn't quite figure out what his tone meant—irony? Anger? A challenge of some kind?

But she had been saving her biggest concern for last. "It's not only multiple rounds of gunshots I've heard near that old ranch area," she said. "And I think this is what actually got the military's attention. There have been explosions, too. Small ones, but more than just shots being fired."

Her boss, the sheriff, had only shaken his head when she'd mentioned them. Told her she had one hell of a female imagination.

In essence, told her to bug off and maybe respond to some phone calls from senior citizens who called the cops claiming they heard things because they wanted some attention.

Like she supposedly was doing despite her lesser age.

"Interesting," Jock said. He asked her questions—cogent ones that indicated he actually believed her, which made her feel a lot better than it should.

But she managed to explain her own patrol duties—both assigned by the department and assumed by herself because of her concern about the growing number of apparent hunters hanging out at the old ranch that had been unused for years but apparently had been purchased recently by a relative of one of the men now living there, according to public records. Or at least it had been purchased by someone with the last name Tisal, but not Nate Tisal, the guy who apparently was in charge of the group.

"If anything, they could be terrorists and not also anarchists," she said, "but when I've spoken with any of them, which is rare, their comments suggest that they hate any kind of authority, not only local."

"If they're either," Jock said, "we need to confirm it and shut them down before anyone's hurt."

"Definitely," Kathlene said. "One thing I'm particularly concerned about is that there have been threats made against at least some of the Clifford County Commissioners. A friend of mine who's a commissioner told me about some anonymous emails with sources that couldn't be traced, as well as actual letters mailed to the County Administration Building from other parts of the country. They apparently tell the commission to back off from enacting some laws currently under consideration that would help enforce state regulations to protect wildlife and require the arrest of poachers. The sheriff said he's got some officers looking into it but nothing's been found so far. It's not certain that the anarchists are to blame, of course—but with the timing and all, that's my suspicion."

"Got it," Jock said. "We'll look into that, too. Right now, though, let's go over our cover story."

"Yeah," Ralf said. He'd been leaning against the cabin wall beside the table sipping water. "Jock's your old buddy, and we're both insurance salesmen from Seattle, which is where Jock supposedly lives these days, too. Don't we look like insurance salesmen?" He mugged a little toward Kathlene and she laughed.

"'Course we do," Jock said. "Risk and liability and all that kind of stuff, right?"

"Right," Ralf responded. "And high premiums, too."

Both men laughed this time. Great. They apparently had a good working relationship. But Kathlene hadn't figured out what Alpha Force was and why it was considered a particularly special military team.

Good thing she had made friends in college with Bill Grantham, whose dad had been an army colonel then. Now he was a general working at the Pentagon. Kathlene, frustrated and not knowing what else to do, had wound up explaining her concerns to Bill about what was going on in Clifford County. General Grantham had listened, then suggested sending in help to scope out their validity. The result had been the deployment here of members of this covert unit. But why Alpha Force? What was Alpha Force all about? Kathlene had no idea…yet. But she would definitely learn.

"You'll need to explain insurance to me one of these days," she made herself joke. Then she got serious. "And also about what your special unit's all about and how you'll be dealing with the situation here."

"Sure," Jock responded. "Once we've done our recon and we see what we're actually up against."

But why was it that Kathlene had the sense that the last thing that hot, amusing, obviously determined Jock Larabey wanted to do was to let her know what Alpha Force was really about?

"I'll give you my schedule," she told them. "I'll want to be with you as much as possible."

"No need," Jock said. "We'll handle it."

She glanced at him. He was sharing a look with Ralf that clearly excluded her. What weren't they saying?

"My participation, helping out? That's part of the plan," she said coolly.

"Not exactly."

"Yes, exactly."

He just glared at her, but only for a moment before moving on as if she hadn't spoken. "Now, as I started to say, we're here from Seattle, which is where we ostensibly live. Right now we're here visiting my old buddy Kathlene on our way to tour Yellowstone once we've done some sightseeing and real camping around here. We love this area, though, and will explore it for fun— or that's what it'll look like. But we'll do some nosing around to find out more about it. That will include where you indicate your anarchists are living."

"Fine," she said. "I unfortunately don't have vacation time I can take right now but I'll visit you a lot here at the cabin, camp out with you on nights when I don't have to report for duty early the next day. And—"

"No, not necessary. We'll hang out in town with you some of the time, get together for lunch or dinner in public, that kind of thing. We're the ones here undercover, and we'll handle all the covert investigation stuff. No need for you to get involved."

Kathlene felt herself rise to a half stand. Her shoulders were tense. Her whole body was stiff, in fact.

Was this man telling her, as her boss, the sheriff, did, that women had no place in down and dirty law-enforcement matters—maybe just pushing paper or bringing coffee?

If that was what he wasn't saying—but meant—Jock Larabey was going to learn that exactly the opposite was true.

Especially with her.

Chapter 2

Kathlene decided not to push the point with this man. Not yet. Instead, she suggested that she give them a quick tour of Cliffordsville.

Even though they must have driven through the town to get here, she could give them a different perspective on it, both as a resident and a peace officer.

Not to mention being the person who thought the town—and possibly way beyond—needed help.

"Sounds like a good idea," Jock said, and Ralf agreed.

They concurred that Kathlene should drive them. Her chauffeuring them around would help substantiate their cover of Jock being an old friend of hers.

"Kathlene and I are going to talk a little bit first," Jock told Ralf as they reached her car. "Why don't you meet us at the front gate to this place? You won't mind stopping there for a minute, will you, Kathlene?"

The cabin-filled motel area was surrounded by a decorative wooden fence, with a gate near the office that was almost always open. "No, that's fine," Kathlene said, although she wondered what was really going on after the two men exchanged looks that appeared to hold a brief, silent conversation. Some Alpha Force business that they weren't going to tell her about?

If so, that was okay—for now. But it made her even more determined to learn what they really were about.

She looked in the rearview mirror after backing her vehicle out of its space in front of the row of cabins where these men were staying. Only a few other cars were around, including a black, nondescript sedan, which, considering its proximity to their cabin, was the one she assumed they had come in.

She glanced again into the mirror after aiming her SUV toward the entrance and saw that Ralf still stood there, apparently waiting for her to leave the area before doing whatever he and Jock had communicated about.

That only piqued her curiosity all the more.

"So how long have you lived in Cliffordsville?" Jock asked as she drove slowly toward the parking area near the entrance.

"About six years," she said, glancing toward the hot-looking man who was getting her to think about sex a whole lot more than she had in ages. Well, she could think about it all she wanted. But the only action around here would be the impending demise of the anarchist group if it presented the kind of threat she believed it did.

"Did you live in Missoula before you went to college there?"

"Yes." She knew her voice sounded curt with that answer, but he was now edging too close to topics she refused to discuss. Like her childhood and background. Sex? Hah. She was now being turned off by this man thanks to his chosen topic of conversation.

They passed three other rows of identical cabins before reaching the much larger one that served as the reception area and offices. She pulled into a space nearest the exit gate and parked.

To preclude Jock's continuing her interrogation, she decided it was time for one of her own. "So tell me about Alpha Force," she said.

His craggy, handsome face seemed to shutter, but only for an instant. Then he smiled. "I'm sure you've been told that we're a covert military group, and we can't discuss our methodology with anyone, either other military personnel or civilians."

"But in a situation like this, where I know you've been picked out particularly because of whatever it is you do to look into what's going on here—"

"So did you always know you wanted to go into law enforcement?" His tone was smooth, but his expression was both wry and warning.

He wasn't going to tell her anything.

Well, she wasn't going to tell him anything, either, unless she was sure it would help her cause.

Another car pulled through the gate and parked close to the office. Kathlene pretended to study it.

That was when she saw Ralf approaching on foot from the direction from which they'd driven.

Good. This conversation was clearly over.

Ralf was now ensconced in the backseat. Although Kathlene turned the car toward town as they exited the motel's entrance driveway, she told Jock she would drive them farther along this road on their return—past the entry to the formerly abandoned ranch where the people she believed to be anarchists now lived and multiplied.

"That's where we'll do whatever recon we decide on later," she said. "But I figured I'd get you started by showing you the town and innocently drive past the area on our return to your motel room."

"Thanks," Jock said. "That'll work. And I'd like you to tell us everything you know and suspect so Ralf and I will be able to do our job here."

She heard between the lines. They thought they were going to exclude her.

They weren't.

Right now, as promised, she headed toward town.

As she drove down Main Street, she chatted about Cliffordsville, the shops they passed, the nature of the place before the anarchists had started appearing. They drove along a well-stocked commercial area, with stores ranging from name-brand casual clothes to a men's suit outlet to a variety of restaurants from fast-food to nice, sit-down dining.

Main Street was pretty much a straight line, with a few traffic lights to allow drivers to pull onto it from the myriad side streets, some of which were also commercial, and others led to residential areas.

They didn't drive far enough down it to reach the County Administration Building, City Hall and the Sheriff's Department. The official part of town sat on the outskirts of the business area.

Kathlene liked Cliffordsville. A lot. She had made it her home.

Unlike Missoula, where she had grown up, it held only good memories for her—at least before.

Nothing controversial.

Not till recently, at least.

But her mind veered in different directions from all she was talking about. She was determining how she was going to take a stand and make it clear to Jock that she would participate in the investigation. Period.

"Where do you live?" Jock asked out of the blue. They had just turned down a side street so she could show them some of the closest residential areas—but she hadn't intended to show them her house.

A jolt rocked through her body nonetheless. She knew he wasn't asking to come home with her, yet the idea suddenly heated up her insides as if he had suggested they engage in some down and dirty sex.

Damn. She'd already convinced herself not to feel turned on by this man—hadn't she? She wanted them to be comrades in arms, conspirators in figuring out what was really going on in that odd and growing encampment outside town.

She knew what would turn her off. Fast.

"I own a house in the same general direction we just turned," she told him as casually as she could muster. "It's in a small residential neighborhood within the city limits, though. The cabins where you're staying are in an area considered to be outside town, although still within Clifford County, which means they're within the sheriff's department's jurisdiction." She paused. "As I said before, I'll be spending time with you at your cabin. That'll help us look like the old friends we're supposed to be. I'll also accompany you if you go camping. That way, I'll be able to help in your surveillance."

There. The gauntlet had been thrown down once more, but this time she had given a cursory reason why she should be with them at least part of the time as they worked.

Jock said nothing. But as Kathlene reached Main Street again and stopped for a traffic light, she looked over at him.

He seemed to be staring out the windshield, but his large hands were fisted in his lap. What was he thinking?

She had a feeling she wouldn't like it. But she was dying to know.

The woman was trying to drive him nuts—and not just because she was so hot that he didn't really want to keep his hands off her. But he would. Sex would only complicate things even further.

She had to keep her nose out of what Ralf and he were doing. Hell, Jock knew she had no idea about the facts.

First of all, when he did his surveillance of the supposed anarchists' camp, he wouldn't look like he did at the moment.

No. He would look a lot more like his cover dog, Click. The dog Ralf had gone to check on in the cabin next door before they left their motel.

Click must have been fine, or Ralf would have stayed behind. Or at least said something.

Jock glanced quickly into the backseat. Ralf remained there, of course. Looking all nice and neutral—and interested. But staying out of the conversation.

A good thing? Maybe. But it might be better if his aide participated. Even took over for him. Ralf was good at being discreet, keeping things calm.

Keeping Jock in line, both in human and in wolf form.

At the moment, Jock knew he had to make his position clear with Kathlene. Not give her all the facts. But even though she had been the one to trigger Alpha Force's involvement by taking her concerns to the right government contacts, now she had to stay back and let him do what was necessary—and only with Ralf's help, not hers.

He thought more about Ralf and what he should do. What he should say.

And how their commanding officer, Major Drew Connell—the man who had approved Jock's enlistment into the military and into Alpha Force, the man who had first created the very special elixir that gave Alpha Force's shifting members such an edge over other shapeshifters, other *people*—would handle this.

Discretion is the key, he reminded himself.

He let himself respond to Kathlene's challenge at last.

"I appreciate your offer to help out," he lied, but he did manage to keep his tone calm and level. "The thing is, you may not know it, but Alpha Force's position is that, once we accept a mission, we work alone, without outside help." Another lie, but it made sense, especially now.

"That may work sometimes," Kathlene said, her tone as flat as his, "but not here. Not now. I need to stay involved because I *am* involved."

"But you could get hurt!" Damn. He hadn't meant to blast that out that way. It was what was on his mind, though.

Always. Especially in a situation like this.

"I won't," she countered, her voice raised as much as his. He wanted to grab her and shake some sense into her. But he couldn't. Not with her driving.

Besides, he found Deputy Kathlene Baylor so attractive, so sexy, that touching her again for any reason would be a huge mistake. All he would want to do, despite all his common sense, would be to get her under the covers.

And then what would happen to the mission she had gotten him into?

His attraction to her was a huge part of the problem, though. He couldn't help comparing this lovely, determined woman with Jill, his high school sweetheart.

Jill, a shapeshifter like him.

Jill, who had gone into law enforcement like Kathlene.

And who had been killed during her first year on the job, not while shifted but while in human form on a dangerous assignment.

Would Jill have survived if she'd been a man? If she had been in wolf form? Unlikely, of course, and he knew that even wondering about it allowed him no closure, especially after all this time.

But one thing Jock was sure of. He didn't like it at all when women he felt attracted to got into perilous circumstances. If he happened to be there, he'd save them.

There was no way of his being certain he could be with them at the crucial time, though. He knew what a dinosaur he might be—yet, thanks to what had happened to Jill, he couldn't help thinking it was a lot more foolish of women, even trained ones, to put themselves into hazardous situations than it was for men.

Because they were not physically as strong, they were more likely to get killed.

"Jock?" Her challenging tone shrieked irritation. She was waiting for his further response.

He still said nothing. He wasn't about to explain his beliefs to her—or his rationale for them.

"Jock, tell you what. I appreciate your protective attitude." She sounded anything but appreciative, yet she

continued. "But I'll prove to you that I can take care of
myself. I'm a skilled law-enforcement officer. I've been
trained in everything from accuracy in shooting guns
of nearly all types to hand-to-hand combat. I'm challenging you, Jock. We'll start when we get back to the
cabin. If I can pin you to the floor in a hand-to-hand
fight, then you'll let me be there when you do your surveillance and more."

Silly? Foolish? Absurd to the max? All of the above.
But the challenge had been impulsive, a way to show him
who she was and what she really was made of.

And now? Well, she had no choice. She could do it.
She *would* do it.

Notwithstanding her inability to fully read Jock's expression when he looked at her so incredulously.

There seemed to be an angry set to his brow.

A heated look in his blue eyes that suggested her
words had turned him on.

Since it was now early evening, she went through a
fast-food drive-in lane and they all got their meals, which
they ate in the car. Fine with her. She was on a mission of
sorts and didn't want any further interruptions just now.

Next, she did as she had planned from the moment
they had set out on this drive. She made a left turn at one
of the traffic lights, then drove them onto the narrowing
lane they had come from before.

This time, though, she went beyond where the cabin
motel lay, heading down the road even farther.

There was a sparse number of homes along it, some
tiny, others large, mostly in good condition, but a few
were run-down cottages that had been there forever. All
were set in the midst of large stands of trees, some with

branches carved back to avoid blocking the road and others somewhat in the way.

Eventually, she reached the turnoff she had been looking for, a very narrow, nondescript driveway. No one could tell from this better-traveled drag what lay beyond.

She knew. She had visited it, several times. And had seen the huge chain-link fence that had been built in the middle of nowhere.

Farther down the drive, the guard at the gate had not let her through, claiming that it was private property and everything was fine there. No need for law enforcement's interference...er, help.

"That's the way to the enclave in question." She slowed and pointed in that direction.

"All the way out here?" Ralf leaned forward so his head was between the front seats. "Guess that could make someone suspicious in itself."

Was he questioning her thought processes? Kathlene would have expected that more from Jock—although she really didn't know Ralf any better than she knew her supposed friend from the past.

"But it looks innocent enough," Jock observed.

Okay. No surprise. He was questioning her, too.

"From here, yes," she acknowledged. "Farther along... well, I'm sure you'll see for yourselves soon." *With me along,* she thought, but didn't voice it just then.

Now, though, it was time to go back.

She found the turnoff she was looking for a mile down the road, then maneuvered her SUV to return in the direction from which they'd come.

Once again, they drove along the narrow road with conifers looming overhead—lodgepole pines, junipers, cedars, firs. Every once in a while the blue sky showed through, but the roadway was mostly shaded.

Kathlene knew it would be unpleasant to come here at night, and she hadn't done so…yet. But she suspected she would. Maybe with these Alpha Force men.

Soon they again reached the area where the motel cabins lay. Kathlene smiled grimly to herself, wondering what awaited her here this time.

Was she really going to fight Jock?

Hell, yes, if that was the only way to get him to cooperate.

She had done extremely well as a rookie, training to become a deputy sheriff. She had outfought all of the other would-be deputies, male and female.

Sheriff Frawley had yet to acknowledge her skills—even though she still engaged in training exercises with other deputies more experienced than she was.

Would surprising Jock, toppling him, be enough to convince him?

Even if it didn't, it would certainly improve her frustrated state of mind.

Although, considering how sexy she found the muscular guy staring at the narrow, barely paved road in front of them, it was bound to cause her another kind of frustration.

Jock hadn't actually responded to her dare. But the moment they reached the large cabin at the front of the development that contained the offices, he jumped out.

After one cold stare and shake of his head, he turned away from Kathlene.

Fine with her. She waited until Ralf got out of the backseat. Would he try to talk her out of her challenge?

She'd gathered, from the way the two men interacted,

that Jock was probably the superior-ranking military officer, with Ralf perhaps reporting to him.

That was something else she wanted to know, in addition to what Alpha Force was really about.

How could these men, members of this particular unit, help to figure out what was going on here better than other cops or military members?

Well, if she won their fight, Jock would owe her. He'd have to let her help in their investigation.

And he'd also have to tell her more, including about Alpha Force.

But would he?

He damn well better.

They'd gone back to the cabin. All three of them.

"So…thanks for showing us around, Kathlene," Jock said, finally glancing at her. She'd been helpful, but now it was time for her to go. "We'll get more of the lay of the land tomorrow morning on our own. What's your schedule? Can we meet you for lunch? That'll fit with our cover story."

"Yes," she said curtly. "It will. And I'll be glad to meet you then. But my next day off is Friday, the day after tomorrow. We'll get together in between, too, when I can. You'll keep me apprised in between by phone or meeting, let me know what you learn. I'll join up with you as much as I can."

She looked so attractive as she snarled at him, her hair still pulled back from that gorgeous face.

But she was still trying to take control of a situation that *he* controlled.

Wasn't going to happen.

"We'll keep you apprised," he agreed mildly. "Let us

know what time you can take off for lunch tomorrow. And we'll let you know every step we've taken." After we take it. But he didn't say that aloud.

She obviously figured it out, though. "No, like I said, I'm going to be part of this. You remember my challenge?"

"Now look, Kathlene," Ralf said. "We know you were joking, but—"

"I wasn't," she responded curtly, still staring at Jock.

"Of course I remember it," he retorted. "But Ralf's right. It was—"

"Then let's get started," she interrupted. "You win and I'll comply with what you've said. *I* win, and I'm dead center in the middle of the operation. Got it?"

"Yes, but—"

He was shocked. Amused. And taken by surprise as the lovely, slim woman removed her sheriff's department jacket, belt with its holster and radio, and dropped them on the floor.

And then she approached him fast, hands out, and grabbed him by the arms.

Chapter 3

Jock Larabey's body felt just as muscular as it looked. Kathlene wasn't surprised by that. In fact, she'd felt it before, when they'd hugged.

She'd only hoped to take *him* by surprise, here in the middle of the cabin's main room on its polished wood floor, between the beds and sitting area she had checked out previously. She had to get him to take her seriously, and defeating him like one of the guys should help.

"Hey!" Ralf shouted, and out of the corner of her eye Kathlene saw him approaching, his hands out, too, as if he intended to pull her away.

She wouldn't let him. But fighting two muscular men at once?

That could be a problem.

She was gratified, therefore, to hear Jock snap out, "Stay back, Ralf. In fact, get out of here. I've got this covered."

He didn't, of course, but fortunately Ralf backed off and stormed out of the cabin. Good.

But why had Jock done that? So Ralf wouldn't see his humiliation? Doubtful. He had to believe he would win.

She'd inhaled as she moved and, now even more aware of her breathing and what was around her, she smelled the sweet combo of aromas of whatever had been used to clean this space for the next occupants.

But she quickly threw all of that out of her consciousness. She had to focus on what she was doing.

At the same time as she had grabbed Jock, she'd twisted her body, her legs around his, to trip him and take him down.

It was like trying to pull down a sturdy steel pipe.

"Hey!" he yelled, but he didn't fall. That was okay. She'd conducted a lot of hand-to-hand combat training with men as well as women, and some were not only muscular but big-bellied, too, unlike Jock. She'd always managed to defeat even them.

She knew her best moves.

She turned and rose at once, putting herself out of Jock's arms' reach temporarily. Or so she thought.

One of his hands was suddenly on her middle, the other grasping for her neck. Was he going to strangle her? Maybe the military was trained to do their worst, act harshly as if prepared to kill even its own, presuming that the other guy was as well trained and could get out of it.

Well, she could, too.

"No!" she yelled, another kind of distraction as she twisted away from him, then quickly turned and attempted to swing her arm and aim at his face while her leg again moved around his.

This time, he apparently let her. No resistance. At

first. But before she could trip him, he moved once more and had one of his arms about her chest while the other moved farther below.

Interesting, to have him touching her there. All over. Apparently, he thought so, too, since she heard a whoosh from him that sounded like what she had heard sometimes in her training sessions with men—surprise, maybe. And interest.

His hand on her breasts moved. Squeezing just a little. Damn, but it felt good. She couldn't allow it to distract her, though—even if it distracted him.

She pretended to start going limp, then straightened, leaped back and turned, facing him again.

And noticing the thick bulge in his jeans as he, too, faced her once more, bent slightly forward, his arms at his sides, clenching and unclenching his fists.

This was definitely more heated, in many ways, than the hug they had previously shared.

Why did that position look so sexy? Or was it just her touching him—and seeing how his body appeared to be reacting?

"Enough?" he asked. He was breathing hard, even though what they'd done so far wasn't especially active.

"Not unless you give in and agree I'm part of your team."

She anticipated his rush forward. She turned sideways to make it harder for him to grab her in crucially vulnerable spots to bring her down.

That ended with her hip pressed right against that bulge she had noticed before. She drew in her breath.

Lord, how she wanted him just then. Which was crazy. She didn't know him. And she needed him to do a job here that could protect her friends, her fellow Clifford

County residents and maybe even more citizens of the United States.

Would her seducing Jock cause him to do a better job? Hardly.

Even if it did, that didn't mean he would let her help.

And she was going to help, no matter what he thought.

"Okay, then, yes," he said. "You're part of the team." Was it over that quickly? "The part of it that I say you are. And that means staying out of danger." As if he believed he had distracted her, he rushed forward, upper part of his body bent, and attempted to tackle her.

She quickly moved away, grabbing at his head and smelling his musky scent as she let herself fall, pulling him down with her.

Amazingly, he fell, too. Onto the floor. Beside where she now knelt. She flipped over, heaving her entire being on top of him. Using every ounce of her weight to press him down.

Feeling his thick muscles everywhere tense beneath her. His chest. His legs.

And the protrusion at his core that thrust up at her as she refused to move.

"You're busted!" she exclaimed triumphantly. "I win. I'm a part of your team—the way *I* say I am."

He didn't move. Didn't say anything. Not for several heartbeats—and she believed hers was somehow synced with his.

His hips moved, and his erection was thrust up against her gut, making her own insides heat and churn and ache with a desire that would not, could not, be fulfilled. Not now or ever. Not with this man.

She continued to watch his face, which, as handsome as it was, somehow remained blank, as if all thoughts, all emotions, all desires, had been erased from within him by her victory.

Even if he rocked her off him now, she still had won, so his pretending to ignore her wouldn't work. Or at least it wouldn't gain him a win over her.

And then a horrible thought struck her. "Did you let me win, Larabey?" she demanded. Well, even if he had, she was still on top—in more ways than one.

She couldn't quite read the expression that passed quickly over his face before disappearing. Smugness? Anger?

"You think I want you to join us in danger? Forget it." The movement of his chest as he spoke bumped against her, causing her breasts to tense along his muscular body. Oh, that heat within her. She'd better get off. Quickly.

"You don't need to worry about me," she said. "I can take care of myself."

"So I've just learned." She appreciated the irony in his tone. "In this kind of situation. But even so, Kathlene, you have to realize that what we're likely to be up against, if you're right about those guys being anarchists, is—"

She had to shut him up. She bent her head forward— and covered those still-moving lips of his with her own.

He responded. Oh, did he ever. His voice stopped immediately, but the movement of his lips didn't. He fastened them on her as he thrust his tongue into her mouth, hot and moving as enticingly as his body below suggested by its pressure against her, imitating the dance of sensuality that she had already imagined going on be-tween them.

"Kathlene," he murmured against her. She responded by drawing his tongue even farther into her mouth, teasing it with hers as suggestively as he played with her.

She couldn't think. Couldn't react with the sanity of a deputy sheriff in danger. For this was danger, maybe even a kind Jock had been warning her about.

Danger that would be magnified by her joining his team. Working with him. Seeing him often while he was here, till they had accomplished—

"Hell." A familiar male voice from the doorway interrupted her thoughts that were already disjointed, thanks to Jock's continuing to drive her nuts with the movement of his body. She turned her head to see Ralf standing there. He'd come back. "Didn't mean to interrupt anything like…I'll go take another walk."

Jock's body heaved slightly from beneath her. He grabbed her with his hands and lowered her gently to the floor as he stood. "Not what it looks like," he told his fellow Alpha Force member. "We were just demonstrating some fighting moves we'd each learned."

"Right," Ralf said. His deep complexion had grown ruddy with embarrassment.

"It's true." Jock was standing now. He bent to offer his hand to help her to her feet.

She accepted, still looking at the floor. Kathlene didn't dare glance toward Ralf. Not just yet.

"Kathlene and I have reached an agreement of sorts," Jock said. "She wants to work with us. Be part of our team as we investigate those potential anarchists. She'd wanted to show me some of her fighting skills to prove that she could hold her own, and I now agree with her. Kathlene is now definitely a part of our team."

Had he let her win? Jock didn't think so, but he had allowed her to distract him enough with her so-sexy body in motion that the result had been inevitable.

Besides, he'd felt reluctant to fight a female at all. Could that have been his wolf side reacting? Unlikely. That part of him illustrated his wildness, not holding back when it was in his best interests. Even so...well, it was over now.

She had stayed for just a short while as they planned their next meet-up—lunch the next day. Meantime, Ralf and he would do a little recon on their own before getting together with her, studying the layout of Cliffordsville and its environs even more, maybe even doing an initial check of the area containing the anarchists' habitat tonight.

Little did she know how he would check it.

And that was one of the biggest problems of her working with them as a team. That, and the potential danger.

He could protect her. Would protect her.

But what would she think if she knew what he was, and why he, rather than a member of any other military unit, had been sent here?

Now, after their brief discussion inside the cabin, he walked her to her car. She said goodbye to them—for now. It was getting late, darkness was falling and she said she was heading home.

She used her key to unlock the driver's door of her SUV, and he opened it for her.

"Sorry I embarrassed you in front of your partner," she said as she faced him before getting inside. Her lovely face was flushed a bit, too. Her smile seemed ironic, drawing her full lips up just a bit at the corners.

He couldn't help it. He bent and gave her another kiss.

Oh, not as sensual as last time. It was, in comparison, just a peck. But it still managed to evoke the feelings he had captured before—feelings of her firm but curva-ceous body against him.

She pulled away first. "Bye, Jock. I'll be thinking about you tonight." Before he could react, she said, "About our team. And how best to investigate the anar-chists together." She ducked into the car and pulled the door shut. She turned the key in the ignition and waved to him as she drove off.

"You've got an interesting way of sealing the deal, making her part of the team." Ralf and Click had come up to Jock as Kathlene's car vanished around a curve. "And I thought the last thing you wanted was for her to *help* us—and potentially learn what Alpha Force is all about."

Jock turned and motioned for Ralf to follow him back toward the cabin. "I don't know yet what kind of help she might be, but she does know people around here as well as locations. Plus, she was the one who revealed that there was a potential issue here and was credible enough for those in charge to follow up. Maybe she can help, and maybe not. But as far as her learning about Alpha Force—and me—we'll just have to make sure she doesn't. At least not unless we decide it's to our advan-tage for her to know—which I doubt. Speaking of which, now that she's gone, I think it'll be time soon for some very special reconnaissance."

The drive back to her home was a short distance along narrow streets now illuminated by artificial light, but Kathlene considered it a huge way from where she had left Jock. What had she been thinking?

Apparently, she *hadn't* been thinking. A hand-to-hand combat battle to convince him to let her help in finding out what was up with those anarchists?

Well, he was military, she was in law enforcement, and engaging in that kind of confrontation may have made sense...*may* being the operative word.

At least it had worked out. He had acknowledged that she would be part of his team.

Kathlene reached the cottage-style redbrick house on the residential street that she called home. She pulled into the driveway and pushed the button for the garage door to open.

She knew she wouldn't sleep much that night. She would be thinking too much about Jock Larabey, their workout together...and the feel of his body, and lips, against hers.

She made herself rehash their final conversation—and realized it felt too easy. They were going to look around. Preliminarily check out the town and the anarchists' site that she had pointed out to them. Tomorrow morning?

Maybe. But she had a feeling that these men would not wait. She turned the key in the ignition, closed her garage door and backed out of her driveway again.

They might be checking out the anarchists' location that night. If not, she'd just return here, no harm, no foul.

But if they were checking it out—well, she'd be checking *them* out.

"This should do it." Jock had allowed Ralf to drive him back along the route they had taken when Kathlene pointed out the turnoff toward where she'd indicated the possible anarchists were living. Then they had cruised a bit longer until they had found what appeared to be a nearby solitary and abandoned home, at least from what they could tell in the near absolute darkness of this forested area. The place had been built of wood in a style that looked like some bygone era's, and that wood was rotting.

Its emptiness made it a good place to conduct what they now needed to do.

Ralf had pulled behind the structure, just in case. They didn't want their car to be seen from the road if any of the people they wanted to surveil happened to drive by.

Plus, what they now needed to do could not be done with any normal, non–Alpha Force human around.

It was a secret from all other eyes. It was the heart of their supercovert military unit.

They both were out of the car. Click had remained locked in the rented cabin next door to theirs. He was vital to this part of their assignment—but only because he closely resembled the wolf into which Jock was about to change. If anyone happened to see Jock, Ralf and he would laugh it off. Show off the dog later and say it had always been Click.

"You ready, sir?" Ralf asked. He had pulled his large backpack out of the rear seat of the car and was holding out a vial of the very special Alpha Force shifting elixir.

That elixir alone was enough to entice shapeshifters to join Alpha Force. It had been developed by some of the unit's members, starting with its commanding officer, Major Drew Connell, and enhanced by formulas that other members had created independently that provided additional qualities.

"'Sir'? You're too military, bro." Ralf was a staff sergeant. Jock, as a lieutenant, was, in fact, his superior officer. But Alpha Forcers worked together too closely to stand much on military protocol. "But yeah, I'm ready."

They had decided, to save time, to have Jock shift outside the house, at least for this change. Then, when he was off performing his recon, Ralf would find a way to get inside and check the place out.

Now the only illumination was from the penlight that Ralf had taken from his sack and turned on, plus a bit of natural light from the starlit sky, visible now and then through the canopy of trees and over the road where they had been cleared. No full moon, not for another couple of weeks. Jock took the bottle of elixir and downed it slowly. It tasted somewhat minty and a bit like citrus fruit. Drinkable, but that didn't matter.

When he had finished it, he handed back the empty vial, took a deep breath and said, "Now."

Ralf aimed the other light he had taken from the backpack toward Jock, the one that, turned on, resembled the illumination of a full moon.

Jock immediately felt the stretching and pulling sensations begin. He smiled, then growled, as his body began morphing into the form of a wolf.

He prowled through the forest, in the direction of the distant sounds and scents of a large human habitat.

The one that was his target. The target of Alpha Force.

Tonight would be an overview by a wolf seeking information—one with the perception of a human, thanks to the elixir—to see what was there, to help plan what would come next.

He smelled the aromas of the woodlands—the trees. Small creatures whose sounds he heard in the underbrush, fleeing from him. Larger animals—a bobcat. A bear. Perhaps a wolverine. He scented them all, but none was near him.

A good thing. He wanted neither to flee nor to fight. Not this night.

He soon arrived at his destination. He smelled a legion of humans. Saw the compound surrounded by a tall chain-link fence.

He slowly began circling it, careful to stay far enough away in the trees not to be spotted by curious human eyes.

He smelled fire and approached the wooded area closest to where it seemed to originate. Yes. Beyond the fence, a group of humans sat around a large campfire, apparently talking and drinking. He could smell beer and some harder stuff. Despite his keen hearing, he could only make out a hum of conversation, not specifically what they were saying.

Was it true? Were these men bent on evading—or toppling—authority and harming other humans? Or were they just a group of hunters banding together in a bond of yearning to kill wildlife?

As much as he despised that, it would not be something that merited Alpha Force intervention.

Killing or even threatening other humans did.

He needed to learn more. But he had done most of what he had intended for this night.

Observing, using his other senses that were much keener than those of a human, he nevertheless waited for another twenty minutes, but that yielded little further useful information except for the scent of gunpowder, which fit with who these people were. Explosives? Maybe, but if so they had been set off a while back.

But what he sought could still be on the property, hidden, perhaps being stored without being utilized, for now. This was not the time to check—but he would in the near future.

He had determined where the gates to this property

were, including the one staffed by a guard. Other areas
where the fencing was not rooted as well. Ways he could
enter if he had to.

Still others where the trees and bushes and under-
growth did not end at the fence line but extended onto
the property—and could hide a wolf who happened to
stalk into them and hide.

He would return here.

Soon.

And then, as he began to leave, he inhaled a scent.
A familiar human scent, one that trumped all he had
smelled previously.

He had to be wrong. And yet his special senses were
never wrong about things like that.

A woman with the anarchists?

No. Near them.

Kathlene.

What was going on?

Kathlene had headed back to the area of the cabins
and arrived just in time to see the car driven by Ralf
exit through the motel's gates and head in the direction
of the anarchists' area. She'd had to stay far back, even
drive without using her headlights, to ensure that she
wouldn't be seen.

She'd watched as their car pulled into the driveway of
what appeared to be an abandoned house along the road.
She had decided she'd better park along a nearby turn-
out and walk, rather than drive, to keep an eye on them.

And, potentially, protect them. She had taken her
weapon from where she had locked it in her glove compartment and now wore it at her hip.

The night was dark, especially with the canopy of

trees looming overhead, obliterating the light from the half moon and the stars that, in as remote and unlighted an area as this, usually lit up the sky in identifiable constellations. And she had been right. It *was* unpleasant to come to this area at night, especially alone. But she had little choice.

She had carefully stayed on the road, walking slower than she would have liked but trying to make as little noise as possible, staying off the cover of dry leaves on the ground yet trying to remain invisible at the edge of the road. Making her way in the darkness. Staying careful, and as aware of her surroundings, and her solitude, as she possibly could.

That way, it took her a long time to catch up.

She had finally reached the house, looked inside a window, saw Ralf there in the faint illumination of a flashlight—but not Jock.

Had he tried to get inside the compound alone?

Bad move, she'd thought. What if he were seen?

Maybe he'd only intended to walk the perimeter outside the fence, just to take an initial look in the dark when he was less likely to be noticed. That made sense to her.

She'd decided to go check, just in case.

Still careful to walk as silently as possible, she had left the house with Ralf inside and hurried toward the road to the compound.

She'd wished she could use a flashlight, but at least her eyes had acclimated to the darkness. She had soon seen the light from the guardhouse and slipped behind the nearest trees, still carefully drawing closer to the area.

Then she'd started to slowly walk the perimeter. But then she had stopped. What was that?

Some kind of canine. It looked, from where she'd

stood, like a German shepherd mix of some kind—but tawnier. Furrier. Like a wolf. A wild dog, maybe, that was part wolf.

As she'd watched, it seemed to smell the air in her direction. And then it moved on.

Moving cautiously, she tried to watch it but got only occasional glimpses of it. It appeared to stalk the compound outside the fence, like her—staying in the cover of the trees. It walked slowly, staring inside the enclosed area as if consciously observing what was there.

And then it disappeared. Even so, she continued to watch the area of the old ranch from her cover.

Now she had returned to an area not far from the driveway, hoping to see Jock, assuming he had come on foot to check the place out.

But after half an hour, she didn't see him. She was tired. Disappointed. Maybe she had been wrong about what the Alpha Force members intended to do this night besides exclude her.

She still didn't know what Ralf had been doing at that house. Where was Jock? Did it matter?

That wolf had most likely been hunting for food and had nothing to do with what else was going on around here.

Right?

But why was it she couldn't quite accept that?

Still careful, she headed back to where she had parked her car.

Maybe she would get some answers tomorrow.

Chapter 4

"She was there."

While still a wolf, Jock had loped through the woods back to the house near which he'd previously shifted. As planned, Ralf had gotten inside and had opened the door for him when he'd returned.

Jock had just morphed back to his human form. He'd grabbed the clothes that Ralf had folded neatly and left on a cleaned spot on the floor, then threw them on.

Now, inside the dismal and filthy hovel, he was dressed and angry and wanted to slam something. Except for spotting a few flaws in their security and some possible entry points, his initial observation had been totally inconclusive. He still had no sense of the extent of the likelihood for peril looming around the former ranch, but he definitely hadn't ruled out the conceivability of those now staying there being at least skilled and dedicated terrorists and possible anarchists, as well.

He needed to get inside, though, to check for the extent of their weaponry.

Now he knew all his frustration was evident as he spoke to Ralf.

"Who? Kathlene? Where was she?" Ralf had placed his equipment on the floor and was now stowing it in his backpack again. He stopped, though, facing Jock in the dim glow of the flashlight he had left on for illumination.

"Near the old ranch, outside the fence like I was, also hiding in the woods. But I scented and heard her, then saw her. Damn the woman. She must have been following us. Does she like throwing herself into potential danger?"

"I think you know the answer to that," Ralf said drily. Which only made Jock want to slam something all the more, like the wall. Not Ralf, and certainly not Kathlene—although, had she been nearby, it wouldn't have been outside the realm of possibility for him to grab and shake her.

And he knew what a bad idea that would be…touching her again at all. He'd want to kiss those defiant lips, and more.

Well, he would have time to cool down before seeing her at lunch again tomorrow.

By then he would have thought of a brilliant way to convince her to back off and let Ralf and him do their jobs.

At least he hoped so.

"Did she know it was you?" Ralf asked, interrupting his thoughts.

"Of course not." But Jock wondered nevertheless. Had she just shown up there because that was what she did—

keeping an eye on the place where she thought a lot of dangerous people were gathering? That was a viable theory, of course. But unlikely for this evening.

Had she instead followed them—him?

That was something else he would have to check into tomorrow.

Kathlene was tired when she reported to work the next morning.

That wasn't surprising. She hadn't slept much.

Her mind kept buzzing around thoughts of her new Alpha Force best friends. Especially the so very sexy Jock Larabey, her supposed old buddy.

And their attempts to exclude her from the investigation.

Plus that strange visit of hers to the anarchists' enclave last night, thinking she would see Jock hanging around outside, near where she was, after leaving Ralf at that old house...but instead seeing only a wolf.

A particularly strange-acting wolf...

Now, inside the sheriff's station, in the assembly room waiting for the day's instructions, she kept herself from yawning by sheer willpower.

The dozens of other deputies taking their seats on folding chairs around her would only rib her about it if they saw.

The noise around her was growing—loud male voices hailing each other, chairs being dragged around the wooden floor, shrill feedback from a microphone that Sheriff Melton Frawley's top assistant, Undersheriff George Kerringston, was testing from the row of chairs up front that faced the rest.

Hardly any sound of female voices. Oh, yes, there

were a couple of other deputies toughing it out like Kathlene. Or, actually, not like Kathlene. Deputy Betsy Alvers and Deputy Alberta Sheyne were perfectly happy being obedient underlings who did as Melton said, filling out paperwork at the station and bringing coffee to the big, brave men in the department.

The other couple of female deputies had resigned and moved away. There wasn't even a local police department for them to join, since the county sheriff's department was the only law enforcement in this area other than the state highway patrol on the major nearby roads. Only Kathlene attempted to keep up the job as they had once all known it.

That had become a daily fight. But she was no quitter.

And now, with her concerns about the apparent anarchists, she felt she owed it to the town, to the many people who remained her friends, to see this through.

"Hey, good lookin'."

A thin man dressed just like her sat down on the empty chair beside her, sliding over so their hips met.

"Hey, ugly guy," she said back, turning to smile up into the face of Senior Deputy Tommy Xavier Jones, the man who appeared to be her only supporter in the higher ranks of the department.

Tommy X had been a deputy for nearly twenty years. He had short gray hair, a long, almost equine face and a lot of wrinkles. He was the tallest member of the department, was great friends with the town's ranking politicians and dated a county commissioner, who also happened to be Kathlene's friend.

He could get away with bucking the current regime within the Sheriff's Department—and did.

And fortunately, he remained Kathlene's champion, too.

"So—do you anticipate anything exciting today?" he asked, nodding toward the front of the room where Sheriff Frawley was about to take the microphone.

"Here? Nope. But I'm having lunch with my old college friend Jock, the one I told you about. I saw him briefly yesterday. He's here with a friend on the way to Yellowstone and I'll spend as much time as I can with them before they leave."

Even with someone as close to her as Tommy X, Kathlene had decided to maintain the cover story—partly because she'd been instructed to if she wanted continuing help from the elite and covert Alpha Force, whatever it was, and partly because she didn't dare allow her personal investigation of the anarchists become the knowledge of anyone here, not even Tommy X. Tommy X was a nice guy, trustworthy—but if he let even a hint of what was going on drop in front of anyone here who wanted to curry favor with Sheriff Frawley, she'd be toast.

"Attention, please." That was Kerringston, shouting into the microphone although he didn't have to. He knew that. He'd been told nearly daily since his promotion to undersheriff six months earlier, when the former sheriff had retired and Melton Frawley was promoted into his position.

Before the good old days had ended, Kathlene thought. Unlike today.

Kerringston gave his greeting and handed the mike to his boss. Melton did his usual song and dance of thanking his people, telling them to do a good job, going over the stuff that had been investigated yesterday—which amounted to nearly nothing unless one was impressed with local traffic stops.

And then the sheriff finished. He didn't look toward Kathlene. He didn't have to.

But she knew exactly whom he spoke to next, since he did so often.

"Now, we've had a few more local applications for hunting licenses. Like always. Nice for the economy since the licenses aren't cheap, plus some of the sportsmen—that's what they consider themselves, you know—are joining the others already here who're practicing their shooting skills and all. I've talked to them. They talk to me. No one's been hurt as they do their target practice—still. And no one will be hurt."

He stopped, looking over the heads of nearly all the deputies quietly facing him, some jabbing each other in the sides with their elbows as they nodded toward Kathlene and laughed.

"So…today's a new day. Anyone want to ruin our meeting by objecting to our visitors?" This time, he shot a look right at Kathlene, challenging her, even as he guffawed aloud.

She said nothing. Just looked down as if there was something loose on her utility belt that she had to check.

Same as every day. Even as she felt her face flush, her insides churn.

His discussions with the *sportsmen* suggested they didn't mind authority, so they couldn't be anarchists, could they? Or was he being wooed by them so he'd leave them alone?

Melton obviously wanted her to quit and run. She knew it. And she was tempted daily. Like now. After he had humiliated her—again.

"You okay?" Tommy X whispered without looking at her. He'd already told her that his standing up and arguing in her favor would only garner more reaction from the sheriff and nearly all his minions.

"Fine," she said. As always.

This time, though, she had something to add. For once.

"But I'm really looking forward to having lunch today with my dear old college friend," she told Tommy X.

In the late morning gloom, Kathlene had walked briskly down the busy Cliffordsville sidewalk from the sheriff's station toward the Clifford Café, the place she had chosen to meet Jock and Ralf. She'd called to let them know the address.

She had gotten there first and grabbed a table in a corner. Now she looked around. She knew maybe a half dozen patrons there, some waiting for their meals and others eating already. As she caught the eyes of a few, she smiled and lifted her hand in a wave of greeting. She remained in uniform since she would return to duty in a little less than an hour, so they clearly knew who, or at least what, she was.

This wasn't usually where she spent her lunchtime, but it seemed an appropriate place for today.

The place smelled delicious, with the aroma of grilled meats and baking bread in the air. The sound of voices was mostly a low hum. She couldn't make out what was said in any conversations, but that was fine with her.

Even so, none of the tables in this busy joint was completely immune from eavesdropping by the nosy locals who frequented it. In a way, that was a good thing. Word would get out that Kathlene had publicly dined with those friends she'd been talking about. Nothing sneaky about that. Not worth anyone spending any time puzzling over or talking about.

Unless, of course, those *friends* of hers were successful in outing, and taking federal custody of, some or all of the *sportsmen*. If word got out, that might be something worth more than some lunchtime gossip.

In any event, this wasn't Kathlene's usual midday meal. Her favorite lunch on days she was on duty was to grab a sandwich to go at one of the chains where she could choose everything from the bread to the meat and all other ingredients. That way, she could stuff it with all the salad makings she could want.

It was too hard to eat salads in patrol cars. And fortunately, the guy who was usually her partner, chosen especially for that role by her buddy Sheriff Frawley, could also get all the unhealthy menu items he wanted, too.

That way, Deputy Jimmy Korling didn't gripe at her. At least no more than usual.

Today he had griped, though, since she was actually taking an hour to have lunch by herself. Well, not exactly by herself. With her old college buddy Jock and his traveling companion, Ralf.

"Can I bring you a drink to start with, Deputy Baylor?" The server had obviously read Kathlene's name tag. She wore a dress with a short skirt covered by a dainty apron—the kind of woman, Kathlene was sure, that Sheriff Frawley expected all his female deputies to be. Not that she had anything but complete respect for this server, who also wore a name tag. Hers said she was Addie. But Addie had chosen to take on this kind of job.

Kathlene hadn't.

"Just a cup of coffee," Kathlene said, smiling. "And a recommendation for what I should order after my friends arrive."

As she said that, she glanced past the server's shoulder

toward the front entrance. There they were—Jock and
Ralf were just entering the restaurant. As they looked
around, Kathlene half stood and waved.

"Are your friends here now?" Addie asked.

"Yes. I'm sure we'll be ready to order soon. Your sug-
gestions?"

Addie described the specials—a turkey club sandwich, a meat-loaf platter, the soups of the day. By the
time she was through, she went over them again as Jock
and Ralf pulled their chairs from beneath the table and
took their seats. "I'll give you a few minutes to decide,"
she said after taking their drink orders.

Kathlene noticed how the pretty brunette server's eyes
skimmed approvingly over Jock, who smiled back. Oh,
yeah, the server had noticed how sexy he was. How could
she help it? But that didn't matter to Kathlene. Couldn't
matter.

So why did she want to shake the waitress and tell her
to go get their drinks? Fast.

"Do you have any other recommendations?" Ralf
asked. This time his T-shirt was blue with a circular
logo representing the Montana flag in the middle, along
with the state motto *"Oro Y Plata"*—gold and silver.
He'd definitely done his homework before coming here,
probably ordered his shirt online. His toothy grin was
friendly, not suggesting at all that he was anything but
what he pretended to be: a visitor who'd come here along
with a friend on a road trip.

Jock, on the other hand, was also in jeans but with
a snug black T-shirt on top. It hugged his ample muscles and emphasized the tightness of his hot body. He
wasn't smiling at Kathlene, though. Instead, his hazel
eyes regarded her with an expression she couldn't quite

read. Curiosity? Irritation? Challenge? Maybe all of the above—but she was entitled to feel each of those emotions even more than he did.

Although she had no doubt that he believed otherwise.

She turned back to Ralf. "I don't eat here often, but when I do I usually order one of the specials. I've never had a bad meal at this place, though, so just pick whatever sounds best to you."

At least here, sitting at a table, she could order a salad. The Cobb salad at this café was one of the best she had ever tasted, so she knew that would be her selection.

The server returned. Ralf ordered the meat-loaf special, Jock the sandwich and Kathlene her salad.

Then it was time for them to put on their act, pretend for those surrounding them to be longtime friends.

But Kathlene needed to give these men a reminder. They'd apparently tried to do something without her last night. Today, to maintain cordiality in their relationship, she could understand and agree with it, but only on a limited basis. And she would first make it clear that they hadn't gotten rid of her for this evening.

"So did you sleep well last night?" she began, aiming an enormous, friendly smile toward Jock.

His return grin was wry—an utterly sexy look on his craggy face. "Sure did. How about you?"

"Eventually, sure. But you know, I remembered something I wanted to tell you after I left and decided to go back rather than to just call you. Imagine my surprise when I saw you driving away down the road." She kept her smile large but her voice was very low. "I knew you didn't intend to check on that…place I'd told you about, since you'd have let me know and invited me to come along, as we agreed. Sure enough, I noticed that you'd stopped not there but farther down the road, only…" She wasn't quite sure how to continue. Things had become murky after that, and she hadn't really been able to observe either of these men or what they'd been up to. She'd essentially lost them in darkness, and neither had shown up in the area she expected they would.

Addie returned to their table and placed their food in front of them. "Enjoy," she said, "and let me know if there's anything else you need."

Oh, there was something else Kathlene needed, all right, but the server wasn't the one who could help her. Addie lingered a bit more than necessary, refilling their water glasses and making a point of joking a little with Jock, who responded as if he enjoyed it. As if flirting with their waitress was the best thing that had happened to him that day.

Which only annoyed Kathlene all the more.

Ignoring Jock, she turned to Ralf after Addie had left. "I admire the way you discovered that old, abandoned house down the road, but I wasn't sure what you were up to." Once again, she kept her voice muted even as she all but batted her eyelashes at him so anyone observing them would think she was having a grand old time flirting with her buddy's friend. "Just looking for a closer venue to use as headquarters for the investigation we'll be conducting at the ranch?"

Ralf's features seemed to grow even darker. He glanced at the man who was evidently his commanding officer.

"You could say that." Jock's smile was rigid now, his voice low but sharp. "And we will include you when it makes sense. But it didn't last night during our preliminary recon." He paused, and his hazel eyes grew icy.

"You have no business following us. For all you know, there could have been some major danger there and we might not have known you were around to help protect you."

That again. He seemed determined to keep her out of danger, out of trouble. The idea should have warmed her, but instead it made her chill. Had they made no progress at all after her demonstration that she could protect herself, at least in hand-to-hand combat?

But this wasn't the place to encourage a major argument with Jock Larabey. Not with so many people around who might overhear them, especially if they raised their voices.

"I get it," she said as neutrally as she could. "But look, I really need to be able to trust you both. At least tell me what you're going to do, where you're going to go." She hesitated. "And it frustrated me last night when I lost track of you. I didn't see you anywhere near the ranch when I got there. I only saw a…well, it looked like a wolf. It seemed to be stalking the outside of the compound. Were you around? Did you see it—and me—too?"

There was no immediate response from either man. They glanced at each other, though, as if their silence spoke volumes between them.

What was going on?

"Those guys purport to be hunters," she went on when they still said nothing. "I had the sense that the wolf had some purpose to be there. Isn't that silly? But I'd have hated to see one of them shoot the animal. There is no license for killing wolves this early in the year, but I wouldn't have been surprised if they used the poor thing for target practice, anyway."

She'd been watching their expressions as she talked.

Once again Jock's look appeared to say lots that she couldn't read. But he finally spoke. "You're right, Kathlene," he said, amazing her—only she wasn't sure what she was right about. "There's something we'll show you and explain after lunch. Will you have a few minutes?"

Not really, but she wasn't about to tell him that. She'd just have to face the wrath of her partner, Jimmy, after calling him to tell him she'd be late.

And dealing with his anger wouldn't be pleasant.

But she had a feeling it would be worth it…to learn whatever Jock Larabey was now willing to tell her.

Chapter 5

She had seen him. Just as he had suspected.

And she might wind up seeing him again as their investigation progressed.

Therefore, Jock figured it was already time to nip any suspicions she might have in the bud.

Not that she was likely to assume that the canine she saw was anything but a genuine wolf or dog or whatever.

He took a sip of water from the glass in front of him. He'd already told Ralf his opinion by his glance.

Jock hadn't been a member of the military and Alpha Force for very long so far, but Ralf had enlisted in the army years ago. He was an astute soldier and a smart aide to a shifting Alpha Force member—him.

Ralf knew by Jock's glance what he was saying. Jock felt certain of it.

It was time, after lunch, to go introduce Kathlene to Click.

* * *

She had insisted on driving her own vehicle since she had to return to duty soon.

Jock sent Ralf back with the car they had driven here as part of their cover—a nice but slightly beat-up black sedan that was owned by Uncle Sam, but with plates registered to Mr. Jock Larabey of Seattle, Washington.

He rode in the passenger's seat of Kathlene's SUV. She'd indicated that her partner was in current possession of her sheriff's department cruiser.

They had been relatively silent on the drive from town, with Ralf staying right behind them. Jock had insisted on paying for their lunch, and she'd thanked him. He didn't need to tell her it was part of his government expense account.

He wondered what she was thinking as they drove along the lane that would take them to the driveway to the Clifford Cabins—that also, eventually, would pass by the area that was the object of their investigation.

But they weren't going that far. Not this afternoon.

"So tell me what made you decide to move to Cliffordsville for your law-enforcement career," he finally said. It was similar to what they'd talked about yesterday, noncontroversial—although she had grown quiet when he had asked about her early background.

"I'd just heard that Clifford County was looking for new deputies here," she said, glancing toward him.

Lord, was she gorgeous, even decked out in that uniform with her hair pulled back. Or maybe having her face barely adorned like that added to how beautiful she was, with nothing artificial making her look like anything but herself. Oh, she did wear some lip gloss. Maybe she had a little makeup on, too.

But mostly, she looked like one lovely lady. One lovely, hot, enticing lady.

"Did they hire you right away?"

She nodded. "But that was Sheriff Chrissoula. Before our current sheriff, Melton Frawley, took over after Chrissoula retired six months ago."

"And was that around when the anarchist group started to move in?"

She again shot him a glance. "How did you know? Or did you just guess? Yes, it's my belief that Sheriff Frawley may have rolled out the welcome mat. Or even if he didn't, he also didn't tell the group to get lost."

"Do you think he's one of them?"

She shrugged her shoulders that still somehow managed to look slim and sexy despite her uniform. "I hope not, but I can't say for sure. Now—" she turned her car onto the driveway toward the cabins "—what is it you want to show me here?"

"You'll see. I think it'll explain a lot to you, at least about last night."

She parked, and Ralf pulled in beside her. The parking lot had a few more cars in it now, but no other people were visible around the row of rustic cabins surrounding the parking area.

Kathlene didn't wait for Jock to open the door for her, but he hadn't really expected her to. She clearly didn't want to rely on anyone behaving in a gentlemanly manner.

And somehow her independence only added to her attractiveness to him. To a point. Ignoring politeness was fine.

Ignoring danger was not.

She began walking along the paved path toward the

cabin where Ralf and he were staying. "No," Jock called. "This way." He gestured toward the cabin next door. "Got the key, Ralf?"

"Sure do."

His aide moved to the front of the group, holding the key card in his hand.

"You've rented this cabin, too?" Kathlene looked confused.

Why did he want to kiss that puzzled frown away…?

"I'd like you to meet Click," Jock said, and nodded to Ralf.

Ralf pushed the door open and was nearly bowled over as Click leaped out, eagerly wagging his tail and greeting one of the humans who was his closest friend.

"You brought a dog?" Kathlene asked. She shook her head, then smiled. "The dog I saw last night? He's not a wolf, then? He's a pet?"

Instead of waiting for his answers, she dashed off toward where Click and Ralf were now roughhousing.

She obviously liked canines.

Couldn't he find anything to dislike about this woman—except for her carelessness in the face of danger?

He wasn't sure he wanted to find out.

At first all Kathlene wanted to do was hug the obviously excited dog. He looked familiar—moderate sized, with shining, light brown eyes, pert ears and lots of tawny fur that looked almost silvery in the light. He clearly loved people, since he bounded from Ralf to her and back again in this cabin that looked nearly identical inside to the one where the men were staying. Click basked in the attention they both gave him and snugged his head against her for multiple pats.

"He's so sweet!" she exclaimed, kneeling with one hand on the floor to keep her balance as the dog pushed at her for attention and made snuffling noises. She loved dogs. Meant to adopt a rescue someday when her work schedule was less crazy and more predictable. If it ever was. "Is Click yours, Ralf? Or Jock's?"

Why did the men exchange glances about that? It was an easy question.

Wasn't it? And if not…

"He's mine," Jock said, and he joined the excited doggy love fest, too.

But the hesitation before he knelt and roughhoused with Click had reminded Kathlene of all the mystery surrounding this dog. Why hadn't they mentioned they had brought a pet along?

She asked them. "I can understand your wanting to have a dog with you. Is Click a trained search dog?" Or was there some other reason he'd been brought here— then hidden?

And why hide him from *her?*

"That's right." Jock stepped back. "He's trained to do other things, too, like sniff out particular subjects we need to find and follow."

"Is that why he was wandering around the ranch compound last night?"

Of course it had been Click. And yet there was something about the shape of his head, the length of his legs, the fullness of his coat, that didn't look exactly the way Kathlene remembered. But she'd been stressed then. Her recollections might not be entirely accurate. Plus, she hadn't been that close to the dog.

"Yes, that's right," Jock said. "He's got some other skills we're working on, too. He's not fully trained, so we weren't sure at first about bringing him, and when we decided to we just figured we'd keep him hidden, at least initially, until we decided how best to use him."

Kathlene supposed that made sense—but she wasn't fully convinced.

And yet why would they lie to her about that?

She stood, leaned down and stroked the soft fur around Click's shoulders as she looked straight into Jock's eyes.

The guy looked the picture of innocence, as if all he had told her was the absolute truth, even if it sounded somewhat contrived.

He clearly wasn't going to give her any explanation of why he might be prevaricating.

"You look like a good friend of Click's, too," Kathlene said to Ralf. "Are either of you skilled trainers, or does someone else do that?"

"A little of both," Ralf said. "I like to work with canines, tell them what to do, that kind of thing." He gave a big grin that he aimed at Jock, whose return smile looked almost nasty.

What was the gist of their unspoken conversation?

They obviously weren't going to tell her, any more than they'd explained Alpha Force or included her in their planning.

"Can we take him for a walk now?" she asked the men.

Another hesitation before Jock said, "Sure. There aren't likely to be a lot of people around now, in the middle of the day when they're off doing whatever they're here to do."

Which again didn't make sense to Kathlene. They apparently didn't want Click to be seen by many people. When did they walk him, then?

After dark, at least. That was the one obvious time. Early morning, before many people were up and about? That still wouldn't allow Click to relieve himself in the middle of the day as well as other times, which might be hard on the poor dog.

She knew she wasn't going to get answers now, so she didn't bother asking.

"Great," she said. "I'll bet you're glad to go for a walk now, aren't you, Click?"

Hearing his name, the dog looked up at her expectantly. Did he understand the word *walk?* Probably. She had the sense that, as playful as he was, he was also a smart pooch.

"So are we all going?" Kathlene said after Ralf brought over Click's leash.

"Just you, me and Click," Jock said. Ralf just nodded, not appearing particularly unhappy about being left out.

It bothered Kathlene, though. She'd be more or less alone with the man who was driving her a bit nuts. His sexiness didn't let her state of mind settle down in his presence. His secretiveness drove her nuts in other ways.

Well, she couldn't—wouldn't—do anything about the former. The latter she could get around. She could be sweet or professional or just darned pushy.

But one way or another she would find out what these men had planned to do to start their investigation.

"Here we go, boy." Jock spoke to Click as he attached his leash inside the cabin. "You ready to join us?" he asked Kathlene.

"Definitely." She smiled, although it faded quickly.

"I can only stay here for another few minutes, though. I need to get back on duty."

"We'll make it short, then." Jock gave a gentle tug on the leash and let Click lead them out of the cabin.

Jock was glad to have an opportunity to walk Click. Mostly, it was Ralf who figured out the best times to go out with the dog, when they were least likely to be seen.

On the other hand, he and his aide had talked often about potential timing for Jock to be the one to walk his cover dog. People seeing them together was generally a good thing. They would know there were two entities, Jock and the dog. They wouldn't think Jock even slightly resembled the pet he had brought here. Or that he was, sometimes, a canine himself.

Not that most regular humans would even imagine the possibility.

And of those that might…well, there weren't any people they needed to demonstrate anything to here, in this motel area.

Maybe not anywhere in this town. At least not yet.

Except for Kathlene.

He was both glad and sorry for the opportunity to take a walk with her. The best thing for his cover would be for them to stay as alone as possible here.

But that would be worst for his sense of self-control. He wanted this woman. He knew it, and being in her presence only kept his desires at the forefront of his thoughts.

As well as his physical reactions—which were uncomfortable at times, but definitely stimulating.

She was a bundle of contradictions, and that attracted him. A lot.

Maybe because he, too, wasn't all that he appeared to be.

"Let's take Click into the woods," he told Kathlene once they were outside. He held Click's leash. "He loves the scents there."

"I noticed," she said, then shrugged. "Fine with me."

He chose to say nothing about the woods in this motel area being any different from what surrounded the compound that was the target of their observation. In many ways, it was the same.

Although he himself had detected a lot of differences in the smells around there from what was here.

Gunpowder and explosives, for example. If Click had really been there, Jock had no doubt he'd have scented them, too, despite how they seemed to be muted by distance or age. He'd also have some sense of urgency about them, since he was a trained military K9. But he'd have waited for orders to determine what to do about them.

Jock would need to figure that out for himself, although he would discuss it, if necessary, with his commanding officers, as well as Ralf.

The closest part of the woods began only a few feet away, behind the row of cabins. Jock pulled Click's leash slightly to aim him between the rustic structures toward that direction.

"So tell me," said Kathlene once they had gone beyond the narrow lawn area and beneath the trees. "What is our next plan of action? Did you learn anything by sending Click to the encampment of those supposed sportsmen last night?"

"Click's presence there did give us some ideas," Jock said. Rather, it was his own presence. And it certainly had triggered what he intended to be their next course of action.

In wolf form, he had looked for—and found—some portions of the surrounding chain-link fence that were less secure and more penetrable by a canine observer than the rest of it.

He intended to return tonight under cover of darkness, and in his wolfen form.

He'd not seen or heard enough to understand what was really going on there, let alone how best to deal with it.

"What do you smell, boy?" Kathlene was talking to Click, whose nose was all but buried in a stack of dead leaves.

Jock scented it, too, of course. His sense of smell was much more acute than any person's besides other shifters, even when in human form. But he was hardly going to tell Kathlene that the dog was fascinated by the odor of a pile of pheasant droppings.

"Must be something interesting," Jock said mildly. "But we'd better keep on the move."

He nevertheless waited until Click lifted his leg to imbue the area with his own canine smell. And then they continued on.

"So what are those ideas you came up with?" Kathlene asked, walking directly behind him as they made their way through the towering trees that had a sweet, piney aroma.

Unfortunately, she hadn't been fully distracted by Click and his reaction to the odors of the woods.

"We need more information about what's going on inside the compound," Jock said. "For one thing, we'll want to know where the *sportsmen* hang out when they're in town. If possible, we'll act like we're of the same hunting mind-set and also want to engage in target practice and have the fun of killing whatever game is in season."

Even though that was contrary to his way of thinking. There were plenty of farm animals raised to be meat. He might feel sorry for them, but he was definitely carnivorous. He was a wolf in human form.

But in his opinion creatures that were wild, like wolves, should be permitted to stay that way. Survival of the fittest would allow them to feed on their own kinds of prey.

Humans did not need to kill or eat them.

"I can give you some information about that," Kathlene said. "There are a couple of bars in town where the sheriff's department has been called in because of some altercations between our townsfolk and some nonresidents. One's a sports bar near our headquarters—Arnie's. At least some of those who've gotten out of control came to town from that ranch."

"Good. We'll work that out soon, then."

"But not tonight?" She sounded curious. Too curious. He knew what was coming next.

"No, not tonight."

"Then what are we doing tonight?" she asked.

We. Of course she would assume it would be *we.*

Which it was. But that *we* included only Ralf and him. Not her. Not for what he had planned tonight.

Click stopped to circle slightly before defecating. Good. That gave Jock an opportunity to stop, too, and turn and face Kathlene.

He drew himself up as much as possible and looked down on her slim, yet official-looking form in her deputy sheriff's uniform.

But for this purpose, he was in charge, her job notwithstanding.

"Ralf and Click and I are going to do pretty much as we did last night," he told her. "Observation and reconnaissance at the perimeter of the target facility. Just us." He raised his hand to stop her as she opened her mouth to protest. "I know you're part of our team. You won that right. But we can't spend our time worrying about where you are and if you're okay, especially when we're just doing our preliminary examinations. You can work with us, participate in other aspects of what we're doing—but only if you listen to what I'm telling you now." *And obey me,* but he knew better than to say that.

She glared up at him. Damn, but that firm chin, that angry scowl on such a beautiful face…it turned him on. Even more than her presence already generated reactions inside—and outside—him that he'd never have imagined would occur with a woman in uniform, especially when that uniform was not one associated with Alpha Force.

"Then you promise that this will be the only time you'll not include me in your plans from now on." It wasn't a question but a statement. Her voice was chilly, but not even that forced his body to lose interest.

"Yes," he lied as he stooped to clean up after Click. "I promise—as long as you promise not to interfere with what we're doing tonight."

Chapter 6

Sure, Kathlene had given her promise.

She needed to make sure Jock considered her a member of their team, so what else could she do? She didn't want to fight him again, at least not yet. Besides, he claimed it would only be this one time they would exclude her.

Ha!

On her drive back to department headquarters that afternoon, along the winding road outside town, and even when she reached the main streets, she stewed.

Damn the man and his overprotective, exclusionary attitude!

Was it going to be like this all the time? Would Jock tell her each day that she'd be included in their plans... tomorrow. But not today?

Well, she might not be officially included in their recon plans that night.

But unofficially?

She'd been there last night observing.

She would do the same tonight.

They'd followed Kathlene back into town. No, not followed her. Not exactly. But Jock had made sure that Click was settled back in his cabin. Then he drove their car, with Ralf in the passenger's seat, in the direction that Kathlene had headed.

When they reached Cliffordsville, their first plan of attack was to drive by the sheriff's department.

Kathlene's car had been parked in the large outside lot. Was she inside the building?

She could be out on patrol already. And each sheriff's department vehicle, parked in rows nearest the building, looked like the rest, with their white color, gold logo and lights on top. Jock could definitely distinguish them from the unofficial ones also parked in that lot where Kathlene had left her car among a bunch of others—ones probably also belonging to the deputies and other department employees.

It didn't matter where she was, not now. Or it shouldn't matter.

But now that Jock had met her, he worried about her safety—her training and the way she had demonstrated her prowess in hand-to-hand notwithstanding.

Would she listen to him and stay away that night?

He doubted it.

But he had to trust her…didn't he?

"So where are we going?" Ralf asked from beside him.

"Any games on TV now? I saw a sports bar not far from the restaurant where we had lunch, and it might be the one Kathlene mentioned. I think this would be a good time for beer and conversation if the place is likely to have any kind of crowd."

Ralf pulled his smartphone out of his pocket and slid his fingers over it. "Baseball, of course. But I'm not sure what teams they follow in Montana. There aren't any major league teams here. Maybe college teams. There's a baseball game between the Minnesota Twins and New York Yankees being played in the East tonight, starting about now. Maybe they watch stuff like that in the bars, even though it's not local."

"We'll go see," Jock said.

Sure enough, Arnie's Bar, along Main Street, had a big-screen TV on the wall, and it was tuned to that baseball game. The crowd seemed rather sparse, but of course Jock was used to seeing lots of people gather in bars in the Baltimore area when he and other Alpha Force members decided to join regular humans in their celebration of the teams nearest to their headquarters at Ft. Lukman on Maryland's Eastern Shore.

Jock motioned for Ralf to join him on a couple of empty stools at the tall wooden bar where most of those present had congregated.

"Hi," he said, the epitome of friendly visitor when the bartender, a short, middle-aged guy who looked as if he enjoyed both the drinks and food he served, came over to take their orders. Both chose a locally brewed bottled beer. Jock liked beer, and drinking one that originated from around here should provide an additional topic of conversation, if they needed one besides sports. Oh, and who besides them were visitors here?

Jock glanced around at the others surrounding the bar. All eyes were focused on the large screen occupying the wall behind where the bartender bustled around filling orders. Jock looked at the score at the bottom of the picture. Close game. Just one run separated the two teams, but it was only the second inning. Plenty of time for them to jostle for position before one or the other won.

The bartender plopped bottles and glasses down in front of both Ralf and him without offering to pour. That was fine with Jock. In fact, drinking directly from the bottle seemed more appropriate to this apparent guy hangout.

He lifted his bottle in a silent toast, and Ralf did the same. Both took swigs just as some members of the small crowd around them started to cheer. Jock looked up to see the screen filled with two players dashing to the next bases. The batter for New York must have hit a double, or at least his teammates were treating it like one.

"Hey," Jock said to the guy on his left side. "Good game, huh?"

"It's okay, but it may be over already since the Yanks have scored again."

"I'm from Seattle," Jock said, "just visiting here. I wouldn't mind if the Yanks won. How about you?"

"The Twins are my team," he said shortly.

"Are you from Minnesota?" Jock asked. "Or do you live here?" He kept his tone light, as if all he was doing was making polite conversation rather than conducting his first interrogation here.

"Neither." The guy took a swig of his own beer and stared back up at the screen. Interesting, Jock thought. He might just have been lucky enough to start out finding one of the possible anarchists—or sportsmen, as Kathlene was calling them. Although the guy could, of course, just be visiting friends or relatives here, or even have business to conduct in Cliffordsville.

But his disinclination to answer suggested some degree of secrecy. Jock couldn't rule him out as being one of those hanging out at the old ranch for possibly nefarious purposes.

He felt Ralf elbow him gently and turned toward his aide. "Hey, Jock," Ralf said. "This is Hal." He gestured toward the man on his other side. "He's just visiting town for a while, like us. He's doing some target practice on a ranch not far from the motel where we're staying."

Jock leaned so he could check out Hal from behind Ralf. He held out his hand. "Hi, Hal. Good to meet you. You a hunter?" He kept his tone light and nonjudgmental. Heck, if he were to ask, probably ninety percent of the regular humans who lived in an area like this most likely engaged in hunting, for food or sport or both and probably most complied with the laws. Just because he identified with some of the wildlife they might go after didn't mean he should give them a hard time about it.

"Sure am," Hal said. He was a moderate-sized guy and, if Jock were to guess, he probably worked out regularly with weights, judging by the way his arm muscles bulged as he, too, reached around Ralf to shake Jock's hand.

"Me, too," Jock lied. "We're only here for a short time visiting an old friend of mine, but target practice sounds like fun. Any possibility of our joining in?" Of course, they'd have to find reasons not to if it turned out this guy's target practice wasn't at the old ranch as part of whatever was going on there.

"Could be," Hal said. He stood and walked behind Ralf and Jock, approaching the guy at Jock's other side. That guy didn't look too pleased, especially when Hal said, "Hey, Nate, we got room to enlist some other hunters?" If Jock wasn't mistaken, Hal, who was even taller than Jock had first thought and had a substantially receding hairline, half winked toward the man he called Nate.

"Probably not just now," Nate said, not sounding especially inviting. "But I can check. You guys done much shooting before?"

Jock started making up a whole story of how he'd loved hunting since he was a kid. He added what he thought might help make up this Nate's mind if he was one of the leaders and the group actually was composed of anarchists. "Thing is," he ended up saying, "there are so many damned laws about who can own guns and where you can shoot them and what you can shoot where we come from—well, it's just damned frustrating."

"Yeah," Nate said. "Where I'm from, too." He held out his hand. "I'm Nate Tisal."

Jock introduced himself and Ralf, too.

Tisal appeared to be in his fifties, with a lot of gray in his dark hair and divots resembling parentheses emphasizing the narrowness of his lips. His light brown eyes seemed to study Jock, as if he were trying to dig into his mind and learn what he really thought about hunting and guns.

"Where's that?" Jock asked in a tone that was studiedly casual yet friendly.

"Another state," the guy dissembled. "How long you here for?"

Obviously turning the topic back to him, Jock thought. "Just a few days. Ralf and I are on our way to Yellowstone, but I wanted to take the opportunity to visit a friend from my college days who lives here."

"Who's that?" Nate immediately shot back.

Jock had already talked about this with Ralf. Since they were likely to be seen in town with Kathlene, who wore her deputy sheriff's uniform a lot, it would be better to be up front about that so none of the possible anarchists they met would assume they were talking to the authorities about their newest acquaintances.

Even though they would be.

"My old buddy Kathlene Baylor. Who'd a thunk back then that she would go into law enforcement? She's with the local sheriff's department, of all things." He shook his head as if he was totally befuddled by the idea.

"She is?" Despite the casualness of Tisal's tone, he sounded interested. Worried? Probably not.

"Yeah. I don't get it. But damned if she doesn't look good in a uniform." Jock looked around. "Hey," he said, and waved toward the bartender. "I'd like another beer. How about you?" He looked at Nate. "I'm buying. And you, Hal?"

Jock paid for a round of beers for the four of them, who were now good buddies. Or at least he had made some inroads, he hoped, into finding out more about these men and those with them—and whether they were, in fact, terrorists or more.

He realized he hadn't fully established, not yet, that they were among those hanging out at the old ranch. But he'd have bet another round of drinks for everyone there, including the additional dozen or so guys also still at the bar, that these two were part of that group.

And were they anti-law? Anti-government? That remained to be seen.

But with their initial attitude about hunting and guns... well, he couldn't rule it out, either.

* * *

"Hey, the sheriff's got a job for you for tomorrow afternoon."

Kathlene had just gotten back to work, logged in and contacted her partner, Jimmy Korling, who was going to come by and pick her up in their patrol car. She was heading outside to wait for him when Undersheriff George Kerringston hustled from the doorway to catch up with her.

She pivoted to face George. If Sheriff Frawley had personally chosen an assignment for her, it probably involved hanging out in their cruiser on the street where some town muckety-muck's kid was having a birthday party inside.

George Kerringston had been with the sheriff's department for twenty years and bragged about that often. He was slightly tall, slightly plump and all dazed most of the time. Kathlene had wondered whether their old boss, Sheriff Lon Chrissoula, had kept George on out of kindness to him or to his large and needy family, and had thought their supervisor particularly sweet to have done so. Back then, George was just a deputy, like her.

But Sheriff Frawley had promoted him. Kerringston couldn't have been happier. Or more loyal. He probably had few thoughts of his own, anyway, so he'd undoubtedly been delighted to become Melton's second in command and pass along anything and everything his boss told him to.

"Thanks, George," Kathlene made herself say. "Do you know what the assignment is?" She braced herself for something minor and useless that she'd hate.

Instead, though, it was something potentially important. "Yeah. You and a few others are being sent to patrol tomorrow afternoon's meeting of the county commissioners."

"Oh? Great. I'm on my way out now but will check more about it when I go off duty later."

"Okay." He looked her square in the face, then let his gaze roll lustfully down over her body, which made her freeze and want to go take a shower. When she glared angrily back at him, she'd have sworn he was about to drool.

Before she could say anything, he turned. Lord, couldn't the man even remember to tuck in his uniform shirt? He wasn't only a sleazy, unintelligent goon, but he was also a slob who only made the sheriff's department look bad.

But Melton obviously didn't care. He had this guy's undivided allegiance.

Some other deputies were just entering the building. They looked at her curiously, and she just shot them a smug smile that was intended to tell them this was a fine day and she was doing just great, thank you. Never mind what she was thinking inside.

She wondered what overprotective Jock Larabey would have thought about her exchange with Kerringston. Good thing he wasn't here.

At least her trading of lustful expressions with Jock was mutual—and they both understood that acting on any real sexual interest between them simply wouldn't happen.

Kathlene scanned the street in front of her. There were only a few pedestrians along the sidewalk. Not much automobile traffic, either. She wasn't sure where Jimmy was, but he was obviously taking his time getting here to pick her up.

Well, that was fine. She would use the time to her benefit. She decided to make a quick phone call—to Commission Chair Myra Enager. Myra was Tommy X's lady friend. She was also a friend of Kathlene's. Maybe even a reason why Kathlene remained with the Clifford County Sheriff's Department. Myra was both a role model for a woman's being in charge of something important around here and a sounding board for Kathlene to vent when things here didn't go well.

Not that she would abuse her authority and tell Sheriff Frawley where to go on Kathlene's behalf. And that was fine with Kathlene. She would handle this, like everything else in her life, herself.

As she would tonight, when she was supposed to pretend that she wasn't part of the team she had gotten in place here. Jock and Ralf might have heard her promise to stay away this time.

But she would use her own definition of staying away.

"Hi, Myra," she said after a secretary at the commissioners' offices had gotten her on the line. "I hear there's a meeting tomorrow afternoon."

"That's right," Myra said. "I was going to contact you about it. You might want to attend. The main topic to be discussed is my proposal for the enactment of local laws to help enforce state regulations that protect wildlife and require the arrest of poachers."

Passage of those laws locally should have been a no-brainer. They were simply following what was already enacted in the state.

But there were opponents on the commission.

And even more, the timing of the arrival of the first of the supposed sportsmen had begun just after Myra initially proposed enactment of the local law—right after Sheriff Chrissoula retired six months ago.

"Great. Not only will I be there to hear it, but I've been told I'll be on duty then, with other deputies, as well. I don't know about Tommy X, though."

Silence on the other end. Then Myra said, "Your boss is anticipating some controversy, then." It wasn't a question but a statement.

"Guess so, although I haven't talked to him directly."

"Well, don't." Myra, more than anyone, knew how much Kathlene hated conversations with her highest-up boss. "We'll be fine, especially with some of the best deputies in your department there keeping the peace. And you're definitely the best."

"Thanks, Myra. We should grab a cup of coffee one of these days." Should Kathlene tell her friend more about what she was up to? "I've got something in the works that just might help get your law passed. If nothing else, I'm checking out my theory that those guys who're showing up in town need to either get arrested or leave."

"You're not doing anything foolish, are you, Kathlene?" Now Myra sounded worried.

Kathlene glimpsed her patrol car driven by Jimmy pulling up at the curb. "Gotta run," she said. "And no, I'm not doing anything foolish. You know me better than that. See you tomorrow."

She wondered, as she hurried to the car, what Myra would really think if she knew Kathlene had not only gotten the federal government involved, but a secret military unit that wouldn't reveal, even to her, what they were really about.

Chapter 7

They were back at the cabin. After Jock and Ralf had returned, they'd taken Click for a walk around the motel area, saying hi to the few other guests and staff members they ran into.

The place seemed to be getting busier, but that was okay. They still maintained their extra cabin for Click, and his being seen with Jock now and then was a good thing.

Now they were inside, ready to report to their superior officer, Major Drew Connell of Alpha Force. He was at Ft. Lukman, and it was a couple of hours later there, nearly nine o'clock.

Drew didn't mind. The members of Alpha Force were sent all over the country and abroad for special assignments, and he'd made it clear to Jock that he expected periodic call-ins, no matter what the time.

Jock didn't have a lot to say…yet. But he knew it was time to make a call.

He motioned for Ralf to join him on the couch. Each had a bottle of water on the low table in front of them.

No more alcohol that day. Or that night. They still had something to accomplish after this call.

"Anything in particular you think we need to report?" Jock asked Ralf, then chugged some water from his bottle.

They discussed all they'd seen and heard in Clifford County so far, underscoring to one another what sounded most important. Then Jock took his phone from his pocket and keyed in the number for their commanding officer. He pressed the button that would put the call on speaker.

"Jock?" The major's voice sounded alert and interested. He was obviously using caller ID. "Ralf with you?"

"We're both here, Drew," Jock responded. "Just wanted to give you a rundown of what we've learned so far, which isn't much."

"Go ahead."

Jock proceeded to relate all that had happened in the past couple of days, from Deputy Kathlene Baylor's showing up at the cabin she had reserved for them soon after he'd called to let her know they'd arrived, to the brief interchange with the guys at the bar that afternoon.

He stressed what they had done last night. Of course. It was the crux of why Alpha Force was involved. "I shifted into wolf form and prowled outside the enclosed area," he told Drew. "Ralf stayed at the deserted house where I'd changed. I was able to find some potentially vulnerable points of entry into the encampment but I mostly stayed in the surrounding forest using all my senses just to orient myself. I'll be going back tonight, once we're done talking, to do a bit more digging."

"Anybody see you shifted?" Drew asked.

"I'm pretty sure none of the hunters or whoever they are inside the fence did, but Deputy Baylor did."

He didn't mention that he had told the stubborn woman to stay away from them, nor did he tell his commanding officer that the deputy now believed she was an integral part of their team. Jock had to deal with all of that in the best way he could. Kathlene's proclivity for involving herself was his problem, not Drew's. He could deal with it, although he might avail himself of Ralf's help now and then.

What he also hoped he could deal with—no, he *would* deal with it—was his attraction to the strong, determined and completely frustrating woman.

"We diffused any concerns she might have about seeing a wolflike dog at the site by introducing her to Click," he added. He didn't tell Drew that she appeared to be fond of canines. That was irrelevant.

"And those men at the bar—you think they're among those hanging out at that site, the possible anarchists?"

"Maybe," Jock said. "We started to foster a good relationship with them, although how good remains to be seen."

"Carry on, then." Drew paused. "Oh, and Jock?"

"Yes, sir?"

"Be damned careful—but do a good job. We need to maintain our stellar reputation."

"We will. Count on it."

His affirmative reply was seconded by Ralf.

The two men grinned at each other as they hung up. But then Ralf's expression faded. "You think there's a problem with Alpha Force's reputation?" he asked.

"Not with Drew in charge."

Every member of Alpha Force knew the covert unit's background. It was started a few years back by Drew, who was a shifter. He had begun developing the extraordinary elixir that helped shapeshifters change not only during the full moon, but at any time they chose, as well. Not only that, they could also keep their human mind, and knowledge, intact while in shifted form.

The unit consisted of shifters from wolves to lynxes to hawks. It also included aides for each of them.

Not to mention their cover animals, as close to the others' shifted forms as Click was to Jock's.

The unit's operations had occurred all over the U.S. and occasionally elsewhere, and had involved rooting out terrorists, including some who had intended to create biological weapons, and others who had aimed to destroy glaciers much faster than global warming and effect all the harm that could involve.

It was definitely a covert unit, and yet Drew and his operatives always kept their eyes peeled for other shifters they could recruit.

Like Jock himself had been about a year ago.

He hadn't regretted it. Not for a moment.

He had mostly worked with other Alpha Force operatives before. This was his first assignment in which he was the sole shifter, in charge of initial surveillance and determination if more Alpha Force members were needed to stop any harm from being inflicted on people or this country.

He definitely would perform as Drew had commanded—and do a good job.

"Let's get ready," he finally said to Ralf, who was playing with Click. "We need to put him in his cabin and then head for that deserted house again. I intend to learn a lot more about what goes on beyond that fence tonight."

Jock thought about Kathlene. He didn't feel guilty at all about leaving her out of whatever was to occur. This time he had even told her to butt out, though he would do as promised and include her as part of their team. Whenever he could. Whenever it wasn't too dangerous for her.

For tonight at least, team member or not, she was safe.

Kathlene drove a circuitous route toward the back of the fenced-in compound, lights turned off, then parked off-road so her car couldn't be seen from what passed as a partially paved lane way off in the forest.

This time she'd had plenty of time to change out of her uniform. Tonight she wore a long-sleeved knit shirt and jeans, both black. So were her athletic shoes. Unlike when she was on duty, she hadn't clipped her long hair behind her head. Its dark color might even help hide the lightness of her facial skin, in case anyone happened to glance in her direction.

She stared into the blackness of the forest and saw nothing. That was good. It meant she was unlikely to be seen, too.

She sat motionless for a few minutes, going over plans in her mind.

She had once again hung out near that old hovel of a house, observing from a distance as the two men went in, but only the dog came out. She hadn't seen Click at first, but they were clearly relying on him to observe what was going on at the nearby enclosed ranch.

And then she had carefully slipped away and driven here.

By being there, she wasn't disobeying orders. Sexy

but annoying Jock Larabey might be in charge of Ralf Nunnoz and whatever he was doing here, but he wasn't in charge of her. He wasn't her superior officer, and he had no authority to tell her what to do.

And extorting her cooperation by telling her when she was, and wasn't, a member of his team, simply didn't work.

She cracked her window just a bit. A light breeze was blowing. She heard a couple of owls hooting not far away. No other wildlife, though.

And no Click barking anywhere around. Not that a dog as well trained as he seemed to be would be making noise when he shouldn't.

Jock had told her that Ralf and he—or apparently just Click again—would be conducting some kind of surveillance at the old ranch once more that night. She wasn't sure what that would accomplish, unless the group centered there had decided to conduct an exercise under cover of darkness. Did they ever do that? Maybe.

They at least practiced the use of different kinds of weapons, although the muted explosions she'd heard a few weeks ago had been late in the day, but not nighttime.

She didn't really know what they did, though, except act secretive and threatening while pretending to be nice guys off to practice hunting skills. As sportsmen.

As they planned some nasty uses in the future of the weapons they tested now…? That was her fear.

But hanging out here tonight was likely to be fruitless, just as last night had been.

Still, if Jock decided that Alpha Force would check the compound out again that night, then so would she.

She hated doing everything in near total darkness, but fortunately, in the area where she was now, the trees weren't quite as close together so there was a little illumination from the stars overhead.

Lovely to see them this way, the constellations and all. The moon was only a sliver, so it didn't provide much light, but she loved looking up in the sky toward the stars.

Not that she dared do that very much. She had more important things to watch.

For now she would just stay in this area and conduct her own little bit of surveillance.

If she didn't see anything, she would carefully move toward where she had first seen Click maneuvering around the compound last night.

Surely she could glean more information than a dog could. Or even if she couldn't compete with its superior senses, she could certainly verbally divulge a lot more than a canine could.

Unless…she hadn't asked, but maybe they had equipped the dog with some kind of camera or other recording equipment. That would make sense.

And if she was part of the team, they should not only tell her but also show her what had been filmed.

She could take some shots herself. She pulled her phone out of her pocket, held it down so any illumination wouldn't be visible outside her car and reset it so it showed no lights—but would nevertheless take pictures.

No other kinds of shots, though. Not tonight. She purposely left her Glock in the glove compartment of her car.

She wasn't here as a deputy, but as a curious and concerned citizen.

But now it was time. She cautiously opened the door of her vehicle, prepared to get out quickly, even though she'd turned off the interior lights, too. This far from the fencing no one was likely to see her, anyway, but just in case...

She slid out fast and pushed the door closed, careful not to make any slamming sounds. Then she stood still for a few minutes to orient herself.

The air smelled tangy and moist, as if humidity was hovering, determining when a rain shower should begin to pummel the earth.

She heard nothing now, not owls or anything else. It was time to draw closer to the perimeter of the compound. And watch for Click, who would probably be circling the whole thing.

She had done a bit of surveillance before trying to enlist help from the federal government, but she hadn't done this.

Nor had she been competing to convince anyone to keep her involved. She had, back then, been the only one who'd tried to do anything.

And now, if she was lucky, she would get a lot more useful stuff than the dog did. Show Jock that she was an important part of the team.

Show Jock that—

"Hands up, lady." The voice that growled at her was off to her side, and she was suddenly bathed in so much light that she was blinded and couldn't see its source. "What the hell are you doing here?"

"I was just—" she stammered.

"Don't matter. You're coming with me."

Damn!
While preparing to sneak in through a particularly vulnerable and worn area of fencing, Jock had caught the scent of Kathlene in the distance.

The woman was impossible. Never listened.

Always put herself in danger.

And once he had loped in her direction in his shifted form, careful to stay hidden in the trees, he had seen that she had been captured.

The man who had found her kept a gun trained on her back. He marched her toward a nearby gate in the fence—one that had been secured and was not a potential entry point for Jock. He watched as Kathlene was forced to go through the gate and onto the fenced-in site.

He tore back to one of the vulnerable areas he had located before, where the chain-link fencing had apparently been hit by a car or otherwise damaged. There was enough of a gap that a canine could squeeze through it.

He did.

He looked around cautiously, engaged all his senses to ensure that there were no humans nearer than those now congregating around Kathlene and the man who had captured her.

He knew how to help her—maybe. And then only if she was astute enough to follow his lead.

Too bad he hadn't come with a collar and leash to further resemble the dog who was his cover. But he would improvise, and so, he hoped, would Kathlene.

Assuming a submissive position, he all but crawled on his stomach, using all four legs.

As he maneuvered, he listened to the conversation. Rather, the way Kathlene was being chewed out and threatened.

"Why the hell are you here?" "Ain't you a deputy sheriff?" "You don't belong here. We don't like snoops." "Tell us what you want here." "Let's just shoot the nosy bitch. No one will ever know."

Jock wanted to growl. To attack. But his human mind overshadowed his wild-animal instincts. Instead, he just continued to draw himself closer.

"What's that dog doing here?" he heard one of the men say. "That's no dog. It's a wolf."

Jock maneuvered his way up to Kathlene's side, pretending to ignore the crowd of ill-smelling, menacing hunters who surrounded her in what appeared to be a stable yard of the old ranch. A floodlight had been turned on and illuminated the entire area. When he glanced up briefly, he recognized one of the men Ralf and he had seen in the bar earlier.

That man—Nate Tisal—appeared to be in charge.

Jock smelled Kathlene's fear, but the woman stood straight, chin up, scowling at her captors...until she saw him.

"Click!" she exclaimed, as if he was her savior.

In some ways he was—if she figured out how to play this.

He hurried up to her, nuzzled her side with his nose, whined a little as if in fear.

"There you are," she said. "You bad dog." Did she get it? It sounded as if she did. "He belongs to some friends of mine who're visiting. I love dogs but don't have one right now, so I was walking him for them. He apparently likes to go into the woods and usually stays near the road, but this time he ran away. I was out here looking for him." She slipped to her knees and hugged him. He wished he could hug her back but instead licked her cheek.

She tasted sweet and salty and nervous.

"You were walking a dog out here?" Tisal's tone was scornful.

"No," she said, rising again to look the tall, hefty, scowling man in his gleaming brown eyes. "Like I said, I was walking him in the area, a distance from here, near the road, but he ran away and I've been looking all over for him."

She sounded affronted and sure of herself.

"I'm sorry if I bothered you, Mr. Tisal. Although," she continued, "I don't understand why you're all so defensive. Are you doing something here that you shouldn't be?"

Damn her! If he could have, he'd have slapped a muzzle on her to shut her up.

But then he realized why she'd done it. To maintain her character, since at least some of these men apparently knew she was a deputy sheriff.

"Not at all," Tisal countered smoothly. "It's just that most of us were heading for bed and it was startling that someone spotted a prowler. We weren't sure if you were doing something here that you shouldn't be. Were you?"

"Of course not. Just looking for my friends' dog. And now I won't even have to tell them he went missing. I'll just take him and go home." She looked at him. "I left his collar and leash, though. Do you happen to have a rope that I can use to lead him?"

"Yeah." Tisal nodded toward one of his minions, who dashed off. "Okay. You can go home with your dog. No harm, no foul. I apologize that some of my friends might have sounded too harsh but we were all startled by your being here. And in case anyone asks, I hope it's clear enough to you that we're not doing anything wrong, just hanging out and practicing till hunting season."

"I got it," she said. "And I can certainly understand why your friends overreacted." Jock wished she would *aim such a bright smile toward him but realized how false it really was.*

And he felt sure she didn't forgive them for their threats—which convinced him more that she'd been correct about the nature of these guys and what they were doing.

Smart lady, he thought again. Turning the situation so it appeared as if it was resolved in favor of these men.

And maybe it was. Would real anarchists rehearsing for some terrorist attack actually let her go?

Or were they simply using Kathlene as a foil?

And if the latter, she should only remain in danger as long as these men were around.

Chapter 8

One of the men, a guy in an open shirt and jeans, stayed with Kathlene while she walked Click back through the woods to her car. She tromped in the near total darkness on uneven clumps of dead leaves, not caring about the noise she made now and not looking at the guy—but aware every moment of his presence.

The odor of impending rain filled her lungs, or maybe they just felt constricted because of the nervousness she had felt before, with vestiges still hanging on now.

Fortunately, the man who'd gone after a rope had found something that let her keep Click secured loosely at her side. She just hoped their escort didn't insist on her showing him Click's actual collar and leash. She'd have to go into an act about how she'd thought she had left it in the car but must have instead lost it in the woods when she let the dog run free.

She reached her car in about five minutes, yanked the key from her pocket and pushed the button to unlock the doors. She opened the one on the passenger's side and gently pulled the rope around Click's neck to get him to jump in first. Then she nodded to their unwelcome companion without saying anything as she circled the car, slid into the driver's seat and locked the doors.

Only then did she feel she could breathe again.

"That wasn't any fun," she said to Click as the light inside the car faded. "Those guys are definitely nasty."

He whined, and she interpreted it as agreement with her. But the way the wolflike dog looked at her—it seemed like a glare, scolding her for having been there in the first place.

"I'm reading too much of your master into you, guy," she told the dog. And despite knowing she would be scolded, at a minimum, by Jock, she half wished he were there, too. No, more than half.

Whatever Alpha Force was, she would really have appreciated it if the strong, determined Jock had had her back during this ugly incident.

Well, his dog had had her back, and the situation had ended a whole lot better than she'd figured it would.

And Click? Well, she really liked this dog. Appreciated his help.

Still wondered why she had recalled his head as being flatter, his legs longer, his coat a little shorter and less wolflike.

Well, no matter. She turned the key in the ignition and drove off slowly through the woods toward the barely paved road.

If she hadn't had Click with her, she'd have driven

straight home. Maybe had a glass of wine to help calm her nerves. Or two glasses.

But since Click was with her she needed to take him back to Jock and Ralf. That meant she would have to explain to them what had happened.

Where she had been.

And how their dog had been a lifesaver.

This time she didn't turn off her exterior lights. She soon reached the main road, which was a shred better maintained than the one she'd been on. It only took another few minutes to arrive at the hovel that the Alpha Force guys had settled into as their apparent local command center. She pulled into what passed for a driveway and parked.

"Come on, boy." She again took hold of the rope that looped around Click's neck and remained careful not to pull it too hard, not wanting to choke him.

But the dog didn't seem to want to go to the house's main door. Instead, he pulled slightly toward the back area, then led her to the rear door. Interesting. But of course Click had been here before with the two men, and maybe they had started using this as their main entrance. It was less visible from the nearby road, so that made sense, especially since they had also parked in back. Maybe she should have, too.

As she knocked on the door, Click raised one of his fur-covered legs and pawed at it. That made Kathlene smile. The dog was clearly trained to act at least somewhat human.

The door was pulled open nearly immediately. Ralf stood there, and he looked downward toward Click first, then let his gaze dart upward toward Kathlene's face.

"Er…Hi, Kathlene. Come in. How did you—where did you find Click?"

"I'll tell you all about it but I'd rather just describe it one time, to both Jock and you. It wasn't pretty, but it'd have been a lot worse if Click hadn't been there to save me."

"What?" His tone sounded aghast, and his dark eyes turned huge.

Kathlene managed a laugh. "I'll explain." She glanced around. "Where is Jock?"

"Uh…he's probably out looking for Click. He…went with Click to check out the exterior of the ranch again. And since Click is here with you, he's probably still there searching for…for the dog."

Ralf seemed to be hiding something, but Kathlene had no idea what it could be. No matter.

"I'll wait here with you, then, till he shows up."

"No!" Ralf's tone was sharp. He ran his thick hand over his short crop of graying hair. What the heck was really going on? "No, Jock and I already made plans for this kind of situation. I'm to take Click back to our cabin and wait there. If…if Jock doesn't show up within a short while, I'm to head back here to wait for him. Since you probably won't see him tonight, it'd be better if you just gave me a brief description of what happened that I can convey to him, then you can go home and get some sleep. We'll all talk about it more tomorrow."

He clearly wanted her to spill her story then leave. At the moment he hadn't really even let her go very far inside. They stood near the door, talking.

Maybe that was a good thing. The place smelled musty and unpleasant. But she didn't need to stay there long. Only long enough for Jock to arrive and listen to her story.

She didn't want to argue, though. Ralf obviously didn't want her to wait for Jock. And as exhausted and frustrated as she felt, going home sounded great.

"Okay," she said. "Let me sit down, and I'll tell you what happened."

Ralf showed her to a rickety chair that had apparently remained in this disaster of a house. She gave him the abridged version of her horror at being caught, threatened and virtually imprisoned, and how she had been able to use the very unexpected presence of Click inside the property's fence to make up a good enough story that, even if the anarchists didn't buy it, they wound up letting her and the dog leave, anyway.

Ralf, seated on another equally decrepit chair, kept exclaiming and shaking his head.

Surprisingly, Click stayed at her feet, sitting there and seeming to enjoy the sound of her voice. At least the dog kept looking up at her and even made some small whining noises in his throat.

When she finished with how it had felt to slip into the car with Click and drive away, Ralf leaped to his feet. He took her hands and squeezed them.

"I'm just glad you're okay. Jock'll be glad, too. I've got to go look for him now since he won't have his phone on. You go ahead home and get some sleep. I know he'll want to talk to you more about it, so plan on getting together with us sometime tomorrow."

She told him about the county commissioners' upcoming meeting and that she would be there on duty. "And I'm glad—since I heard that some measures that might evoke reactions from those sportsmen are being discussed. It's a public meeting, so I'd suggest that Jock and you attend, too. I'll go off duty shortly after it's over, so we can grab coffee and talk."

"Sounds like a plan." Ralf glanced down at Click, then back up into Kathlene's face. "We'll see you there."

And then he ushered her back out the door.

She rehashed a lot of things as she drove back home as quickly as she could: her horrible situation with those men. How that smart dog, who was unbelievably sweet despite resembling a combo between a wolf and German shepherd, had helped her diffuse and escape.

And then Ralf's attitude, and the absence of Jock.

She absolutely had to get those men to explain Alpha Force. Something about that covert military unit would clarify at least some of their part of what she had just undergone. She felt sure of it.

Those two men should not keep her in the dark any longer.

Jock sat on the chair that Kathlene had vacated half an hour before, his hands clasped, his head bent as he attempted to maintain his temper.

He had spent part of that time shifting back to human form and getting dressed.

Now he was ready to head back to their cabins with Ralf. To check on the real Click and make sure he was okay.

And grab a drink, not at the bar where they'd met up with Tisal but by themselves. By *him*self, preferably.

He knew that Ralf was full of questions but had been astute enough not to ask them—yet.

What he did ask, though, was, "You okay, Lieutenant? I mean, Jock."

Jock shot a glare at his aide, who again sat in the chair he had occupied when Kathlene was here. Ralf was grinning, knowing he was intentionally prodding Jock's dander by doing as he'd been ordered not to—acting even somewhat military right now.

"I'm fine," he grumbled back.

"Except for wanting to strangle Deputy Baylor, right?"

Jock closed his eyes and counted to five before opening them again. "Yeah," he said. "Except for wanting to strangle Deputy Baylor. But that would be most imprudent considering I pretty much saved her ass before, while shifted."

"Yes, she does have a pretty ass." That grin of Ralf's twitched, and Jock knew he was only trying to goad him. And succeeding.

"Maybe I should strangle you, instead, Staff Sergeant." Jock started to rise, but only got a laugh out of Ralf.

"Maybe I can just pin you to the floor like Deputy Baylor did," Ralf countered. He paused and continued more seriously, "I know you don't like her putting herself in danger like that, Jock. I don't, either. But until we figure out what's going on around here and stop it, you know she's just going to keep at it. And if she hadn't wound up calling in federal help and getting Alpha Force here she'd probably have remained in the thick of it all by herself."

"Yeah, I know," Jock conceded. "But she did wind up with us here, even if she didn't know exactly what she was getting. And like it or not, I realize we'd better plan on her inclusion and interference."

"And maybe on her finding out what Alpha Force is really about."

"Not if I—" Jock stopped himself. "Maybe you're

right. Whether or not we want her to. But I suspect a woman like that, once she got over the shock, might not hate the idea."

"We may just find that out," Ralf said.

"True." He forced himself not to sigh or react in any other way—this time. "Now, let's go back and see how I—rather, my counterpart Click—is doing right now, shall we?"

"Yes, sir," Ralf said.

"On the way, let's discuss what we're likely to hear at tomorrow's county commissioners' meeting, okay?"

"I just happen to have downloaded their agenda onto my smartphone while you were out playing wonder dog and saving Deputy Kathlene's butt. I'll drive—which I should, anyway, since your body may still be morphing here and there—and you can look it over. The agenda, that is. Not our deputy's butt. Or ass. Or whatever."

Jock glared at Ralf. He shouldn't give a damn that his aide happened to have noticed Kathlene's lovely, firm, enticing rear area. What red-blooded male wouldn't have?

And just because he found the woman much too damned sexy didn't mean he had any priority over any other man in looking at, or wanting, her.

He'd have to keep telling himself that in the next few days, especially since he had no doubt that she would insist on staying involved.

And that meant he actually had to treat her as part of their team—at least enough to keep an eye on her and attempt to keep her out of trouble.

"You ready, Kathlene?" asked Deputy Jimmy Korling, checking his duty belt without glancing at her. Jimmy was a somewhat nice-looking guy, with short, wavy black hair and a youthfully muscular body.

He was also clearly not pleased about having a woman as his very first partner after joining the department. Most of the time he was very cordial, if remote.

Most of the time…

"Just about. How about you?" She, like her partner, was confirming that her uniform, including the equipment on her belt, was complete and that she was ready to report to the county commissioners' meeting as one of the law-enforcement officers there on duty.

"I sure am," Jimmy said.

"Great. Just give me another minute." She worked to finalize her check.

Right now it was the morning after her unpleasant visit to the sportsmen's ranch. She was at the department headquarters, in the dispatch room, where all officers congregated before heading off to duty. It had chairs for them to sit, plus mirrors on the wall so they could get last-minute glimpses of themselves and assure that they appeared professional and ready for the day's assignment.

She had arrived at department headquarters right on time that morning despite the wet roads after some overnight rainfall—and after getting little sleep the night before.

That was mostly because of her nighttime rescue, thanks to a dog, from the people she deemed to be anarchists. Thinking about it—the situation, and how she had managed to exit it relatively gracefully—had occupied her mind much of the night.

But she wasn't about to tell any of her colleagues about that. Would the men from the ranch mention it to any locals?

To Sheriff Frawley?

Kathlene didn't like the idea but couldn't assume it wouldn't happen.

And where had Jock been? Had Ralf found him? Were they back at their cabin?

She believed so. She hadn't wanted to call them in case they were sleeping in, or were up early and out and about doing whatever they were doing undercover, maybe hanging out in local restaurants pretending to be visitors.

She was their team member, though, and they should have let her know.

She'd texted Jock just before reporting for duty, while still in her car. She'd received a brief response:

All fine. Glad Click helped you yesterday. See you later.

The only question he'd seemed to answer was whether he'd gotten back with Ralf and Click. Unless, of course, Ralf was responding on Jock's behalf.

She knew she was one suspicious lady. But she was an officer of the law. Suspicion was her job, even when she wasn't involved in a potentially threatening situation—like now.

But she wasn't going to resolve anything here. Would she at the upcoming meeting?

No, but it might turn out to be quite interesting—and the discussions there could be highly enlightening.

"Okay, partner," she finally said, aiming one last look at the mirror on the wall, then facing Jimmy, who now seemed to be studiously ignoring her. "Let's go."

As she had been ordered, Kathlene, in uniform and with her weapon in its holster at her side, stood just inside the door to the large public meeting room in the 1950s-style building that housed the Clifford County government offices. Straight and alert, she maintained a position that wasn't quite at attention, but nor was it at ease.

Far from it.

She was there to be visible as well as to watch all that was going on. Her gaze scanned the room, confirming that everything looked peaceful and friendly and not in need of official sheriff's department intervention. Not yet, at least.

She scented perfumes and shaving lotions as people walked by her to enter. She heard snatches of conversations, received a few friendly hellos, which she responded to, but otherwise stayed silent and alert.

She knew most of the people walking in. So far, they hadn't included Jock or Ralf. Where were they? Today's session could be important to their ability to determine who those who'd infiltrated that old ranch were and what they wanted.

Even if it wasn't, they should be here to find out.

At least none of the men who'd accosted her when she'd been saved by Click had arrived yet, either. But she felt fairly certain that Nate Tisal, who'd appeared to be in charge of the sportsmen's outpost, would be here.

Her partner, Jimmy, was stationed at the door directly across the room from her. He appeared bored and not especially alert, but the meeting hadn't yet gotten started.

Kathlene hoped he would do his job. Same went for the other couple of deputies who'd been deployed here, both of whom stood outside in the hallway at the moment. She wasn't sure when or if they'd come inside.

A lot of people had already entered the assembly room. Most were seated in the folding metal chairs that had been lined up in ten long rows. A few stood in the aisles at each end of the rows, chatting. The noise level was high in this room that had clearly not been built for the best acoustics, but Kathlene knew the sound would level off once the meeting began.

She glanced at her watch. Five more minutes. That's when the commissioners would enter the room and begin their session.

She had attended county commissioners' meetings before, mostly as a local resident interested in what was going on in the area.

Now, though, the commission had requested a visible presence by the sheriff's department for the third time—and each of those times Kathlene had attended in uniform.

Which she had been glad to do. She had discussed the situation with her friend Commission Chair Myra Enager each time, before the session and after. Both of the prior times, there'd been at least a few of the men hanging out at the old ranch who'd come in and even tried to speak. But they hadn't followed the commission protocol so they'd not been able to present their opinions.

Not vocally. But their glares had spoken volumes.

So had the anonymous and general threats delivered by email and otherwise afterward, although no one could definitely attribute any of them to the apparent anarchist group.

These sessions and what had occurred afterward had added to Kathlene's concerns about who the people were who were staying at the old ranch. But it didn't take a law-enforcement officer to note the cold stares leveled by the visitors who appeared at those earlier meetings and sat at the front of the room when something about hunting restrictions or gun licensing was being discussed.

Today the mayor of Cliffordsville, Larry Davonne, was also there, sitting in the front row with some of his aides. He wasn't in charge of anything here, since he was a city official and this was a county meeting. But Kathlene felt certain that the commissioners had requested his presence to ensure that he knew what was going on. Maybe to get his input.

Kathlene had been watching for the mayor, since Jimmy and she had been told to pay special attention to him and to a couple of commissioners who had expressly requested the law-enforcement presence and surveillance. The deputies were to make it clear that the crowd at the meeting was under guard, if necessary.

That included Myra, of course, and her closest ally on the commission, Wendy Ingerton. The other five members were men. All appeared to get along reasonably well, but the members besides Myra and Wendy had been fairly tight-lipped about their opinions on the matters that clearly riled the visitors: local laws to help enforce new state regulations that protected wildlife and required the arrest of poachers. A certain amount of gun control was involved in those matters, too—licensing, at least, and some background checks for the purchase of ammunition.

Despite the controversy surrounding those concepts even among members of the sheriff's department, Kathlene thought them quite reasonable to impose on strangers whose real purpose for being here remained hazy—and potentially threatening.

"Hello, Kathlene." The low voice at her ear caused a soft shiver of pleasure to ripple through her body. She tried not to smile, to stay professional, as she turned to see its source.

"Well, hi, Jock," she said. "Hi, Ralf." It was okay to smile now, since she was playing the role of longtime friend of the tall, sexy, grinning man who stood closest to her after slipping in the door near her. "So you decided to see how my town works? Good. I'm glad. Go ahead and grab a seat. I'm on duty, like I told you."

But she felt a lot more comfortable with these two men in the room—which was also perversely irritating. She knew they were military men, probably could handle a lot of stuff, but she was the official law-enforcement officer here, not them.

"I should have told you to save us some seats near you," Jock said softly. It was true; most of the chairs on her side of the room had filled up.

But there were a couple near the back, although not on the aisle. "How about there?" At the moment, it really didn't matter if they were close by. Even so, the idea of their having her back, even unofficially, allowed her to relax just a little and ignore her internal grumpiness.

"Okay."

Ralf waved at her as he followed Jock through what was left of the crowd in the aisle. Nearly everyone had found seats.

Kathlene glanced at her watch. Time for the fun to begin.

As if she had called them, the county commissioners began filing into the room from the door near the front that led to a separate hallway to their offices.

That was when Kathlene saw Tisal and some others she recognized from her confrontation the night before begin to enter the chamber from the door nearest Jimmy.

Showtime.

Chapter 9

Jock didn't like this, but he wasn't surprised.

The possible anarchists slipping into the commissioners' meeting at the last minute could just have been because they were running late—as Ralf and he had been. They'd just spoken with Major Drew Connell again, this time about the day's proposed agenda, and had gotten a delayed start.

But with the newcomers, including that guy Tisal, who'd been involved in the nastiness against Kathlene last night—well, they'd wait and see if those guys tried to disrupt anything, but Jock wasn't at all pleased to see them even if they kept quiet and just listened. Not that he was surprised by their presence.

"Let's come to order here." That was the woman in the middle of the group of seven commissioners, all seated at a long table facing their audience on a slightly raised stage. Her name was Myra Enager, Jock found out a moment later as she introduced herself and the other commissioners. She was the chairperson, an efficient and serious-looking, middle-aged woman, who didn't look like she would brook any nonsense from this group.

Jock had heard of her and wasn't surprised. The information Kathlene had provided that resulted in Alpha Force being deployed here had mentioned Myra's name and status on the commission.

It had additionally said what proposed local laws the commission had been considering, and the nonspecific threats to its members had been part of why the military presence was determined to be critical. The situation had sounded potentially way beyond the ability of locals to resolve peacefully, if at all.

Myra also introduced Mayor Laurence Davonne, who sat at one side of the audience and appeared to be surrounded by assistants dressed much like he was in dark suits. He waved but didn't seem very enthused about being mentioned.

"Now here are the items we will be considering today," Myra continued. "We've had some changes in our agenda."

Interesting. The woman leveled a glare toward the part of the room now occupied by the group who'd stomped in at the last minute—Tisal and his gang.

"We'll once again defer consideration of the matters I have proposed to the commission, those regarding enactment of county statutes to help enforce the latest state regulations to protect wildlife and to arrest and incarcerate anyone found poaching."

"What? Why defer it again?" This was another of the commissioners, one toward the end of the table—Grabling was his name, per Myra's intro. He half stood and glared at the chairperson.

"From the start, I intended my proposal to be helpful, not controversial. However, for the past several months it has generated a lot of discussion at our open meetings—and more." Myra glared into the audience toward the corner of the room where the newcomers still stood. They glared right back. Jock figured that what she wasn't saying was that the arrival of that group had made her decide to remove the controversial matters from the agenda.

Possibly due to prior bad experience.

Tisal raised his hand as if he wanted to be called on to speak.

"We are currently not open to any further discussion, at least not here and now," Myra said.

Jock glanced toward Kathlene. She was obviously on alert, standing stiffly with her hand poised over her firearm. He doubted she would use it—unless she had no choice.

But just the gesture should make any sane person in this audience back down.

Tisal didn't. His hand was still raised, and it was waving. "Madam Chairwoman," he shouted. "I wish to be heard."

"There is nothing for you to be heard about, sir," Myra called back to him. "We have no motions on the table, and in fact, we are about to adjourn."

"But we haven't done anything," Grabling protested. "We owe it to our county residents who've come here this afternoon to at least describe what they came to learn more about—your damned…er, your proposals regarding hunting. We and they can talk about those proposals further and put them to a vote if not this afternoon, then next time for sure."

"If anyone here is unhappy about this, I do apologize," Myra said, "but in the interest of safety and security of all of us—"

"At least tell us what proposals are still on the table." That was Tisal. He was no longer with his gang at the back of the room but strode forward toward the podium. "We're curious, that's all. Then you can adjourn or do whatever you'd like, Madam Chairperson."

He spoke completely reasonable words in a completely reasonable way—and Jock didn't trust any of it. Not after his own supposedly innocent discussions with Tisal, the *sportsman*—or the way Tisal had allowed Kathlene to be badgered last night.

By now the entire crowd was stirring, mostly chattering in apparent support of Tisal. Kathlene was still alert, her expression suggesting incredulity. Were the apparent anarchists always so rational-sounding in public? Unlikely, but they were garnering a lot of support here.

Two other deputies were now inside, too. They stood near the other uniformed guy across the room, apparently listening.

Or not. They all seemed to glare at Myra as if she was being unreasonable, and maybe she was.

Or maybe she was just being smart. And protective.

"I think we can accommodate that gentleman," Grabling said. "Here's what we are considering, sir. Earlier this year, our state named some additional wild animals as endangered and requested that individual counties where hunting permits are granted add those animals to their lists. We're also requested to step up our gun laws and the penalties that can be imposed for violating them."

"We told everyone that before," said Wendy Ingerton, the other woman on the commission. "And making it public generated all sorts of…well, let's just call it discussion."

"And threats," Myra added. "Even though we assured people that we're not against hunting when done appropriately and in accordance with law. Nor are we against using guns, again if they're used safely and in accordance with law. And never used against people." She shot a glance in Kathlene's direction. "Except when enforcing the law, of course." Then Myra moved her gaze toward Tisal. "You wouldn't know anything about that, would you, sir?"

The man's smile was so sorrowful that it all but shouted its falseness to Jock. But others in the room might buy it. The buzz of conversation grew louder.

"Are you accusing me of something, Madam Chairperson?" Tisal asked in a soft tone that mirrored his expression.

"Only if the shoe fits," Myra said.

"But I'm sure you're just speculating," Tisal responded. "Can you provide proof to these nice people?"

"I think we're adjourned," Wendy Ingerton said. "All in favor?"

Myra's hand went up immediately. "Aye."

Grabling seemed to want to protest, but Myra's accusatory stare was leveled next at him. "Aye," he echoed.

So did enough of the others at the table to actually adjourn the meeting.

But as everyone poured out of the room, including the mayor and his minions, Tisal and some of his gang flowed forward while the council members filed out.

"We'll see you all next time," Tisal said as he reached some of those council members, his smile still innocent but his eyes full of malice.

* * *

Before she left, Myra gestured an invitation toward Kathlene, who hurried to join her at the front of the room on an edge of the raised meeting platform. Myra's charcoal suit looked rumpled, her face looked stressed.

"I'd like for you to come with me," Myra said. "I've called for a private session to start now. I don't think my colleagues are thrilled about it, and they may even let those…men know. If you could just stand there, looking official and guarding us, it might help."

"Of course." Kathlene would need to report in to let her superiors know what she was doing, but she doubted they'd mind an extension of the assignment they had given her earlier.

She glanced around. The rest of the room was nearly empty of people. She saw Jock and Ralf move in her direction. She wanted to talk to them, to get their take on what had happened at the meeting, but that would need to wait until they could go somewhere private.

The expression on Jock's face was icy and serious, but when she motioned for him to join them his look softened—after he gave her one sexy, assessing look.

"Come here, you guys," Kathlene said cheerfully. "I want you to meet Commission Chair Myra Enager. Myra, Jock is an old friend from college, and Ralf is one of his friends." She quickly told Myra their cover story about the men being from Washington State and stopping to see her before heading to Yellowstone.

Could she tell her friend about bringing in a covert military unit to help confront the *sportsmen?* Maybe, but she'd been sworn to secrecy. And if she told Myra, Tommy X would undoubtedly hear about it, too.

"I found your meeting very interesting," Jock said to

Myra. "But I was really concerned when you mentioned threats. What kind of threats?"

He actually knew more about them, of course, Kathlene thought. The threats to the council had all been part of the reports she had submitted when she sought help. But she figured he wanted Myra's description, too.

As well as how concerned she really felt about those threats. But Kathlene knew that Myra was an intelligent, sensitive and politically savvy woman. And in their discussions about the threats, she might have laughed them off a bit in what she said, but the seriousness of her tone and expression told a different tale.

"I don't have time to talk about them now," Myra said. "My private meeting's about to begin. But Kathlene knows about them. She'll be with me at that session but I'm sure she can fill you in later. Nice meeting you." Without another glance, Myra headed out of the room.

"I do need to be with her," Kathlene said. "But I'll want to get together later. Dinner?"

"Sure," Jock said after sharing a glance with Ralf. "An early one."

"What's going on later?" she demanded. They weren't going to keep her out of it this time, no matter what it was.

"We'll talk about it at dinner," Jock said cryptically. Kathlene wanted to strangle it out of him.

Better yet, kiss it out of him...

No. She wouldn't think like that, no matter how much his amused, hot gaze turned her on. He was just trying to discombobulate her. And succeeding.

"I'll call you as soon as this meeting is over," she told him.

And as she followed Myra down the hall she made

another call—one to Tommy X. He was high enough in the food chain that he could report to those who needed to know about what she was doing, and a close enough friend that he wouldn't argue about it.

Pizza. That was what they were going to have for dinner that night, Kathlene learned after the relocated and abbreviated commission meeting was finally over.

Her first phone call had been to Jock, and his deep voice, filled with amusement and charm, asked first where she was, how she was, whether she needed backup, all of which made her feel both annoyed at his lack of confidence in her and gooey that he seemed to give a damn. And then they talked about where to eat—in about half an hour.

She was walking along the relatively empty sidewalks of Cliffordsville now, back to the sheriff's department to officially sign out for the day and get on her way to meet Jock and Ralf. There wasn't much traffic on the streets, either. She simply strolled between official administration buildings, almost alone. The sun was going down, and the structures cast shadows along the pavement, keeping her comfortably cool.

Nothing much had been accomplished at the reconvened meeting. Not unexpectedly, the seven members were divided into two factions: Myra and Wendy Ingerton on one side, along with one of the men. Three men, including Grabling, were decisively on the anti-legislation side when it had to do with more restrictions on hunting or weapons. And one guy was undecided, so they might as well not have met again. That commissioner, Mertas, was likely to be accosted by lots of attempts to sway him to one side or the other, Kathlene felt sure.

She called Jimmy after her conversation with Jock ended, a courtesy since he was her partner. He seemed a bit grateful that he hadn't been enlisted to stay, too.

She finally reached the department headquarters and went inside. Asking around, she learned that the sheriff and his head deputies were in a meeting of their own. They might not even have known—yet—that Kathlene had remained at the county commissioners building after the main meeting broke up.

Tommy X, ducking out of that meeting for a restroom break, took her aside briefly in the department's main admin room as she signed out for the day. "What actually happened?" he asked. "I've heard all sorts of versions. Is Myra okay? Was there any trouble?"

"She's fine and, no, there wasn't any trouble—not at the private, post-meeting meeting," Kathlene told her tall, middle-aged ally, who leaned on the nearby wall for extra support. Of course he would be most concerned about the woman he was dating.

Now that she wasn't in the middle of things, Kathlene could relax—and she felt exhausted. Good thing they were alone in this vast room, at least for the moment. She just wished she was out of her uniform and into something a lot more comfortable. "I suspect there was a lot that churned in the background and remained unsaid at the adjourned public meeting. The an…er, the sportsmen now living at the old ranch had a presence, and they seemed very well behaved, but that doesn't mean they weren't the source of the threats."

It wasn't appropriate to call those men *anarchists* in Tommy X's presence. She'd run that by him before, and, despite his awareness that there was some animosity toward Myra, he wasn't buying Kathlene's accusation, not without more proof. Continuing to call them sportsmen was a good compromise.

"It doesn't mean they were, either." Tommy X's gray eyebrows knitted in a chastising frown. "I know you don't like or trust them. But don't let your opinions cloud your thinking."

Good thing he didn't know about her trespassing the night before, Kathlene thought. Or how it had turned out.

"I won't," she said. "See you tomorrow."

Jock and Ralf were already seated at a table at the pizza joint when Kathlene walked in, still in her uniform as usual on a day she was on duty.

She made the outfit look almost beautiful—because she was beautiful.

She also looked tired, Jock thought. Being on duty in the middle of an overtly peaceful yet underlyingly antagonistic crowd must have been wearing on her.

The restaurant was only moderately crowded and smelled of a lot of tangy spices. Even regular humans would probably sense the sharp cheese, oregano, peppers and more.

Kathlene spotted them in the middle of the room nearly immediately, and Ralf waved toward her. As soon as she was near them, Jock rose to pull her chair out for her.

"Hi," she said softly, looking up at him. He could imagine her sleepy blue eyes trained on him similarly in the dark after an exhausting, fulfilling bout of lovemaking.

His body reacted to the image, and he moved quickly to get her seated and resume his own chair.

Surprisingly, she ordered a beer. He'd have assumed that would put her right to sleep. But she seemed to perk up a bit as they started talking.

"What did you think of Tisal and the way he acted at the meeting?" she asked them. "I mean, he mostly just seemed so nice and low-key, like any other attendee. And yet—"

"And yet it didn't take anyone with psychic ability, if there is such a thing, to know what he was thinking," Ralf said. He'd been dressed in a nice shirt and slacks at the meeting but they'd had time to return to their cabin and change. And check on Click. Now Ralf wore a Cliffordsville T-shirt that he had just bought.

Jock had stuck with a solid color navy knit shirt. "Or implying," he added. "Threats? Who, him? He acted so innocent that it should have been obvious to anyone who knew there'd been some threats that they'd come from him or his gang."

"Amen," Kathlene said.

Their server brought their beers and they ordered a large pizza with a variety of toppings that they would all split. Kathlene also ordered a small salad.

For the rest of their time together, they discussed what should come next—in lowered voices and language couched in tourist kinds of planning.

Kathlene pushed for details, reminding him that he'd said they'd discuss plans over dinner. He kept things general, though, mostly talking about how Ralf and he were still determining their best approach to learn more about the men at that compound. For one thing, he told her, they'd already started acting interested in joining the group as hunters and would follow up on that.

Jock didn't mention how far along their intended process really was, or that their plans didn't really start the next day, but sooner. He had a feeling that there'd be some interesting discussions that night at the anarchists' hangout.

He wanted to listen to them. And the best way to do that would be to shift first.

That wasn't something Kathlene needed to know.

When they were all done eating, they squabbled a bit over the check but Jock remained adamant, hinting about their expense account. It wasn't really that generous, but, although he didn't want to admit it to himself, he did feel just a touch guilty about not letting Kathlene know more of the truth. Not that he wanted her to know he was a shapeshifter, of course, but he also wasn't telling her that the Alpha Force members at this table were again excluding her from their team for what they intended to do that night.

"No need to follow me home," Kathlene told them when they were outside after eating. "I need to grab my car at the department lot. I'll just be heading back to my place. I almost got my second wind while eating with you, but I'll sleep well tonight."

The look she aimed at him was almost challenging, as if she was hinting that she wouldn't mind company.

That was just wishful thinking, but he didn't hide his own lust from his eyes as he said, "Okay, then. Good night. We'll meet again for lunch tomorrow and let you know if our sightseeing in the morning in the areas of gun shops and all yields us anything useful."

"Great," she said. "Good night."

He wished that he could turn that last smile of hers into a very different activity with those gorgeous, full lips.

She had gotten her second wind, fortunately.

Kathlene had also learned something about the Alpha

Force guys who were supposed to treat her as a member of their team.

They did what they pleased when it came to making plans to surveil the presumed anarchists. She knew they weren't telling her everything. And after the events of today, when Tisal and others had shown up so unbelievably innocently at the meeting, she had no doubt something was about to happen.

And that her best buddy Jock and his friend Ralf thought the same thing. And intended to go check it out...without her.

That was why she broke speed limits getting back to her home and quickly changed clothes into a dark-colored, long-sleeved shirt and snug pants, along with black athletic shoes.

She was going into surreptitious mode.

Once more she hurried, driving her car toward the hovel where Jock and Ralf had hung out for the past couple of nights, sending Click to the anarchists' outpost to do whatever recon they had planned.

Best she could figure, as she'd considered before, the dog must somehow have a video camera that recorded what he came up against. Only, when she had been with Click that previous night, there'd been no indication of even a collar, let alone any electronic wonder toy attached to it or to the dog.

Well, she intended to hide in that house and see and listen to whatever transpired before the men took Click to the old ranch area to do his unexplained assignment there.

She again drove faster than she should. Once more, she parked some distance from her goal, hiding her car behind some trees near the crumbling roadway.

She walked quickly but quietly to the house—and was delighted to find that she was, in fact, there before the men had arrived.

Assuming they did show up there that night. And she had a feeling, a very strong feeling, that they would.

She'd have to play it all by ear…but she relished the thought of, tomorrow, telling all to an astonished Jock— that she had figured out what they were up to and showed up there to learn more. She would once again outmaneuver the hot and commanding man who had gotten her body to react in ways she hadn't felt in years. If ever.

And wouldn't she have fun laughing at him? Oh, yeah.

Her only fear was that Click would scent or hear her and give her away before he was taken out and about for his task for the night.

As a result, she maneuvered her way into the dilapidated house and, using a flashlight, looked around the foul-smelling place, knowing she had to be careful about where she ended up. And *up* was the operative word. She found an area above what had once been the living room where she could climb the wall thanks to some holes in the deteriorating plaster that revealed wooden framing strong enough to act as a ladder and also opened into her target area. It was up above the ceiling but below the roof. Even if Click smelled or heard her and started barking about something above them, they surely wouldn't suspect there was a person up there—let alone her.

She hoped.

She was glad her arms were strong from her training, as she had to mostly pull herself up since the footholds in the wall weren't plentiful, but eventually she was exactly where she had hoped.

She settled in as best she could into the uncomfortable and uneven area that consisted of broken slats above a partially plastered ceiling. And waited.

And hoped she had been right that the men would show up here for a third night in a row.

After maybe half an hour, she heard something outside—a car engine that was quickly cut off.

Good. Only…was it definitely the men she hoped it was?

Well, she would see.

And she wasn't stupid. She had brought her service weapon, just in case she ran into trouble.

Sure enough, though, she soon saw, through the hole in the ceiling that she had adopted as her viewing point, the faces of Jock and Ralf illuminated slightly by the flashlights they carried.

She held her breath, watching for Click, waiting for the dog to sense her and react.

But she didn't see him. Didn't hear him.

Had they left him back at the cabins that night? Had they dropped him off at the ranch by himself? Or were their plans to conduct some other kind of surveillance?

They didn't hide what they said, so she listened.

"You ready?" Ralf asked. He had put what she assumed, in the faint light, was a backpack on the floor and was digging in it. She couldn't tell what it was that he extracted.

"Sure am," responded Jock.

Ralf handed him something that looked like a large bottle, and Jock drank from it. Kathlene wondered what it was. Did he need to fortify himself with alcohol to do whatever it was they had planned?

When he had apparently finished it, he sat down on the floor. "Okay," he told Ralf. "It's time."

"Yes, sir," Ralf said, and laughed as he turned on some kind of bright light and shone it on Jock. He was nude! But why? Did it matter? Maybe not, but she wanted to learn more.

Lord, was his nude body gorgeous. As masculine and sexy as she'd imagined when he was fully clothed. She loved the view…at first.

But in a minute, Kathlene had to chomp on her hand to prevent herself from calling out. She couldn't believe what she thought she saw as Jock began to roll around on the floor. And moan. And change.

Oh, how he changed. His limbs seemed to tighten. His face grew longer. He grew fur all over his body.

And when it was all over, Kathlene could finally understand why she had seen Click around here but not Jock. Not at the same time. Not after Ralf and he had been at this house before.

Understand? No, not really.

But Jock Larabey had become the wolflike dog who had rescued her yesterday in the anarchists' compound.

Jock Larabey was a werewolf.

Chapter 10

A werewolf? A shapeshifter? She didn't believe in such things. She was a peace officer. A realist. A... An incredulous fool.

For she had seen what she had seen. She couldn't deny that, even though everything inside her screamed that she was hallucinating.

But she knew she wasn't.

Kathlene attempted not to move. She knew she hadn't cried out; she'd stuck her fist in her mouth to prevent it, not an easy feat considering the cramped position she was in here, above the room.

Even so, once he had stabilized and stopped changing, the wolf—Jock—froze in place, then moved his head to stare straight up in her direction. He growled, but only for a second. And then he barked.

Ralf followed the canine's gaze, moving his head to look up toward her. Could he see her?

"What is it, Jock?" Ralf asked. "Something up there?"

The dog nodded, growled again, pawed the floor with one paw, then stopped right beneath her.

"You want me to check it out." It wasn't a question but a statement. And why not? Kathlene figured that, if what she'd seen was true, Ralf had done something to help Jock change. He might be able to help him in other ways.

"I didn't see a ladder, but it looks like I can scale that messed-up wall. Maybe. I'll try to go up and…"

"No need," Kathlene called down in a small, defeated tone. "He—whatever he is—knows I'm here."

"Kathlene!" Ralf's voice was sharp and angry. Kathlene could only imagine what Jock would say, and how he would say it, if he could actually talk now. "What are you doing up there?"

"Right now, I don't know. I'm coming down."

She hadn't really thought through how she would retreat from the area above the ceiling but figured she would just do as she'd done to climb here, only in reverse. It wasn't quite that easy, not with using flimsy handholds and places to stick her feet into the partly destroyed wall areas, but, with Ralf's help, she managed.

And when she was back down on the main level, she just stood there, staring. At the wolf, who stared right back at her.

She was anthropomorphizing, sure, but with good cause, when she read in the canine's gaze anger and frustration and a need to chew her out.

"Is this what your Alpha Force is about?" she finally demanded, looking first at the wolf, then at Ralf. "Why didn't you just tell me?"

"As if you'd have believed it," Ralf countered. His dark eyes looked even darker now as he frowned at her, his thick arms crossed over his chest. "And now what are we going to do with you?"

The wolf gave a quick bark. He dashed toward the large bag that Ralf had carried into the house and pawed at it.

In moments, he dipped his muzzle in and extracted a leash.

"You want me to take you for another walk...Click?" Her hand raised to her mouth. "Not Click. It wasn't Click yesterday, either, at the ranch, was it?"

"Nope," Ralf answered.

Jock brought the leash to Kathlene. But instead of holding it for her to take and try to attach it to him— without a collar—he took an end, dropped it on the floor, then held the other end in his mouth and, slowly circling her, wrapped it around her legs.

"You want to leash me?" she asked incredulously.

The canine looked at her, then at Ralf, and nodded his head.

"We've worked out some ways of communicating without talking," Ralf said. "I'm interpreting this to mean that he wants you to stay here while he conducts the recon we already planned. He'll change back on his return, then we'll talk. Right, Jock?"

The wolf-dog gave one bark and nodded once more.

"And if I don't want to stay? If I want to just get out of here and digest what I just saw, and—"

Jock growled again, then sat down on her leashed feet.

Kathlene thought about how funny this situation could be if it were played out in a movie or TV show. But the reality?

It felt anything but funny to her.

Was she nuts? Were they all nuts? Had they somehow drugged her or... Well, she wasn't going to find out now.

She wouldn't find out until they had that conversation that Ralf had mentioned.

"Okay," she finally said with a sigh. "I'll wait here with Ralf. But I expect you both to fill me in later. On everything."

And if she could, she'd push for Ralf to tell all in Jock's absence.

But she had a feeling that lower-ranking members of this supersecret Alpha Force military unit wouldn't do anything without their superior officer's verbal, human-type, okay.

She had seen him shift.

Jock loped through the woods now, toward the encampment that was his target. Again.

He had to concentrate on his mission, what he needed to accomplish this night.

How he needed to accomplish it.

But his mind was filled with human thoughts other than those he had to focus on.

She had seen him shift.

She had seen him naked, and that somehow made him glad. He wanted her to return the favor. Soon.

But she had also seen his fleeting but intense discomfort as he had changed from human form into wolfen.

And then they had communicated somewhat. She had agreed to stay. To obey his command.

But he knew better. If he had been in human form and gave her orders, she would never have agreed to do as he'd said.

She was confused. Unsure what to do, so she was heeding him. For now.

But later…

Why hadn't he scented her before he shifted? He had caught her fragrant scent before when she had been where she wasn't supposed to be. The old house was filled with ugly smells, so why not pick out one good one from the rest?

His only excuse was that he had been focused on shifting. If he had smelled her, he might have sloughed it off, anyway, as a residual scent from yesterday.

There. He had arrived at the area just outside the fence.

Time to concentrate. Time to meander around and eavesdrop and see if those inside were discussing the meeting that had occurred today—and how their presence, even acting like interested bystanders, had changed the outcome.

And if he were lucky, he would overhear how they intended next to levy their threats on the county commissioners who wanted to put further restrictions on their abilities to hunt and arm themselves...and hurt people.

That was why he was here: to learn what they were actually up to.

And to stop them.

A good time for it, too. For the first time since he had started recon on this old ranch, he heard an explosion. Small and muffled, yes. But he needed to find out more about it—and the very slight scent of plastic, perhaps C-4 explosives, that accompanied it.

Kathlene had gotten Ralf talking. Not a lot, and not comfortably.

But at least she knew a little more now than when Jock had stalked away toward the ranch site.

Rather than on the dilapidated chairs, they sat on the

warped wood of the house's floor with the flashlight pointing toward the base of the wall to give off a minimum amount of illumination that could let them see around them. She leaned against the wall, her legs bent with her knees pointing toward the ceiling where she had been hiding before. Ralf had his legs crossed and looked highly uneasy.

But he had answered a few of her questions—*few* being the operative word. Some responses were interesting and hinted at even more fascinating data behind them. But none were in depth.

"So Alpha Force somehow recruits different kinds of shapeshifters—mostly wolves, but also lynxes and cougars and even hawks," she repeated back to Ralf, trying to buy into the concept. But she'd seen a shift with her own eyes. If a man could change into a wolf, why not all the other kinds of animals, too?

"That's right," Ralf said. "But I can't tell you anything about the recruitment process or how they're utilized on missions or anything else, really."

"Are you a shifter, too?"

"No, but I was a member of Special Forces before I was recruited into Alpha Force. I'd gained the trust of my commanding officers so they must have figured I could handle this…different…kind of assignment."

"Do you like it?"

"Oh, yeah. I always liked trying something new and outrageous, and you can't get much more outrageous than this."

Kathlene pondered what else to ask that wouldn't trigger a refusal to answer. "What do you do as an aide?"

"Whatever's necessary—but some of it's classified so I can't answer any more of your questions about it."

"Right." She tried to sound perky and understanding and accepting of all he said. What else could she do? He could be lying about everything, but after what she had seen she might believe stuff that was even crazier than reality—like, was Ralf himself going to shapeshift in a few minutes into King Kong?

How could she be certain that he couldn't?

A noise sounded at the front door, like something scratching on it. A dog's paw?

Ralf must have heard it, too, since he stood quickly and dashed over then opened the door.

Sure enough, a silver-furred figure leaped inside, panting. A dog. A wolf.

Jock.

"All okay, sir?" Ralf asked, obviously trying to be funny. For her, or for his commanding officer, or both?

Kathlene had already figured out that, whatever happened to Jock when he shifted, he obviously maintained his ability to understand what people said, even if he couldn't respond in kind. Otherwise, how could he have helped her so much at the ranch compound last night?

And how could Ralf joke with him?

The sound Jock made in response was like a muted growl. Maybe he didn't find Ralf so funny after all. He barked again and loped over to Ralf's backpack that still lay on the floor. He pawed at it.

And then he stared at Kathlene.

"He wants to shift back right now," Ralf said. "He could do it on his own in time, but I can help him do it faster with the light. But the thing is, when he shifts back he'll be...er..."

"Naked. I got a glimpse when he shifted into being

a wolf before," Kathlene reminded him. "No problem. I can just leave now."

Jock barked again, giving a decisively negative shake of his head.

"He wants you to stay," Ralf interpreted unnecessarily. "Maybe he saw or heard something that means danger if you go outside now. Tell you what. Why don't you just turn your back?"

"Sure," she said, pivoting to face the wall that had been nearest her back in the house's main, and most decrepit, room.

But she couldn't help it. She turned just slightly, enough to see that Ralf had his back to her as he pulled the light from his backpack and aimed it at Jock.

Jock wasn't looking at her, either. Especially not when he growled, then moaned as his body started lengthening, the fur pelt receding into him, his muzzle and pointed ears retracting.

The process was fascinating. Kathlene couldn't have forced herself to turn away even if she'd wanted to.

Which she didn't.

The most intriguing part of the process was to see Jock's taut, all-masculine, human muscles forming and tightening once more.

Not to mention the nether part of his body. His sexual organs, before the evident but not so interesting form of a canine's, morphing into all human, large and erect and utterly enticing.

Why did he have an erection? Did he know she was staring at him or was this what always happened to him?

The process was nearly over now. Both men would be more aware of her presence very soon.

At least now Kathlene was able to force herself to turn back toward the wall.

And go over, in her mind, the miraculous change she had just witnessed.

How often did he do this? How much did it hurt?

Why did it seem so sexy to her?

She suddenly heard whispering behind her. It was so soft that she couldn't make out what the men were saying.

Too bad *she* didn't have any canine abilities. Dogs had excellent hearing. Did a werewolf?

She prepared to call out, ask if it was okay to turn around, if Jock was decent.

But before she could, someone touched her elbow, startling her. Why hadn't she heard movement on this irregular wood floor?

"Kathlene," said Jock's voice. She turned to see him standing right behind her, tall, fully dressed and with an ominous look on his handsome, chiseled—and now all human—face.

"Oh, hi," she said, making an attempt to act nonchalant and unaffected by the night's offbeat occurrences. "I'd really like for you to tell me more about what's going on."

"Yeah, I will. I hope you're not tired tonight, because we have to talk—right now."

Could they trust her?

They had to. Jock knew that. But he wanted to make sure she understood there would be consequences if she even unintentionally alluded to what she'd seen in front of any of her sheriff's department people, or anyone else, for that matter.

"Okay," she said. "But could we go someplace more

comfortable to have this conversation? Your cabin would be a whole lot better than this."

"Fine," Jock said. "I'll ride with you."

He didn't really believe she'd try to drive off and ignore them, or, worse, shout what she had seen to the world, but just in case...

"Okay."

Was it that easy? He'd anticipated some argument from her.

But on the other hand, she'd made it clear that she had a lot of questions. Maybe she thought he'd answer them more freely if they were one-on-one.

And maybe he would, depending on her reactions.

"We'll see you back at the cabins," Jock told Ralf, meeting his aide's eyes in an attempt at reassurance that this was the best way. "If you could take care of Click first, that would be great. We'll wait for you in the other cabin before we have any major discussion." That part was for Kathlene. Maybe he'd talk with her in the car and maybe he wouldn't, but the main part of their conversation would have to wait. "Although you both should know that I heard one small explosion this time—like the ones you described, Kathlene, that helped in the decision to send Alpha Force here."

Both Kathlene and Ralf reacted to that. "Interesting timing," Ralf said.

"Sure was," Jock agreed. What neither said was that the information would need to be passed along to their Alpha Force superiors.

At least waiting to talk more about his shifting would also give him time to consider the best way to present the facts—and which ones he actually would tell her.

"I want to hear more about what you heard," Kathlene said. But she was clearly distracted by his shifting, which was okay. He'd rather talk about that now. Give her an explanation that she—and he—could live with. "Although...well, was the dog you introduced me to in your cabin next door actually Click?" Kathlene had started walking with him toward the house's back door.

"Yes. He's my cover dog," Jock explained.

"Yeah. That gives me two canines to take care of." Ralf, always willing to joke to lighten a difficult situation, followed them. He'd picked up his backpack, and as they all exited the house he was the one to make sure the door was shut behind them.

"Interesting," Kathlene said. She paused and looked up into Jock's face in the near total darkness outside. "That's why I was so confused—one reason, at least. I'd seen you, and I'd seen Click, and I thought there were even some differences in appearance between that dog and the one who saved me yesterday, but that didn't make sense to me...before. And I never even considered the possibility of your—do you call it shapeshifting?"

"That's right," he said, then asked, "Where did you park your car?"

"Just down the road a little ways, in a small clearing in the woods."

"Okay. We'll see you in a few, Ralf." Jock picked up his pace a bit, taking Kathlene's hand. "So neither of us falls in the dark," he explained to her. It was partially true. It was also true that he didn't want her to dash off and leave him here—although at this moment he doubted she would do that. And if she did, he had his phone along and could call Ralf to pick him up—and to chase her with him.

What he hadn't counted on, though, was what it did

to him to have her firm, warm hand in his. It somehow seemed to irradiate a path of heat from their fingertips all the way inside him to his groin, where an unbidden erection started to grow once more.

Last time, as his shift ended, it had also been because of Kathlene, because he knew she was peeking, saw him naked.

This woman was going to drive him nuts in more ways than one.

They reached her car quickly and he did his usual thing of opening her door for her, then getting into the passenger's seat. She drove slowly at first, which gave him an opportunity to sense their surroundings by sight and scent as they reached the road.

Nothing out of the ordinary. That was a good thing.

Her next question wasn't such a good thing, though.

"Why, Jock? I mean, what causes you to shapeshift? Have you always done it? I thought werewolves changed under full moons, although that's not even true anymore sometimes in movies. But what's the reality? Do you like it? And—I think I'd better shut up." Her gaze was straight out the windshield. She didn't even glance toward him, but he could smell a slight tangy scent that suggested she was afraid.

Of him?

Damn.

"I'm not going to hurt you, Kathlene," he said softly, reaching over to stroke her warm, smooth cheek with the back of his hand. She tensed up, but only for a moment as he continued to touch her.

"I know," she responded, but he heard the slight tremor in her voice.

Touching her like this, even just to be friendly, wasn't

a good idea. It gave his body thoughts of touching her all over—and not just with his hand.

"Tell you what," he said. "This isn't the kind of conversation to have in the car, and what I need to talk to you about with Ralf along isn't going to touch on what you asked, either. Once we've had that conversation, I intend to see you back to your home, anyway, since, even though I didn't hear anything threatening at the ranch compound before, after that county commission meeting today I don't trust anyone in this town. Especially around you, since you and your fellow officers were there representing local authority, and you've already made noises against the group in question. I'll answer your questions then, okay?"

She hesitated, but only for a moment. Was she still afraid of him?

Or of herself? For when she finally aimed a brief glance at him before turning from the small road onto the main highway, he saw something on her face and scented something other than fear and her underlying perfume.

Something that suggested that she might feel as turned on, and interested in touching and more, as he did.

But her ultimate response made him smile.

"Okay," she agreed.

Chapter 11

They were back in the motel cabin she had reserved for the two men from Alpha Force, once more sitting on one of the two chairs. Ralf was already inside with Click when they'd arrived. He had walked the dog briefly and had fed him a late dinner.

Kathlene studied Click as he now sat near the cabin's kitchenette. Yes, he looked similar to the wolf-dog she had seen earlier after Jock had shifted, but they were not identical. As she had noted but not understood before, his head was flatter, his legs longer, and the color and fullness of his coat, although similar, was less of a tawny-silver than Jock's.

Jock's. Jock, the shapeshifter, the human-wolf combo.

She liked dogs. A lot.

But she liked Jock in human form even better. He was gorgeous. Even more, he was hot. Maybe the sexiest guy she had ever met.

Shouldn't the fact that he was so…different…turn her off?

Maybe so, but it didn't. How weird was that?

He'd sat beside her briefly but had stood to confer with Ralf and pat the dog that looked so much like him—sometimes. Were they discussing the sounds he had heard? She hoped so.

She finally felt more vindicated. She'd want to talk more about them, too, later.

But for this moment, she wanted to know more about Alpha Force—and Jock.

He returned and handed Kathlene a glass of soda with ice in it. "Now," he said, "let's talk."

That sounded ominous. But she knew what he was going to say.

"Okay," she said, and waited for his orders.

As she'd anticipated, they were, in fact, directives. Jock leaned toward her, his hands clasped near her knees as if he would grab and shake her if she dared to argue with what he said. Kathlene glanced toward Ralf, not expecting any support from the other military man. Ralf sat beside Click, who had lain down on the cabin's polished wooden floor. Everyone's eyes seemed to be on her, waiting for her reaction.

Even Click's.

"I know you have questions," Jock began, "and we'll go over them later, the way we discussed. But right now I need to be sure that you understand the circumstances. Alpha Force is a highly covert military unit, and I'm a member."

When he paused, she nodded to signify she understood and didn't disagree. At least not yet.

"You saw me shapeshift. That's fine, since we've already established that we're on the same team. But you can't mention, can't even hint about it, to anyone. Do you understand?"

She nodded. "Yes."

"And do you agree?"

"Of course. But—well, I know you said we could talk later about what shapeshifting is and all that, but I'd love to understand why Alpha Force was sent here to help in this situation."

Jock looked a little irritated that she had dared to interrupt what he intended to say, but his expression softened immediately. "Because things here, if they're as you represented, could get pretty dangerous if the only undercover personnel deployed here happened to be all human."

Kathlene laughed and was a little surprised that both men did, too.

"We have a general idea how you asked for help," Jock continued, "but why don't you describe that to us now and maybe it'll help us explain."

She ran through the facts. She had seen—and heard—what appeared to be going on at the old ranch, and more men with guns appeared to arrive daily. When no one here, especially not Sheriff Melton Frawley or even town mayor Laurence Davonne, had paid attention to her, she knew she needed help.

She told them now how she'd stayed in touch with her friend from college, Bill Grantham, whose father had been an army colonel then but was now a general working at the Pentagon. Bill had listened to her, and so had the general.

Despite asking, Kathlene had never been told why he'd decided to call in Alpha Force. All she knew was that he'd contacted her and discussed the cover that the military men to be deployed to Cliffordsville would undertake. She'd been glad that they'd taken her seriously, at least.

"Got it," Jock said. "I know of General Grantham. He's a friend of the general who oversees Alpha Force, General Greg Yarrow. Guess that's why we were called in to help. General Yarrow knows all about us, who we are and what we can do."

"Yeah," Ralf said. "If they'd brought in the usual kind of military or other guys to go undercover, they might have been able to infiltrate that group as fellow sportsmen to see what's going on, and Jock and I still might resort to doing that, depending. But we have the choice of what'll work best, unlike anyone else."

"You sound proud of Alpha Force," Kathlene noted.

"Damn straight!" Ralf responded.

"Then it sounds like I did the right thing." Kathlene sure hoped so.

But the ultimate success of the team consisting of Jock, Ralf, Click and her still remained to be seen.

They talked a little longer about Alpha Force without going into detail about how many there were in the unit or what kinds of missions they'd undertaken before.

But the upshot was that Kathlene was definitely a temporary member of their team now—since she knew what she knew.

And if she blew their trust, she would be sorry.

Eventually, she found herself stifling a yawn.

"Guess it's time to get you back safely to your place," Jock said. He told Ralf that he would follow Kathlene to assure her safety.

She wanted to tell Jock that she'd be fine. She could head home alone.

And yet she could hardly wait for the private conversation Jock had promised her.

She wanted to know more about shapeshifting and shapeshifters and what they thought and how they felt.

"Sounds good," she said. "Good night, Ralf." She headed toward Click, then bent and hugged the wolf-like dog, whose tail was wagging fiercely. "Good night, Click. See you tomorrow—although Jock and I need to discuss tomorrow's plan of action."

She looked at the man who waited near the door for her. His mouth had thinned as if he didn't like what he'd heard, but then his stance relaxed.

"I guess we do," he said.

Once again, Jock followed Kathlene as she drove. This time, at least, he would get to see where she lived.

He had the address, of course. He'd contacted the military computer geeks who unearthed all private information when necessary for Alpha Force. So far, he hadn't felt a need to go there.

Tonight would have been different even if she hadn't agreed for him to follow her.

Before he had left, he told Ralf to call Drew Connell. He was sure that the major would be very interested in the report of his hearing that explosion, though not particularly strong—this time—at the old ranch, as well as getting the small, yet distinct, scent of explosives.

He wasn't surprised to see Kathlene pull off the main Cliffordsville streets into a nice residential neighborhood. After a few turns, she pulled into the driveway of a small but pretty redbrick home on a block of other similar, well-maintained houses.

Jock parked on the street and followed her to the front door.

For her safety and security, he reminded himself. That was all.

"Nice place," he said.

"Thanks." She opened the front door with a key she had taken from the large bag she carried—which he felt sure hid her weapon. And then she walked inside, with him close behind her.

They entered into a living room with textured beige walls, floral-patterned and fluffy sofa and chairs and a huge wide-screen TV along one wall. It smelled of tangy cleaning fluids and unlit jasmine-scented candles on the end tables.

The woman was a bundle of contrasts. A peace officer with feminine furniture and aromas in her home.

But the ability to watch the news in high definition.

He told himself yet again that he wasn't here because he found her attractive—and so sexy that he wanted to take her into his arms and undress her, seduce her and make love till she screamed.

He'd never considered getting close to anyone outside of his old home neighborhood or Alpha Force.

He'd certainly never thought about getting close to a deputy sheriff.

But that was before he had met Kathlene Baylor.

Still, making love with her, a supposed team member with whom he would have to continue to work until this assignment was complete? Bad idea.

He would just have to keep his thoughts, and body, in check.

"It's a little late for coffee," Kathlene said. "Would you like a glass of wine? A bottle of beer?"

"Just water will be fine," Jock told her. He was looking closely at her TV.

"I can turn that on for you, if you'd like." She figured, though, that he could do it easily by himself.

"No. I don't think it would make good background noise for our talk."

"Right." She went through the doorway in the far wall and entered her kitchen, glad to be out of Jock's presence for even just a minute.

What had she been thinking, inviting him to her house?

Even though what they'd said they would talk about fascinated her.

Good thing he hadn't taken her up on her offer of alcohol. She didn't want any, either. She needed her wits about her.

Otherwise—well, she might just jump Jock Larabey's bones here, knowing they were alone.

Knowing he was the sexiest man she had ever laid eyes—and lips—on.

As long as he was in the form of a man.

She quickly brought him a glass of water and carried one for herself as she joined him on the sofa.

"Now," she said, "tell me all about what it's like to be a—do you call yourself a shapeshifter? A werewolf? What?"

"Either is fine. And I love who and what I am."

He described growing up in the less-populated areas of Wisconsin with his family and other shifters around. "I don't know whether the regular humans around had any idea of who we really were, but if they did they were still friendly and pretty much left us alone."

"Amazing," she said. What would she have done as a kid if she'd known there were actually such things as shapeshifters, and some lived near her? She'd have been fascinated.

She'd always loved to watch sci-fi shows on TV and in movies.

But that's what they were. Science *fiction*.

Or so she had always believed…until now.

"And Alpha Force?" she asked. "How did you learn about it?"

"They found me," he said. "The unit is always on the lookout for shifters who would fit a specialized career in the military. And Alpha Force—well, I can't really talk much about it, but one of the perks is the special elixir we use that gives us a lot of benefits that regular shifters don't have."

"Like not having to wait until a full moon?" she asked. "I always thought the original legends said that werewolves only changed then."

"And it's true," he said. "Except for Alpha Force members and others who've found a way to get around it. Plus, we can keep a lot more of our human awareness and intelligence with Alpha Force's elixir. But like the other information you now have about Alpha Force, that's something you can't talk about." His hazel eyes bored into hers as if attempting to see inside her brain for her thoughts about whether to blab all to the world.

"I get it," she said. "And, yes, I'll keep it to myself."

Those eyes stayed on her, but their expression changed from icy inquisitiveness to something warmer. A whole lot warmer.

Which made her smile even as her insides turned molten.

Oh, yes, it was a bad idea to have Jock here alone with her in her home.

"Would you like some more water?" she asked quickly, needing a reason to stand up and run away, even by just a few feet.

But his glass wasn't empty.

"No, thanks. So, your turn now. Tell me, Kathlene. Why did you decide to go into law enforcement?"

She didn't have to tell him. It wasn't something she talked about much, if at all.

But he had been honest with her. She supposed it was her turn.

"I wanted to fight for justice," she said with an ironic grin. "As if there really was any out there."

"Because…?" he prompted, his gaze still not leaving hers.

For this moment, at least, her body stiffened and had no interest in doing anything but leaving the room, leaving the topic.

Instead, she said as nonchalantly as she could, "My parents owned a convenience store in Missoula. One day, a couple of thugs came in to steal their cash and wound up murdering them. My folks' killers were caught and prosecuted and went to prison—for all of a year. But they appealed their conviction and got off on a technicality. Now they're free. Maybe even robbing and killing other people, but maybe not. I keep track of them as best I can. Justice? Maybe I can't create it, but I sure as hell can seek it and try to make sure it sticks."

"I'm so sorry, Kathlene." His expression had turned full of compassion. And suddenly, she found herself in his embrace.

She closed her eyes. She couldn't allow herself to give in to her desire because this man—no, man-wolf—was also a really nice and caring guy.

Only…as his mouth sought, then captured, hers, she realized for a fleeting moment that this was what she had been hoping for all day long.

No, from the moment she had first met Jock Larabey.

They were going to make love. She knew it. She also knew how foolish it was.

But for this moment, foolishness be damned. She opened her own lips, allowed her tongue to seek out his, even as her body pressed up against him.

Her breasts became the epitome of sensitivity…especially when, as they stood, she felt his hard erection pushing against her. She sighed, even as she maneuvered herself closer.

"Jock," she whispered against his hot, searching mouth.

"Yes," he responded without missing a moment of their increasingly sensual kiss.

"My bedroom is just down the hall."

Jock had promised himself before to keep his libido in check. His wayward body parts, too.

But his erection had a mind of its own. Oh, yeah.

And the erotic dance with this woman on their way to her bedroom was filled with deep, deep kisses, not to mention hugs and caresses and touches outside his clothes to his most sensitive and responsive areas. Which he reciprocated, and then some.

He couldn't wait to strip. And to strip Kathlene, too.

The thought aroused him even more, if that was possible.

Her scent was spicy and salty and altogether sexually incredible. The atmosphere was enhanced by the sound of her deep, irregular breathing, her soft, sexy moans.

"In here," Kathlene gasped momentarily against his mouth, and he responded by kissing her even more deeply, even as she guided him through a doorway and flicked on the lights.

To her bedroom.

Like the furniture he had already seen, this room, when he managed to pry open his eyes and look at it, had a floral motif, from the carvings on the mirror over the dresser to the rose-and-lilac design on the comforter on the bed.

The bed. That was the way they were heading. Good idea.

Better idea was how he at last started removing Kathlene's clothes on the way over to it. First her knit shirt over her head. Then his hands on the buttons on her slacks, and they soon slid to the floor.

"Now me," she said, and it was his turn to lose his shirt, his pants, his briefs. He was naked first.

Fine by him. He quickly got the rest of Kathlene's stuff off, too.

And then they tumbled right onto that pretty, flowery bed.

Yes, oh yes, Kathlene thought. She refused to even consider how unwise this was.

Not with Jock's gorgeous, hot, muscular body on top of hers, writhing gently, obviously trying to feel all of her against him without squashing her with his substantial, tense weight.

He was still kissing her mouth. At this angle, she couldn't do much more than kiss him back, squeeze his delightful, firm buttocks in her hands.

Feel his thick arousal pressing against her.

But she wanted more. A lot more.

She wriggled, whispered, "My turn," and maneuvered so she could get loose from beneath his body.

He let her, without removing his hands. Which was a good thing. Otherwise, she would have felt bereft if she no longer had his touch upon her.

As it was, he gently grasped her breasts, rubbing his thumbs against her nipples so erotically that it made her feel like crying.

Instead, she moved, curling up a bit so he could no longer reach her chest…but she could reach his hard shaft, which she took into her mouth.

And reveled in the sound of his gasp even as she tasted its heat and hardness and enticement.

"Now," she heard him say, and it sounded as if he spoke through gritted teeth.

But she couldn't quite comply with what he said.

If she remembered correctly…she pulled away from him entirely and left the bed, giving only a quick glance to his narrowed eyes that stared at her so sexily.

She opened the top drawer of the nightstand nearest her and reached past the makeup and other inappropriate contents toward the back.

And found exactly what she sought: a box of condoms. Unopened. There for years, a box of unfulfilled hope that she'd never been tempted to use with any man she'd met recently.

Until now.

She pulled it open, took out a foil packet and tore it, holding it out toward Jock.

"You do it," he said. "I'm busy." That was when he reached toward her, claimed her hot and wet and aroused area with his hand and stroked it, inserted a finger, then two…

She cried out even as she got the condom in place over him. He pulled her onto the bed, rolled her back into the position she had been in before, beneath him, and entered her.

She reached a climax nearly immediately and was happy to hear Jock's own cry of fulfillment.

In moments, his body became a loose weight on top of her. He panted as he laughed, moved off her and said, "Too fast. We've got to get in more practice."

More?

Did she want to do this again with this man?

Oh, yeah.

Chapter 12

Lying there beside Jock, Kathlene was still breathing heavily from what they had just done together when he asked to stay the night.

She graciously said yes. Heck, she wasn't just being gracious. He was fulfilling her dream. Her desire.

For even though they both talked about how tired they were, she knew that they would make love again. And, maybe, again.

First, though, he left her bedroom, ostensibly to use the bathroom. She saw him grab his phone from his trousers before he left. Her head on her pillow, her body beneath the sheet, she soon heard his voice as he talked to someone else. Ralf?

She couldn't distinguish much of what Jock said, but she did hear the word *protection*. Was that what he called what they had done?

More likely, he was just giving an excuse to Ralf for staying here.

But if protection was really on his mind…

No. He surely wasn't using his body to try to control her, to make her more amenable to his staying around her. Protecting her.

She didn't need that.

He returned to the room. She sat up, ready to confront him, to make sure he continued to remember, despite their amazing lovemaking, that she wasn't just some needy woman, a female who wanted a man around who would take care of her.

She could do it all by herself.

But as she sat up, the sheet dropped from her…and her upper body showed. Her breasts.

They began tingling as he looked at them.

And when he slid back onto the bed with her and reached out for them, touched them, slid his fingers back and forth over their sensitive nubs, she forgot all of what she intended to say.

He actually got some sleep that night. In between delicious interludes of lovemaking with this all-human, all-female woman who knew his secrets. Was she somehow turned on by what he was? Or did it simply make no difference to her?

He counted at least three more times when he rolled over in her erotically smelling bed to find her awake, too. Or maybe they were simply in sync.

They made love over and over, and then he slept.

Not that he felt well rested when he awoke in the morning, listening.

He heard sounds outside—Kathlene's neighbors walking their dogs and chatting with their kids, cars driving by, noises that were not familiar to him in this area while staying in the remote cabins.

"Good morning," whispered a soft voice from beside him.

He rolled over to find Kathlene's half-open blue eyes looking at him, her still-sleepy face smiling.

Why did that look sexy? He didn't know, except that there they were, still in bed, still nude. He reached for her, and they made love yet again.

"Are you interested in breakfast?" Kathlene asked once she had returned to her bedroom after showering.

Jock and she had finally arisen after their most recent round of luscious sex that took enough out of her that she could have stayed in bed all day. Except that she had to report for duty in about an hour.

And except that spending any more bed time with Jock nearby was not a good idea. She had questions. He probably had answers. They had discussed only the generalities of Alpha Force last night at his cabin, and more specifics about his shapeshifting when they had arrived here at her home. But she had other questions about what he did. And if they didn't get up, she wouldn't even be able to try to draw responses out of him. They'd be too busy engaging in other, more enjoyable things. Assuming they could find any more energy after last night.

So she had tossed him out of the bedroom first to shower. Then she'd dashed to her wonderfully appointed kitchen—her favorite room in the house—in his absence, still in the robe she had thrown on, to see what she had in the way of breakfast fixings.

Fortunately, she had a few eggs, some bread, cereal and plenty of milk. Coffee, too.

"Sure," he said now. "Where would you like to go?" He undoubtedly meant for her to pick a restaurant.

Instead, she said, "Down the hall, to my kitchen. I'll take care of it." She gave him her available choices. Seemingly glad about her offer to cook their breakfast, he chose toast and coffee, with a couple of scrambled eggs thrown in when she said she was making some for herself.

But she liked the fact that he apparently didn't want to create extra work for her, even when she offered it.

A short while later, they both sat at her oval wooden kitchen table, their plates of eggs and toast, and large white mugs of coffee, on red woven place mats in front of them.

Jock once again wore the outfit he had had on last night, of course—T-shirt and jeans, his and Ralf's usual undercover uniform.

She, on the other hand, wore her deputy sheriff's uniform.

"Now let's backtrack a bit," Kathlene said, smiling as Jock took one bite after another of the eggs that she had seasoned with thyme and oregano to add a slightly Italian flair to them.

"Okay," he said. "This is really good, by the way."

"Glad you like it." Kathlene took a sip of her hot coffee. "Now, last night. When you were wandering around the old ranch area."

"When I was shifted," he said with a nod, gazing at her as if waiting for her reaction this morning, after she'd had time to sleep on her initial thoughts.

Well, heck, neither one of them had actually slept much....

"That's right," she said. "Tell me more about what you saw and heard. And whatever else you did while you were—while you were a wolf."

His grin at her was obviously meant to be a sexy leer. "I'm always a wolf, but which kind depends on what form I'm in."

"Right," she said drily. "While you looked like a wolf."

"Sure." Their limited repartee had been enough for him, she figured, for he spent the next few minutes describing what he had seen and heard as he walked, in wolf form, around the outside of the old ranch's fence. "I heard a couple of guys I couldn't see talk about the county commissioners' meeting and how they needed to teach the town a few lessons about backing off when it came to adding any possible limits on hunting."

"Did you see who they were?"

"No, but I might be able to identify them through their voices and scents, although I was too far away to be sure."

"Oh. Of course." His other senses besides sight were undoubtedly sharper when he was actually a wolf, she figured.

Which gave more credence to why the feds would send this kind of secret unit here to deal with the situation she had described.

"Then there was the noise I heard—probably like the explosions you had mentioned hearing a while back. I wasn't close enough to really get a good scent, but I thought I smelled a hint of plastic, like C-4. The sound was muffled, though, so could be they were just experimenting and keeping it under wraps—troublesome, anyway. Something we need more information about, as well as the ability to disarm anything that has the potential of injuring anyone, including the county commissioners this group clearly has no love for."

Kathlene shivered. She felt vindicated, but that didn't really make her feel good. The danger still existed.

"I'm glad you heard it, too," she said. "And smelled it. And are checking into it, even though no one else around here seems concerned."

"Nothing but peaceful target practice," Jock acknowledged. "And if I believed that's all that was going on there, Ralf and I would be on our way to Yellowstone— or that's what we'd tell anyone here who asked. Which is probably no one."

"Do we need to get you more involved in the community?" She had wondered about that. Maybe they needed to be more than just her buddies. But how?

His smile looked both amazed and…tender? A teasing warmth crept up her back. She was beginning to care too much for this man, and she had to get it under control. He was only here for a short time, till he accomplished his very important mission.

Then there was the fact that he was so different from her…

"I knew we were on the same wavelength," he said, "but I didn't think you'd anticipate this. And maybe you haven't. But here's what I wanted to tell you. Let me preface it by explaining there was another thing I heard. Something else you might be particularly interested in."

Her curiosity was suddenly almost overwhelming. "What's that?"

"I want you to bring me to your sheriff's department this morning, introduce me to all your coworkers as your longtime buddy, even though I've already met some of them, okay?"

"Sure," she said, but he hadn't answered her question. She needed to know more. "But tell me why."

"Because one of the things I heard and sensed last night was a presence I didn't expect. Or maybe I did, but you might not."

"Who's that?" she asked.

"Sheriff Melton Frawley."

Jock took another bite of the delicious eggs that Kathlene had cooked while waiting for her response.

Her beautiful blue eyes had widened, and she was staring at him. "Sheriff Frawley." It wasn't a question, but a statement. "Did you hear anything he said?"

Clearly, she had suspected his involvement.

But then again, why wouldn't she? From what she had told her friend that had led to Alpha Force's being deployed here, she'd tried to get her boss's support in investigating the people she had become concerned were anarchists and had gotten nowhere.

"Sure," Jock responded. "That's how I knew he was there. I recognized his voice from when I'd heard him before, yesterday at the commissioners' meeting. But if you're asking if he said anything that would implicate him as being part of whatever those guys are doing, the answer's no."

"What did he say, then?"

"All the most circumspect stuff, thanking Tisal—I heard his voice, too—for inviting him there and showing him around…again. That wasn't his first time there, apparently. And also apologizing for the way the county appeared to be criticizing a group of licensed hunters like the people camping out there."

"Really? He…he sounded as if he assumed someone was eavesdropping on him."

Jock nodded. "I wouldn't be surprised if that's what he thought. Not that he would assume it would be a shapeshifter, but there are a lot of tiny, hard-to-find electronic bugs these days. He certainly did sound like he was covering his butt."

"He also seemed to be protecting the guys who are hanging out there." Kathlene looked so affronted and woeful that Jock had to fight the urge to kiss away her bad mood—or at least try. "What are we going to do?"

"Okay, team member," he said. "Here's what I want. Like I said, you'll need to introduce Ralf and me to your colleagues, including the higher-ups. And pretty soon, you and I, old buddy, are going to have a very public difference of opinion—when Ralf and I make it clear that we're sportsmen, too. We like hunting and are all for those who don't want to add any more protections to the animals that should be fair game for us all. Period."

"And then?" The worry on Kathlene's face only got more obvious.

"Ralf and I are going to join the anarchists."

"But how will you do your shapeshifting then?"

Kathlene knew she was acting almost confrontational with Jock, but she now realized that there was a good reason for Alpha Force to have sent members here to deal with the possible anarchist situation.

Yes, she liked the idea of the two men going undercover with the people she suspected were anarchists to find out what they really were up to.

But if Jock was there with them, she might not be able to communicate with him anymore except in apparent anger.

And his very special abilities, which might help lead to more answers than just some ordinary—even well-conducted—undercover work might wind up being extraneous and unusable.

"Don't worry about that," Jock said. "You can be sure I'll work it out." He stood up from the table, his now-empty plate in his hand. He took it over to the sink, rinsed it and placed it in her dishwasher.

Which she liked. He was a guy who didn't assume that women were the ones who had to do all the cleanup chores, unlike so many of the men she now worked with.

He returned to the table and picked up his coffee mug. He didn't ask her to refill it for him but instead went to the tile counter and picked the half-filled pot off the coffeemaker and poured more into it. And then he brought the pot over and refreshed her coffee, too.

That made her smile. She looked up at him, right into his intense hazel eyes that were so much like the eyes of the wolf he was while shifted—and like Click's eyes, too.

As much as she wanted to stand up, place herself close to him, into his arms, she pulled her gaze away, took her phone from her pocket and checked the time on it.

It was getting late. She had to go.

"Time for me to head to work," she said. "You go ahead and pick up Ralf. Maybe give me an extra half hour to see who's around and figure out the best way to handle your further introductions at the department—and get you in a position to speak with Sheriff Frawley. We'll have to figure out later how best to keep our *friendship* going on, in secret if necessary. Okay?"

"Okay," he said, and he was the one to take her coffee mug and place it back on the table, then pull her into his arms. "One for the road," he said, then engaged her in another deep, sexy kiss.

Chapter 13

Kathlene's uniform felt fresh, slightly stiff and generally comfortable, as it always did—but she was entirely conscious of being dressed as she drove to the department headquarters building along the pleasant town streets of Cliffordsville.

Dressed wasn't how she had been for the entire night—in Jock's arms.

But she commanded herself not to think only about him and sex as she headed to work.

She could think about him some, yes. In fact, she could think of little else—especially in light of the secret she now knew about him.

Yet instead of constantly recalling who and what he was, and—somehow, amazingly, even more mindboggling—how incredible their bouts of lovemaking had been, she had to consider Jock in the scheming she needed to do.

She had to figure out the best plan for bringing Jock and Ralf in to meet up with Sheriff Frawley in a manner that wouldn't appear odd or suspicious.

The two secret Alpha Force members needed to interrogate Melton about his relationship with the group of sportsmen in a way that couldn't possibly be interpreted to indicate that one of them had actually discovered the sheriff at the old ranch and overheard at least some of his conversation there.

Not that Sheriff Frawley, or anyone else who was reasonably sane, for that matter, would have the slightest glimmer of what Jock Larabey actually was or how he might have seen the sheriff, and even eavesdropped on him, during his visit to the possible anarchists' camp.

And once the scheming Kathlene was involved in bore fruit, she reminded herself, and the sportsmen's true nature was determined and dealt with, Jock would be gone. Out of here.

Leaving her to maintain the position she loved, as a deputy sheriff in Clifford County.

Which was the perfect reason to enjoy him while he was here, but not get emotionally involved.

Hear that, heart? she made her mind assert to herself.

Her heart's only reply was to continue to beat. A good thing.

She would survive this interlude with Jock. And then she would survive without him.

Better that way, of course. She didn't know how she had somehow accepted that he was a shapeshifter, but that was all the more reason not to form any relationship with him. At least no more than she already had—an amazing one, yes, but definitely short-term.

At least now, with what she knew, Jock and Ralf

couldn't treat her as someone outside their team. She could always blackmail them into including her. They didn't know that wasn't her way. And she wasn't going to tell them…yet.

Kathlene soon pulled her SUV into one of the spaces behind the sheriff's department headquarters and got out. She wasn't the only one arriving then, which wasn't surprising. The daily meeting in the assembly room for those on duty during this regular shift would begin in— she checked her cell phone—ten minutes.

She still hadn't decided how to achieve what she needed to do. But she knew she would figure it out.

She glanced around at the others who were also heading toward the rear entrance to the building. Her partner, Jimmy Korling, was among them, but she didn't hurry to catch up with him. They'd have enough time together that day when they headed out on patrol.

She spied Deputy Betsy Alvers, one of the other few remaining female deputies. Kathlene usually went out of her way to avoid her overweight and irritatingly accommodating counterpart because Betsy's way of dealing with the strife at the department was to simper and smile and act as if that was the way things should be.

Consequently, Sheriff Frawley and Undersheriff George Kerringston seemed utterly pleased that Betsy was one of their deputies—especially since she seemed thrilled to bring them coffee and agree with everything they said.

Unlike Kathlene.

But maybe Betsy was the ideal person for her to talk to now. Whatever she told the young and obnoxious deputy would undoubtedly be passed along to the brass.

She had to finesse this well, though. More often than

not, Kathlene avoided talking to Betsy since it was so difficult not to show her scorn—and that would be highly inappropriate behavior for someone who wanted to keep her job around here.

So she would need to find a way to get Betsy to address her first. Then it would be impolite of her *not* to respond. All would look good then…she hoped.

She sped up a bit as she headed toward the door. She figured that spacey, controversy-avoiding Betsy might be best approached as if Kathlene was in the throes of sadness. She put her head down and turned her mouth into a sorrowful pout.

She met up with Betsy as they neared the door. "Hi," Kathlene said, glancing up with a tiny smile that she intended to appear more mournful than false.

"Hi, Kathlene," Betsy gushed in her usually enthusiastic tone. "How are you?" But before Kathlene could respond, Betsy got the gist of what she was faking. "Oh, is something wrong?"

"No," Kathlene said hurriedly, reaching for the door handle. "Well…maybe."

She held the door open so Betsy could enter first. Fortunately, there was a gap between them and the next group of deputies heading in their direction, and the lobby area into which they entered was already empty. Everyone must have headed to the assembly room right away.

"You want to talk about it?" Betsy's dark brows were raised sympathetically over her small brown eyes. She wore too much makeup and her puffy rouged cheeks looked as if she had been in the sun too long. Her white-blond hair was pulled into a clip at the back of her head, as all female law-enforcement personnel were directed to do. The result almost made her look like a large, overdone doll. An overdone deputy doll, since she, too, wore a uniform—hers larger and more rounded out than Kathlene's.

Kathlene felt a snap of conscience. The young woman was actually acting nice. And in fact, she usually did. The problem was with how she caved under the orders of the most chauvinistic men around here.

She might really make a good deputy, given a chance to prove herself besides exercising her waitress and secretarial skills.

The room they'd gone into was more of an entry that led to a variety of hallways within the building, including a stairway at one end. They'd need to scale it to reach the assembly room. But for the moment Kathlene moseyed in a way she hoped looked sorrowful toward a far corner.

"It's really not much," Kathlene said. "And I probably shouldn't be talking about it at all." *Especially to you,* she thought—except now, when she hoped to use the deputy, who had good connections thanks to her submissive nature.

"Sometimes it helps to talk about things," Betsy encouraged. Kathlene wondered how often others had caved in to the young woman's sympathetic demeanor and revealed stuff they shouldn't—and had it used against them.

She, at least, would only say things she wanted to get to the ears of their bosses.

"I guess. And really—well, it's not so bad. I'm just feeling a little disappointed. One of my old-time friends is in town, a guy I've known since college. He brought another friend along with them, and the two of them told me that they plan to leave here sooner than they originally said."

She looked up at Betsy's face, hoping her expression showed both frustration and sadness.

"Did they tell you why?" Betsy asked. Good. Kathlene didn't have to prompt her to ask that question.

"Well…yes. They live in Washington State and came to visit me before going on to visit Yellowstone. I didn't know they'd had the idea of doing some hunting in Montana. Or maybe they hadn't thought about it before. But they're looking into the possibility. The thing is, they attended the county commissioners' meeting yesterday out of curiosity and were…well, concerned about the issues being discussed that might outlaw hunting completely in this area. I told them that wasn't the case, and even further limits were somewhat iffy, but they decided they'd only stay another couple of days, anyway."

"But didn't they understand that there's a nice, solid faction here that is discouraging the commissioners from passing any more laws that would make it hard for people to hunt in this county?" Betsy peered at Kathlene. "Or are they mostly upset with you, since I gather that you're in favor of that kind of law."

Kathlene shrugged. "It could be partly that, I guess, even though I try not to get into my opinions with them too much. But no, they just think this area's government may be too dictatorial. Or at least that's what I assume."

"What if someone talked to them, tried to convince them otherwise?"

Kathlene forbore from rolling her eyes, instead attempting to look happy and pleadingly into Betsy's face. "Oh, would you?"

Betsy shrugged. "I'm probably not the best person. Maybe someone who's a hunter, or who at least is in favor of allowing hunting, would be better."

"Do you know someone who'd talk to them?" Kathlene hoped she appeared the picture of clueless innocence.

"I've got a couple of ideas," Betsy said. "Let me ask around."

"That would be wonderful," Kathlene gushed. "My friends will be here in about half an hour. I told them to come so I could give them a quick tour after our assembly but before Jimmy and I go out on patrol. They were interested in seeing where I work and what the local sheriff's station looks like."

"Fine," Betsy said. She glanced at a watch on her puffy wrist. "We'd better go upstairs. And I'm not sure I can get anyone to talk to them this soon, but I'll see what I can do."

"Thanks so much," Kathlene said, and followed Betsy to the flight of stairs across the room.

Jock and Ralf entered the reception area at the front of the sheriff's department building. They approached the desk and told a uniformed guy behind it who they were—at least who their undercover identities were—and that Deputy Kathlene Baylor was expecting them.

"I'll let her know as soon as the meeting she's in is over," the smooth-faced deputy, who looked as if he still belonged in high school, told them.

"Thanks."

Ralf and he sat down on chairs at the room's perimeter. Jock picked up a couple of magazines and leafed through them—some on law enforcement and on the wonders and delights of Montana.

Two women sat across the room from them. A man and woman entered behind them and also approached the reception desk. "We want to file a complaint," the man said. "One of our neighbors has a dog that he lets do his business in our front yard."

"I'll give you the paperwork to file a complaint," the deputy told them.

Jock glanced at Ralf. "Sounds like this town has some nondog people," he said with a rueful shrug.

"Yeah. Maybe we should get their address so you can leave a deposit in their yard sometime." Ralf had kept his voice very low. His smile looked as if he was trying to appear diabolical but he failed.

Jock couldn't help laughing back.

He looked up as other people in uniforms started entering the area both from the stairs and from the couple of doors into the room. "Guess the meeting's over," Jock said.

"Guess so," Ralf agreed.

In a minute Kathlene hurried down the stairway toward them. How could she look so beautiful and sexy with her dark hair pulled starkly away from her face, and in a unisex gray uniform?

Maybe it was the beauty of her face. The way she filled out the uniform.

The way he could visualize, from experience, what was beneath it.

"Hi," she said. "Are you ready for your tour?"

"We sure are. You ready to show us around?"

"Absolutely," she said, loud enough for others to hear her. "I definitely want to show you where I work." And then, more softly, she added, "I tried to initiate something that'll get you an audience with one of the guys in charge—preferably Tisal. But we'll just have to see whether it works."

* * *

Jock played his role well, or at least he intended to.

Ralf and he had both dressed in button-down shirts and nice trousers as an ostensible show of respect while getting a tour of the sheriff's department headquarters, Kathlene's base of operations as a deputy. Dressing well wouldn't guarantee them the meeting that they hoped for, but it probably wouldn't hurt.

The three of them had discussed their approach before—definitely treating Kathlene as a member of their team.

She, in turn, was following through quite well. She was in uniform and acted utterly professional.

Now, leading them down hallways and into various rooms, Kathlene spoke loudly enough for anyone around them to hear what she was up to. She repeated often that she really couldn't spend much time doing this since she and her partner were scheduled to go on patrol in less than half an hour.

In turn, Jock acted, in reaction to Kathlene's cheerful prattle about what he was seeing, as if he appreciated what she said but wasn't overly impressed. Ralf undoubtedly appeared to be the nicer of the two of them. Maybe that was actually the case.

After all, the man Jock was supposed to be at the moment was a potentially frustrated hunter who wasn't particularly happy with this town that considered enacting further hunting restrictions.

A hunter who in fact wasn't wild about towns or any other kind of government authority that attempted to tell its citizens what to do.

In other words, a budding anarchist.

Ralf? Well, his assumed character had similar values but perhaps wasn't as vocal about them.

They'd reached the end of the second-floor hallway and Kathlene had just pointed out the assembly room where she and her fellow officers met daily for a general assessment of what was going on and what to look out for before being sent off on their assignments.

"Now let's go up another couple of floors to the offices of the sheriff and his primary officers and staff," Kathlene said with a wide, too-bright smile. "That will have to be the end of the tour, at least for now. I've got to go on patrol in just a few minutes."

"Sounds good," Ralf said. "I'm really enjoying this. How about you, Jock?" The guy certainly knew how to play his role well. All his Alpha Force roles.

There wasn't any better aide to shifters than his was, and Jock knew it.

Especially since they'd also had a talk about Kathlene. Ralf wasn't stupid. He knew what was going on. Was nonjudgmental. Only told Jock to be careful, which he was.

"Definitely," Jock replied to Ralf. "But let's hurry. I don't want to hold you up any more, Kathlene."

A couple of other people in uniform were standing nearby, conversing. If any of them eavesdropped, they'd most likely believe exactly as Jock wanted them to. All was well. His old buddy Kathlene was merely showing him and his friend around where she worked. Everything was aboveboard. No underlying issues or goals.

False.

They'd started out on the lower levels, where Kathlene had pointed out the rooms of emergency staff and others who responded to phone calls, as well as locker rooms, storage areas and places that were of great use but wouldn't yield them the information they were after.

But that was part of the act. They really had to behave as if this was a genuine tour of the building—even though they were only just now about to dig into what was important here.

Rather than waiting for an elevator, Kathlene showed them up the couple of flights of steps to the upper echelons of this building.

They emerged into a hallway much wider and more brightly lit than those downstairs. The floor was gleaming wood. The walls between the numerous doors were covered with photos of faces of smiling men in uniforms, probably former sheriffs and their seconds in command.

"I don't get up here very often," Kathlene said. "The officers stationed up here mostly come downstairs if they want to interact with us. But—"

A door at the far end of the hall opened, and Sheriff Melton Frawley emerged. With him was a young uniformed deputy, a woman. Jock assumed she was the person Kathlene had said she would talk to about Ralf and him and their opinions about the town.

The woman who had Frawley's ear because she did as he said and waited on him hand and foot, if what Kathlene had said was true. And Jock had no doubt that it was.

Frawley strode toward them. Kathlene smiled again in a way that struck Jock as nervous yet determined. Instinctively, he moved to her side and was glad to see Ralf do the same.

"Deputy Baylor," the sheriff said, "what're you doing on this floor?" To his credit, the guy wasn't scowling at her, and his tone sounded more curious than angry or dictatorial.

Sheriff Melton Frawley struck Jock as being a tall stick of a man who'd fought his way into a job with power and would do anything to maintain it. When Jock had seen him the previous night at the old ranch, the guy had been in his uniform as he was now, maybe to assert himself as in charge, or maybe just because he hadn't had time to change. In either event, he'd swaggered a bit while talking to Tisal and the others in charge of the supposed sportsmen.

"I was just giving my friends Jock and Ralf a tour of our headquarters, sir, but we're done. I'm off to find Deputy Korling so we can go out on patrol."

"You do that," said Frawley. And then the man turned to Jock and Ralf. "Meantime, I'll continue with your friends' tour." The man grinned, and Jock figured that the other lady deputy had done as Kathlene had hoped: told their story to this man.

And with luck, Ralf and he would get an invitation to meet the sportsmen in person. Tonight.

While Jock was still in human form.

Chapter 14

As the sheriff spoke, Betsy Alvers had remained just behind him, peeking around to aim a sympathetic smile toward Kathlene that said she'd done as Kathlene had anticipated and revealed to the boss the earlier conversation they'd had—whether or not Kathlene had expected some discretion from her.

But fortunately, Kathlene had expected exactly what had happened.

And the results? Well, now Sheriff Frawley must know how concerned Kathlene was that her dear long-term friend Jock and his buddy Ralf weren't on the same page as Kathlene about hunting and hunting laws and maybe even about people who tried to restrict other people's rights.

So as Kathlene hurried downstairs to meet up with her partner, she kept telling herself those results were perfect, just what she'd wanted: a probable conversation between the undercover Alpha Force guys and the sheriff, one that could lead to her team members learning a whole lot more about what was going on with the sportsmen and what they were up to.

So why did Kathlene feel so bummed out now?

As if she didn't know.

What they were doing wouldn't, couldn't, include her.

At least not right now...

She reached the downstairs area where Jimmy waited for her, nearly alone since others in their shift had already hit the road.

"You ready to go, partner?" Jimmy asked, frowning in what she interpreted to be barely concealed irritation.

"I sure am. Let's sign out and get on our way."

They'd both officially gone on duty before the morning's assembly, but now they followed the standard process to confirm that they were about to enter the patrol car assigned to them and get out there to protect the town and county.

"Let's go," Kathlene said a minute later when she had completed her entry on the department computer system, tossing a grim smile toward Jimmy. She strode determinedly through the doorway and down the concrete steps to the parking area, hearing him keeping up with her.

Today she had the keys. She would drive them around.

And would get nowhere near the old ranch unless there was a call out for assistance from law enforcement.

That wouldn't happen.

Nor would she get back here, or anywhere else where Jock and Ralf were likely to be hanging out.

No, she would get an update from them later about how their ad hoc meeting with Sheriff Frawley went, and whether they would get a visit to the sportsmen's camp out of it.

Kathlene would have to wait.

And Kathlene was not a patient person.

All had gone perfectly, as if Jock had whispered into the sheriff's ear exactly what he wanted, and the guy had been nothing but an obedient servant—even while Frawley undoubtedly assumed he held all the cards in anyone's pockets around this department and the county where he was in charge.

At the moment, Jock and Ralf were just ending their meeting in Frawley's surprisingly small but neat, and expensively appointed, office.

"We really appreciate all you've said," Jock said, leaning forward in the smooth wooden office chair he'd taken that faced the sheriff's desk.

Ralf was right beside him. "We sure do," he said. "I'd been telling Jock that maybe it was a mistake to come here, at least for any length of time. It's okay for him to say hi to an old friend, but we're on vacation, and the idea of not being able to do any hunting before visiting Yellowstone and then heading home... Well, I, for one, didn't like it."

"And like we said, before we talked to you we really had the impression that things around here were about to get even worse. I mean, your county commissioners' ideas about passing even more restrictions?" Jock shook his head, hoping he was as good an actor as he was trying to be. Those restrictions could save lives, including lives of wolves.

And his kind had an affinity for the true, wild, non-shifting canines as well as for their own.

"Well, when you come tonight to the barbecue, you'll get to meet other people who think like you do."

"We're looking forward to it." Jock knew his smile was genuine. They'd gotten an invitation to visit the ranch. They would be able to talk to the men staying there, listen in on what they were saying to one another, get a better feel—he hoped—for what those explosions were about and whether the residents there genuinely were true sportsmen.

It still was possible that they were innocent of any wrongdoing despite all Jock's doubts, including those raised by the snippets of conversations he had been able to make out while patrolling the area in wolf form. And that one small explosion he'd heard and smelled.

"I'll let them know you're coming, and I'll be there, too, at least for a while." The sheriff stood, still grinning at them. Even if Jock didn't have other reasons to doubt the man's sincerity, that too-bright smile on the narrow, aging, yet falsely friendly face would have given him the same sense of crawly insects along his back as he had now. "And don't you worry about your friendship with Deputy Baylor," Frawley drawled. "I'm a bit older than you gentlemen, and sometimes youthful relationships don't last forever, especially since people often go in different directions that you can't imagine when you're kids in college."

Very philosophical for an old, curmudgeonly—and most likely deceitful—sheriff, Jock thought. But this one had an ax to grind, apparently against anyone who didn't think the same way he did.

"Thanks," Jock said.

"See you later," Ralf added as they both rose and left the room.

* * *

It was late afternoon, and Kathlene was off duty. She was glad that she'd gotten a few minutes to join up with Jock and Ralf at their cabin before they left to go to the barbecue at the fenced-off ranch.

"We need some kind of signal or code," she said. "You can always call me and say it, and then I'll come to help."

Jock had been standing by the cabin's unused fireplace, but now he strode over to her. He was wearing a white T-shirt and jeans with a light hunting jacket over it. Ralf, just coming in with Click on a leash, was dressed similarly.

"Thanks," Jock said, "but we'll be fine." He drew close enough to look down at her, and the heat in his brilliant hazel eyes looked both fond and damnably sexy. Too bad she couldn't just seduce him to keep him from going into what could be a lion's den of trouble.

"Well, will you be able to shapeshift if things get too rocky?"

"No. I don't want to have the equipment and elixir along just in case things do get out of hand, and I doubt we'd be able to slip away long enough to do anything, anyway. But don't worry. We'll be fine. We're well trained by the military, even though we also have some secret kinds of missions that the rest of the troops aren't sent on. I doubt things will get so out of hand that we'll need to engage in any kind of self-defense or combat, but if so, we'll deal with it."

"Yeah, but Kathlene already bested you in hand-to-hand," Ralf called from behind them. "No wonder she's worried."

She couldn't help smiling, but only for a moment.

"That's not the point. I should find a way to go with you, to help if—"

"No need," Jock interrupted.

"But—" Kathlene didn't get to finish. She was suddenly in Jock's arms, held tightly against his muscular body, his mouth silencing her with a hot kiss.

When he finally let go of her—just a little—Jock pulled his head back and looked down at her again.

"We'll be fine," he repeated. "And I'll call you just as soon as we're far enough away from there to have no repercussions. I'll tell you what we learn, I promise."

Kathlene wanted to contradict him yet again. Sure, he could distract her with an unexpected kiss, but only for a moment, and not from her deepest concerns.

None of them spoke much more before the two men left shortly thereafter—although Kathlene had to glare at Ralf to fend off his amused glances. When they were gone, Kathlene stayed in their cabin just a little longer, glad to have at least Click's company this time.

She sat on one of the two rustic chairs, and the dog seemed to sense her malaise. He came over and sat on the wooden floor beside her, putting his head onto her lap.

"Thanks, Click," she whispered, bending over to hug the dog. She patted him for a while, then reached for the TV remote. Maybe she'd find some brainless sitcom to take her mind off those men—that man—and his attitude, and the potential danger to both of them.

But that was impossible. She was damned worried.

She was part of their team. They'd confirmed it before, and her knowledge about the nature of Alpha Force now made it even more critical that they accept her.

They had, therefore, told her all that they'd said in their discussion with her boss, or so she believed. Sheriff Frawley had undoubtedly invited them that night because of her. His sportsmen should supposedly be able to convince these visitors that there were others in and around Clifford County who weren't like her and who didn't like the kind of authority that she espoused.

She was concerned, of course, that the sportsmen just wanted to get to know Jock and Ralf better, to learn if they truly were of a similar mind-set to them—or potential enemies, as she was.

They were aware that she and Jock were supposedly old friends, so that could give them cause to mistrust him, no matter what he told them.

Her showing up with them for this barbecue, as part of their team, wouldn't work. She knew that.

But she could at least wait here, on their turf, for their return.

Unless…

This felt novel. Instead of Jock's creeping around while in wolf form, Ralf drove their car right up the narrow, pitted driveway through the woods to the locked metal gate in the fence surrounding the old ranch.

It late now. Evening was falling. A good time for a party, Jock supposed.

A guard came out of the small shed that was right next door, a guy in a camo uniform, of all things. If this group was composed of anarchists, why did any of them want to look like official military members?

Or was this just for show, to make any visitors realize that not just anyone could enter here?

Jock got out of the car and approached. He was careful not to raise his chin or do anything else that might look unusual, but he did use his stronger senses to check out the area a bit. There was nothing unusual, though, except the hint of a fire in the distance, probably the barbecue.

That didn't mean the entire facility was pristine.

"Hello," the guard called through the gate. He looked like he must have been around for a while, a senior citizen with a wrinkled face and suspicious frown. A longtime anarchist?

Jock motioned for Ralf to join him. Ralf turned off the engine and they both walked toward the gate. "Hi," Jock called. "Sheriff Frawley invited us to the barbecue here tonight."

When the guard didn't move for a moment except to study them with dark, distrustful eyes, Jock thought of Kathlene and what she had said and her concern for them.

Maybe she'd been right—not that he doubted they could be putting themselves in a dangerous position just by coming here. But maybe they should have called in backup first.

Their orders, though, were that backup would be readily available, but no Alpha Force members would be flown in until their surveillance yielded more than suspicions that these guys were ready to blow up civilians and others to support their hatred of authority.

Jock had put his superior officer, Drew Connell, on alert after hearing, and scenting, that one explosion, but more was needed.

And Kathlene as backup? No way! He needed to ensure her safety, but not vice versa.

"Your names?" the guy finally called.

Beside Jock, Ralf moved a little. He apparently felt uncomfortable with this situation, too. "I'm Ralf Nunnoz," he called, "and this is my friend Jock Larabey. We visited with Sheriff Frawley at his office this morning, so if there's any question about our being here, you can call him."

His aide at work. Jock suppressed his grim smile. He knew he could always count on Ralf to have his back.

"No need. He's been in touch. You can come in." The senior guy moved away and pulled something out of his pocket. It must have been a control of some kind since the gate started to roll sideways as it opened.

"Thanks," Ralf called. Both returned to the car and Ralf slowly drove them inside.

The guard approached the driver's window, which Ralf opened. He told them to continue down the narrow road until they saw a parking lot. They were to leave their car there and someone would meet them.

Once again, Ralf thanked the man, and they followed his instructions. Jock was surprised to see that the parking lot was fairly substantial in size and nearly full. Perhaps twenty cars were there beneath the canopy of overhanging trees. It was still light enough that Jock could see that, straight ahead, there was a clearing beyond a narrow row of vegetation, and in it was a structure he'd noticed before, while prowling the area, that looked like a ranch house.

Sure enough, as the guard had said, they were met by a man walking from that direction. He looked familiar—one of those they'd met at the bar and at the county commissioners' meeting.

Ralf had parked in one of the few empty spaces and the guy joined them. He was tall and appeared as muscular in his bright green knit shirt and jeans as Jock remembered him. "Hi," he said. "Welcome. We met before. I'm Hal."

"Hi, Hal." Jock reintroduced himself and Ralf. "This

is really nice, our being invited here. I understand from the sheriff that there are a bunch of you and that you're into hunting."

"That's right. Come on and I'll introduce you to some of the others." Hal motioned with his long arm, and both Jock and Ralf followed him along the unpaved path through the trees. "I hear you're not from Montana," he continued as they walked.

"That's right," Jock said. "I went to school in Missoula but I live in Washington State now."

"I gather that you wanted to do some hunting here, but this isn't a good time, and we've got some strict laws against poaching. People generally have to apply for permits before now, and there's a lot of game that's not yet in season. But we'll fill you in."

"Don't you have a way to get around that?" Ralf inquired. He was staying closer to Hal's side than Jock, which was fine. It gave Jock more of an opportunity to view what they were passing—and use his more powerful senses to also scout the area.

"Like I said," Hal responded, "we'll fill you in."

They reached the clearing. At its far side was the large wooden ranch house that was painted a deep red. There was a white door in its center, and equal-sized wings on each side.

He couldn't tell the depth, but Jock had the sense that quite a few *sportsmen* could be housed right here, for as long as they were needed to train…or whatever.

Jock smelled the aromas of barbecuing meats and the fire cooking them more strongly here. He also scented a number of different people, although there were enough that he couldn't distinguish one from another—not the way he'd have been able to in wolf form. He did think, though, that he smelled the other person, Tisal, whom he'd met at the bar and who had gone to the commissioners' meeting.

Sure enough, when Hal led them around the back to a large stone-paved patio filled with chattering men, most with beer cans in their hands, Tisal was the first in the crowd to approach them. Jock didn't see the sheriff there, but he might come later.

"Welcome, gentlemen," the man said. "As you know, I'm Nate Tisal, and I guess I'm the guy in charge here. As Sheriff Frawley probably told you, we're a little selective in who we invite since there are a lot of people these days who're tree huggers and don't like what we do—hunting."

"That's not us," Jock said immediately. "In fact, we told the sheriff that our inability to hunt around here was making us leave sooner than we'd originally anticipated."

"Well, we might be able to help with that. Come on, let's grab you some beers and I'll introduce you around."

The next hour or so would have been enjoyable under other circumstances. Tisal introduced them to everyone there—all men, and all dressed casually in clothing that ranged from snug, sleeveless T-shirts and jeans to full hunting apparel.

Food was served buffet-style on a table near the barbecue pit, and all the guys grabbed seats at the three rows of picnic tables on the large patio.

"Good stuff," Jock said after tasting the meat. "What is it?" He knew, of course. Venison. But as far as he knew deer wasn't yet in season here.

"What do you think?" Tisal asked. He'd sat down at the same table, as had Hal and four other guys.

"Venison?" Ralf said.

"Well, if anyone outside these gates asks, you had some damned good steak," said one of the other men.

"That's right," Tisal said. "There aren't any poachers around here." They all started to laugh.

"Definitely not." Jock made himself grin as he took another bite. Of course they were poachers. But the sheriff probably knew that and had no intention of arresting them.

Nor would Alpha Force have any interest in hauling these guys in if that was the only kind of law they were breaking…although if the poaching included wolves, wild cats or birds there'd be a bunch of controversy within their very special military ranks.

For now Jock just ate and stayed as quiet as possible. Ralf knew the deal. He was the friendly one who answered questions and asked some of his own about how this group had moved into the ranch area and started growing. The men described how they all were sportsmen who practiced at a shooting range on the property that their latest visitors would be shown after dinner. How they nearly all had their hunting licenses already and would brag about using them in town when the time was right—but not talk about anything else they might be using their guns for before that.

And Jock? Well, he listened to the conversation and chimed in now and then. He looked around them, believing he could, through some breaks in the trees around this part of the property, get a glimpse of the chain-link fence surrounding the ranch thanks to the lights that had been lit on the property, since it was already nightfall.

But mostly he used his acute hearing to eavesdrop on what those at other tables were saying.

And, yes, some were complaining about the laws that

wouldn't let them legally hunt much now, and the talk that those laws might even be made stronger.

There were also complaints about government in general, and how other people, who claimed they had rights under stupid laws that should never have been passed, should be shot for telling these guys what they could and couldn't do.

These guys, as they continued to swig down beer after beer, complained even more. And said they would do something about those laws and the people proposing and enacting and enforcing them.

General stuff, though. Not enough to call in reinforcements to bring this group to justice. Were they planning to do something to back up their complaints?

Jock didn't hear anything like that—but Ralf and he cheered what they did hear and made it sound like they agreed with everything said at their table.

A while later, four new guys who hadn't been there previously joined the party. Jock had heard a car enter the parking lot at the other side of the house, so they'd apparently just arrived. They all wore black and seemed highly muscular beneath their tight shirts, but otherwise they didn't resemble one another at all. Two were bald, though one of them, a short guy, had a dark mustache and the other was probably six foot five. One newcomer with short dark hair had a skinny, lined face and the final guy, with fuzzy light hair, looked about sixteen. Their scents varied, too, from popular aftershaves to sweat and garlic.

Jock was curious about them, especially when Tisal rose quickly from the table to join them. With all the other conversation going on, increasingly loud and rowdy as the men drank a lot of beer, all Jock could make out were a few words—ones that concerned him. Words like *follow-up* and *warning*.

But when he rose to ostensibly go after another helping of food, all four guys seemed to melt into the crowd.

Even so, despite how interesting this was, it didn't
dispel the suspicions they had about this group; neither
did it scream out that they were all dedicated anarchists
who planned to do something about it…like kill people.

At least this evening was a foot in the door. Hopefully, Ralf and he were making friends and contacts, and
would be invited back to interact and listen some more.

Maybe get the lowdown on the men who'd arrived late.

And…

Jock froze suddenly, then lowered his fork to his plate.
He wanted to raise his head, to aim his nose into the air
so he could verify that what he'd thought he had smelled
was real.

But that would look damned odd to this group, so instead he sat quietly, allowing himself to inhale as unno-
ticeably as possible.

Yes. There it was, the scent he'd thought he smelled.

Two scents.

Somewhere beyond the patio, beyond the fencing that
he could only glimpse here and there…

Were Kathlene and Click.

Chapter 15

Good thing Click was well trained, Kathlene thought. Otherwise, he'd surely be barking at what was going on beyond the trees and fence, maybe even tugging at his leash.

She had stopped at an area where the trees were thick but she still, after angling herself, could see inside the well-lighted compound. Click undoubtedly could sense a lot more, but the wolflike dog sat down, panting slightly as if expressing frustration and glancing up at her often.

"Good boy," she whispered and patted his furry head while she stood there looking. And worrying.

The night was warm, the air still and dry. She heard rustling in the trees around her, possibly from creatures of the night, but fortunately Click didn't react to them. Nor did he react to the pulsing sounds of noises beyond the fence, as if people were partying. They sometimes raised their voices to cheer.

Was that where the night's dinner was being served? Probably.

As far as she knew, this was Click's first time here. The other visits to the exterior area of the ranch had not been by the actual dog, but by Jock, while shapeshifted.

Shapeshifted. Amazing, but she had accepted the idea. She had no choice, after what she had seen. But that didn't keep her from worrying.

Maybe Jock could take excellent care of himself when he was in wolf form. But tonight he was pretty much all human.

In case he needed to shift, though, she had brought the backpack that was usually in Ralf's possession. It contained the stuff she'd seen the two men use to get Jock shifted.

She had also brought her Glock.

She had come here because she was worried. She still didn't know if that worry was justified.

She hadn't stayed long at the cabin after the Alpha Force members had left for the evening to do their undercover work—without her, their team member. This time, she understood and agreed with it. If a deputy sheriff turned up at the supposed sportsmen's complex for dinner, she'd no idea what their reaction would be, but it certainly would be as bad as she'd experienced when they'd caught her in the area before. Maybe worse, since she was supposed to have learned her lesson.

So tonight she'd intended to simply head home and wait for Jock to call and tell all that had occurred, as he'd promised.

But things hadn't turned out that easy. When she started to leave the cabin area, she'd parked at the opening to the main road to check her bag because she'd wanted to make sure she hadn't left her phone at the cabin. She wasn't sure why she'd turned off the engine, but it was a good thing she had.

Despite her car lights being off, thanks to the minimal illumination outside the registration cabin she'd seen a reflection on the side of a vehicle driving down the road without its lights on, either. It appeared large and dark.

It headed in the direction of the old ranch.

Her law-enforcement instincts had immediately shrieked silently at her that something was wrong. After all, she, too, kept her lights turned off at times she didn't want to be seen while driving at night. But she knew her own motives, and they were essentially law-abiding.

What were the motives of whoever was in this vehicle?

She didn't know for sure, of course, that the sportsmen's compound was the car's destination. Nor did she have any reason to believe that her teammates would be in trouble.

She didn't know that they wouldn't be, either. And the idea of something happening to either of them, particularly Jock, especially when she might be able to help... Well, she had hurried back to the cabin and gotten Click, just in case she again needed an excuse to be out and about if she were caught. It hadn't worked well last time but at least it had worked.

And this time, with a real dog instead of Jock in wolf form...

It didn't matter. She had to be there in case she was needed.

So here she was.

Filled with frustration. She couldn't be certain that this compound was where that car had been heading, but she hadn't seen it again when she'd driven in this direction a few minutes after spotting it.

She didn't know who had been inside the vehicle, had no real idea why she'd worried so much about Jock and Ralf…except that she had learned to trust her instincts.

Plus, she admitted to herself, she had come to care much more than she should for her teammates. Especially for one of them.

Jock.

Was he okay? Were things within the compound—

Wait. There.

In the bright lights beyond the fence, she saw more movement than she had before. The area she observed appeared to be an outer wall of a house, and she'd caught sight of cars parked to one side and heard noises like a party beyond it.

She hadn't seen any people…before. But now several men appeared to be walking from the noisy area toward where the cars were parked.

Four or five men.

They included Jock and Ralf.

Those two appeared to be engaged in a rollicking conversation with their companions. Having fun.

Maybe Kathlene's instincts had been all wrong. That could be a good thing.

She and Click would leave soon. Carefully. At least, having seen Jock, she could assume that he was okay.

She stifled a gasp and a laugh. Oh, yes, he was okay. As she watched, he lifted his hands as if aiming a rifle. He was evidently getting into his role there as a hunter. But while he was pretending, one of his hands went over his head. His hand moved in a strange gesture. As if he knew she was there and he firmly motioned her away.

He turned, and the group headed back toward the party area. She'd no idea why—other than he was protecting her, keeping anyone from driving away while Click and she headed from the area toward where she had parked her car.

Instead of her protecting him, he had wound up protecting her.

She didn't like that...and yet she appreciated it.

And she would have to tell him so.

Fortunately, no one had blinked when Jock, in a completely friendly manner, asked for a short tour of the property. He'd acted as if he'd drunk too much beer and was in the mood to see the shooting range, maybe fire a few rounds, which gave him the ability to perform his gesture to Kathlene without anyone suspecting that he was doing anything but being an idiot who'd OD'd on alcohol.

He'd asked Hal to show him around and invited lots of others. Only a few had come along.

When they'd reached the area pointed out to them as the firing range, a cleared area surrounded by trees that he believed to be near the back of the property, no one had given in to his requests to practice firing any guns, even at targets, with him in such a soused condition. No matter what these men were, they at least didn't agree to put themselves in danger. Not here. Not now.

But the other goal of his performance, trying to get closer to the men who'd slipped in late, hadn't been successful. They had dropped a few more words that captured his attention, hints about other, bigger, more powerful guns that they may have brought that were perhaps still stashed in their vehicle.

But then they had shut up and begun just partying, too.

Ralf had gone along with him. His aide knew him well

enough to realize he had a reason for acting so loony. But not even his looniness got him close enough to the large black SUV the latecomers had driven here except to see it at a distance. Were there guns hidden inside? Were there other guns more powerful than regular hunting weapons already hidden somewhere on the ranch?

He needed to look, to find out somehow. But that wouldn't happen tonight.

It would happen soon, though. He had to make sure of it.

Now Ralf and he were back on the patio. He started to wind down, then approached Hal again.

"Sorry," he muttered. "I'm not…I'd better go back to our cabin now. Thanks so much for inviting us. I'd love to come again."

"Me, too," Ralf said. He put a hand under Jock's elbow, as if trying to steady him. Good. That added another element of believability to the act he was putting on.

"Of course, of course." That was Tisal, who had joined them. "Glad you came."

He got a little closer, making Jock more uncomfortable although he didn't show it. What was the guy up to?

"We're always interested in having men of similar interests…and ideas…join us. I know you don't plan to be here long, but consider that."

Jock suddenly wanted to do a fist pump but of course stayed still. They were being accepted. Right?

Or was this just an act so these *sportsmen* could keep an eye on them?

No matter. Ralf and he had achieved most of what they'd hoped to do on this visit—including some level of being accepted here. Now they were leaving, but they would return. By invitation.

First thing he wanted to do after leaving this compound?

Go find Kathlene, give her a big kiss…then chew her out for showing up here and potentially endangering all of them.

A noise at the door woke Kathlene, followed by the excited scratching of doggy nails on the wooden floor as Click jumped around near the cabin's entry.

She hadn't intended to fall asleep, but after seeing Jock's motions that told her to leave, she had headed back to the cabins to return Click. Then she'd decided to stay for just a short while to see if Jock and Ralf came back quickly.

She'd sat down on the bed and picked up a brochure on the Clifford County area that the motel had left in the cabin for its visitors…and that was all she remembered until now.

She wasn't sure what time it was, but she knew she'd been here awhile.

Click's excitement told her who was about to enter the cabin. Even so, her law-enforcement instincts kicked in and she reached toward the weapon she had placed in her bag and left on the floor near the bed.

When Jock and Ralf entered and were jumped on in greeting by Click, she put her bag back down, relaxed and smiled at them. But only for a moment.

Jock was scowling at her.

"Hi." She attempted to sound friendly and ignore what she assumed was his irritation.

"Hi, Kathlene," Ralf said as he knelt to hug the ecstatic dog. "What are you doing here?"

"More important, what were you doing around the

ranch? Didn't you learn your lesson last time?" Jock
stood with his arms folded across his buff chest that was
now covered by a white T-shirt and open hunting jacket.
If it weren't for his attitude, she might have felt turned
on by his stance, his obviously toned body.

Instead, she made herself ignore what he looked like
as she responded, "Yes, I keep learning lessons around
here. But I also know that there are times my primary
focus is to protect people. I hadn't intended to go to the
ranch, but I saw something that worried me."

"What's that?" Jock's response was immediate.

"Possible invaders. They might have been hiding from
whatever they left behind, or whatever was in front of
them, but I needed to make sure you two remained un-
harmed." Standing to face them, her own arms folded
across her chest, Kathlene described the darkened car
she had followed and why it had worried her. "Once I
got there, I didn't see them anymore so I figured they'd
driven into the compound. I walked around it with Click
to try to make sure that, whoever they were, they weren't
doing anything to harm either of you."

"Even if they were slaughtering us, why on earth did
you think you and Click would be able to do anything
about it?" Clearly Jock wasn't going to back down.

She wasn't going to allow him to get away with his
attitude. Not now. "You mean you're the only one who
can act protective? Hell, I'm the one in law enforcement
around here. You're—"

"I'm one of the people you called in for help. Don't
forget that."

She wilted, but just a little. "You're right," she acknowledged. "And tonight? If I'd seen you in trouble, I'd
have called for help…but it couldn't have been a standard

call-out of my department. Not when the sheriff himself is apparently allied with that group. I'm just…"

"Just?" Jock prompted when she stopped talking and looked over at Click, who sat between the legs of the two men facing her.

"Just glad you're both okay." She lifted her eyes, looking first at Ralf, whose gaze was clearly sympathetic, and then at Jock, who at least wasn't scowling at her now. In fact, his expression had softened quite a bit. Enough to make her want to throw herself into his arms, so she could feel, as well as see, that he was all right.

But she wouldn't do that now, even if they'd been alone. Maybe he was right. Was she worrying too much about him? He was a big boy, a soldier…and more. He surely could take care of himself as well as she did for herself.

"It's getting late," she finally said. "I'd better head for home."

"Yes," Jock said, "but not yet. We need to make sure none of my newest best friends followed us here. If they see a nonallied deputy sheriff leaving here, that could blow everything."

"Oh." Kathlene realized she should have considered that. She had been so wound up in her concerns about the men's treatment at the ranch that she hadn't thought about what might happen next around here. "I'm parked back in the lot outside. Umm…maybe I could sneak out behind this cabin and you could…" But she couldn't figure out how to move her car in a way that she wouldn't be spotted if they were under surveillance.

"No, best thing is for us to go out and check." Jock turned to look at Ralf, and they exchanged glances that seemed to communicate volumes.

Volumes Kathlene could read, too.

"You're going to shift and go out as if you're Click," she stated.

"Exactly."

That would mean... Hell, she was a professional. The fact that Jock would have to get nude again was just part of the process, and she didn't have to react to it, even if she observed it. "I'll help," she said.

"What do you mean?"

She pointed toward the backpack that now lay on the floor near the cabin's couple of chairs, near where Ralf had left it before. "I'd brought that along on my venture, just in case you'd need to shift to get out of there. I wasn't sure how, but I figured it didn't hurt to be prepared. I saw you shift before, and even if I have to stay in here while Ralf walks the canine who looks like Click, I can assist Ralf in doing his part to help you change—pour your elixir, maybe, or get the light ready, or—"

"You've really bought into the reality that I'm a shifter." Jock's grin was huge now.

"I don't actually need assistance," Ralf added, "but I'd be glad to show you what I'm up to, step by step, so you'll be ready if you ever have to do it on your own someday."

"Great! How soon should we get started?"

"How about now?" Jock answered, and his flashing hazel eyes caught hers.

He knew what she was thinking...and he started to remove his clothes.

He made it look good.

Jock didn't bother to glance toward his aide. Ralf would know exactly what he was doing.

Teasing, tempting the hot woman who was staring at

him. Not that they could do anything about sexual urges now, and he knew better than to give in to them later.

But he might as well have fun for the few minutes it took for him to shift.

True to her word, Kathlene stood beside Ralf. She held the vial that had stored the elixir, which Jock had already drunk. She knelt beside Ralf as he aimed the light toward Jock.

And watched closely, very closely, with eyes that shouted appreciation and more, as Jock finally removed the rest of his clothes.

He didn't have much time, though, to continue the silent seduction of the woman who watched him strip. The pulling began inside him, outside him along his skin, and the discomfort turned into more.

He was changing. Fast.

Kathlene watched…everything. As much as she appreciated seeing Jock's hard, bared body—and how his erection grew and pulsed as if aware of how intensely she watched it and the rest of him—she also found herself amazed and intrigued as that wonderful male body changed and contorted, shrinking in many places, growing in others, sprouting the same kind of fur that covered Click.

Click. The dog had been banished to the other room for this process. Had he seen it before? Interacted with the man who looked, when all was through, so much like the dog?

No matter. The process seemed to take forever, yet no time at all.

And in just a few minutes, it was complete.

After another short time frame, Ralf glanced at Kathlene. "It's time for our walk. Click will stay here with you. Everything okay?"

Kathlene admired how the man who had undoubtedly watched this process countless times could act so nonchalant. She looked into Ralf's dark, inquisitive eyes and said, "I'm fine. I'll be here. Go ahead."

Ralf slipped a collar around Jock's neck and attached a leash. "Okay, my friend," he said. "Let's go."

Chapter 16

*T*he area around the cabins was busier this night than Jock had seen before. He did not know the identity of any of those who darted between cars and into other buildings.

That did not matter.

As Ralf and he walked around the area, Jock continued to use his enhanced wolfen senses, his sense of smell, his hearing, to determine if anyone here had also been at the old ranch this day.

He detected no one from there.

He continued to stay at Ralf's side, sniffing the ground, occasionally lifting his leg, doing as he would if he truly were Click or another domesticated canine.

Ralf, above him, whispered now and then, asking if there was anywhere Jock wanted to go, to examine more closely.

Each time, Jock shook himself as a dog would do, signifying that the answer was no.

They remained this way for quite a while, although Jock, in this form, was not certain how much time had passed even with his enhanced human abilities thanks to the elixir.

Eventually, Ralf said, "We've been around the whole place twice. Is there anything else we need to do?"

Once more, Jock shook himself. Then he pulled forward a bit on the leash that he forced himself not to resent.

He much preferred freedom while in shifted form. Freedom to roam. To be as wolfen as he desired.

But in this situation, he had to conform.

In a few more minutes, they had returned to the cabin. The cabin that still contained Kathlene...for now.

Since he had sensed no others around who could harm them, it was time for her to go home.

She would be glad.

And so would he.

They were back, on the wooden platform outside the door.

The real Click's skittering around on the bathroom floor, where he'd been temporarily confined, confirmed that, and so did his soft woofs.

It had taken all the self-control Kathlene possessed not to follow the man and apparent dog, not even to pull back the curtains and peek out to watch what she could, knowing they might not be in her line of sight at all.

They walked into the cabin, Ralf still holding the leash attached to the collar around Jock's neck.

"Did you see anyone?" she asked Ralf as he bent to

remove the collar from around the gorgeous, wild-looking wolf.

"No, and Jock didn't sense anyone, either."

"Is that what he told you?" She couldn't help the smart-alecky question. Or was it? Despite earlier conversations in his presence, for all she knew this werewolf did actually know how to talk to his aide in English.

"He communicated it, yes." The smile on Ralf's dark-toned face appeared smug, as if he was proud of his ability to understand his shifted charge.

That charge, sitting on the floor beside Ralf, cocked his head and gave a muted bark—one that Kathlene interpreted to mean that he might choose to honor her with direct communication, too, if she earned it.

Okay, this was weird. Definitely. And yet knowing someone who shifted—and not only knowing him, but being part of his team, at least for now—was a whole lot more fun, a whole lot more intriguing, than she could ever have imagined while reading books or seeing movies or TV shows that featured shapeshifters. Fictional shapeshifters, at least in those media.

But never, ever, had she considered the fact any part of that could be real.

Till now.

"Are you going to shift back now? I mean—" She'd started aiming the question at Jock as if he would be responding directly, but she gave a short laugh and looked back at Ralf. "Will he be shifting back now?"

But Jock did in fact provide the first response. His pointed ears moved farther forward and his head nodded. He gave a short "woof" in emphasis.

"That means yes," Ralf said unnecessarily. "When Alpha Force shifters take that elixir so they don't have to rely on a full moon, they'll shift back on their own in a few hours. But like I've said, we can help them by aiming that same light on them, which quickens the process. I don't know how it works. I only know it does." He had been looking at Kathlene but now turned and looked down at Jock. "You ready to change back?"

Again his ears moved, along with a nod and muted bark.

"Good." Ralf looked around. He apparently spied his backpack in a corner along the wall, where Kathlene had seen him put it after returning the elixir container and light once Jock had shifted. Ralf approached it and pulled out the light.

"Let's go," Ralf said.

Kathlene braced herself. The amazing immediate transformation she had seen before was about to happen again.

And this time, when it was complete, Jock the man would be there.

Once again in the nude.

And also this time, neither of them, Ralf nor Jock, had told her to leave or even to look away.

She watched, feeling sorry for the tawny-silver wolf as he began writhing and moving and changing in the light, his fur receding, his body elongating…and then, very soon, it was Jock lying there on the floor, unclothed and buff and enticingly gorgeous.

You're a professional, she reminded herself—even if it was law enforcement and nothing related to what she was watching. She pasted a vaguely interested expression on her face and stood near the wall, behind Jock's head so he wouldn't see her.

Not that he'd be surprised she was still there.

"You okay, bro?" Ralf soon asked his charge.

"Yeah," Jock said somewhat breathily. Kathlene had anticipated his panting like that. That shift looked terribly uncomfortable, probably painful. "Yeah," he repeated and sat up—shielding the most intriguing parts of his body from Kathlene, but not before she had gotten a really good glimpse of them again. Now her best view was of his back, including his butt resting on the floor. His firm, amazingly great-looking butt...

Jock looked around as if he wanted to confirm her presence.

"Hi," she said when his eyes landed on her. He'd swiveled a bit on the floor—and Ralf had grabbed Jock's clothes and dumped them on his lap, hiding a lot from view.

"Hi," he said. His expression was taunting, and it became even more challenging as he stood without putting on a stitch of his clothing first. Then, without rushing, he donned the outfit Ralf had tossed to him.

If he was trying to turn her on, he was succeeding, but Kathlene was not about to give him any indication of it. Keeping her tone cool and professional, she said, "Since you didn't see or hear anyone who shouldn't be here, there's no reason I can't head back to my place now."

"That's fine," Jock said. His acknowledgment should make her feel good, feel free—and yet she experienced a pang of sorrow. He obviously didn't care that they'd be parting for the night now that he'd done his duty and ensured her safe departure.

"Tomorrow is Friday, my day off," she continued, "so I won't be at the department. We should be able to get together early and also plan what happens next. My idea? We'll meet someplace private first, maybe my home. I want to hear everything you both saw and heard at that place."

"Yeah, you'll find it interesting," Ralf said. "I think we just reached the tip of the iceberg, but anarchists? I'd say so. They definitely appear to be looking at things their own way."

"And did you achieve what you wanted to—cozying up to them, showing them that you have attitudes in common?"

"We did," Jock acknowledged. He was fully dressed now but no longer wearing the jacket that had made him appear like a hunter. He'd donned only the white T-shirt and jeans. "And I think you were right, by the way, about the ones in that darkened car. We can tell you all about what we learned tomorrow, after we've all gotten some sleep. Your place is fine."

"After that," Kathlene said, "we should go out in public again since you're still supposedly my buddy, Jock, maybe for breakfast. But after we do whatever planning we decide on, let's have a very public argument so you can stomp back to the ranch and vent about your former friend and her nasty, official-government-loving approach to the world."

Jock laughed. "Good idea. In fact, that was also what I was going to suggest."

As they'd spoken, Ralf had gone to the bathroom door and let Click loose at last. Kathlene supposed that worked well now since there were no further canines around to confuse anyone who might be watching them.

Although, after the patrol by the man and wolf a while ago, it appeared unlikely that they were under observation by the anarchists—and therefore probably by no one.

Click jumped around, leaping first on Ralf and then

on Jock, his two humans…at the moment. Then he came over to sniff Kathlene again, and she patted his head.

"Great," she told Jock. "I'll be up early, so let's talk first thing. Plan on being at my place at…let's say seven o'clock?"

"Okay," Jock said. As Kathlene headed for the door, he added, "Oh, and by the way. Don't be surprised if you see a vehicle following you on your way home."

"You don't need to do that." Kathlene let exasperation pour from her tone, even though she realized she felt a bit of relief. And more. Was she really starting to accept this man's too-protective ways? No. That couldn't happen.

"Maybe not," Jock said calmly. "But like I said, don't be surprised."

He didn't have to tell her he'd be right behind her, Jock thought as he followed Kathlene in his car while she headed back to her place. But she was a cautious person. She might be…displeased if she just happened to see someone following her, even in a car she recognized.

But one way or another, he did have to follow her.

He hardly trusted anyone.

Fellow Alpha Forcers, yes. And Kathlene? Yes, partly because she had brought Alpha Force in to investigate a situation that could be highly dangerous to a lot of people if it was as she, and now he, believed.

Those guys at the ranch? The *sportsmen?* He trusted none of them. At all. And the fact that he had checked around in shifted form and found no indication that any of them was near his cabin was a good thing, but it didn't mean Kathlene was safe.

Now that Ralf and he were potential members of their group, they might even think it'd guarantee the newcomers' joining up if the gang did something to neutralize Jock's *friend,* who was now giving him a hard time.

But the ride was seamless. As alert as Jock was, he saw no indication that anyone else on the road had any interest in Kathlene—or him, for that matter.

This late, there was little traffic so it didn't take them much time to reach her home.

And of course Jock wasn't about to let Kathlene enter that house without an escort…just in case.

He parked on the street after watching her pull down her driveway and into her garage. She waved at him, as if she figured he would be on his way.

Eventually, he would. But first he had to make sure she got into her house okay.

He didn't see her go in. She shut her garage door, and presumably that was the way she entered.

Was she okay? He went to the front door and waited for a minute or so, listening with his enhanced hearing. Scenting the air to ensure that there were no odors of intruders wafting through her home.

Even so, he had to make certain. He canvassed her neighborhood as he stood there. No cars creeping down the street, with or without their headlights on. No neighbors apparently peering out their windows at him, and that could be either a good thing or bad. No one was watching out for Kathlene or anyone else.

And no people out in the yards or street, even, at this hour, walking their dogs.

Safe? Maybe. Probably. But even so… He reached up to ring the doorbell.

And was startled as the outside light came on and the door opened.

Kathlene stood there, one hand holding the door and the other on her slender, sexy hip.

"What are you waiting for?" she asked. "Everything's fine in here, but come on in and see for yourself."

She'd have known he was following her even if he hadn't warned her.

She always watched her surroundings, but she was especially on alert tonight after her little jaunt once that car with no lights had headed down the road.

He should have known that.

But she also realized that this guy's protectiveness never quit.

She told him now that she would wait in the kitchen while he looked through her place and assured himself all was well. As he left her there, she opened her refrigerator door and brought out a couple of bottles of beer. He didn't have to come here, and she might as well reward him.

What she wanted to reward him—and herself—with wasn't beer, of course. But inviting him to make love to her—again—was beyond the realm of rationality. Been there, done that, and despite how enjoyable it had been, it had to be a one-time event. This was not a man—or whatever—that she dared to get any further involved with.

No matter how attracted she felt toward him.

While waiting, she opened her beer and took a swig, needing the kick to slow down her thoughts—and desires. But she knew better than to think that would work.

He was only gone for a few minutes, but she heard his footsteps here and there on her hardwood floors, including upstairs where her bedroom was.

When he returned, he just stood there at the kitchen door. Looking at her with those intense, erotically enticing hazel eyes.

"Everything okay?" she asked, forcing herself to stay cool.

"More or less."

"Do you want to stay for a few minutes? Have a beer?"

"Yes," he said, "and no. Here's what I want."

In less than a heartbeat he had joined her, taken her into his arms.

And lowered his hot, teasing lips to hers.

Chapter 17

Bad idea. But Jock wasn't about to stop. Not now. Not unless Kathlene pushed him away.

At least for the moment he would revel in the feel of her curvaceous, hot body against his, the taste of sweetness and heat in her mouth.

She apparently had reservations, too, since without backing up she said, "You should go." But her words didn't match her actions. Not at all. Her lips didn't stop exploring his, nor did her tongue, and her hands roved along his back and down into his jeans, pulling him closer where he grew and ached for her.

"Later," he said. "But now… Let's go upstairs." He had been up there while checking to make sure there was no one hiding in her house. Had glanced into her bedroom and sloughed off—sort of—his memories of being in it before with Kathlene.

That had been a few moments ago. And now…

"Okay," she whispered against him. She moved away and took his hand, leading him toward the stairway before he could scoop her up in his arms and carry her.

That was fine. It seemed more by mutual consent this way rather than some demanding guy dragging her to her room.

And he knew too well that Kathlene preferred to stay in control. Maybe that was one of the things that he liked about her. No matter how frustrating…

She was almost running now, and he smiled as he kept up with her so she wouldn't have to drag him, either, to where he actually wanted to go.

Her stairway was wide, the steps bare and polished wood with a white railing. In only a minute they were upstairs, then a short distance down the hall and into her room.

She flicked on the overhead light, but only for a moment as if to gain perspective of where her bed was: still right in the middle. And then, lights out, they were on top of the fluffy floral-print cover. He didn't wait before pulling Kathlene's shirt over her head, then reaching down to remove her slacks.

Meantime, they nearly formed a knot as she, too, stripped him. Which was fine, but only the tiniest bit unfair since she had seen him nude that night—twice. It was his turn.

When he was finally finished getting her clothes off, he could see her thanks to the dim glow radiating from the hallway. She was beautiful, every bit as lovely as he remembered. He smiled before reaching toward her breasts, beginning to caress them softly, reveling in the feel of how the initial small contact caused her nipples to bud and grow. He had to taste them, and so he did, even as he continued to touch her, to stroke her, to ease his hands downward along her warm, smooth skin until he touched her buttocks, then moved so he could touch her hot, moist core and begin stroking her there.

He loved the sound of her gasp, then followed it with one of his own as she gently grabbed his erection and began pumping it, driving him mad with need of her.

But his mind wasn't completely gone. He stopped long enough to feel around for his pants and reach into a pocket. He pulled out a condom and handed it to her. These days, he planned ahead, just in case....

"Would you care to do the honors?" he said in a tight, raspy voice he barely recognized.

"Yes," she rasped back, and he all but moaned as she pulled the taut rubber over him.

Kathlene refused to listen to the chiding voice in her head that still repeated how sorry she would be later. She wouldn't be sorry. No, this man wasn't the right person to form a long-lasting relationship with. One way or another he'd be out of her life soon.

But for now she might as well enjoy his sexy presence.

She cried out as he moved over her, touched her again down there where she was burning with desire, and then plunged his shaft into her. He began to drive into her, in and out, making her feel as if the wholeness of her being was centered on him and what he was doing and how he was making her feel—hot and excited and needy and wanting even more...

Until she screamed out when her orgasm surrounded her, and she heard Jock, too, groan as he apparently also reached his climax.

For a long moment he perched on his arms above her, connecting with her only down below where her thoughts and feelings were entirely centered.

And then he lowered himself gently on top of her, his breathing hard and irregular as hers.

"Wow," he said softly.

"Yes, wow," she agreed.

He hadn't intended to stay the night, but after his earlier shift to ensure Kathlene's safety, followed by his check of her house and, most exhausting and rewarding, their lovemaking, he had fallen asleep beside her on her bed.

She must have moved or made a small sound, since suddenly he was awake. He became aware immediately of where he was. Who he was with.

Why he was there.

He didn't move, not at first. It struck him that being here with Kathlene in her bed, both of them sated with lovemaking, felt right.

Right? Yeah, sure. He remained all too aware that the woman was a peace officer who threw herself into danger without a moment's thought. He still wanted to protect her, whether she wanted it or not—*not* being her usual scenario.

At the moment, they had to maintain a relationship while Ralf and he fulfilled the mission for Alpha Force. But he and his aide would be heading back to Ft. Lukman as soon as they dealt with the presumed anarchists, which he hoped would be soon.

The truth that he enjoyed being here with Kathlene, loved it, in fact, didn't make any difference.

Okay. He realized that, on top of his enjoyment of their

incredible physical encounters, he was somehow being swayed by her apparent ability to accept who and what he was…and he actually wasn't sure what she thought about it.

Maybe he'd ask her. Tomorrow.

For now… "Are you awake?" he asked her.

"Yes," she said. "I guess you are, too."

He heard the smile in her voice—and that was enough.

He reached for her, smiled himself as he felt her warm, naked flesh and began making love to her once more.

The next time Kathlene awoke in the middle of the night, she was the one to check on Jock. She woke him, too, but he didn't seem to mind.

Neither did she.

A little later, still lying there, out of breath and definitely happy, she realized she could get used to this kind of impulsive, immediate lovemaking.

She also realized she had better enjoy it while she could.

Tomorrow, who knew what would happen? After all, Jock and his buddy Ralf might be about to become anarchists. If they went deeper undercover in that capacity, they might even have to stay at the old ranch.

Where Kathlene would be absolutely unwelcome, even if she wanted to go there.

Which she didn't, except as an observer.

"You okay?" Jock asked, his voice hoarse. He was lying on his back beside her. She, too, remained on her back. But, heck, she might as well milk this one night for all she could get out of it.

She was too tired, too spent, to make love again—at this moment. But a snuggle wouldn't hurt.

"I'm fine," she responded, still a bit out of breath. She turned anyway to lie on her side, her arm over his irregularly rising and falling, and utterly warm, chest. He maneuvered his arm around her and she rested her cheek on his shoulder.

She must have fallen asleep, since she jumped sometime later when her cell phone pealed its musical ringtone. She'd left it on the nightstand and immediately turned on her back and reached for it.

The caller ID said that it was Myra Enager.

Kathlene turned and got out of bed. She felt Jock reach for her but needed to take this call.

"Hi, Myra," she said, then glanced again at the phone screen. It was barely six o'clock in the morning. Myra and she were friends, but this was the first time she'd ever called this early. "Everything okay?"

"I don't know," Myra said. "I need to talk to you and wanted to see you in person. I'm in my car, just down the block from your place. Could you let me in by the back door? I'll try to avoid being seen."

"What—?"

"I'll tell you in a minute," Myra interrupted. "Okay?"

"Of course."

Kathlene pushed the button to turn off her phone, then glanced back toward the bed.

Jock was sitting up, his back resting on pillows against the headboard. He'd pulled the sheet over him so she wasn't able to see much of his body. She felt a sigh of regret, but it was better that way. "What's going on?" he asked. "Who was that?"

"Myra Enager," Kathlene responded. "She's here, or will be in a minute. She needs to talk to me." Her mind somersaulted over whether she should kick Jock out, let him stay somewhere that Myra couldn't see him or let him in on whatever this meeting was about. He'd come to town in an undercover role, so would it be okay for Myra to know he was here now?

Myra had been told that Jock was a longtime friend who was here visiting Kathlene. Maybe she wouldn't be surprised that an old buddy from way back—especially one who looked like Jock—had stayed the night.

But part of the role Jock had undertaken here was to attempt to infiltrate the anarchists. Myra and the *sportsmen* were antagonistic. Maybe he should—

He took the decision away from her. "It'd probably be better if she didn't know I was hanging out here. With my new best friends acting out the way they did against the county commissioners, I'd probably have to snap at her to stay in character and that might mean she won't confide whatever's on her mind to you." He stared into her eyes from across the room. "Is that okay with you?"

"Definitely." Kathlene had moved toward her closet, where she pulled out a plaid button-down shirt and dark jeans. "But she's coming to the back door, so something must be wrong. I'll let you out the front."

"No, why don't you make coffee for the two of you and join her in the kitchen? Your living room is fairly close, and I can sneak back in there after you're settled in to hear what she says. Okay?"

Kathlene had a feeling that if she objected he would spout a bunch of reasons why his way was the only way.

But she actually thought he was right. And so she said, "Okay."

After they both hurriedly dressed, Jock hid out in the bathroom near the closed door when Kathlene let Myra

Enager into the house via her back entrance. Kathlene had already started some coffee brewing, and although it smelled inviting to him he held off sneaking some out, not wanting Myra to suspect there was someone else around.

"What's going on?" he heard Kathlene say. He used his enhanced senses just a little, since she'd raised her voice a bit as if to help him to hear.

Sweet of her, but he didn't need that kind of assistance—which she probably knew. Maybe she was just nervous.

"Something awful." The other woman's tone was high and shaky.

"Well, here," Kathlene said soothingly. "Come on into the kitchen. Sit down right here at the table, and I'll get you a cup of coffee. Then you tell me everything."

There was a little shuffling of feet and chairs and whatever Kathlene put on the table. Jock again inhaled the scent of good, strong coffee, plus some milk that Kathlene must have made available to the other woman.

He cracked the white wooden door open just a little. He didn't need help to hear, but it gave him a bit more freedom to sense what was happening and to determine what, if anything, he should do next.

What he heard Myra tell Kathlene didn't stun him. It didn't even surprise him. In fact, he was even a little pleased to hear it.

What was going on just might bring his mission here to a close very soon.

Kathlene considered giving her obviously terrified friend a reassuring hug.

But all she did was remain on one of the shallow calico pillows tied to a chair by her oval wooden table and lean forward, her hands around her white coffee mug.

Myra's age-textured hand remained on the handle of her mug, shaking a little. The older woman did not look as seasoned and professional and together as Kathlene was used to seeing the county commission's chairwoman. Instead, her salon-darkened hair was in disarray and the wrinkles on her face appeared deeper, as if she hadn't used whatever age-defying lotions and makeup she usually daubed on before leaving home.

Or maybe it was whatever was on her mind that made her appear ten years older.

"All right," Myra finally said, looking directly at Kathlene's face with stressed-looking brown eyes. "Here's what's happened. Yesterday, late in the afternoon, a couple of my colleagues on the commission asked for me to call a special session today. A special *public* session, where we'll go over the same issues we've been discussing, but they'll make a couple of additional motions for us to act on."

"Does that happen often?" Kathlene aimed a sympathetic glance toward her friend. She knew Myra loved being part of the government. Until recently, Kathlene had been interested in what Myra did but hadn't been involved professionally.

Yet she had a feeling that Myra had come here this morning not just because she needed a friend, but she also needed someone in law enforcement to hear what she had to say.

Would anything they discussed help to further Jock's investigation?

It might, so she kept her voice raised a bit to make sure he could hear—not that she doubted he could.

"Not really," Myra answered. "There have been some other local issues where the commission's factions were at loggerheads, but voting always seemed to resolve them." Myra shook her head, and her lips narrowed even further. "Not this time."

"When is your meeting, then?" Kathlene asked. This was her day off. She could possibly attend but she couldn't go there in any official capacity. Just as well. The sheriff had already made it clear that all gun control and wildlife-preservation issues around there were a whole lot less important than hunting abilities. He was hardly likely to send anyone off duty there, on overtime, to look official and stave off any physical altercations potentially resulting from the commission's consideration of preservation issues, even if they followed the state's latest guidelines.

But maybe she could find a way to get someone else who wasn't so eager to take sides to go there—Tommy X, maybe?

"It'll start around 10:00 a.m.," Myra said. "And—" Her sip of coffee seemed as much to give her time to think as it was to give her a caffeine lift.

"And?" Kathlene prompted.

"And I'm damned scared," Myra practically exploded. "Things around here are definitely not normal. I…I had a visitor last night at my home, at around nine-thirty at night. Or it may have been more than one person. I don't know. But someone unscrewed the bulb from the light on my porch. That could have been done earlier, I suppose. In any event, I didn't notice until the doorbell rang and I looked out the view hole in my door. I didn't see anyone, so I opened it. And…well, no one was there. But this was."

She bent down to where she had placed her small black leather handbag on the floor and pulled out a piece of paper. It had printing on it and looked as if it could have come from any generic computer.

Kathlene reached for it carefully, touching only the edges so she wouldn't smear any fingerprints. But she had a feeling that whoever might have done this knew how to avoid being identified.

The paper had large letters on it in a font that was not unusual.

Those letters said WE KNOW WHERE YOU LIVE.

Because she knew Jock was listening, she read it out loud. And then she said to Myra, "This isn't a threat in itself, but the time and way it was delivered…well, I'm glad you contacted me. Let me take this and have it checked for prints."

There had been threats before, of course, but not specific and not aimed directly at any individual commissioner.

This was different. And even more disquieting.

As Kathlene had figured, Myra also said, "Okay, but I'll bet you don't find any. Or the computer this was printed on, or anything about the person who came to my house."

That was probably true. But the situation—and the time—certainly made Kathlene even more suspicious.

The vehicle that had driven down the main road near the cabins and ranch last night had arrived there not long after 9:30 p.m. with its lights out, indicating whoever was inside did not want to be recognized.

"That may be," Kathlene said slowly, "but I'll have it looked at, anyway."

"And that's not all," Myra said.

Kathlene's insides were already churning. Whatever was going on with those self-proclaimed sportsmen was polarizing, and damaging, the town she had come to love. Not to mention at least one person that she cared about: Myra.

"What else is there?" She made certain that her voice was strong, not only for Jock but for herself, too. If there was something worse, she might hate to hear it, but she needed to know.

"I was scared enough last night that I called not only Tommy X but also some of my colleagues on the commission—those allied with me on the wildlife protection and gun-control issues. Wendy Ingerton, for one. She told me the same thing had happened to her. I let Tommy X know that, too."

That was a good thing. Even if Sheriff Frawley wouldn't want to hear Kathlene's concerns, Tommy X remained on the sheriff's good side despite his relationship with Myra. Or at least he had till now.

"So where do things stand now?" Kathlene asked.

"I told Tommy X to protect Wendy. He didn't like it, but I told him I was coming here."

"Good. You can stay with me till the meeting." Kathlene would have to figure out a way to sneak Jock out, but he'd understand.

"No. I'm going home to get ready for the meeting. I'm nervous, of course, and I wanted to let someone else know what was going on. If something happens to me…"

"Stay with me," Kathlene said again. "We don't know who threatened you or, really, why."

"I think the *why* is fairly clear. The *who*…well, I've got some ideas, don't you?" Myra took a long swig of coffee, then stood. "I'd like for you to come to the meeting."

"I will, but I won't be on duty."

"Your position is clearer than most, so just having you there, a deputy sheriff not aligned with those terrorists—"

"But I am just that—a deputy. I don't have much authority, and—"

"But you do have integrity. I'll feel better having you there. I'd imagine that Wendy will, too. And we'll all be happy that Tommy X will also attend. I don't want this meeting to be a showdown, but that could happen. And I intend to vote my conscience—again."

"Okay, I'll be there, officially or not." Kathlene enunciated carefully and raised her voice a little. She suspected she'd get an argument from Jock, but so be it.

Whatever happened at the meeting might help—or hinder—the outcome of his determining what the *sportsmen* were up to, as well as preventing them from harming anyone.

She hoped.

Chapter 18

Jock had taken a seat on top of the closed toilet lid. With the keenness of his hearing, he didn't need to remain at the door to hear the ongoing conversation. He'd already checked out the size of the bathroom window along the wall beside him. It would be tight, but if necessary he could fit through it. Yet even though this was the first floor the window was high, and it would be a problem to reach the ground without injury, especially in human form.

Plus, if he tried it, he'd have to be careful not to be seen by anyone in the nearest house, of similar structure to Kathlene's, not far beyond the wooden fence separating the yards. No, it would be better not to leave via the window.

He wondered if, despite Myra's initial refusal, Kathlene would insist that Myra hang out here at her house until the commission meeting was scheduled to begin.

Since she'd been threatened, it would be a good idea for Myra to remain in the company of a friendly law-enforcement officer.

But if she stayed here, he'd have to leave the bathroom, and he wasn't quite sure how to finesse his presence there—especially since it was so vital that he continue to develop his alliance with the sportsmen's group.

Under these circumstances, they might expect him to do something to the commissioner, or at least let them know she was here. That was presuming that whoever had threatened her was one of the group at the ranch.

The most obvious possibilities were those guys who had shown up late yesterday, the ones Kathlene had indicated were trying to hide their presence on the roads. Had they just come from leaving the threats at Myra's and other commissioners who maintained positions against the sportsmen's? And what about the hints they'd given regarding weapons in their car? He'd have to figure out a way to ask without making it sound accusatory, just interested.

In any event, he couldn't just stay in the bathroom. If nothing else, Myra might eventually want to use the facilities and come this way. Kathlene's only other bathroom was upstairs.

More important, inaction was not in his vocabulary. He had to do something that went with his undercover role—without, of course, embarrassing Kathlene about how she'd spent her night and who she'd spent it with.

He decided it was finally time for him to magically appear at Kathlene's doorstep, too. Even though this old friend of hers was now supposedly at odds with her about something going on in her town, they'd still see each other while he was here.

His decision was underscored even before he acted when Kathlene began to push Myra the way he'd anticipated.

"Myra, please. You really should stay here with me till you're ready to head to the meeting," she insisted.

Jock waited for the commissioner's concurrence, even if it was reluctant. She was wise enough to come here in the first place, so she'd clearly also be smart in this—having somewhere safe to hang out till she had to put herself in front of the county's citizens and visitors once more. Then, no matter which side they might be on personally, the sheriff's department officers on duty would have to protect everyone including the commissioners, at least during the meeting.

He was surprised, therefore, when Myra responded, "No. Really. I'll be okay. But I need to go home now, not only to change clothes but to go over my notes and computer files so I'll be fully prepared to counter any negative arguments at the meeting."

Jock was not surprised at Kathlene's response, but he wasn't happy about it. In fact, he was downright angry. "Then I'll come with you to make sure you're okay," she said.

Didn't the woman ever avoid putting herself into dangerous situations?

Hell, he knew the answer to that.

He also knew that he, too, would be heading to Myra Enager's home.

Kathlene checked the street to ensure that there were no strangers, no occupied cars, no other apparent dangers. Then she saw Myra out the door and into her car.

She hadn't spoken to Jock yet but felt certain he knew

what she was doing. Myra and she hadn't been whispering—not that the sound level would likely make much difference to Jock.

She also figured he wasn't pleased about it. Right now Kathlene rode in the passenger's seat of Myra's hybrid car. For the moment she believed she was doing everything possible to keep her friend safe.

Jock would undoubtedly have a different opinion about the safety of what she was doing.

To be fair, she should give him the opportunity to bawl her out. Not that it would make any difference.

She told Myra she needed to make a phone call.

"Sure thing," Myra said. "I'd hold my ears if I didn't need my hands to drive."

Kathlene gave the laugh she figured was expected, then pushed numbers on her phone. "Hi, Jock," she said perkily when he answered.

"What the hell are you doing?"

"Yes, it's me," she responded as if he had said something friendly rather than argumentative. Myra should only be able to hear her end of the call. "I'm going to a friend's house now, since it's my day off work, and then I'll go watch the county commissioners' meeting. Maybe we could hook up there. Are you free for lunch?"

"I'm free to wring your neck," he muttered.

"Oh, I know you'd never do that. But I have a feeling that the meeting's going to be a bit wild. Even though I'm not on duty, maybe I can help out if there's any disturbance. You could watch me in action. Of course you have before, but it'll give you even more reason to understand why I became a deputy sheriff." She glanced over at Myra. "People don't always wind up doing what it looks like they're headed for in school, do they? My buddy Jock probably thought I'd go into journalism, since that was my field of study." It actually had been—until her parents had been killed....

"Did you figure he'd wind up doing what he did?"

"You mean insurance?" She talked back into the phone. "How about you, Jock? Did you think, in school, that you'd wind up where you are now?"

"Actually, not exactly. But—"

"So there. Anyway, we'll talk later." She pressed the button to hang up. She didn't really want to hear any more of his criticism. She might not be able to avoid it later, but for now she'd do as she wanted.

Help her friend.

And her town.

He followed them, of course. As unobtrusively as possible.

She should have at least allowed him to enter and check out the nice, huge house that was apparently Myra's, since they pulled up the driveway and into the garage. For now he remained in his car, listening for any disturbance. Presumably, Kathlene had brought her service weapon with her, just in case.

She didn't call out, didn't call him, and nothing sounded strange.

Consequently, he hung out for only a few more minutes. Then he knew where he had to go.

He called Ralf on the way. "I'd like for Click and you to go observe the street where Kathlene has gone to protect her friend on the county commission."

"Yes, sir," Ralf said.

"At ease, Sergeant." Jock couldn't help smiling, if only a little.

"Where are you off to?"

"I'm about to visit my newest best friends again. I have a feeling that, after the warnings handed out last night, this county commissioners' meeting might be the ignition for whatever they have in mind—unless, of course, everything turns around and the vote goes exactly as they want."

"Even then," Ralf began.

"Yeah, even then. I saw their attitude last night, and I don't think these guys are going to suddenly settle down and become nice, calm, law-abiding hunters and all-around citizens."

"Me, neither. You…you want to shift?"

"I will, but not now. Besides, I want Click to hang out with you for now, and you know what a bad idea having another dog around that looks like him, during daylight and with everything else going on, would be."

"Got it." Ralf paused. "Keep in touch, Jock."

Jock grinned. "Yes, sir."

As Jock had anticipated, the sportsmen weren't just sitting around drinking beer—or even, at this hour of the morning, coffee. He had no problem checking in with the guy at the gate, and when he parked and headed toward the ranch house he saw a lot of them around talking. They weren't even at the shooting range engaged in target practice.

What were they up to?

He was one of them now…kind of. He could just ask what was going on.

He saw tall Hal with the receding hairline almost immediately. The guy was decked out in a hunting jacket, as were most of the men around the house and parking area.

Jock approached and asked, "What's going on?"

"There's another of those damned public county commissioners' meetings today. Better than their private ones, but they're still trying to tell us what to do, and since it didn't work last time they're going at it again. We're heading there to…make a statement."

"Good idea," Jock said. "I'll come, too." He pretended to hesitate. "But what'll we do if the same damned thing happens and they enact more laws about our hunting the wildlife that was put on this earth for men to shoot and kill?" He hated even to say stuff like that, but it was necessary here for the role he was playing.

Hal smiled. It was the kind of smile that made Jock's skin crawl. "Oh, we've got some plans to take care of it."

"What kind of plans?" Jock pasted an eager grin on his face. "I want in."

"Good. We'll need all of our followers to get involved. But we're just in the planning stage right now. You'll be filled in at the appropriate time."

"Soon?" Jock asked.

"Yeah, real soon."

Jock stood there for a few minutes. The crowd seemed to ebb and flow, with men joining one group, and then some moved on to form another. With all the people, all the activity, Jock figured everyone would be too preoccupied to pay much attention to him. A good thing.

He began walking around the ranch, moving with the crowds as if he was part of them.

He grinned as he saw men massing together and working each other up into an angry frenzy. Who dared to tell them what to do? He was with them, shared their mindset. Or so he pretended.

He walked among them and between the buildings as

if attempting to meet and support them all. How many were there? Dozens, yes. A hundred, maybe?

And finally, as most began moving toward the front of the property to prepare to go to the commissioners' meeting, he found his opportunity. He headed carefully, by himself, toward the shooting range.

There were a few remote buildings near the outdoor range area that intrigued him. Was that where the weapons brought by the guys who'd driven that SUV in the dark were stored? Were there more than what they had brought?

And were they regular hunting rifles, or something more?

Plus, where did they keep the C-4 explosives that he'd smelled?

For now it made sense to explore this property in human form. A canine would be way out of place. But an undercover military man worked out just fine…he hoped. And he'd been close enough to the main ranch building itself to pretty much rule it out as a storage area—no concentrated scent of gunpowder or anything else close by, although he could smell some near the sportsmen themselves when they were armed.

He kept his pace easy, as if he had nothing on his mind except perhaps finding a bathroom. Too bad it was morning, though. The cover of darkness would be preferable. At least the back of the property, near the shooting range, hadn't been cleared of all trees, so there was some cover available.

The double door to the first black metal shed Jock came to closest to the shooting range was open. That suggested all the sportsmen were welcome there. It wasn't what he was looking for. Nor was there any scent of interest.

He stopped and listened. Lots of voices were audible to his enhanced senses—near the front of the place. A pep rally of sorts was going on now.

That didn't mean he was alone here, though. He stopped and focused his enhanced senses. Without moving his head, he sniffed the air for any scents of people nearby but smelled none. He listened but heard no one around.

Even so, he would remain cautious.

He moved onward as if he hadn't a concern in the world, just a curious man checking out a place he'd hardly visited before. And of course he was interested in the shooting range and practicing there someday.

The next shed he reached was open, too. But there was also what appeared to be the ranch's old stable a short distance away, large and decrepit and hidden among tall bushes and trees, as if it had been allowed to fall into disrepair. And yet when he made his way there, its most visible doors that faced the interior area of the ranch were locked.

That made him all the more determined to get inside. This could be what he was looking for.

He edged his way around to the back and found another door, a single, sliding one. Carefully, he tried it… and it moved. Did that mean the stable contained nothing of interest, too? He believed he should check this one out—partly because of the sharper smells he sensed. Different kinds of gunpowder? He ducked inside and closed the door behind him.

No horses. Not now. But several of the stalls were filled with boxes. It was also dark inside. All windows had been boarded up, which was a good thing. He couldn't be seen.

He pulled his phone out of his pocket and turned on its light, shielding it to ensure that it remained dim as he checked the place out.

The closest boxes had rifles in them. Regular hunting rifles, the kinds that real sportsmen might use. Which frustrated Jock. He knew these guys weren't real sportsmen, but he needed proof.

A short while later, he found himself grinning as he checked through other boxes at the bottom of the piles of crates where the regular rifles were stored.

They were semiautomatic rifles, M-16s, like the military used, and there were a lot of them.

He wondered if they might even have been stolen from the military. He'd have to check.

Could they be used for hunting? Maybe. But why so many? And why were they hidden?

A couple of boxes also held handguns, Berettas and SIG Sauers.

Why would ordinary hunters need them?

Answer? They wouldn't.

Plus, he did, in fact, find some crates that were sealed, and yet he smelled the plastic scent that told him they contained C-4.

Jock had found what he needed. Maybe not all of the guns he'd found were illegal, but he'd no doubt that their collection was not for any law-abiding, neutral purpose.

And now it was time to go back to playing his role of supporting the anti-government position of these supposed sportsmen.

He cautiously edged his way back out of this shed, silently applauding Kathlene.

By contacting Alpha Force, she may have saved a lot of lives.

* * *

It was time now to head to the Clifford County Building. According to Myra, the meeting was scheduled to begin in about half an hour.

"Are you ready?" Kathlene asked. Myra had changed into a dark suit and white blouse, one that looked even more professional than the charcoal outfit she had worn to the last meeting. Kathlene wasn't sure whether Myra's attitude had shaved ten years off her appearance or if the makeup she had applied, along with her determined expression, had done the job, but at least for now Myra looked ready to face anything.

"I sure am," Myra responded.

"Then let's go."

Once again Myra drove, since Kathlene had left her car at her place.

"So tell me what the agenda is today," Kathlene said, although she had a pretty good idea.

"About the same as last time. We'll be talking about those gun-control laws that were passed in closed chambers after the last meeting. There've been some complaints, some challenges to the point of order, that claim statutes passed in private, without the opportunity of citizen comment and discussion, are not valid. Our county counsel will be talking about that, disputing it, but even so, we on the commission have decided to take that vote again. In front of everyone. After allowing the discussion, including any threats, tacit or explicit."

"Really?" Kathlene wished now that she was on duty that day. She would have much preferred being in uniform, acting officially to help control whatever issues were bound to come up with those discussions...like the threats. "Are you all nuts?"

Myra laughed. "No, but this is important around

here—especially with that element that's come to town that argues against everything. They don't really have a say—but they were undoubtedly involved in the threats against me and the others. I appreciate your letting me stay with you before while I felt discombobulated, but I'm fine now. They can't hurt me—even if they wound or kill me."

"What?"

"I mean, it's more hurtful to me to cower and give in. And I think I'm not the only commissioner who feels that way. Wendy's said the same thing. Besides, Tommy X will be there officially. So will the sheriff himself, I've been promised."

"But…er, Sheriff Frawley…" Kathlene seldom was at a loss for words, but she knew her commanding officer at least favored the *sportsmen* and might actually be one of them.

Myra had stopped at a stop sign and glanced toward Kathlene. "If you're trying to say that your boss is as much of an outspoken creep in favor of guns and killing people and protected animals as well as breaking state laws as the rest of them, I'm not going to argue with you. But this has to be resolved. Now. So are you with me?"

Kathlene felt certain this was not going to lead to anything good—not until the anarchists were shown to be what they were and brought down.

But she had to answer the question the way she believed. "Yes," she said, "I'm with you. But Myra—"

"It'll all work out," Myra interrupted. "You'll see."

Kathlene knew her friend was right—but not for the reason Myra thought.

She wondered where Jock was at that moment.

And whether she would see him at the commissioners' meeting.

* * *

Jock had made some calls on his way to pick up Ralf.

The most important was to Major Drew Connell.

The others had been to fellow Alpha Force members, shifters like him.

It was time. He knew things were coming to a head around here. He would soon need backup.

It would be dangerous. He knew that, and he made it clear to Drew and the others.

This group of anarchists—and, yes, he felt certain now that was what they were—were out for blood. Maybe things would go their way in the upcoming session, but if they didn't, they would want to exact revenge on those who dared to oppose them.

Like Commission Chair Myra Enager.

And those who supported their opponents—like Deputy Kathlene Baylor.

Jock was not about to let anything happen to either of them.

Especially Kathlene.

Now he pulled into the area behind the cabins he shared with Ralf and Click, got out and went inside the first one.

His aide was there with his cover dog. "I just took Click for a walk," Ralf said. "I'm ready to go."

"Good. Let's hurry."

They got to downtown Cliffordsville in ten minutes, and Jock drove the city streets for a short while before finding a place to park.

By the time they got to the County Administration Building's main entrance, a huge crowd had gathered there. The sportsmen? Yes. But the town's entire population also seemed to be heading inside.

For genuine interest, or to witness a showdown?

It didn't matter. Nor did Jock give a damn whether they got seats in the assembly room.

They would be there.

He didn't see Kathlene at first as Ralf and he joined the crowd heading to the same location. But when they got inside, he noticed her right away. She sat at the end of a row in the middle of the room.

Two empty seats were beside her, and she appeared to be defending them.

Her gorgeous blue eyes met his nearly immediately, as if she'd been watching for him. She smiled and waved Ralf and him in her direction.

When they eased their way through the crowd to Kathlene's side, she stood, grabbed his hand for a quick squeeze, then motioned toward those chairs.

"I've been saving these for you," she said.

Kathlene pushed back a little as Jock and Ralf edged by her to the seats she'd kept empty, with effort, for them. Jock faced her as he slid by. His chest, in a navy T-shirt, just touched the tips of her breasts that were covered by the dressy blouse she had quickly donned over slacks for this outing. His quick, meaningless touch made her insides tingle—with relief, she told herself. She was glad he was here. Ralf, too.

She hadn't been positive they would come because it wasn't exactly within their cover here to observe the local government. Since they'd attended the previous meeting, maybe being here today would feel like too much.

On the other hand, Jock had apparently been doing fairly well in establishing himself as a potential member of the sportsmen, and a whole bunch of them were here.

The guys who'd mostly come dressed in hunting jackets like Nate Tisal, and who hung out with him, were part of that group.

Sitting near her might not be Jock's best choice. On the other hand, ostensibly knowing her was what had brought him to town in the first place. He could always hold a public argument with her if that turned out to be in the best interests of their investigation.

Even if she'd hate it.

Ralf took the vacant seat farthest from her. Jock sat beside her.

"Hi," she said. "Good to see you."

"Likewise." But his tone wasn't especially friendly. She understood. In the role he had taken on, he was now supposed to be pulling away from her as part of the sportsmen's group.

But despite recognizing, and even admiring, his acting ability, she couldn't quite keep a pang of hurt from stabbing her.

She considered how she'd react if who he was pretending to be was real, what someone in her position— what *she*—would say to her soon-to-be-former friend.

Before she figured it out, she heard a stirring through the audience and looked up. The seven county commissioners were taking their places at the table facing the onlookers. With them was Mayor Laurence Davonne.

The show was about to begin.

She hazarded a glance toward Jock. He was looking at her, his stare hard and challenging and unfriendly.

She knew now how someone in her position, how she, would feel when the person she had presumably thought of as a longtime friend had backed away. Maybe even turned on her.

"Jock," she began.

But she got no further. "Hello, everyone, and welcome," said the mayor. "Let's get started."

Jock gave a decisive nod in the direction of the front as if commanding Kathlene to pay attention.

Feeling irrationally hurt at his attitude, Kathlene nevertheless obeyed.

Chapter 19

Under other circumstances, Jock would have reached over and taken his *friend* Kathlene's hand.

The tension in the room was almost palpable. Everyone stared at the people in front, and the undercurrent of grumbling, especially loud to Jock but clearly discernible to everyone else, made the mayor speak even more directly into the microphone in his hand.

Even though Kathlene wasn't on duty, two people in uniforms similar to hers stood at the doors, arms crossed. One Jock recognized as her friend, Senior Deputy Tommy X. He didn't know the other one, a young woman. Would they be able to keep the peace?

Surely this crowd wasn't going to get out of hand right here and now…he hoped.

Jock shot a look toward Ralf. His aide's face was placid, as if all was fine.

And in fact, if Jock had really been recruited into the sportsmen and in turn convinced his friend to join, all would, in fact, have seemed fine.

Even with a buddy like Kathlene. He knew he had to act as if their friendship was fraying. It was damned hard to put on an act like that, when what he wanted to do was to wrap his arms around her and usher her from this room and all of the controversy and potential for danger being initiated here.

But he had a role to maintain.

He hadn't had a chance to tell her what he'd found yet. Maybe that was just as well—for now. He'd let her in on it when he could, but for the moment, for her protection, it might be better if she wasn't aware that additional evidence supported her theory.

The mayor, standing near the end of the table with the commissioners mostly behind him, had started to explain the reason for this assembly of the county commissioners so soon after the last one. "I requested the meeting," Mayor Davonne said, "because of how important I think it is for all aspects of our government to be transparent, to be open and aboveboard." He turned slightly as if trying to solicit the commissioners' opinions.

Kathlene's friend Myra had pasted a completely blank expression on her face. A couple of the others were nodding, including the man whose name card on the table in front of him reminded Jock he was Commissioner Grabling.

Not Commissioner Ingerton, though. She sat right beside Myra Enager. From this distance, her face seemed pale, her expression stoic yet scared, as if she expected someone to hit her. With all of the people present in this room, Jock could not be certain he'd picked out her scent from the rest, but he'd little doubt that, if he were closer, he would distinguish the smell of her fear.

"Now you all know," the mayor said, "that things were rather out of order at the last meeting. It was dissolved, and the commissioners went off by themselves and voted on some of the matters before them. Before *us*."

"Now, just a minute, Mr. Mayor." Myra had stood and moved to speak into the microphone without taking it.

Davonne pulled it away, turning his back as he continued to talk. "Point of order," he said. "I have the floor."

"But this is a meeting of the commissioners of Clifford County," Myra shouted so she could be heard. "You are an official of the City of Cliffordsville."

The mayor ignored her. "All sessions where matters of public importance are to be voted on should be held in front of our citizens. That didn't happen, and so I requested—no, demanded—that this new meeting be held. The commission should vacate whatever was decided in private chambers before. We need to ensure that laws enacted that affect all, or a significant part of our citizenry, be discussed and voted on in public."

"Mr. Mayor," Myra said. "We acted in good faith. And—"

"Excuse me, Madam Chairwoman," the mayor said smoothly. "Let me continue."

Interesting, Jock thought. Maybe he had a point.

Or would this situation be different if the laws to be discussed in private and potentially enacted did not affect those who might be prone to violence?

If all that happened was to keep hunting laws as they were, Jock might not like it personally but it wouldn't necessarily be inappropriate.

Even failing to enact stricter gun-control laws might

be acceptable. That was definitely a sore subject in many places in this country.

But the county commissioners had acted in what Jock—and he assumed others, too—considered to be good faith to adopt local laws that followed and clarified for local enforcement those their state had recently passed to affect everyone who lived within its borders.

Feeling a stirring beside him, Jock glanced toward Kathlene. She was biting her lower lip. She looked ready to spring up and chew out the mayor, too.

Maybe it was out of character—or maybe not. He reached over and took her hand.

She looked shocked as she glanced back at him. And then she seemed to relax, if just a little.

She nodded slightly, as if he had offered her an explanation of his actions. And then she sat still once more.

This was such a travesty, Kathlene thought. This place, Cliffordsville, Clifford County, was her home now. And yet the mayor was acting as if he wasn't an elected official but a dictator.

But Jock was right. If nothing else, what was happening here this morning might cause a reaction in the people she believed to be anarchists. She could be proven correct. Vindicated.

But more important, it would then be time for Jock and Ralf to fix things around here. And she would help.

Somehow, whether he liked it or not, she would remain on Jock's team for that.

To the extent possible—and she realized how difficult it might be—she would stay by his side.

The mayor continued to speak for a while. Was this a

kind of local equivalent of a filibuster? He didn't seem inclined to cede the floor for anything.

Not until Myra faded back and Commissioner Grabling stood and walked up beside him.

"We very much appreciate your position, Mr. Mayor," the thin, nearly bald guy in the plaid suit said. "In fact, let me be the first on the commission to say that I, too, believe that our vote in secrecy is not effective. We can all vote the same way as we did then, of course, but we need public comment first. Anyone?"

He looked out over the sea of people.

Kathlene looked around, too, and noticed that her boss, Sheriff Melton Frawley, had arrived, and so had Undersheriff George Kerringston. They remained near the door where Deputy Betsy Alvers stood, one of those on duty today.

Still, Kathlene was glad. The more law-enforcement personnel who were here and obvious, the less this place was likely to get out of hand. She hoped.

Although she wasn't certain what Sheriff Frawley's position would be on that, or on what was being discussed.

Kathlene wasn't surprised when the first person to stand was Tisal. The tall, hefty man had come in his hunter's jacket, as had many of his friends. He hurried onto the stage and took the microphone from Grabling.

Kathlene hazarded a glance at Jock. His expression, as he stared toward the man, looked pleased. Until he looked back at her, and for an instant she could read anger in his gaze, and she knew that, despite what other people who might catch it might think, it wasn't really aimed at her.

She didn't allow herself to smile.

"Thank you, Commissioner Grabling. And Mayor

Davonne. My name is Nate Tisal. I'd just like to say that I, and some of my friends, came here to Clifford County temporarily at first, just to meet up and engage in some sporting activities like target practice and hunting. We've found we really like it here and want to stay. But I have to say that what's going on here, at this meeting, is important to us. We've discussed it as a group. We're very concerned not only about where and how new laws are passed, but also the fact that there are new laws at all. Any laws can be too much if they restrict citizens' rights. Yes, we understand that the mayor's in charge of the city, and the commissioners are in charge of the larger county, but none of them, no one, should be in charge of the populace. And so, having this open forum, ensuring that any vote that's taken is in front of all of us—well, we really appreciate it."

Kathlene again looked swiftly toward Jock. Tisal had done it—nearly. He had all but admitted that he and his group were anarchists, against any kind of laws or government.

That in itself didn't make them dangerous. And yet their engaging in target practice—and in setting off the explosives she had heard—seemed to vindicate her, show that her position was correct.

Were they dangerous, though? She believed so, but so far they hadn't demonstrated it.

Unless, of course, some of them were behind the threats sent to Myra and at least one of her fellow commissioners—and Kathlene felt sure that was the case.

Myra must have thought so, too. She rose suddenly once more and placed herself firmly beside the man who now held the microphone. She grabbed his arm, apparently startling him, since he didn't yank it away.

"Thank you, Mr. Tisal," she said, and somehow managed to take the microphone into her own hand. "And thank you, Mr. Mayor. As I mentioned before, this is a meeting of the Clifford County Commissioners, and I am its chairperson. We do appreciate the opinions of our citizens, and our potential citizens like you, Mr. Tisal. We normally do like to hold all of our meetings in public to get citizens' comments. This time, though, considering how our last meeting fell apart, we decided to act in private. We regret that some of our county's citizens are unhappy about that, and we will be glad to take a new vote—although I don't think that the results will change. I can see why some people might think otherwise. You see, a few of us, myself included, have received some very frightening threats that make us fear for our lives. Now, I'm not accusing anyone in particular, but considering the timing and what went on at the last meeting—and what's gone on so far here—I believe that anyone who is uncomfortable with our local government and how we enact laws or anything else, doesn't need to come to our meeting or even stay here." She turned to glance at the mayor, then at Tisal and then at Sheriff Melton Frawley. "So who here, in this room, is ready to admit they issued those threats?" She looked down into the audience, and her gaze stopped in the area populated by men in hunting jackets. And then she again looked at Tisal. "Who's first?" she goaded.

Tisal was not at all polite as he wrested the microphone back into his possession. "I think you are accusing us, Commissioner. Without any proof. You represent the government here in Clifford County. Do you think it's any wonder that I, and my friends, are not fond of the government—or you?"

His turn to look down at his gang, who all stood and started leaving the room.

"We like it here, even if we don't like you," Tisal continued. "You can be sure that we will stay here, at least for a while. On our own terms. And you can certainly expect some changes around here very soon—to your government and otherwise."

The sportsmen were gone quickly. And among them were Jock and Ralf, who hadn't even bothered to excuse themselves as they edged out of their seats around her.

Which was only appropriate under the circumstances, Kathlene thought. Even though she wanted to talk to Jock. Maybe even receive a hug of reassurance that all would be well.

But he was doing as he must in his undercover role.

He would remain safe. He had to. But she felt almost desperate to talk to him. Surely they would find a way to stay in touch.

The citizens who were still there were mostly familiar-looking to Kathlene. Myra, again in charge of the microphone, told her fellow commissioners that it was finally time to discuss in public the measures they had passed in private before.

She looked pale to Kathlene, and scared.

Kathlene looked toward the door where Sheriff Frawley, Undersheriff Kerringston and Deputy Alvers stood. Most of the sportsmen had exited that way, and none of the officers had followed.

Was that a good thing?

No one else in the audience seemed inclined to speak. There was obvious tension on the stage where the commissioners remained, particularly when they took their vote.

The matters before them passed. Again. In public.

Unsurprisingly, no one looked thrilled.

And as they finally followed the crowd out of the assembly room, Kathlene felt her phone in her pocket.

Did she dare call Jock?

No. That might only increase the danger to him. But he had assets, methods his new allies couldn't possibly know about.

He would be safe.

He would come back to her—temporarily, of course. But despite his dangerous undercover role, he would stay alive.

Wouldn't he...?

Ralf drove Jock to the ranch. On the way the two of them mostly discussed their strategy.

"I'm not sure how long it'll take for the rest of the Alpha Force team assigned to this situation to get here," Jock said. "They've been on alert, so I doubt it'll take long, especially since they can get a military jet to fly them into Billings or a closer small airport."

"Meantime, we're sportsmen, all in a huff because the county commissioners ignored what our leader, Tisal, had to say." Ralf jutted out his lower jaw and nodded his head. "We'll join up with our fellow sportsmen and grumble and...well, whatever."

"Exactly," Jock said. "Whatever. Or at least we'll get to see what their *whatever* is, hopefully in time to give a heads-up to the rest of the Alpha Force team before they arrive so we can plan in advance how to handle the sportsmen. We may not be able to stall them from starting their *whatever,* but we'll be able to keep our eyes on that weapons cache to make sure no one gets into them, at least not before Alpha Force can take over."

"Maybe we can lock the stable down," Ralf said, "and even, if necessary, destroy it. It's in bad enough condition that it shouldn't be hard to set it on fire."

"Maybe," Jock agreed, "but I'd rather have its contents available as evidence—and not destroy any people along with it, either."

"You're right, of course, sir." Ralf smiled. And then he grew more serious. "Too bad we don't really know what they're up to."

"Yeah. And it'd sure be easier for our Alpha Force members to deal with if those sportsmen stay on the ranch till nightfall. And that might make sense if they intend attacks on civilians. Why not do it under cover of darkness?"

"Exactly," said Ralf.

"Let's hope that's what they have in mind," Jock said. "That would make it a whole lot easier for shifted Alpha Force members to shut them down." He intended to take on Tisal himself. But in any event, no matter what precautions the sportsmen were taking, no matter what kind of opposition they anticipated, an attack by a pack of wolves would not likely be what they prepared for.

Once again, Ralf and Jock were admitted onto the ranch grounds with hardly a glance by the guard. They were now accepted members, which could only help.

They immediately parked and began mingling among the crowd on the grounds of the ranch house and around the firing range. Jock heard a lot of angry grumbles, intermixed with mention of the talk Tisal was about to give.

Jock's mind seldom left Kathlene and what she was up to. She had come to this area nearly every time he had gone undercover here.

He understood that she believed she was doing the right thing to keep civilians safe.

Even as she endangered herself.

Just in case, he had called her briefly before, while they drove. She had sounded happy to hear from him but he cut her off quickly. "You need to go home," he'd said.

"But—"

"Please, just do it. I promise you'll be included in our handling of the situation. But I can't explain everything. Not now. Just know that I've found some evidence that I'll try to fill you in on later."

There had been a silence. And then she'd said, "Okay. I'm heading home…for now."

That, at least, was something. Once he learned what the plans were around here, he would figure out a good excuse to leave temporarily, go and find her—and take her along when he met up with the Alpha Force unit as they arrived. Kathlene could definitely provide good background information to his teammates. She could work with their aides, do as they did, mostly observing and being ready to assist their shifted superior officers.

Stay with them—and remain safe.

It was midafternoon by the time Tisal had his sportsmen all assemble in the courtyard behind the ranch house where barbecues had previously been set up. Now chips and beer made the rounds but nothing more substantial.

Except what the crowd heard.

They still mostly wore hunting jackets over jeans. There were a lot of them—around sixty, if Jock's count was correct. He'd overestimated before thanks to their moving around the property so much, which was probably a good thing. He was sure the guys he had overheard talking about how much they despised government were here, and so, undoubtedly, were the ones who'd arrived at this ranch with a dark SUV containing weapons, even if he couldn't pick any of them out of the crowd.

But there certainly were enough of them present to wreak a whole lot of damage if they used the weapons of terrorists.

Tisal stood on top of a picnic table, and everyone quieted down and watched him expectantly.

"Did you hear what those damned county commissioners said today, my friends?" Tisal shouted.

"Yeah!" came the response that was nearly in unison.

"Wasn't it bad enough that there were already laws in place that supposedly told us what to do with our guns and hunting and other things important to us?"

"Yeah!"

"And now they're imposing even more governmental restrictions on us. Saying that we are even more limited in our ability to shoot game that should be available to us. Thinking that they have rights to tell us what to do, when we're the ones who should have rights."

"Yeah!"

"Well, that's not gonna happen. Not more restrictions. No laws should apply to us, anyway, and no one should attempt to foist any more on us, right, my friends?"

"Yeah!"

It wasn't as if Jock hadn't seen other maniacs get crowds stirred up by using their dynamics, the psychology of groups aroused by outspoken individuals. Even though he attempted to be low-key in nearly all he did to keep the secret part of his identity completely hidden, as a college student years ago, and even once he had joined the military, he had observed how crowds worked now and then. Plus, there had been enough in the media about revolutions throughout the world to underscore how groups of people working together fed off one another to get riled into action.

But here, on this small ranch in the middle of nowhere, the dynamics seemed as potent as some huge crowds with common goals.

Something was going to happen in little Clifford County. Something dangerous to its populace. Something in which those dangerous weapons would be used.

Unless Alpha Force could stop it.

"You think we're going to be allowed to leave here easily?" Ralf whispered into his ear as Tisal continued his cheered-on rant.

"Of course," Jock whispered back. "Just play along."

They stayed until Tisal had finished. The man's plans were not explicit, but he did make it clear that they would show these miserable locals tonight that they could not mess with men who had absolute rights to freedom.

The crowd started to disperse. It was time for Jock to make his play.

He couldn't reach Tisal, who was surrounded by his admirers and laughing along with their enthusiasm.

But Tisal's peon Hal was at the fringe of the crowd. Jock, motioning to Ralf, approached him.

"That was so outstanding!" Jock exclaimed to Hal. "I never thought there were others who hated restrictions as much as I did—except for my friend Ralf, here." He nudged his aide. "But I always figured I might get so mad someday that I'd take a stand. Fight, no matter what the consequences." He paused. "You know, to prepare for it I've been collecting some pretty special weaponry, though I have to dismantle and disguise it if I fly or otherwise get subject to some government jerks looking over my things. We left what we've got in the cabins where we're staying here. I'm not sure what Tisal has in mind, but a couple of AK-47s and an Uzi won't hurt."

"Really? Well, yeah, go get them," Hal said. "I'm not sure if we need them or if there'll any questions if you leave right now, but extra stuff might come in handy."

Extra? That did imply the existence of what Jock had found but wasn't exactly an admission. Not that it mattered.

"Just tell the guard to call me if there's any problem," Hal finished.

"Sure thing," Jock said. "We'll be back soon. Looking forward to being part of whatever happens tonight."

Sure enough, they were permitted to leave.

Only when Ralf drove them through the gate and they got on the road away from the ranch did Jock breathe a sigh of relief.

"To the cabins first," he told Ralf. "To get Click."

"Not our collection of imaginary weapons?"

"Well, those, too." Jock grinned. And then he grew more somber again. "Next stop will be Kathlene's. We'll go pick her up. By then we should have an update about the progress of our Alpha Force teammates—and where we'll need to go pick them up, too."

It was going to be a long—and eventful—night.

Chapter 20

At home, alone and waiting, Kathlene entered the kitchen she had fallen in love with when she had first bought this house yet had hardly ever used for cooking large meals and entertaining. It contained a stove with two ovens, an island in the center for food preparation, a state-of-the-art microwave and a side-by-side metallic refrigerator, all synchronized by the pale wood of the cabinets that matched the oval table, and the yellow tile counters and floor.

She had most recently cooked breakfast for Jock and her here, and then had brewed coffee when Myra was visiting. But the room definitely wasn't used as much as she had initially planned.

She employed the fridge and microwave the most, depending on fruit and veggies and prepackaged meals for herself. She had no time for fussing over food.

Deputy sheriffs had very little time of their own, since even when off duty they could be called in for emergencies. And despite how small Clifford County was, it seemed to have more than its share of car accidents and vandalism and even thefts and robberies.

Now she sat on a stool at the island in that kitchen, staring around the room as if it belonged to a stranger. She had made herself a cup of herbal tea after heating the water in the microwave. She'd considered something stronger, something with alcohol, but she needed all her wits about her.

Tonight was key in the potential showdown that had started months ago, that had haunted her, frightened her. Made her stronger, even as she had reached out for help.

She sat still, using all of her strength to remain there, sipping tea while wanting to scream. To act.

To be with Jock, one of the men who had come here because of her quest for assistance in dealing with this potentially horrible situation.

The man, yet more than a man.

Was he learning anything now that would help in the upcoming fight? For she felt certain there would be a fight. The anarchists seemed to be spoiling for one. Maybe they had come to small, remote Clifford County because they thought they could win here, could use it as a hopping-off place to take over the state. The country. The world.

Or maybe her imagination was just working overtime in her fear for her friends and her adopted hometown.

She thought about her parents, and how she had lost them to those hoodlums who had robbed their convenience store and shot them.

No, she would not allow the bad guys to win, no matter who they were, or how many, or—

Her phone rang. She snatched it from her pocket. Was Jock checking in?

But no, the caller ID said it was Myra.

"Hi," Kathlene said. "Are you okay?"

A short, ironic laugh was the response. "That's exactly what I was going to ask you."

Kathlene's turn to laugh, but only a little. "I'm fine, but really concerned about what's going on. I was just considering a drive to the sheriff's station to check out how things are around there."

"No need," Myra said. "I happen to have a senior deputy here who just left the department a little while ago. He wanted to check on me, too."

"Tommy X? Let me speak with him."

She heard a mumbling away from the phone, and then, "Kathlene? You okay?"

Once again Kathlene smiled. "That's a pretty common question tonight. I'm glad you're keeping watch over Myra."

"Me, too. I'm also heading to Wendy's soon to check on her. I really didn't like how things went at the meeting earlier. Combined with those written threats—well, I tried to get Melton's attention while I was still on duty but he didn't seem concerned."

No, he wouldn't. But Kathlene didn't want to tell Tommy X her suspicions about the sheriff and his leanings and the possible confirmation she'd learned about from Jock. And Kathlene also didn't want him asking questions about her visiting friends that she wouldn't want to answer.

Instead, she said, "I wondered about that. I get the

impression that Sheriff Frawley may have some sympathy for the positions those sportsmen have taken against additional hunting laws."

"Maybe, but I think there's more to those sportsmen than simply wanting to go shoot some animals."

"It sure sounded like it tonight," Kathlene agreed. "We'll just all have to be on our guard, especially our county commissioners. I'm glad to hear that you're checking on them." She hesitated, trying to figure out what to say next. "My friends are going to be leaving town soon, I think, and once they're gone I'll be able to help out even more."

At least that told Tommy X, her true long-term friend in this area, that she was on his side, the county's side, but had some distractions at the moment.

If he only knew what those distractions were…

Her doorbell rang, and her heart leaped into her throat. She made herself calm down just a little as she got off her stool and started walking from the kitchen to the hall toward the front door. "I've got to run now, Tommy X. I'm really glad Myra and you called and that everyone's okay." For now. "My friends just arrived." She hoped. Oh, did she hope. Who else could be at her door?

The anarchists?

As she finished saying goodbye, she stopped at the small bureau near the entryway that had a tall mirror on top and reached into the back of the top drawer. She pulled out the Glock she used on the job, checked it quickly to ensure that it was loaded, then walked up to the door. She looked out the peephole.

And almost melted in relief.

She had told Tommy X the truth. Jock and Ralf had arrived.

She returned the gun to its drawer, pulled open the door and smiled. "Hi. Come in," she said loudly. But in case any neighbors—or sportsmen—were around listening, she said more softly, "I want to hear everything you did tonight."

They both entered. If Kathlene hadn't known better, she could have assumed they truly were part of the sportsmen-anarchists. They wore hunting jackets over their casual outfits.

Before she shut the door, Jock said loudly, "We just have a few minutes. Some errands to run, including heading back to our cabins soon."

When they were all inside and the door had been closed and locked, Jock said, "There's a lot going down tonight. I want you with us. We're heading back to the cabins, ostensibly to pick up the wonderful weapons I promised our fearless leaders at the ranch. But we're not going to be alone there, and I want you to be with us when we meet the people who're showing up."

"Who's there?" Kathlene asked.

"Alpha Force."

Without moving from the doorway, Jock explained to Kathlene that he'd found some pretty major, potentially lethal weapons at the ranch. After that, anticipating the tone, if not the results, of the meeting before, he had already called in his special unit, and the plane containing his backup would be landing soon if it hadn't already.

"We communicated with them with phones no one'll be able to hack," Ralf confirmed, leaning his back against the nearest wall in the house's entry, arms folded across his chest.

Ralf was definitely acting the role of a good aide. He

looked and sounded calm in the face of what could be total chaos if they were unsuccessful tonight. But that wouldn't happen.

"We've got them scheduled to meet us at the cabins," Ralf continued. "There's a rental car I reserved for them and I provided them with GPS coordinates."

"I'd really like for you to come with us and meet them," Jock emphasized to Kathlene. He stood just in front of her, looking down into those skeptical blue eyes in her lovely, pale face. He wanted to take her into his arms, kiss the sternness from her lips. Reassure her that he was telling the truth. Which he was.

But what he wasn't telling her was that he simply did not want to leave her alone tonight.

He wasn't sure how things would go down, but he expected some major confrontations. The anarchists—no more euphemisms from him about their nature, either in his mind or spoken—had issued their threats. No matter what else they had planned to make their point, they had threatened several important people, including county commissioners.

And they had the means to really make good on their threats.

The sheriff's department did not look primed to protect them, so Alpha Force would take that on as well as controlling whatever other damage the anarchists intended to do.

Jock had wanted to pick his fellow Alpha Force members up at the Billings Logan International Airport, where the decision had been made for them to land to maintain better anonymity around here.

But after discussions with them, Jock had figured it would be better, in case Ralf and he were being followed, to have his backup team members meet them at the motel, where they had already booked cabins in names that couldn't be traced.

"That's why we're here now." Jock reached out to touch Kathlene's arm, very gently. She had changed from the dressy outfit she'd worn to the meeting to jeans and a royal blue knit shirt that hugged her curves. "I'll tell you a bit about what happened at the ranch tonight, but for now let's just say things are coming to a head, fast. We said we'd hidden some very special weapons of our own at the cabins that we'll bring back for our fellow anarchists to use, too, if necessary, since we're not supposed to know, at least not yet, about what the group already has. That's how we got away easily. My coming here to see you shouldn't be too suspicious if we're being followed, but I'd like for you to pretend that I'm coercing you to come with us—as if we want to keep an eye on my old buddy the deputy sheriff, rather than leaving you loose to do something against our interests."

"I guess that's okay, but why do they think you'd have been in communication with me again if you're supposedly part of their team?"

"Oh, we're just being wonderful sportsmen," Ralf said with a laugh. "We all saw you at the commissioners' meeting and knew you weren't happy. Jock's your old buddy, so to show how much he's wanting things to go well for the anarchists he offered to give them those really fun weapons, and if they ask we'll both say we didn't like your attitude so, while we were out and about anyway, we decided to take you into our control."

Kathlene's eyes widened and she took several deep breaths, seemingly to calm herself. "This is all just an act, right? I mean, the fun weapons—and your supposedly taking control of me."

"Right. No actual Uzis or AK-47s in our possession at the moment," Jock assured her, "although I've warned my Alpha Force team and they're bringing along some heavy-duty military gear. And, yes, you're our team member." His wanting to keep an eye on her, to protect her, was part of that teamwork, but he wasn't going to mention that to her and rile her all the more. "Now, we'd better get on our way. Please come, Kathlene."

He wasn't sure what he would do if she dug in her heels to stay, as unlikely as that might be. She'd always wanted to be included as part of their team.

But despite his not saying so, if she realized he wanted her along mostly for her protection there was a chance that she'd balk.

If she did, forcing her would not be a good idea—even though that was the show he wanted to put on as they left here. He wanted her genuine cooperation.

He wanted…more. Whatever it might be. He wasn't sure. But he might need to convince her that, like it or not, he recognized she could help Alpha Force succeed if she chose to.

She certainly could deter it from succeeding, at least for a short time, if she didn't go along.

He looked directly into her eyes, wanting to read her thoughts.

Thinking he saw…lust? Oh, yeah. Or was that just wishful thinking? Even if he was right, they couldn't do anything about it, but just maybe, if it was true, it would encourage her to go along with them.

"All right," she said. "Let's go."

* * *

Kathlene hated playing games. Always had. She much preferred directness, especially on the job.

She'd rather arrest someone, a robber or whoever, rather than pretend he was simply a person who'd had a tough life and made some bad decisions and now had to suffer needlessly for them.

Ha. But this situation could be a matter of life or death. Not for her, but for her friend Myra and other commissioners who thought like her.

Not to mention Jock. And Ralf. And even innocent civilians.

And so, as she left her house with the two men, a substantial-sized handbag over her shoulder, she pretended to hesitate as she shut her front door behind them. She wasn't surprised when Jock took her arm beneath the elbow and tugged on it not so gently. Not enough to hurt her, of course, but enough to show he meant business to anyone who might be watching.

She appreciated his touch. Even liked knowing he was this close.

But this was playing a game, one she could not avoid going along with.

She didn't have to pretend much to show some resentment. And when he opened the rear car door for her she stumbled as she resisted getting in.

"No tricks!" Jock shouted. In a lower voice he asked, "Are you okay?"

"Yes," she whispered. Aloud she said, "Shove it, Jock. Some old friend you are." She slid onto the seat, tossed her bag onto the floor and yanked at the seat belt. He got into the passenger's seat in front of her and let Ralf drive.

* * *

Okay. She was playing along.

She also felt excited. They were going to meet up with some other members of the military unit to which Jock and Ralf belonged.

"Can you tell if we're being followed?" she asked. With her own skills as an officer of the law she had been keeping watch but did not see any vehicle or person that appeared to be spying on them.

Perhaps Alpha Force members had better skills in figuring that out, although she didn't know how, on the road.

"Doesn't look like it," Ralf confirmed. "Jock?"

"Nothing that I see, either."

"But then sight isn't your best sense," Ralf said, shooting a glance across the front seat to his superior officer.

Jock gave him the finger, obviously in jest, and then turned back toward Kathlene. "You okay back there?"

"Fine, except that I've just been kidnapped by a shape-shifter pretending to be an anarchist." If they could jest in this time of stress, so could she—although what she had said wasn't exactly a joke.

"You got it."

A phone rang in the front, and Kathlene saw Jock check the screen before answering. "It's Drew," he said to Ralf, then glanced back toward Kathlene. "Our commanding officer."

For the next few minutes Jock talked about logistics. The rest of the Alpha Force team was apparently nearing Cliffordsville. From what Jock relayed to Ralf, they'd check into their cabins and then happen to be out walking their dogs when Jock and Ralf walked Click. And yes, they'd brought some military weaponry, although they didn't expect to have to resort to that.

"Sounds good."

A short while later, Ralf turned onto the road that led first to the cabins and, farther on, to the ranch. Kathlene opened her eyes even wider. Even if they hadn't been followed, they were much more likely to be seen by the anarchists now.

Assuming that they all hadn't gathered already at the ranch to prepare for whatever mayhem they were planning.

A lot of cars were parked at the motel complex so the place appeared busy, but Jock said that, fortunately, there had been enough empty rooms to reserve some for the people they were expecting. Ralf parked in the same space as he had before, and they all got out of the car.

"Do you need to arm wrestle me or aim a gun at me?" Kathlene asked Jock.

"You tell me. But it would be better if you appeared angry but accepting of whatever's going on."

"I'm not much of an actress," Kathlene said, but she pasted a scowl on her face, grabbed her bag and stalked irritably up to the door of the main cabin they'd rented.

"You two have fun arguing," Ralf said. "I'll go take care of Click, then bring him over to our cabin to wait for the walk you and I take later, when anyone watching will assume I'm accompanying Click again."

"Right." Jock edged past Kathlene and used a key card to open the door. He motioned for her to enter.

She shot him a mock-furious glare, then stomped in. He followed and shut the door behind them.

When they were inside, Kathlene faced Jock. He looked wound up. Edgy. And damned handsome.

Never mind that they were likely to encounter danger from the anarchists sooner rather than later that night.

Never mind that she was supposed to be angry with him for controlling her.

He had, in fact, sought and received her cooperation. In effect asked for her help, to the extent she could provide it to him and the rest of his team that night.

Had, in effect, treated her as a genuine member of his team.

"Kathlene," he began, "I want you to know—"

She didn't let him finish. Instead, impulsively—or maybe she had planned it all along—she put down her bag, threw herself against his hard, hot body, pulled his face down and met his lips with a provocative, needy, suggestive and entirely inappropriate kiss.

Chapter 21

Kathlene was tired of telling herself what a bad idea this was. It was a good idea. A damned good idea. Her active, eager mouth told her so. And her whole body... Oh, yes!

She pressed herself even closer as her entire being concentrated on the feel of his lips on hers, his tongue playing taunting games, his arms locked around her so his body pressed against hers even more.

Did he taste her more than she could taste him? He was human now, yes, but he'd said he had enhanced senses even while not shifted. He was both sweet and salty, addictive and enticing. Really enticing.

What did she taste like to him?

She wished he would tear off her clothes and make love to her right there, on the cabin floor. At least her hair was free, not pulled back the way it had to be when she was on duty. Somehow that made her feel sexier and want more in the way of physical contact. Real, deep, urgent physical contact.

But notwithstanding the urgency, the ecstatic pleasure of that kiss, enjoying sex right now with this man was impossible.

Any moment now, Ralf could come in with Click, and they could even be accompanied by whichever of their Alpha Force coworkers had come to town.

Jock knew that as well as she did. Those who could burst in were people he knew. He should be the one to call this off. Now.

And yet his mouth only pressed on hers with even more urgency. Continuing to kiss and taste and experience the rush of being near him, she knew her sensibility was about to dive out of her brain, maybe causing her to start tearing her own clothes off.

No. She was too smart for that. Too well grounded.

She enjoyed being with Jock, that was all, even while knowing there was no future in it. She might as well take advantage of—

A sound. A song. A cell phone. Jock's.

It broke the spell. He pulled away, leaving her wanting more. Wondering if that was the last time they would ever get to be that close.

He glanced at it, then, with a regretful look toward her, he lifted the phone to his ear. "Yes, Ralf? Where?" A pause. "Good. We'll be right there." Lowering the phone, he pushed a button. "Ralf has run into the rest of the gang from Alpha Force. We need to go meet them."

"Of course." Kathlene tried to even her breathing and make her voice sound calm and cheerful.

"This isn't over." Jock's shining hazel eyes locked on hers. His chin rose, and his handsome, chiseled features seemed to grow even stronger in apparent resolve. As if, by his saying so, they owed each other a time to finish what they had begun. Again.

Kathlene wished it were true.

She smiled. "I think we have a busy night ahead of us. After that…well, we'll see."

"Yes," Jock responded forcefully. "We will." He took her hand, and the feel of its strength protecting hers somehow made her believe that whatever might come that night, it would end well.

And maybe, just maybe, she could hope for one more night with Jock.

Ralf had told Jock that the gang had met up in the parking lot outside the reception cabin where the new arrivals had just checked in.

How amazing. They were a bunch of strangers with similar dogs who happened to run into each other and connect because of their pets—or so they all intended it to appear.

That was the scenario Jock described to Kathlene as they left the cabin and strode in that direction in the shadows of late afternoon. "We're all going to become great buddies, thanks to the coincidence of the three dogs, including Click, looking so much alike. Of course the other guys already knew one another and came here together to do a little hunting, but it was a real kick to see another dog so similar that Ralf got to talking to them…et cetera."

"Et cetera," Kathlene repeated, smiling at him. She kept pace with him along both the lawns and paved areas of the motel as they headed toward the front. He had an urge to take her hand, ostensibly to make sure she kept

her balance on the shifting ground, but actually because
he regretted, would continue to regret, that they'd had to
cut that amazing, hot kiss so short.

But no need to give the guys they were meeting up
with any indication of something between Kathlene and
him besides their cover story of prior friendship and
their actual alliance to check out, and bring down, the
anarchists.

Plus, just in case those anarchists had eyes on them
somehow, Kathlene and he needed to continue to appear
as if their former friendship was fraying.

Of course he'd seen no evidence of their being observed, but he knew better than to trust anyone around
these cabins as being as innocent as they seemed.

Besides, the anarchists might be watching him to try
to get hold of the imaginary weapons he claimed to have
brought here. And might also be wondering why he was
taking so long to bring those weapons to their compound.

So instead of taking Kathlene's hand, he put one of
his at the back of her neck as if controlling where she
was going.

She glanced at him quizzically, and then, obviously
getting it, looked down as if upset.

"I have a pretty good idea which Alpha Force members will be here, but I'll wait and introduce you to them
as we see them, okay?"

"Sure." Her stride seemed to break for just an instant
before she continued walking, and when he glanced at
her gorgeous face it looked actually, and not artificially,
troubled.

"What's wrong?" he demanded.

Her smile appeared rueful. "I'm somewhat aware of

what makes your Alpha Force so special. I assume that some of its other members are like you—shifters, right?"

"Right." He kept his tone light despite his continued scowl for effect. "And one of the good things is that we all get the advantages I've told you about from the elixir you've seen me take."

"I get it. But…well, are all the people who've come here shifters like you? And do they all shift into wolves?"

"I'll have to confirm who all is here," he responded. "I know at least one aide was being sent, and aides are like Ralf: nonshifters. I think I mentioned that some Alpha Force members can shift into other types of animals, but as far as I know only wolf shifters were coming here— for ease of blending into the background, for one thing."

"The wild wolf population around here isn't huge," Kathlene said. "But there are some."

"Which makes those potential changes to wildlife protection laws of great interest to us." He stopped as they reached the front parking lot. "Here we are. And there they are." He gestured toward the left where a small group of people were hanging out with some dogs— three dogs that resembled wolves, in fact, including Click. "And it looks like we have two more shifters here, brothers—although I only see one aide. Come on and I'll introduce you."

Their names were Simon and Quinn Parran and Noel Chuma. Kathlene knew she would have no trouble remembering who was who—even though all her questions hadn't yet been answered. Which were shapeshifters? The brothers, right? And Noel was their aide?

And why on earth did that fascinate her so much?

The men stood with Ralf and Click at the edge of the

parking lot, with the three dogs on long leashes availing themselves of the nearby lawn that led to the reception cabin on one side and several of the motel cabins beyond. The dogs did look similar and, if she'd guessed, might have assumed they were all at least part wolf, with otherwise varying canine lines that probably included some German shepherd or deep brown, furry Labradors—all good-sized for dogs, and all in breeds considered smart.

Even if Kathlene hadn't known, she would probably have guessed that the three newcomers might be in the military or law enforcement. Not that they were in uniform. And their hair wasn't military short. But they all appeared muscular and sure of themselves. They seemed to be having a great time talking together. That probably wasn't just part of their cover stories.

The guy introduced as Noel was shorter than the others but looked just as strong. His complexion was dark, and he seemed just the slightest bit deferential to the others.

The Parran brothers did look related. Both had black hair and eyebrows and a light trace of beard. Their eyes were golden, their bone structure sharp. Quinn was the taller and seemed more inclined to talk than his brother, Simon.

Ralf was the one to introduce the newcomers. There weren't many other people coming and going in the parking lot, but Kathlene noted that all the men maintained their cover—despite stolen, brief words between Jock and Ralf and these men. Serious words, judging by their facial expressions.

She didn't join in the exchanges. Wasn't invited to. But she did try to maintain her cover.

"Hey, Jock, these guys came here to do a little hunting, too. They're from South Dakota."

"As awesome as this area is," Jock said, "you need to know that there's some politics going on that could affect how fun it is to hunt. Look, why don't we all meet for dinner and we can tell you about it, okay?"

"Fine with me." Quinn turned toward the dog he had on a long leash and gave a slight tug to get his attention. The dog came trotting over. "Good boy, Saber." He looked back at the people around him. "If we can't hunt around here, we'll probably move on."

"Yeah," Noel said. The other two dogs had accompanied Saber, and Noel bent to give Click a pat on the top of his head. The other dog—Simon's cover dog?—was called Diesel.

Time for Kathlene to interject her role. "It's not that hunting is going to be outlawed around here or anything like that," she said. "Our county commissioners have been debating whether our local laws comply with some changes made in state statutes. The laws they're passing are to make sure everything's conformed."

"Deputy Baylor is with the local sheriff's department," Jock said. "She's an old friend of mine, and we came here for a visit because I hadn't seen her in ages. But we don't see eye to eye on a lot of things going on around here."

"I get it." Simon's gaze moved from Jock to Kathlene and back again. "I like this area but yeah, let's get together to chat tonight. I've got a feeling we're not going to stay long, but maybe you can convince us otherwise, Deputy."

"I'll try," she said.

That appeared to be the cue for Jock to go off a short

distance with Simon. To talk about dinner plans? Maybe, but Kathlene figured they'd go into more detail than they had before, would be all wrapped up in their strategizing about how to handle the rest of this evening, too.

And the night.

The two men looked very serious as they conversed, not surprising considering the circumstances. When they were likely to be overheard, they'd have to keep things light.

But what was likely to transpire was anything but light.

In a minute, they returned to the rest of the group. Kathlene, trying to maintain the cover of friends and new acquaintances meeting without a care in the world, barely had time to make over all three dogs and tell the two newcomers how beautiful they were as she patted them and knelt to give them hugs. She noticed the approving look Quinn shot her way, and Noel, too.

"Here's the plan," Jock said. "We're all going to my cabin first to toast the evening before it gets here. Later on, we'll head downtown and see if we can find a bar worth trying out. Maybe a couple. Grab some pizza then. Sound okay to you?"

"Sure does," said Simon. "What kind of beer do you have?"

They were in the main cabin rented by Jock and Ralf, all of them plus the dogs.

"Here's the actual plan," Jock said, standing and facing the rest, his expression solemn. The other humans were all leaning on the sides of the two beds. "It's not nighttime yet, but it's still getting late enough that I'm concerned those guys are already starting whatever they're up to. We'll first go on the prowl in the two cars we have here. Just an initial drive through town to make sure all looks well, and we'll pretend to give a tour to you guys. As long as we don't get a hint of anything starting yet, we'll head to that run-down house past the turnoff for the old ranch—and then start our strategy. But we need to be cautious and assume some of the weapons are now in hands that are more than ready to use them." He paused, then continued, "Oh, and by the way, even though it's not in our plans, if I run into any of our new buddies without being shifted, I'll have to tell them I'm mad as hell that I forgot to pack some strategic parts of the weapons I told them I'd brought along. I already said I carry them in pieces to avoid detection while traveling."

"They won't like that," Ralf said.

"No, but I'll beg to borrow some of their wonderful stuff if the occasion arises. I suspect it won't, though, considering what else will be going on."

Kathlene figured that, as part of their plan, there'd be shapeshifting involved. But she had something else important to ask. "What if you're being observed, Jock? Maybe heading downtown won't look suspicious, but if you come back this way and wind up at that old house—"

"Not a problem," Ralf interjected. "Jock and I came partly prepared for what could be going on here, but these guys are really ready. They brought some amazing satellite surveillance equipment that'll shadow us and let us know if anyone's peeking at what we're up to, following us or otherwise using electronics to snoop into our gear. If there's anyone or anything out there that shouldn't be, they'll jam it. And it contains metal-detecting equipment, too, so we'll be forewarned about who's carrying what."

"Really?" Kathlene couldn't help glancing at Jock,

who'd taken a seat beside her at the edge of his bed, for confirmation.

"Really," he said. "Plus, just so you know in advance, they're not the only Alpha Force members around here now besides us. The others have come into the area in smaller groups so they won't be as obvious. But this way there should be enough military—and other—strength to bring those anarchists down if they try anything or otherwise reveal themselves more." He glanced, as if for confirmation, toward the three men who'd just arrived. Simon must have been the one with the highest military rank since the others looked toward him. He nodded decisively.

"Before we go," Ralf said, "we actually do have some beer here, but I'd suggest that we forgo it for now."

"Agreed," said Simon. "But since we're not likely to stop for drinks of any kind, or even food, do you have any snacks?"

"Yeah," Quinn said. "Some of us in particular are going to need a whole lot of energy to accomplish what we're up to tonight. Especially—" He stopped and looked first at Kathlene, then Jock.

Kathlene knew what he was driving at. He wanted to know how much she knew. She should have remained serious, but instead of responding directly she said, "Oh, you mean Click, Diesel and Saber?"

The three men who'd just arrived shared pointed glances with Jock and Ralf. Jock laughed.

"Don't worry, guys. Kathlene's the one who wound up bringing in Alpha Force. She's been working closely with Ralf and me—and yes, me shifted. She knows what's going on. In fact, she's part of our team."

Which made Kathlene beam and feel warm and fuzzy inside.

Until he added, "Of course we have to ensure that every member of our team stays safe. And that includes our favorite deputy sheriff."

She tried to hide her nervousness in anticipating what was to come by offering a half smile. "Just make sure I remain part of your team, Jock. As you well know, I can take care of myself." Maybe she was being repetitious but then, so was he with his attempts to keep her out of harm's way. Nice, but no thanks. Especially not now.

"Yes, I do know," he said, not sounding thrilled about it. "And in fact, I've a feeling you might get an opportunity tonight to prove it."

It was time to get started. Jock had confirmed it with Quinn Parran, commanding officer of the small visiting group, who'd been designated as the one to keep in closest touch with the rest of the Alpha Force team in the area—for now. Until Quinn, like Jock and his brother Simon, shifted into wolf form.

And then? Well, it would be one of their aides—even though it would be safest for all of them to have as many nonshifted personnel as possible watching their backs as the mission ramped up.

The newcomers, along with their cover dogs, headed back to the cabins they had rented, but only for a minute. They were to pick up their supplies, stick them in their vehicle and then head out to the old house.

Ralf had provided them with directions to get there. Jock knew that the other Alpha Force members in the area would be notified that this group was on the move—and how they intended their operation to proceed.

Jock, tense yet eager to get started, waited for about two minutes then nodded to Ralf. "Go ahead and get

things ready for our departure." Ralf nodded and strode
to where he'd left his backpack against the wall farthest
from the door. He started going through the contents,
undoubtedly checking to make sure the light and elixir,
the most important objects they would need that night,
were there. Then Jock said to Kathlene, who was kneeling on the floor petting Click, "It's our turn to leave. You
still okay with that?"

She looked up at him, suspicion marring her lovely
face. "Why? You want me to head back home and stay
out of trouble?"

Yes, was what he thought—but not what he said. "Actually, no. I've a feeling we're going to need your presence tonight for things to go as smoothly as possible."

Her dark eyebrows arched even more than usual as she
rose to her feet. "Really? Or are you just saying that so
I'll be more receptive when you tell me to run into town
for a bottle of water or some other simple time filler?"

"I don't think that even driving down the side road
here for some water will be simple tonight."

Her face froze. "It's going to be bad, right?"

"We'd better anticipate things'll be rough. But you
can still opt out. We'll make do without you if we have
to." And that would be his preference, given a choice.

"Forget it, Larabey. I'm in." She was standing straight
now. "Just tell me what you want me to do to help. If nothing else, I'll have your back." Turning away from him,
she stalked past Click, who appeared mournful about no
longer being petted. She grabbed her large pocketbook
up from the space along the wall where she'd dropped it
and reached inside. She pulled out the Glock she kept at
her hip while on duty. "I've come prepared."

It wasn't a humorous situation or a humorous evening, but he gave a brief laugh nevertheless. "Why am I not surprised? Okay, Deputy. We'll talk on the way about some of the possibilities, but I think I'm about to deputize you myself—as my aide for tonight. I've got other things for Ralf to do, like act as our main liaison between our group and the other Alpha Force members who're still outside of town." He glanced toward Ralf, who had hefted the backpack up and was jutting his arms through the straps.

Ralf nodded. "Sounds good to me, sir."

Jock shook his head in mock irritation. "Stop calling me sir, Sergeant."

"Yes, sir."

Jock shot a glance at Kathlene, who was looking from one man to the other and shaking her head. "Levity at a time like this?" she scolded, but then she smiled. "It can only help us succeed, guys, so keep it up." She walked to the door then turned back. "Are we bringing Click along?"

"Yes," Jock said. "We'll most likely leave him, along with Diesel and Saber, at the old house, but at least we'll have them close by if we need a little canine cover tonight."

"Got it. You two ready to head to the car?"

"Go ahead," Jock said. "For the moment, I have *your* back."

Chapter 22

Kathlene observed how the three of them walked out to the car, all in their casual jeans and shirts, as if nothing in particular was happening or expected that night, chatting about the weather and how Click was, as usual, sniffing everything in his path—a prepared team pretending to be independent and friendly individuals.

Jock walked beside her, and she appreciated his presence. He bolstered her optimism. Things were going to be fine in Clifford County very soon. Alpha Force was here.

He was here.

Good actors all, in their undercover roles.

But it was nearly evening. Who knew what might still occur tonight?

Despite Jock's presence, she realized that she anticipated some pretty bad stuff to take place before everything was over—especially considering those weapons Jock had found—but surely things would end up well.

After all, hadn't she brought in the military's most elite and covert unit?

She didn't feel like laughing at herself or anything else as she again slid into the backseat of the car, this time with Click. She might have been the catalyst for getting Alpha Force sent here, but she'd hardly asked for their help, not specifically. Who knew what Alpha Force was about—before?

And how would they deal with such nasty weaponry?

Jock was the driver this time. That was probably because Ralf had donned some kind of communications device and had unobtrusive plugs in his ears as well as a tiny microphone attached almost invisibly at the neck of his shirt.

"Are you in touch with them?" Jock asked Ralf as he started the engine and began to drive away.

"Yep," Ralf said. "They followed our directions and found the house. They've parked under the cover of some nearby trees and have gotten inside." He paused, then said, apparently into the microphone, "I was just bringing my team up to date, Alpha One."

"They're Alpha One?" Kathlene asked. "The guys who were just with us?"

"That's right," Jock agreed over his shoulder. "We're Alpha Two. And the ones out there in the ether—our nearby backup—they're Alpha Zero."

"How many of them are there?"

"As many as we'll need," he responded cryptically.

"I'm in touch with them, too," Ralf said. And then, toward the microphone, he asked, "Alpha Zero, do you have us in your scope?" He paused. "Good. And what about the tangos?" Once again, he seemed to listen.

"Isn't *tango* the term for terrorists?" Kathlene asked Jock.

"Sure is," he acknowledged. "And that's what we believe our buddies the sportsmen are, above all else. People who don't like the government but don't act on it are one thing. These guys appear primed to do something to make some kind of statement—or worse."

They'd pulled out of the motel complex and started down the road toward the ranch. Kathlene kept watch for any vehicles or signs of life around but saw nothing. "Do we know what they're doing right now? Are they all hanging out on the ranch?" She doubted her companions could know that with any certainty, though.

Even so, she was pleased when Ralf said, "That's what Alpha Zero's been talking about in my ear—and Alpha One's ears, too. They've got surveillance on them from some pretty clever satellites. At the moment it appears there's a bunch of activity on the ranch, at the shooting range and the old stables. It's not clear what the guys there are doing but heat patterns apparently indicate they're teaming together. Possibly assembling some explosives."

Kathlene drew in her breath. "Getting ready to pull some bad stuff."

"Tonight," Jock said in apparent agreement. "Looks like we're right on time and on target."

They passed the turnoff to the ranch. "And no one's following us?" Kathlene asked Ralf. She couldn't help looking out the car windows nervously.

"According to our overhead resources, the answer's no. That doesn't mean we shouldn't be cautious, though."

"Of course." Kathlene wished she could call in some reinforcements of her own—but at the moment, considering the sheriff's shrugging off what the sportsmen

were doing and even what they said in public, that would
probably be a bad idea.

On the other hand, she still completely trusted Tommy
X. If she got an opportunity later, she would at least no-
tify him. Maybe even find a way to meet up with him
and get his backup when—and not if—she jumped in to
help with this operation.

After a couple more bends in the road, they reached
the area where the old house was back behind some trees.
Jock slowed down and looked into the rearview mirror.
"We still okay?" he asked Ralf, who murmured something into his microphone.

"No indication of anyone paying attention to us at
all," he said.

"Good." Jock quickly made a turn that took them behind the old house. Kathlene glimpsed the rental car the
other Alpha Force guys had been driving behind a bunch
of trees, and Jock pulled behind another stand of growth.

Ralf held on to a metallic briefcase as they went inside. Jock carried Ralf's backpack, which left her in
charge of Click. Quickly, they all headed up the rickety
back steps and inside.

Kathlene noted how well trained all three dogs were.
Neither Diesel nor Saber barked at the intrusion by Jock,
Ralf, Click or her, and Click, too, remained silent as he
traded sniffs with the other two wolflike canines inside
the shell of a house.

She wondered, not for the first time, what this place
smelled like to men with enhanced senses. It stank of rot
and mold and unidentified bad odors even to her.

And for the time being, it was headquarters.

"Glad you could make it." Quinn Parran grinned at
them as he stood in the middle of the dogs, his arms

crossed. The other two men were just beyond him, engaged in a conversation near the rotting wood visible behind the cracked plaster that formed the wall of what had once been the living room. "We're nearly ready to rumble. You?" He aimed his gaze toward Jock.

"I take it that we're handling preliminary recon." Jock glanced toward Ralf, who nodded.

"That's what these guys say. Looks like the sportsmen need to be invaded by only a few highly trained K9s who look like wolves at first to check out what they're up to."

"K9s?" Kathlene asked.

"It'll be more easily explained without giving away Alpha Force's true status if we appear to be our cover dogs while shifted," Jock explained.

Kathlene nodded. That did make sense.

"That should work well," Ralf continued. "And if it's like we think, there's backup galore nearby. In fact—" he paused as if to listen "—I need to head back to town real fast. They can tell by the GPS where to go and I'll be able to tell them when, but they want a little face-to-face dialogue first, more about who's who and what we anticipate." He aimed a stare toward Jock. "That's my job. Yours is to shift, sniff and obey the orders of your ostensible trainers."

Jock laughed. Even Kathlene smiled, despite feeling suddenly quite nervous.

But she couldn't afford to let it show. Especially when Jock said to her, "Confirming that you're my aide for tonight, Deputy. You up for that?"

"Yes, sir," she said and made herself grin.

Simon and Noel joined Quinn beside the dogs. "What's the plan?" Simon asked Jock.

"It's close enough to dusk to give us some cover, especially in the forest. Time for the three of us to shift. Ralf's meeting up with Alpha Zero. That'll leave Noel to act as shifting aide for you two, and Kathlene'll assist me." He glanced at her, even as she realized that the other men were studying her skeptically.

"Hey, I can handle it," she said. "I've observed what Ralf does before, and Noel can always act as my adviser."

"If you three are good with it," Simon said, "then so are we. And afterward, you'll also work with Noel to have our backs and communicate further with Alpha Zero?"

"I—" Kathlene was ready to say yes, but she realized she didn't have proper equipment to do so. "If Noel will advise me on that, too, then sure."

"You got your phone with you?" Jock asked.

"Of course."

"Good. You can always use it to communicate with Ralf. Program your number into her phone," he told Ralf. "And if you can get one for our C.O., Major Drew Connell, that wouldn't hurt, either. I assume that Drew's one of our Alpha Zero team, isn't he?"

"Yeah, but in case he's shifting, too, I'll get her Jonas's number." He looked toward Kathlene. "That's Captain Jonas Truro. He's a medical doctor like Drew and he's also essentially Drew's aide. All us aides will stick together to help our shifters, right?" He winked at Kathlene, who laughed.

"Count me in," she said. She realized that all the repartee was calming her nerves a bit, even as she anticipated some nasty stuff going down tonight. But she'd act as backup—and she would have backup, too, even if it wasn't her standard sheriff's-department gang.

"Okay, then," Ralf said. "I'm out of here. Oh, and it

looks like it's pretty much dusk here, partly thanks to the forest. It's dark enough that you shifters can do your thing anytime now and go check out the place."

"Once they're shifted," Noel added, looking at Kathlene, "we'll go with them to the fence outside the ranch. We won't be able to see everything that happens, but we're equipping all three of them with cameras that'll let us see what they do. They're hooked up to my phone and I'll add the app to yours after we get these guys shifted. We'll be able to report to Ralf and the Alpha Zero folks if we need immediate action or if we can just let these shifters take care of things and record them. Under orders as well-trained K9s, of course."

"Sounds like a plan," Kathlene said, smiling gamely. She just hoped it was a *good* plan.

But she couldn't help feeling impressed by all the technological backup that seemed to be in effect. Who would ever have thought there would not only be an army unit comprised partly of shapeshifters—a pretty ancient myth—but that they would also have ultra-modern cameras and cell phones and satellite equipment working in their favor?

"Okay, Ralf, you can get on your way," Jock said.

"Yes, sir." He grinned then added, "Hey, we'll reconvene later and outline everything we did when this is all behind us. See you later." And then, after giving all three dogs quick pats on the head, Ralf went out the house's back door.

"Okay," Jock said, "the rest of you—ready to get started?"

The three Alpha One guys said yes. Kathlene didn't feel as if she had much choice. But, heck, she was ready, too.

She was going to help Jock shift.

And then he would sneak onto the ranch in wolf form, where there were dozens of anarchists who liked to hunt—and most likely worse.

Her feelings about Jock might be indecipherable even to her, but she cared about him and who he was and what he did—not to mention how much she enjoyed sex with him.

Even though that part was now a thing of the past, she would be damned worried about him this night.

You've got to be okay, she thought, looking at him as the other men moved toward the far side of the room where they'd left a couple of backpacks similar to Ralf's.

Her thoughts must have been legible on her face, since the look Jock gave her seemed to blend certainty and sympathy. "Like Ralf said, we'll all talk about our roles in this and how everything went later, when this is all over and we've rounded up the anarchists. Okay?"

"Okay," Kathlene said, as forcefully as if she was convinced that there couldn't be anything but success before them.

"Then let's do it." Jock retrieved Ralf's backpack and knelt on the floor near Kathlene. The other men had gone into another room, so Jock would have some privacy as he shifted. He pulled out a glass vial filled with liquid. "I'll start with this," he said and downed the elixir as Kathlene dug into the pack and pulled out the special battery-operated light. That meant she wasn't looking directly at Jock as he started to pull off his clothes. "Hey," he said. "You're supposed to be watching."

Kathlene couldn't help but oblige, even as Jock started to strip as though he was an entertainer on stage, pulling his T-shirt over his head first, flexing his perfect, buff chest, then reaching to remove his jeans and underwear.

Kathlene felt her breathing become uneven as she stared at his perfect body—and his long, hard shaft that seemed to grow as she watched.

Too bad this moment would be wasted, at least to her. "Looks good," she said as lightly as she could manage, but heard the aroused catch in her voice. "Here we go." She turned on the light and aimed it at him, then watched, enthralled, as his shift from gorgeous human male to wild wolf took place.

He waited for a collar to be fastened about his neck by Noel so he would have a camera to record all he experienced. Then he waited for his packmates, also with cameras attached, to join him before he left the house where they had shifted.

Kathlene was there, observing. He knew she would continue to be there for him. She would also help to watch the dogs that provided cover for the shifters.

Soon, all three of them in wolf form loped through the forest toward the fence that surrounded the ranch housing the anarchists. Jock showed the others the holes in that fence through which they could enter the compound, careful to listen to be sure that no humans were nearby, that no humans would spot them.

When they were inside the fence and in the deepening shadows around trees and bushes on the old ranch, he nodded toward the firing range to get the others to head carefully in that direction.

Him, too—but beyond. He walked slowly, with caution, using all his senses to ensure no human was following, toward the crumbling stable where weapons more powerful than mere guns were being collected.

He hoped that the cameras on him and his packmates

*were working well. He intended to demonstrate to all
members of Alpha Force who were watching now, or
who later observed what was being recorded, what these
anarchists were really about.*

*There. He sensed a large contingent of humans near
where he was going—that stable. He smelled a heavy
scent of gunpowder and other explosives.*

*He heard laughter and swearing and men discussing
with one another in hushed yet ecstatic tones the idea of
blowing up anyone trying to tell them what to do.*

*Time to get closer. Allow the camera to take pictures
and record voices.*

*And ensure there was enough to bring in the rest of
Alpha Force to handle this ugly but anticipated situation.*

Jock was gone. He had shifted in front of her eyes
again, and she had watched, enthralled. Wanted to touch
him, to understand better the change that had overtaken
him.

Instead, Kathlene had done nothing.

And now Jock had left, stalking his way with the others like him onto the grounds of the ranch, to observe
and, if necessary, to act. Perhaps to attack. To put himself in imminent danger.

Now it was her turn to feel protective without being
able to do anything about it. She wanted to help him. To
keep him from harm. To ensure that the bad guys were
brought to justice, but not at Jock's expense.

Yet here she was. She couldn't help him…could she?

Wait. That wasn't true.

She was still with Noel inside the old house. "I gather
that we're to lock the cover dogs inside here," she said to
him, "so anyone spotting Jock and the rest will assume

they're real dogs who happen to have gotten loose—those belonging to Jock and the guys who've just arrived here, right?"

"That's right, although depending on the circumstances we might admit that they're K9s trained to move around an area for recon, taking pictures from their collars." Noel seemed to study her with his deep brown eyes. He was a nice-enough-looking guy, young, serious, dark-toned skin and maybe even a little bit deferential to her. Because she was a civilian—or at least nonmilitary? Because she was a woman?

Because she was a deputy sheriff?

Heck, none of that mattered. The fact that he was at least listening to her was a good thing.

"Can we go to the area outside the ranch?" she asked. "We can stay beyond the fence but keep an eye on what's happening inside the best we can. Show me how to use the app you added to my phone to its best advantage. I want to see what Jock's looking at."

"Sure." He complied, and she got to see, as if through Jock's eyes, what the inner grounds of the ranch looked like at his level.

He appeared to have stopped near the stable, and she heard loud, boisterous, menacing voices without, at the moment, observing the speaker.

"Let's head toward the ranch to observe better," she said to Noel.

"Okay. I was already about to do that. Ralf and I are in contact and he'll keep in touch with our shifters via their cameras, too, and with the rest of the Alpha Force team sent here to help. He's coordinating."

"Then let him also coordinate with me."

"Okay."

"You can talk to them on the way. Let's start our walk toward the ranch."

Phone to his ear, he followed her.

It didn't take them long to reach the outer area of the ranch. For now they remained in the seclusion of the surrounding woods.

"Here," she whispered, handing Noel her phone. "I also want to see what the guys in Alpha One are up to."

He tweaked her phone, and she then was able to look at the pictures on a split screen. Using her fingers, she was able to enlarge one picture, then the other. For now it appeared that Simon and Quinn were near the ranch's shooting range. They must have been hiding in the shadows near the old stable or maybe the ranch house itself, but they faced a whole bunch of men who looked high on alcohol or maybe testosterone. They were laughing, goading each other. Sounded as if they were telling each other that it was nearly time, and no one would ignore them ever again.

Jock appeared to have stopped to continue listening at the stable.

She decided to call Ralf. They were still a distance from the ranch so she didn't have to maintain total silence.

"Yes, I'm with the Alpha Zero guys now," Jock's aide told her. "They're ready to move in whenever the order's given—and that'll be up to Jock or the other shifters."

"How long will it take them to get here?" she asked.

"Not long. No more than ten minutes. We're close by."

But ten minutes could be an eternity if Jock or the others got into trouble.

She didn't say anything to Ralf, though. He was military. He knew how critical even seconds could be if someone was in trouble.

Was Jock in trouble? She enlarged his camera picture again, listening only to what he heard around the stable.

Men continued to rant and laugh there, too.

And then a voice could be heard that was distinguished from the rest. It sounded familiar. Tisal's?

It said, "Which of you wants to be the first one to detonate one of these babies near that county building, where they thought they could ignore us?"

A lot more voices rang out, volunteering for the assignment. Kathlene froze. It was time for Ralf to call in the rest of his team.

It was also time for her to let her own team, the sheriff's department, in on what was happening, even if she couldn't explain how she knew.

But before she could, another voice yelled, "Hey, what's that? Is that the dog that was prowling here the other day? It looks like a wolf, and in my book wolves are fair game. Time to start our fun."

The next thing Kathlene heard was a volley of gunshots. The picture she was viewing started bouncing. At least Jock must still be alive, but he was in trouble.

And she definitely had to help.

Immediately.

Chapter 23

"Jock's in trouble!" Kathlene yelled to Noel as she started running. "Maybe Simon and Quinn, too." Had they been spotted? She didn't know, but she felt sure they would also go to Jock's rescue and put themselves into this horrible situation. "Get the rest of your guys in there." She knew it was time to call in her own reinforcements, as well. It might be too late. But she had to try.

She pressed the numbers into her phone to call Tommy X.

"I'm near the old ranch," she said, keeping her voice somewhat low. They were almost there, and she didn't want to be heard in case any of the anarchists were out patrolling. "There's trouble brewing. They may be planning on using explosive devices on buildings downtown." She'd heard that, and it was more likely to get the sheriff's department moving than mentioning that a wolf or three might be the sportsmen's current target.

"A bunch of us are already on our way," Tommy X told her. "Sheriff Frawley got a call from some of the sportsmen and they've said something's wrong, like they're under some kind of attack."

By wolves? Or did they somehow know more?

"I'll see you there, then," Kathlene said. "And hurry."

"Who'd you call?" Noel demanded as she pressed more buttons on her phone and concentrated fully on what Jock must be seeing. Trees and bushes and undergrowth along with edges of buildings, and the view was bouncing and veering first one way, then the other. He must be running sideways to evade the shooters. At least they weren't all shooting at once in his direction, but Kathlene did hear the sound of erratic gunshots.

Fortunately, Noel and she had nearly arrived at the fence. She started running toward the front gate.

"Where are you going?" Noel demanded from behind her.

"We need to get onto the ranch. I'm not sure they'll let either of us in. They won't like my badge, and I doubt they'll respect military ID any more than they do mine."

"Then we've got to get in another way. Do you know how Jock got himself and the others inside? Are there vulnerable parts of the fence?"

"I'm sure there are, but he didn't tell me where they are. Look, let's head to the front gate first and see if we can bully our way in."

"I don't like it, but—"

"Neither do I," Kathlene snapped, "but there are already a bunch of mad terrorists inside shooting guns at what they think are wild wolves. Do you think they'll be nicer to a couple of humans if they catch us trying to sneak in?"

"No," Noel admitted. "Let's give it a try."

Hurrying through the woods toward the front gate, Kathlene kept watching the phone screen. The picture continued to move. That meant so did Jock.

She still heard gunfire in the background.

As they reached the front, she saw a couple of official sheriff's-department vehicles arriving at the same time.

Sheriff Frawley was in the first one. Good. Surely even he would have to respond to what she had to tell him.

"Sir," she said as the tall man in his uniform with all its medals showing what a bigwig he was strode toward the front gate. She met him there. "I'm so glad to see you. There's a lot going on here. The men inside are not just sportsmen, they're terrorists. They plan to blow up the County Administration Building, and that may not be all."

The sheriff stopped moving and stared down at her with cold eyes. "I got a call that something was going on here that shouldn't be. We're here to find out what and protect the citizens who've chosen to reside here for a while."

"What!" Kathlene's mind fought for a way to try to give a better explanation without revealing the existence, nature or presence of Alpha Force. "They don't need protection. The rest of our citizens need protection from them."

"Get out of the way, Deputy, or I'll have your badge for insubordination. You're not even on duty, are you?"

"Not right now, sir, but—"

The sheriff strode right by her. So did Undersheriff Kerringston and a couple of deputies.

Tommy X emerged from the second car and approached her. "I tried to get Sheriff Frawley to see reason about the sportsmen, told him there was good reason to arrest them, not defend them." He paused, looking at Kathlene. "There is, isn't there?"

"Yes, absolutely." She watched in horror as the sheriff high-fived the guard who opened the gate to let them in.

She'd known the sheriff was okay with having the sportsmen around, maybe even liked the idea, but had hoped he'd been wise enough to change his mind about them after they showed their true colors and spoke out at the last meeting against any kind of government control.

But he hadn't reacted at all to her report that they were intending to blow up public property—presumably with people inside.

Sheriff Frawley must not only accept them. He must be one of them.

What was she going to do?

And where was Jock? How was Jock? She looked frantically toward Tommy X. "We'll go inside, too. We need to help." She didn't explain who she intended to help, but she figured Tommy X would know it wasn't the sheriff or the terrorists.

"Not a good idea, Deputy," he said. "We don't have any evidence about what you're alleging, and—"

"But we do! Video recordings." She couldn't tell him how they were being collected, although the cover dogs would come in handy for the explanation later.

And then she saw several large black vans barreling down the driveway from the main road.

"Reinforcements have arrived," Noel Chuma told her. He was grinning. "I'll introduce you later, but right now they've work to do."

Kathlene watched as humans in military fatigues, carrying weapons, poured out of the vehicles—along with half a dozen other wolves. They'd already done their shifting.

And now they were going to take over this terrorist installation.

Kathlene grinned briefly toward Tommy X, who looked confused.

"Military?" he asked.

Kathlene nodded. "I'll fill you in later." But not about everything.

One guy with lots of stripes on his camo uniform confronted the guard, who quickly backed down.

Kathlene smiled. "We've got work to do, too," she said to Sgt. Chuma. "Let's follow them inside."

People who called themselves sportsmen...hunters. Those hunters seeing wolves—or what they believed were true wolves. Of course they chased the three canines, shot at them. Perhaps allowed them to be a distraction from their own intent to destroy property and kill more than wildlife, at least for a short while.

Fortunately, there were a lot of shadows at this hour, thanks to buildings and trees. Places where Jock could veer in and out for protection. His shifted companions, Simon and Quinn, were equally adept at staying hidden or out of range, splitting up to make themselves more difficult targets.

But it couldn't last much longer.

Jock stopped behind a large vehicle in the ranch's main parking lot to catch his breath, and to use his senses to learn what was happening. Had Ralf and Noel and Kathlene sent for any reinforcements? If not, it was time.

There were loud, continuous sounds behind him, those

chasing him, those firing shots from automatic weapons each time they believed they saw a moving wolf.

They were drunk. They were human and could not see well in the growing darkness.

Eventually, though, they might get lucky.

But then, he heard sounds before him, toward the main entrance to this encampment. Voices, raised and angry and menacing, and they included that sheriff's, but not only his. Kathlene's. And Major Drew Connell's. Yes! And there were also vehicles, large and military.

His additional backup was here.

That meant he could change things where he was. Fast. And relatively safely.

His shifting companions would not be quite so aware, but he nevertheless lifted his muzzle in the air and howled. The sound was echoed by two more voices— and then several more toward the entry.

Gunshots sounded. One bullet even hit the side of a vehicle near him.

He bared his teeth, wishing he could bite the wrist of whoever dared to raise a weapon and aim it at him.

Not now, though. Not yet.

He carefully lowered himself to the ground, moved forward while crouched on his wolfen legs, veered around one vehicle, then another, using his nose to smell and identify those anarchists who were nearest him.

As he had hoped, expected, one was the out-of-control human in charge who obviously wanted to make an example of what he deemed to be a stupid wolf creature who had dared to enter the property he controlled.

The man named Tisal.

Instead, Jock would make an example of him.

He moved slowly, quietly, around the vehicles, on

cooling, rough concrete that scratched at his stomach, smelled of oil and of vehicles and more, circling back in the direction from which he had come, all the while knowing the camera about his neck continued to record all that occurred.

All the while hearing the noises of allies, both human and wolfen, as well as vehicles, drawing closer.

Not all were allies, though. Yet he believed they, too, were under control since at the moment the voices he heard were curt, giving orders, but without arguing.

And then—yes! He scented Tisal nearby, just beyond a large van. Not far from other human smells, yet not surrounded by them. Jock maneuvered around the vehicle.

And saw Tisal. Alone.

Jock prepared to leap, even as the large, rounded human in his hunting jacket raised his weapon and aimed it at him.

"Don't you dare," shouted an angry female human voice. Kathlene's voice. She was off to the side, and she aimed her own service weapon at the offending anarchist. "Drop it, Tisal. You're under arrest."

The anarchist pivoted, aiming his gun toward Kathlene. She fired, even as Jock leaped onto the man, knocking him to the ground, planting his teeth around the beefy, vulnerable neck, growling, and forcing himself not to bite down and kill the creature who had dared to fire toward Kathlene.

"It's okay, J—er, Click," she said, as if talking to Jock's cover dog. Smart lady. "Good boy. You've done a good job, and I'll be glad to tell your trainer, Ralf. Not that you understand what I'm saying, but I'm fine, and I've got this jackass's weapon. I'll cuff him and then you can go help the others like you. There are a bunch, and *with all the other military backup that's here I have a feeling we've got a really productive bust of these anarchists underway."*

Jock moved back, out of the way, his hackles still raised and his teeth still bared, ready to attack again. But the man remained docile as Kathlene rolled him onto his belly and cuffed him.

"Where's your boss, bitch?" Tisal demanded. "The sheriff will fire you for this. Maybe even arrest you for interfering with citizens' rights. And—"

"That's enough, Mr. Tisal. I'm sorry to say that your friend and my boss, Sheriff Frawley, isn't going to be able to help you."

That was when Jock scented the sheriff barreling in their direction. He stood up and barked.

"What is it, Click?" Kathlene knew Jock was warning her about something but she didn't know what.

But she wasn't overly worried. The Alpha Force contingent who'd come here as backup was now fanning out all over the place. They looked damned official in their uniforms, accompanied by what appeared to be a whole group of trained attack dogs—probably all shifters who were apparently using their own special senses and abilities to help round up every one of the anarchists.

The recordings Jock and the other shifters had made would provide all the evidence necessary to convict every one of them for breaking all sorts of terrorism and conspiracy laws, at a minimum.

"I'm sure everything's okay," she continued, addressing the wolf, who clearly remained in protective mode. "Go ahead and look around. You'll see that your fellow—

er, anyway, there are a lot of these guys being taken into custody now."

"Who the hell you talking to?" Tisal demanded.

"Everyone watching the recording that's being made thanks to the camera around that dog's neck," she said, tugging on the head anarchist, making him rise to his feet with his hands now cuffed behind his back. He leaned on the nearest car, and Kathlene assisted him a bit by manipulating his arms.

But Jock didn't move. Which worried Kathlene. She decided it was time to drag Tisal off to where the others were being taken into custody.

"Let him go, bitch."

Kathlene turned in the direction of the voice. Nearly under the cover of growing darkness, Sheriff Frawley strode out from between two parked sedans. He held a gun, and it was pointed at her.

"No, sir," she said. "We have evidence that this man intends to commit terrorist acts in Clifford County." She gave Tisal a gentle nudge in the back with her elbow.

"So you brought in the military? Are you the reason those jerks confronted me at the gate? Well, I got away and I'm going to make sure that all of the law-abiding sportsmen who have been living here are released by the feds and allowed to go about their business. Right now you're going to come with me and tell them you made a mistake, that you recognize now that these gentlemen are just that—gentlemen. They're sportsmen and hunt legally within the laws, even if they don't want those damned laws made any more onerous."

"And you, sir? Are you willing to obey the laws, whatever they are, and enforce them in your role of sheriff of Clifford County? And arrest people for possession and use of illegal weapons and explosives?" Kathlene had met Jock's eyes. His were more feral than she had ever seen them. He again looked ready to attack.

But she knew he recognized what she was doing and he stood still, at least for now—and allowed the security camera around his neck to do its job.

"What am I willing to do?" the sheriff snapped. "I'm willing to fight for the rights of people who don't want to be weighed down by stupid laws that make them give up their natural-born rights, like those to protect and feed themselves and shoot anyone or anything they damned well please." He suddenly dashed toward Kathlene and put his service weapon to her head. "And you're going to agree with me, Deputy, or you'll be damned sorry."

The angle was bad. She couldn't trip him or otherwise grab control.

Turned out she didn't need to. In seconds, she was released. The gun went off but it fired uselessly into the air as Jock pounced onto the sheriff and weighed him down, his teeth at the anarchistic lawman's throat.

"Get him off me!" The sheriff's voice sounded strangled. Kathlene was angry enough that she considered encouraging Jock to bite down—just a little.

But she got control of herself—a good thing, too. A whole group of Alpha Force members suddenly appeared in the parking lot—humans and wolves. With them was Tommy X, as well as Undersheriff Kerringston, who looked confused but hung back, just watching.

"These folks say they're friends of yours, Deputy Baylor," Tommy X said to her. "There are more of them around here, too, and they're taking a lot of the guys from the ranch into custody."

One of them, a tall guy in a camo uniform with black

hair flecked with silver and shining amber eyes—a non-shifted shifter?—approached with his hand extended toward Kathlene. "Deputy Baylor? I'm Major Drew Connell of Alpha Force. I hear you were instrumental in bringing us here to stave off some potentially pretty nasty terrorist attacks."

"I did ask for help, sir," she acknowledged, shaking his hand.

"Well, we've been more than happy to provide it." He glanced down toward where Jock sat at attention near Kathlene's feet. This soldier must be Jock's commanding officer.

"Well, I thank you, sir. And so will the rest of this town when they fully realize what's been going on."

"I think we'll be informing them about it very soon." That was Tommy X. "Interesting group, this Alpha Force. I'm sure we'll all be interested, too, in how you've trained all those dogs you've brought along who look like wolves to act as your canine backup. They've been wonderful in helping to herd the anarchists together and get them rounded up and into custody."

"Yes," Kathlene said wryly, "I'll be very interested, too, in what explanation Alpha Force provides our citizenry. Will you be taking these guys into your custody?" She gestured toward Frawley and Tisal.

"Yes, we will," said Major Connell.

"Great. Then I'm going to walk around and observe the rest of what's going on around here." She glanced down toward Jock. "And I wouldn't mind at all having a canine companion."

Chapter 24

They walked the perimeter of the fence around the ranch in the darkness, this time on the inside. "That's all so amazing," Kathlene remarked more than once, and Jock, still in glorious wolf form, looked up at her often. She sometimes believed he was smiling and when she knelt and hugged him he licked her cheek.

She was fascinated to watch the teamwork of soldiers and wolves pretending to be trained K9s while they rounded up the dozens of anarchists, disarmed them, herded them into the outdoor assembly area where they had previously plotted against the Clifford County commissioners and government in general, and ensured they remained there.

Jock seemed quite pleased with himself, assuming Kathlene could read wolf body language accurately. He almost pranced at her side, sometimes growling if one of the anarchists appeared at all willing to protest what was going on.

It all seemed so surreal, and yet it was wonderful. What she had feared had been proven true—that these men had intended to harm innocent people as well as the government. And what she had tried so hard to accomplish—getting an appropriate law-enforcement group here to take control—had also come true.

Alpha Force was outstanding.

She was also amazed—well, maybe not so much—when Jock led her to the front gate and walked through, looking back at her with his glistening hazel wolf eyes as if he wanted her to follow. She complied, and they headed for the old house.

Once again, Kathlene assisted him in a shift, this time back to human form.

Once again, she got to aim the light at him and observe his wolfen body morph into his gorgeous human form.

And when he was fully shifted and had caught his breath, still nude, he took her into his arms.

"Kathlene," he said. "Thank you for all you did tonight."

"You're the one who deserves thanks," she whispered to him, and he lowered his mouth to hers.

She knew she would never forget that sexy, sincere and wonderful kiss....

Especially because she feared it would be their last.

He eventually pulled back, if only a little. "You know," he said, looking down at her with an expression she couldn't read—lustful? worried? "you still drive me nuts, putting yourself in danger that way, even when it's to help me."

She pulled back a little, too. "I still don't understand why you're so overprotective. I can take care of myself."

"I know you can. And maybe that's why...I do trust you, Kathlene. But—well, maybe you should know that there was once another woman in my life, a shifter like me. She joined a police department even before I ever thought about getting involved in any kind of military life or law enforcement. She was killed in the line of duty."

Oh. That explained so much. He'd obviously cared about that woman. And now he wanted to protect everyone.

"I'm not her, Jock," she said softly.

"I know," he said, and kissed her again.

Kathlene was glad to see the number of Clifford County residents piling into the assembly room for the ad hoc commissioners' meeting that was convened on the afternoon after the confrontations and arrests at the old ranch, even though it was a Saturday.

She was on duty, guarding the doors while in uniform. Her partner, Jimmy Korling, stood at the other door. He'd been less than friendly with her that day. He had obviously heard of her involvement in what had occurred the night before. Had he wanted to be brought into it?

Maybe Kathlene would have considered that if she'd thought she could trust him. He'd seemed, at least before, like a favorite of Sheriff Frawley's, and that made him less than an ideal cohort to work with her, especially as it had become completely clear whose side the sheriff had been on.

For the moment, Senior Deputy Tommy X was in charge of the sheriff's department, since Sheriff Frawley was unsurprisingly being investigated for his alleged roles as part of the anarchist team, and Undersheriff Kerringston, thanks to his close alliance with the sheriff, was also being scrutinized to determine if he had any role in what had occurred.

First thing that morning, Commissioners Myra Enager, Wendy Ingerton and the others had been briefed—or at least as much as wasn't classified under the control of the federal government. Kathlene had been the one to call Myra, who'd sounded thrilled and relieved.

Unsurprisingly, Tommy X had spoken to Myra, too, and the three of them had gone out to breakfast together to discuss the situation.

By then, Kathlene was alone, since Jock and the others had joined the rest of Alpha Force for the law enforcement events that would occur that day. Kathlene hoped to see him later but wasn't sure when…or even *if*. She figured the members of Alpha Force would leave as soon as they confirmed that all was under control, and that would probably include Jock.

After breakfast, Myra had spoken with the other commissioners, and this afternoon's meeting had been planned nearly immediately. They wanted to inform their constituency about what was going on, even if they didn't know the details.

Unsurprisingly to her, Kathlene hadn't been informed of all that was happening, either. All she knew—and all she needed to know—was that a specialized FBI crime scene team had been flown in from D.C. to the nearest air force base, Malmstrom, in Cascade County, which wasn't too far away. As soon as they arrived, they started collecting evidence, which would be used to charge the anarchists, or at least the leaders of the group, with plotting some pretty major terrorist crimes—like potentially blowing up the County Administration Building. And although the collection of weapons Jock had discovered might not be fully illegal, how they were intended to be used probably was, especially after the threats made to the county commissioners.

And Jock had also learned that a cache of weapons of the type he'd found had been stolen from an army base in Michigan. Serial numbers were being checked to see if they matched.

The recordings made by Jock and the others would also help in the investigation and prosecution, but the more evidence they collected, the more likelihood there was of convictions.

Last Kathlene heard, all the members of Alpha Force who had come here, including Jock and Ralf, were meeting and debriefing themselves and the FBI team.

The commissioners' meeting had started. Myra was the first to explain what had gone down the night before. "A local citizen had believed there was more going on at the old ranch than target practice by a bunch of sportsmen." Meaning *her,* Kathlene knew. "In fact, for those of you who were present yesterday at our most recent commission meeting, some of the sportsmen had spoken out and sounded somewhat threatening. That was followed up by several commissioners, including me, receiving written threats that were delivered anonymously and circuitously to our homes. We suspected who had sent them but couldn't prove it—and yet a series of events not even we know about occurred where evidence was gathered at the ranch, and now a full federal investigation is progressing into prosecuting all of the sportsmen as anarchists and terrorists, or at least those in charge."

"What about Sheriff Frawley and Undersheriff Kerringston?" came a question shouted from the audience.

Myra paused and exchanged a brief glance with Kathlene. "There is some reason to suspect that they might have known what was going on. We don't know that for sure, however. Just in case, the investigation will include them, too."

Before heading to the meeting that afternoon, Kathlene had called Jock, just for an update, she had told him. If there was anything that Alpha Force or the feds had found out, or at least suspected, that the public should know about, she requested that he let her know.

Her mind had been circling a lot around what he had told her about the woman he had lost....

But he'd sounded pretty formal when he responded, and she suspected that she had caught him in the middle of a meeting. What he told her surprised her, but only a little. "Part of what is being looked into," he said, "is some allegations made by several of the top anarchists who said they were invited here by Sheriff Frawley, who promised them a perfect venue to meet and make their plans for doing whatever was necessary to let the world know who they are and why they were a major power to be reckoned with. That's for your information only, for now, Kathlene. Just let the people at the assembly know that a full-out investigation is in the works and that justice will be served."

"Against Sheriff Frawley as well as the others?" she asked, and he agreed.

She had hung up feeling all the more vindicated—and lonely. Whatever she had imagined to be growing between Jock and her was clearly something that had ended with the night's final raid on the terrorist encampment.

She had not told Myra any details before the meeting, but she had confirmed, as Jock had told her, that the investigation was continuing but that there appeared to be sufficient evidence to arrest and put at least some of the anarchists on trial. And that the investigation would also continue to include Sheriff Frawley and Undersheriff Kerringston, but it was premature to assert that they would also be prosecuted. Myra's description at the meeting of their suspected involvement had gone far enough... for now.

That meeting continued for just over an hour. And when it was over, Kathlene stayed as long as she felt she must in her role as one of the deputies protecting the room. She ducked questions, deferring to the commissioners.

When she finally could, she hurried back to the sheriff's department, stayed in the background as much as possible and was relieved when she was once more finally off duty.

Jock loved being a shapeshifter. He always had, always would. He particularly loved being a member of Alpha Force, with all its shifting perks and camaraderie with other shifters and military members.

But right now, it was Sunday, the second day after the invasion of the old ranch and the taking of so many anarchists into custody for further evaluation and, in most instances, prosecution for planned acts of terrorism.

He was in the cabin he still shared with Ralf—for now. Most of the other cabins in this motel had also been taken over by Alpha Force members for at least one more night. They'd all been meeting and debriefing one another and sharing thoughts about what should come next—all of which was presented to their commanding officer, Major Drew Connell. He was their liaison with the FBI and other feds who were now involved with this situation.

Although they'd spoken on the phone, Jock hadn't seen Kathlene since late on the night when the raid on the ranch had been conducted, which had been the day before yesterday. And he was probably leaving Clifford County tomorrow. Forever.

There was a lot of cleanup work awaiting him at Ft. Lukman. Debriefing and planning for whatever his next assignment would be, and who knew what else?

Yet another meeting was scheduled to begin in half an hour at Drew's cabin. Jock would go there. He had to.

Ralf had already strolled over there so he could touch base with all the other shifting aides who'd come to this area, not just Noel Chuma but about half a dozen others who'd helped their shifters change into wolves and invade the camp en masse, the best way of handling it safely for Alpha Force.

Before heading to Drew's cabin, Jock grabbed a bottle of beer from the fridge. Then he picked up his laptop computer.

He was going to say goodbye to Kathlene tomorrow—maybe.

But he also had an idea, and he had to flesh it out now to determine if it might work.

"You've got to be joking," Kathlene said to Myra.

Her friend had called her first thing on that Monday morning and asked her to come to see her at the County Building. She'd had her secretary serve both of them coffee, and now they sat in the tiny conversation area in Myra's office.

"No, although I'm not sure what all it'll take to get approvals for you to be named sheriff. But the other most likely person to be named acting sheriff of Clifford

County, Senior Deputy Tommy X Jones, has already told me, his closest contact on the commission, that he likes things as is. He doesn't want to be promoted, at least not now." Myra had taken her navy suit jacket off, but otherwise she looked every bit the official County Commissioner that she was. Her dark hair was arranged perfectly around a face with just enough makeup to hide her wrinkles and underscore the attractiveness of her large brown eyes.

Kathlene felt underdressed, even though she was wearing exactly what she was supposed to, since she was on duty that day. Her uniform looked as good as it always did, and she'd pulled her hair back into a clip at the base of her neck, as was required.

"I'm not sure I do, either." On the other hand, this might be a perfect time to take on more responsibility like that. Despite all her self-chiding, she already missed Jock, and as far as she knew he remained in town. She'd checked around and learned that the Alpha Force contingent that had arrived on Friday was still present, as were some of the feds, who continued to collect evidence. Others had taken the alleged anarchists somewhere for preliminary incarceration and arraignments or whatever the system required.

She'd last talked to Jock yesterday. She figured he wouldn't be here much longer.

She just hoped he would call to say goodbye. At least that way she'd get some closure.

She realized how odd it was that she had accepted who and what he was and had nevertheless, despite all good sense, fallen for him. It was probably a good thing that he had backed off like this. Her interest was clearly one-sided.

Maybe he could only fall for another shifter, like that woman he had lost.

That should make it easier to forget him…shouldn't it?

Feeling sorrow welling inside her, she took another sip of coffee without looking at Myra. "Tell you what," she said. "Right now I'm against the idea, but I'll think about it. Meantime, there are surely others with more seniority than me who would make a better sheriff. Tell Tommy X my feelings about this, and I'm sure he'll help you figure it out."

"But—"

"I'll think about it, too, Myra. I promise." Her mind wrapped momentarily around her partner, Jimmy Korling, then unwrapped him immediately. Not only was he more junior within the department than she was, but he'd seemed much too accepting of Sheriff Frawley's position. Plus, he wasn't wild about having women as equals, let alone superior officers.

But there were others in the department who'd work out a lot better than he would.

She would start making a list.

"I'll talk to you later," she told Myra. "Right now, I need to head for the department. I'll be officially on duty soon."

Not for another hour, but she didn't need to tell her friend that.

What she'd do for that hour she wasn't sure, but—

No sooner had she exited the County Administration Building and walked out onto the sidewalk than a car pulled up to the curb beside her. She glanced inside.

It was Jock.

She ignored how her heart started racing, how her

mouth almost curved up into an automatic smile, and just nodded. "Hi," she said. "Are you leaving today?"

"Yes, we are." He'd stopped and opened the window. Lord, did he look handsome in his white knit shirt, with a hint of dark shadow at his cheeks and chin.

"So everything's in order. That's good."

"Nothing's final till the prosecutions finish successfully, but it looks good for now. My commanding officers will be in touch to thank you again. And I want to talk to you about that."

"No need to thank me. Stopping those miserable anarchists before they hurt anyone is all I wanted."

All she started out wanting. Now, if she was honest with herself, she knew she wanted some kind of ongoing relationship with Jock.

But that wasn't going to happen.

Even so, she felt a warm glow inside when he said, "Look, this isn't the place for us to talk. Grab some coffee with me, please?" He looked serious, and she figured he, too, just wanted to thank her—but she should probably give him the courtesy of letting him say goodbye gracefully.

"All right. Where—"

"How about your house?"

Interesting. Did he want to indulge in one last lovemaking session for the road?

Well, if so, maybe that would be the best goodbye she could get. "All right."

"Get in and I'll drive us there. No need for you to make the coffee. We'll stop for some on the way."

Their conversation in the car was all about the case. Everything was coming together well.

"And all of the other shifters who came," she said at

one point as if she was discussing a standard form of weapon that was used that night. "I assume they really helped to make all this successful. It looked that way."

"That's for sure."

They stopped at the town's only chain coffee shop and used the drive-through. She ordered a mocha, figuring she deserved the sweet chocolate considering the sourness she was about to experience. A short while later, they were at her house.

This was probably a very bad idea. On the other hand, here they were and she might as well enjoy what she could of this goodbye session, however it occurred.

She didn't wait for him to open the door before getting out of the car and striding up the front walk to her home. She opened the front door and waved for him to go in first.

And closed her eyes briefly as the tall, muscular, amazingly good-looking guy brushed by her, undoubtedly for the last time.

She showed him into her living room and sat down herself at one end of her fluffy, familiar sofa. She put her mocha down on the coffee table in front of them and waited for him to begin.

She expected thanks and congrats and all sorts of standard stuff people would say to strangers they would never see again.

And was shocked to hear him say, "Kathlene, I've got a proposition for you."

She had raised her chin expecting a blow, but now she cocked her head and stared at him. "Like what?"

"Let me preface this by saying that I've run this by some of my superiors at Alpha Force. They're all impressed by how you saw things that other people didn't, or chose not to see. How you put yourself in jeopardy of losing your job and worse by taking a stand to protect the public and never backing down."

They were impressed. What about him?

It was as if he heard her. "Of course I was sure to make that clear to them quite a bit as we were discussing what I'm about to tell you. I'm the first to admit how impressed I've been—even though you've driven me nuts at times by putting yourself in dangerous situations to make your points. They've all been good points, by the way."

At least now she knew why her putting herself in peril bothered him so much. But— "Stop buttering me up and tell me what you're up to." Now she was filled with suspicion, even though her heart felt like it would burst from his compliments.

"Sure. Here it is. Why don't you come to Ft. Lukman and join Alpha Force—as a nonshifting member, of course. You'd be ideal, as a former deputy sheriff, for training members—both shifters and not—in measures to protect themselves and others, and ensuring that justice is served. Oh, and looking for problems and speaking up when they find them."

Ft. Lukman. That was where Alpha Force was headquartered. She would see more of Jock. A lot more.

But he hadn't mentioned that. Not at all. Maybe he didn't really want to see her again. "Why are you suggesting this?" she asked. "Do you and your fellow Alpha Forcers just want to make sure I keep my mouth shut about what I know about the unit?"

"Nope. I already trust you not to announce to the world that we're a bunch of shapeshifters. That could really harm the unit, and I don't think you'd want to do that. Besides, if you did, everyone would consider you a nut case."

She laughed. "I think a lot of people already do, and

I've never even mentioned shapeshifters." But then she grew serious. "I...I don't know, Jock. I'm surprised that I'd even like to consider the offer. I just turned down an offer that might have made me sheriff here, and that's more appropriate."

"Maybe. But...well, okay, let me fill you in on my ulterior motive. The thing is, I've fallen in love with you, Kathlene. And if you might care for me at all, it'd be a good thing for you to see more of Alpha Force in action. We've a lot of shifters married to nonshifters, and those relationships work well, believe it or not."

She felt her eyes widen. "Are you asking me to marry you?"

"Not yet, but that's in my plans if things go as well as I think they will. And I know now very well how you'd handle yourself if any of our assignments wound up putting you in danger. You'd protect me."

She didn't recall rising to her feet or seeing him rise, but she was suddenly in his arms. His kiss was soft and exploratory and still caused waves of heat to pulse through her.

She soon pulled away and looked up into his eyes. "Let's discuss this later, okay? Right here. Can you stay here one more night?"

"I think so," he said softly, "but—"

"I want to give you a night to convince me." She grinned. "And, by the way, I don't think it'll be hard to do. I've fallen in love with you, too, Jock Larabey. You and the sweet wolf inside you. And—"

She couldn't finish since his mouth was on hers again.

But she had a feeling that she would soon be moving to Ft. Lukman...and a whole new, wonderful life.

* * * * *

LINDA THOMAS-SUNDSTROM

Linda Thomas-Sundstrom, author of contemporary and historical paranormal romance novels, writes for Harlequin Nocturne. She lives in the West, juggling teaching, writing, family and caring for a big stretch of land. She swears she has a resident muse who sings so loudly she virtually funds the Post-it company. Eventually Linda hopes to get to all those ideas. Visit Linda at her website, www.lindathomas-sundstrom.com, and the Nocturne Authors' website, www.nocturneauthors.com.

IMMORTAL OBSESSION
Linda Thomas-Sundstrom

To my family, those here and those gone, who always believed I had a story to tell.

Chapter 1

Death was coming in the form of a cold, hard blackness.

Christopher St. John looked for it with his eyes wide open.

He gave the woman down the block a cursory glance, drawn to the shivering gleams of silver coming off whatever she wore as she passed beneath a streetlight, sensing something else about her that he had no time to explore. Though intrigued by all that shine on a gloomy night, no unnatural darkness floated in the woman's wake, so he couldn't afford a second look.

Where was death hiding?

The air he breathed carried an odor of old boots and had the slimy feel of an oxygenated oil slick, as if something nasty had left an indelible imprint. Alerted by that, St. John turned his head and caught sight of an ooze of movement so subtle, human eyes would have missed it.

He watched the shadow pass into the alley on his left. Tuning in, he fired up his senses to determine that shadow's status and to name and categorize the anomaly, which was just another thing that shouldn't exist, but did, hanging on to darkness as if it needed, ate, breathed, required the worst part of a day. Midnight.

"Shade," St. John said, disgusted.

Shades were evil suckers. Unable to possess actual physical form, they couldn't be touched or destroyed by regular physical means. It took cunning, guts and a whole lot of properly functioning know-how to take down something so substantially unsubstantial. And like flies on a fetid carcass, the presence of this Shade meant some poor fool had died in that alley, probably minutes ago.

St. John's fangs dropped, pressing threateningly against his tongue. He worked his jaw to relax himself. It was imperative that Shades and creatures like them were kept away from London's human population, and that they remained underground. He'd have to follow this one and do his bit to mop up the danger before anyone found out.

Taking a step toward the alley, he paused, his attention disturbed by a sudden prickle at the base of his neck. Cutting his eyes to the left, he saw another shadow hugging the building beside the alley. Then he saw a third.

His fangs began to sharpen automatically, chiseling into lethal points as if they recognized danger all on their own and were getting ready to face it. In this case, the fangs were harbingers of doom. Three Shades in the area meant three dead bodies, since Shades were entities uninterested in sharing their spoils. Three dead bodies in a row suggested the presence of vampires. Probably more than one. These Shades had likely been attracted to leftovers.

Death tonight had manifested in the form of a bloodsuckers' blood fest, a vile breach of etiquette in London's trendy West End. Most vampires here, unless newly made, knew better than to trespass on ground owned by their older immortal cousins. The careless vamps heralding the Shades were either really stupid, had been freshly bitten, or they had a death-after-death wish. Same difference in terms of the results.

"Too damn close to mortals to be excused."

St. John again glanced down the street, to where he had seen the shapely woman in silver walking alone. He looked at the row of lights announcing the first of the West End's string of nightclubs, thinking as he always had that these clubs and the people they attracted had become too tempting for the city's extended list of subterranean inhabitants.

The lights were, in essence, like big neon arrows pointing the way to an all-night buffet. But this particular grouping of night creatures currently flouting the rules were truly on the wrong path if they assumed they'd get away with leaving corpses in alleyways so near an immortal's domain. Especially his. Nobody liked gore on their front steps.

Closing his eyes briefly, St. John again felt death's dark touch, a blackness he knew intimately. In a distant part of his subconscious, he pinpointed the nearness of the other uninvited creatures in the area. Vampires, yes. Rogues, giving off signals of rage and insatiable hunger, things he had long ago mastered, though his fangs were empathetically aching.

Something else nagged at his attention besides the

five young vampires emerging from the far end of the alley sporting haughty expressions and exhibiting no evidence of their recent kills. Some other warning had caught hold of him, mixed up in the brief gleam of a woman's silvery light.

Shaking that warning off, St. John watched the tight group of young vampires, reminiscent of a group of wild animals on the prowl, boldly cross the street, heading for the biggest club on the block. The same one the woman in silver stardust had entered.

Striding past the queue of waiting guests, the rogues looked the club's controller up and down until that man stepped aside, but not before he'd sent St. John a silent signal of alarm that rippled across St. John's skin in the form of a really good chill.

St. John nodded his head to the man in reply, wondering if perhaps these ignorant fanged parasites had also seen that dazzling young woman and had been attracted. Scavengers, like crows, loved anything that glowed.

Or maybe they were just trolling for dessert.

A wave of apprehension rolled across his scalp. Keeping tabs on the ever-increasing hordes of fledgling vampires would have been a full-time job for a small army. Keeping them out of his own territory was a personal necessity.

Drawing his hands out of his pockets, St. John pressed his lips over his pulsing, aggression-seeking incisors.

"Wrong road, wrong night, boys," he said aloud, adding in honor of whatever Shades were lurking nearby, "I'll be back for you."

Thinking of what a bunch of unrepentant, openly visible monsters might do to an unsuspecting woman like the one in the intriguing silver getup they were no doubt salivating for, and knowing that *mercy* wasn't a viable word in bloodsucker vocabulary, St. John set his shoulders, squinted at the club's lights and started off in that direction.

He wasn't called the *Protector* for nothing. And that woman, still very much on his mind after only a glimpse, didn't have any idea of the extent of the trouble about to strike.

Chapter 2

It wasn't the first time Madison Chase had downed one too many drinks lately, and by the look of things, it wasn't going to be her last.

She had accepted a martini from the guy dressed in head-to-toe leather at the bar and a shot of something foul from the stiff in the business suit who smelled faintly of clove cigarettes. Some people thought drinking was sexy. She wasn't one of them.

She had tossed those drinks back like they were water and should have been pain-free by now, but the never-ending ache inside her still hurt like hell, not in the slightest bit blurred by alcohol.

Tonight was no different from all the rest of the past three days: roaming around, tempting fate by taking too many chances. Clearly, she was headed for a breakdown if she kept this up. All the signs were present. She just couldn't seem to back off from the wave of momentum sweeping her up.

She might be placing herself in jeopardy by wandering alone in an unfamiliar city, in another country, at night, but an uncanny, persistent idea suggested that a solo recon might turn up information about what had happened to those missing college girls from the States— the reason for ten American television crews, including her own, taking up residence.

An even more important objective, and the reason for this club-hopping, was the search for her brother, who'd been MIA for a full three weeks.

Hopefully, if her stars were in alignment, she'd find Stewart, her fraternal twin. She just needed to do some of her sleuthing after-hours and alone, since the camera crews usually following her around tended to scare people off.

Plus, there was no plausible way to explain to the network guys that she was almost supernaturally aware of her brother's presence in this part of London because the uniqueness of the bond between twins defied explanation.

Stewart Chase, her womb-mate, and younger than herself by only one minute, felt close enough to reach out and touch. His life force seemed to float in the air, whispering things just out of hearing range.

Madison searched the faces closest to her, finding nothing familiar. Yet she knew she'd be the one to find her brother, if anyone could. Respected Florida attorneys like her twin didn't just disappear when sent by their firms to pursue the legal details of a headlining missing girls' case. Neither did most attorneys believe in the paranormal, she'd be willing to bet.

"But you do," she said to Stewart, wherever he was.

The discovery that he had hidden certain aspects of his life from her had been a shock. More surprising still was the magnitude of the secretive research her brother had gathered on the existence of monsters. Stewart thought that monsters had taken over jolly old England's capital, as well as other cities like it, in the manner of a spreading plague.

Monsters. The kind with fangs.

Vampires, for God's sake.

After cracking the password on his laptop and sifting through Stewart's files, she had learned that her brother had been obsessed with the undead for a while. So, was she to conclude that someone that smart and savvy had become mentally unstable in the past year or two, hiding a loose mental screw from her and everyone else? Although gray, aged London was a place where any gothic idea might seem possible, vampires would be the underworld's dirtiest little secret society.

Stewart had listed this nightclub in his notes.

"Absurd. Disgusting. To hell with you, baby brother, for bringing this up and for vanishing without a trace," Madison muttered, worried her instincts were wrong this time about sensing him near her. Worried also that in sharing genes with Stewart, and thinking about vampires, her own mental screws might someday loosen.

She was here on company time. Her ticket to ferreting out why so many people had gone missing in London in the past month had been presented to her in the form of a golden opportunity not to be missed. Accepting the network's assignment to follow the story of four missing Yale grads, now officially being dubbed in the media as the *Yale Four,* had been a timely move.

And though the streets outside of this club were creepy at night, London's hotspot of the moment, called *Space,* was teeming with people.

Conscious of eyes turned her way, Madison again searched the area around her. The guy in the business suit raised his glass. Shaking her head, she said beneath her breath, "Not going to happen. Not with you, buddy."

She turned her attention to the dance floor. If her brother's research had any merit, this was one of the most dangerous clubs in London for humans, and run by a vampire community whose roots ran deep.

That was nuts, of course. Most of the people here seemed normal enough, and were having a good time. Still, the only way she could maintain any hope of getting her brother back was to explore all scenarios that might explain his disappearance, and those included the most fantastical ones.

So, if she were to *try* to believe her brother...

"What the hell is a vampire supposed to look like, anyway? Other than exposed fangs, how would anyone tell them apart from anyone else?" she muttered.

Stewart's notes said that some vampires blended fairly well with the human population. Then again, rumors about vampires in nightclubs could just as easily be a well-planned advertising campaign for thrill seekers to get off on, and completely make-believe.

This was her third club, in as many nights, looking for Stewart and his monsters. The number three was supposed to be charmed—some kind of supernaturally charged digit. With that in mind, Madison continued to scrutinize the faces around her, picking out likely candidates for fangdom in the crowd. Males seemingly too sober, too intense and darkly expressionless as they lurked in the shadows.

There were a few.

However, slightly suspicious males were also the usual fare for dance clubs, so how in hell could Stewart have been sure of what was what? How could she?

Monsters should be required to wear bells.

And okay, now that she had stooped to considering monsters, Madison wondered how someone with a loose mental screw could tighten it.

Her gaze dropped to the table beside her. Another drink would make the tally what? Three? Four? One awful-tasting alcoholic beverage for every monster she thought she perceived around her. Just to take the edge off the game. For more fighting spirit, in case there was any way Stewart had been right, and there actually were vampires everywhere.

"Another drink is definitely the way to go," she said to herself.

Grabbing a glass off the table, Madison sipped the contents, realizing she was walking close enough to the edge of an abyss to see the steep drop. Why? Because it was impossible to delete from her mind the part of Stewart's research proposing that death didn't have to be the end of existence.

And if anything bad had happened to her brother because of his ridiculous beliefs, some part of her actually hoped he was right. Without Stewart, she felt like only half of a whole. At the moment, a tired, ornery half.

The decibel of the music raining down from overhead speakers drowned out her thoughts. With the burn of alcohol in her throat, Madison closed her eyes and picked up the rhythm of the beat. Moving her head and her hips, she began to wind her way through the people on the dance floor, heading for the center of the room, where something other than fear, sadness and regret would hopefully, for a time, give her some peace.

Regretfully, that peace remained as elusive as ever. Someone still watched her. She picked up on this, she assumed, with the special sense of connection to others that some twins possessed. Whoever this particular watcher was had a gaze like a laser beam that made her feel as if she were naked.

She glanced up at the balcony and found the culprit. Her breath caught. Behind the ornate railing stood one of the most beautiful men she had ever seen. Every working woman's version of a wet dream.

Tall and broad-shouldered, the wickedly handsome observer leaned against a pillar with a self-assured, languid pose. Immaculately dressed in black, a visually stunning contrast of fair hair surrounded his sculpted, angular, aristocratic face.

Having noted his interest, Madison figured that any other woman would have run right up to that balcony and handed him her hotel key, desiring his touch and to hear his haughty British accent. Happy to have been singled out by such a creature, they'd have wished for a kiss, a condom and the luck of being chosen as his one-night stand.

Any *other* woman.

She didn't have time for that sort of nonsense, or for anything other than this one dance. It was after midnight, and she'd be on camera in the morning. Plus, finding this guy observing her so intently, her inner warnings about him automatically upgraded to full alert.

He was staring at her rudely. Something in his expression made her imagine he possessed the ability to read her mind, and that what he found there was amusing.

Blinking slowly to break contact and announce to him that she had no intention of accepting his unspoken invitation, Madison ignored the rise in her pulse that he was causing. No one on the planet was that good-looking. She should know; she had interviewed a lot of movie stars up close.

What would Stewart have said about him?

Maybe this guy's beauty was unearthly because he actually was unearthly?

Though that seemed ridiculous, she took Stewart's reasoning one step further.

Maybe one of her brother's secretive research subjects had just crystallized, and the awe-inspiring male exterior encapsulated something not so fine at its core. Hidden inside that full, slightly insolent mouth of his, could be a pair of long, pointed teeth.

Thanks, brother.

Madison now regretted the drinks, and vowed to never touch another one. Defiantly, she whispered to the man on the balcony, "If there are such things as vampires, though, there'd be no doubt about you."

Disturbed that her brother's extraordinary inner world had folded into her own, she gave herself over to the dance, keeping an attentive eye on the other men who were ogling her as if she were an appetizing after-dinner snack.

St. John settled his shoulder against a pillar and stared down from the balcony, his gaze riveted to one particular woman on the dance floor. He had found the woman in silver. When a sensation long dormant in his chest stirred, he hardly recognized it as a bead of honest interest.

Her hair was bloodred. A brilliant, fiery riot of untamed curls that glowed like bonfire flames in the dimness. Hair like that was the colorful embodiment of passion, intelligence and sex. Moist with sweat, several silky strands clung to her pale neck like crimson streams leaking from a puncture wound as she danced, dead center in the room and in the middle of the fifty other gyrating bodies, on the gritty stainless-steel floor.

St. John had never seen anything like her, or the way she moved. She waved bare, slender arms over her head sinuously, with her eyes closed, as if caught up in a trance. Her hips swayed in time to the heavy bass beat of music in a fluid, seductive display.

As she wove intricate patterns with her body in the tight area she'd carved out for herself, heat rose from her in visible waves. All that heat and flame in one sleek outline made it easy for him to assume he wasn't the only male in this club whose gaze was fastened on the sultry redhead. Certainly not the only one with fangs.

No being with functioning genitals, either dead or alive, could have failed to be drawn in by Madison Chase's enticing performance. This close, he would have recognized the American newscaster anywhere.

His fangs remained lengthened and ready for action, which meant that the rogue vampires were here, and nearby. A subtle scent of well-turned soil pervaded the area below, underscoring the rising drifts of sweat and expensive perfume.

The five bloodsuckers he'd seen on the street had been lured from the anonymity of the crowd and onto the outskirts of that dance floor. He sensed them as cold spots in the overheated room. They were bits of darkness broken off from the night outside, misplaced black holes with no perceivable pulse of their own. Deviations among the world of the living, and nothing at all like him, though their eyes and instincts were also trained on the redhead they had followed here.

Bloodsucker presence in this club was unacceptable. Problem was, he was finding it difficult to concentrate on that situation. His body had already started pulsing in time with Madison Chase's.

Rather than searching out the specifics of the creatures he had tracked here, he continued to stare down at her. The sexy femme's solo performance was an added bit of trouble. The fact that rogues had also zeroed in on the lithe dancer leaned toward a notable multiplication of the problem.

That nagging something he'd sensed in the back of his mind while outside, on the street, had reappeared in the form of a woman. He wasn't sure why her presence affected him, beyond the obvious fact that Madison Chase was nothing short of magnetic.

His reaction to her was visceral and soul-stirring. But he had seen Chase on broadcasts and heard her on the radio, and knew why she had come to London, along with all the other television crews from around the globe.

Madison Chase, famous for her determined attitude of withholding nothing newsworthy from the public, could turn out to be a royal pain in the backside if she persisted in nosing around where she didn't belong. It would be even worse if she were here to track vampires and their body counts, taking up where her brother had left off.

Damn, though, if she wasn't a tantalizing half-naked problem, and keen to his well-honed senses.

The parts of her that weren't bare were skimpily covered in a mesh concoction of silver sequins and spandex that was anything but modest. Calves, knees and most of her shapely thighs were exposed. She wore impossibly high-heeled shoes that sparkled and made her long legs seem endless.

He supposed nice girls might be allowed in public underdressed like that in the States, in the current decadent decade, though for this particular woman to call so much attention to herself here was an act approaching suicide. The world wasn't as safe as it once had been.

Tonight, because of her sumptuous looks and moves, Madison's appearance was a health hazard. Her way-too-personal, provocative dance was raising not only the room's temperature, but some of the room's occupants' hormone levels, taking those things precariously close to the critical zone.

She was playing Russian roulette with her life.

"The gun's chamber might be empty this round, but it's only a matter of time," St. John said to her from his observation perch. "Surely you can hear the fangs gnashing?"

She looked up right at that moment, as if she'd heard him. Her eyes widened. When her lips moved, St. John knew he had been right about the trouble. He'd heard what she said.

If there are such things as vampires, there'd be no doubt about you.

"Such a pity," he said, because it wasn't his business to warn Madison Chase about anything. Nor was it his job to rescue her from herself or anyone else. She wasn't supposed to be on his radar at the moment. There was only room for one Chase twin at a time.

All he had to do was turn his back, lure the rogues outside and take care of them. If he didn't do this soon, it looked as if the mindless monsters might make a move on Madison right here. They were stalking her in public, in one of London's busiest, most successful clubs owned by a consortium of ancient immortals—beings who wouldn't condone misbehavior of any kind. Though the Ancients were themselves old vampires, they hated the fanged fledglings as much as mortals would, if mortals truly believed vampires existed.

"Do you believe it, I wonder?" he said to the feisty dancer stirring things up, and who had the potential to become a thorn in every vampire's hide if she were a believer like the brother who looked almost exactly like her, minus the good parts.

"I guess you haven't been paying enough attention to the roadwork your brother laid about the danger," he said to her conversationally, as if they were side by side.

Actually, she probably had no idea how far and how deep the creatures she'd called vampires had long ago dipped their fangs into London society. Likely she hadn't a clue that immortals owned more land in England and had stockpiled more cash in this country than the Queen.

It also had been made abundantly clear, by her reputation as an aggressive television personality and by her visit here tonight, alone, that Madison Chase might be as tenacious as a vine in digging out newsworthy scoops.

No doubt she was here to find her brother.

"Ah, but you are so interesting. So tempting," he said. "It would be a shame to let the monsters have you. Not to mention how quickly your disappearance would become an international incident. I suppose, in that case, I'll have to intervene."

Descending to the dance floor by way of the stairs, instead of taking a graceful, telling leap down, St. John added, "All that glorious, disturbing heat…" as like a wave of barely disturbed air, he edged himself through the crowd.

Chapter 3

St. John came up behind Madison Chase on the dance floor, eyeing two of the vampires, who quickly turned away from the sternness of his gaze. He spoke to her in a husky tone that he willed her to hear above the music.

"You're alone?"

"Not anymore," she replied over her shoulder. "Though you might want to choose a better opening line."

St. John hadn't been fully prepared for the deepness of her voice, or that it might rival her sultry exterior. As the surprise washed over him, he grinned.

"Also, there's a rule about having to dance while on a dance floor," she said, swiveling side to side so that her hips lightly brushed against his thighs.

His reaction to the unexpected touch came in the form of a jolt of pleasure that streaked through his body. Her life, her energy, and all that fire in such a fragile body, were heady draws that for a fleeting moment made him remember what it was like to be a man, aroused.

He quickly compartmentalized the sensation.

"It's crowded here. Would you like something to drink?" he asked, hoping he'd get her to stop this indiscriminate sexual display and back her temporarily into a safer corner, while at the same time hoping she'd go on dancing. She was so very good at what she was doing.

"No, thanks," she replied. "I never drink while I'm working."

Working? Yes, she was working it hard. He'd attest to that. And she had lied about not drinking. The sugary fragrance of an alcoholic beverage emanated from between her lush, parted lips.

This woman, he decided with mixed feelings, was sex on legs. Without thinking, he reached out to touch her wrist with a quick stroke of his fingers, desiring to touch something so fine, but backed off before doing so, satisfied that she really was as hot as she looked. Heat to someone like him was the ultimate turn-on, and so very dangerous for the mortal radiating this much of it.

Out of the corner of his eye, he watched the two disgruntled, freshly christened vampires circle the floor, checking him out. He sent them a second silent warning.

"You're still not dancing," Madison said, looking at him with slightly dilated, incredibly lovely blue eyes.

Aware of the fact that he was beginning to stand out by standing still, St. John matched his rhythm to hers. As he started to move, he searched her, head to toe.

Madison was indeed genetically gifted. She had a fine-featured, delicate face, with flawless skin. Small nose. High cheekbones. Arched brows. The damp red curls clinging to her cheeks were darker than the rest of her hair and a stark contrast to her skin's paleness. Her mouth was glossy with a scarlet lipstick so dark, it had a blue cast under the lights. Much like dried blood.

Only the force of his willpower kept him from grabbing her. The urge to lay his lips on hers, to taste that red shine and run his fangs over her pretty, pale cheek, was close to overwhelming, and an affront to his monk-like existence.

He couldn't recall the last time he had been so taken with a woman's appearance that he'd allow one to lead the direction of a meeting. And if he was so affected, the young monsters nearby had to be in a state approaching frenzy.

He had to get her out of there for her own good, but in spite of the danger edging closer, he wished for more time with her.

"Perhaps you don't like meeting new people," he suggested when she tossed her head, raised her taut, toned arms and continued to sway in time to the beat.

"I like men," she said, "if that's what you're asking."

When viewed in silhouette, her body was slender to the point of sleekness. Her shoulders sloped toward fragile arms and small, firm breasts. No hint of a bra covered those breasts beneath the mesh dress, which led him to focus longer than he should have on a bit of pale pink nipple. Hell, he actually was aroused. His aching fangs weren't the only parts stimulated by the woman.

The reactions to this sensational dancer had hit surprisingly hard, as if he had dived back in time to when those kinds of physical reactions mattered. He nearly smiled again, though keeping his fangs hidden was imperative. Some people might consider him a monster, but he liked to think of himself as a gentleman, when all was said and done.

"You like men, just not this one?" he persisted. "You might prefer a darker complexion or a smaller frame. Maybe you only like Americans."

She shook her head, sending her red curls flying. "You're too good-looking. Hurtful to the eyes. I don't need more pain in my life."

St. John accepted the unusual compliment with another burst of unfamiliar pleasure. Nevertheless, the fact remained that Madison was more naive than her brother had been if she didn't understand how easily he could make her do whatever he wanted with one whisper in her ear. No self-respecting centuries-old immortal hadn't mastered such a basic trick, and he'd had more opportunity than most to use them.

"Is that a compliment and a rebuff, all in one?" he asked. "Also, it's a strange comment, since I believe you haven't really looked at me yet."

"The truth is," she said, stopping so suddenly, she bumped into the person next to her, "I saw you on the balcony. You're hard to miss. Besides, you're not really affected by my comment anyway, are you, since you're not actually a man at all?"

St. John's eyebrows went up out of sheer curiosity. She had pegged him as a vampire, though she wasn't acting as if she truly believed it—which meant he had to consider the possibility that she wasn't serious, and merely engaging in an unusual bit of titillating fantasy foreplay.

He had heard about vampire fans and groupies of popular horror fiction pretending to be bloodsuckers, playing with the concept without confronting the downside.

However, this was Stewart Chase's sister, so he had to take care.

"Not a man. Damn. That's probably not good," he said, eyeing her carefully, trying to decipher what she might be up to.

"Not good for the unsuspecting people here," she agreed, exhibiting an outward calm, though he sensed her heartbeat had begun to rev inside her chest, and the pink buds of her nipples had hardened. Her beautifully bare, formerly fluid shoulders became tense and riddled with chills. Long lashes veiled her eyes.

"If not a man, what do you suppose I am?" he asked, his concentration dropping to the dazzling net of sparkling silver mesh encircling her frame like a garment composed of pure, unobstructed moonlight.

"Don't you know?" she countered with a lilt of cynicism far too worldly for one so young. "Don't you know what you are?"

"For all I know, this could be some kind of test."

"Vampire. You're a vampire," she said. The nonchalant way she stated this set his fangs on edge. The comment also increased his interest. Possibly the Chase twins had done their research together, after all.

"You believe in vampires?" he asked.

She shrugged.

"If you believe I'm one, why aren't you running?"

"You're bigger than the other monsters here and have twice the presence. You outclass them by miles, so I'm guessing you're a lot older, have more experience, and that if I stay here, on the floor, doing what I came here to do, you won't hurt me. At least not in public."

Unable to help himself, St. John let out a soft bark of laughter. Madison's idea of foreplay was exotic and chancy. For him, sexy, brazen and intelligent were characteristics adding up to a deadly irresistible mix.

Yet she had also proved herself to be somewhat enlightened about his breed, and this was cause for concern. And she was scared. The metallic tang of fear seeped from her pores, adding texture to her woodsy perfume and telegraphing to him that there was a fair chance she might actually believe what she was saying.

"You said *work*. Do tell me what it is that you came here for, exactly, given that dancing isn't the only objective," he said.

"One of my goals was to find you," she replied with a further outward calm containment of nerves that St. John supposed could have earned her an award.

"Find me, personally?" he said. "You know who I am?"

She nodded. "And what you can do."

St. John sobered slightly. "Should I be flattered?"

"Are vampires vain enough to accept truth as flattery?"

Now she had even more of his attention, if that was possible. "Of course," he replied. "Some of us, anyway. It's so rare that we deal directly with mortals who aren't sprinting in the opposite direction, you see. So, if you came here to find me, and saw me watching you, then your dancing might have been to lure me to the floor? To you?"

"It worked."

He grinned, conceding the point. Her intention had, in fact, been accomplished to perfection. He had felt in his bones that she'd been dancing for him, and had been drawn to her light and heat like the proverbial moth to a flickering flame. This was an interesting deviation of his character, and one to be considered carefully.

"Now that I'm here, do you want to tell me why you were looking for me?" he asked.

"I've merely been seeking truth in the rumors."

"There are rumors about me?"

"Now who is being naive?" Her gaze rose a few inches, though she didn't make eye contact. She had not resumed her dancing.

"Actually, I was thinking the word *naive* applied to you." St. John alluded to her outfit with a pointed finger. "I came down here to tell you so, and to warn you to watch out for yourself, though not quite so directly. I'd hoped to use some tact."

"Yes, well where I come from, directness is not a flaw. I know what I'm doing."

"I seriously doubt that, Miss Chase, or you wouldn't still be here talking to me."

When she used lean fingers to press a strand of hair back from her face, St. John knew he had surprised her with his own frankness and the use of her name. Her heart rate exploded, one loud boom after another visibly pounding against the bare skin of her long, lovely neck.

His gaze hesitated on that stretch of creamy skin longer than was prudent before realizing that two of the vampires in the periphery had also sensed the rise in Madison's pulse. Out of the corner of his eye, he saw them take several steps onto the crowded floor.

"You know who I am, then?" she asked.

"We Brits aren't as backward as you might think. Some of us even have television sets."

"What else do you know about me?" Her tone was husky now.

"I believe rumors on this end have you as the bane of anyone's existence who tries to get in your way. Is that a fair assessment?"

He expected her to dash for the exit now that personal

truths were being revealed. Instead, she replied with equal candor, "It's a good enough description, I guess."

"Since you're here alone, and looking for vampires, you know pathetically less about us than you give yourself credit for," he said.

"*Us,* as in Brits, pick-up artists or vampires?" she countered.

Right after, and as though something had disturbed her, Madison's attention shifted to one of the ravenous rogues. "This has been fun," she said. "But the question in need of an answer is if you'll help me, now that we've been introduced?"

"Help you how?"

"I think there are others here who are looking at me strangely." Her expression remained unreadable, with her blue eyes again cloaked by lowered lashes. "Will anyone try to harm me right here?"

Had she somehow sensed the other vampires? Nailed that closest rogue as one of them? She had looked directly at the fledgling.

"Not here," he said, checking that fledgling out. "No ruffians will harm you here."

"Why won't they?" she asked with obvious distaste.

"For several reasons, not the least of which is that bloodstains may be difficult to remove from the floor.

She didn't respond to his remark. Didn't smile. Her expression remained unreadable, even for a master like himself, which made him wonder what she might be thinking.

Her heart gave her away, in the end. It beat dramatically, each strike lifting the skin beneath her right ear.

She truly was scared.

Was all that thumping in honor of the presence of

the others she thought might wish her harm, though, or due to his nearness to her? St. John couldn't quite get a handle on that, or which Madison Chase was the real one… The dancer, with her loose, inviting body, or the intruding, borderline-aggressive, slightly frightened and very nosey media insider, who might or might not have a nose for vampires?

He decided that the unique mixture of all those ingredients was what had fascinated him, and also what made him unexpectedly excited by their continued closeness to each other.

"These ruffians you mentioned are also vampires?" she asked, and followed that question rapidly with another. "If that's true, or even if it isn't, will you see that I get out of here, or at least as far as the door?"

The way she tilted her head exposed another dewy length of ivory skin. Her tension made the enticing lacy network of lilac veins in her neck stand out like a road map to the source of every vampire's inherent need. And though he wasn't a vampire, *per se,* he had been created by drinking of the blood of his Makers, and was reminded of this now by a treasonous thud in his chest.

"Then again," she added, "if I'm to be the bane of anyone's existence, including yours, why would you help me at all?"

Since she preferred directness, and was still thinking in terms of vampires, St. John answered in kind. "Isn't it possible, since vampires were once like you, they're not all heathens? If you can't believe this, I wonder about your sources, Miss Chase."

The spine that had so mesmerizingly taunted him just moments ago snapped straight. The rigidity made the woman beside him seem even younger, and more vulnerable.

Had she taken him seriously? She who had brought up this vampire game?

Her sudden show of frailty sent a reactionary shock of emotion, with the force of a fist, slamming against St. John's rib cage, kicking his nerves into overdrive. He didn't want to hurt her; didn't want anyone else to hurt her. Madison Chase was like a rare, glittering jewel, no matter how her mind worked.

"You wanted to find monsters, and that's it?" He spoke to cover his tremendous need to touch her.

"Yes," she replied. "Maybe."

"Now you'll go? Simple as that?"

"If I can."

"If you were hunting vampires, expecting to find some here, I take it you planned for an escape route?" he said.

"Aren't you that escape route? My free pass out of here?"

"Why would you assume so?"

She glanced up. "Don't they call special beings like you Protectors?"

That stunning announcement actually stopped his breathing for a while before St. John reminded himself to take in a lungful of stale, sweaty air. He withheld a blasphemous oath.

It was possible for Madison to know superficial things about his community, since her brother had been interested, but it was damn inconvenient for her to know about his position within it.

Protector.

No one knew of this. This precocious woman's brother certainly hadn't known it when he'd come nosing around.

Yet reason told him that if Madison hadn't been kidding, and that if she knew what kind of beings ran this club, as well as about Protectors, she had to have an informant. One too close to the fold.

The question, though, was still whether she had really pegged him as a vampire? Beyond that, did she actually know that by asking a Protector for help, he was bound to oblige?

The game had changed. Gaining knowledge about what Madison Chase knew about his society was crucial, as was the importance of finding who her informant was. She almost certainly hadn't seen her brother, or she would have been running for the airport to get as far away as possible. If she'd truly been looking for vampires, would she have come to the club alone?

He wasn't sure, couldn't read her. For the sake of the immortal community, as well as his own well-disguised presence in it, though, he was driven to find the answers.

The room seemed to darken somewhat. He had always loathed the dark when there were so many genuine surprises hidden in it.

"You are far from your home and out of your league on this one," he warned, noting that Madison, with good reason, seemed more and more uncomfortable, and was trying hard not to show it. Her arms were taut with long lines of anxious, wiry sinew. Her pretty jaw had set.

He went on. "There will be trouble if you roam the city alone, and probe into issues that don't really concern you. It's best that you forget about this club and the word *vampire* before some real blood hits the fan. There are all sorts of monsters, you know."

Although her lips parted and he expected a comeback, she didn't offer one. The word *blood* had an effect on her. They had wasted far too much time. He had to get her to move. The only way to make her believe the seriousness of her predicament, as well as seek those answers he needed, would be to get her to safety with a minimal amount of damage to anyone here. Two of the rogues, partway onto the dance floor, were losing patience, being taken over by a bloodlust too ferocious for anyone's good. Their gaunt faces were feral in the fall-out of the club's neon lights.

"If the word you use for bodyguard is *Protector*," he said over her silence, "I can help. But if you persist in taunting ruffians of any species, they might hunt you down for sport."

In fact, they already were. And Madison would be like Easter candy to creatures so much better than television journalists at going after their prey.

"To the door, then," she said, bringing him back to those wide blue eyes that nearly met his. "Please escort me there."

"Well, since you asked so nicely..."

Of course, he knew it would be easy to get her to the door, being who and what he was, and also that it was too late for her to take ten steps beyond the exit by herself. Madison, in all her silver-sequined glory, had attracted the attention of too many creatures tonight. The place virtually hummed with ill intent.

Three of the five miscreants had already cleared out, though the dark, gaping hole by the exit suggested they were out there, eagerly awaiting her departure. Their anticipation, excitement and tangible bloodlust rolled across St. John's skin as if it were his own.

When his fangs raked his lower lip, he imagined what using fangs on the woman beside him would be like for those others. They might take their time biting into her, using quick flicks of their teeth to tear apart her flawless flesh. Would they offer a tender kiss to her throat before the final bite, though, or whisper a caress?

Probably not, since those things were issues of control that had to be learned over long spans of time, and most vampires didn't make it past their first year. Although fledglings had Makers, they lacked tutors, as well as self-restraint.

He told himself to stop imagining kisses and caresses and fangs and throats. All of those things were too erotic with his libido this fired up. Care had to be taken not to maintain his closeness to Madison for too long. An immortal's idea of foreplay was different from the norm.

Damn those rogue vampires. Besides needing information from Madison that necessitated his continued contact with her, he wasn't ready to have her removed from the world—and not for any altruistic reasons. He wanted to bask in her heat awhile longer. Part of him longed to feel the remembered humanness and anticipation of indulging in an all-encompassing man-woman attraction. Since mortals and immortals didn't mix or play well together, he'd had no desire before this to explore those things.

Madison Chase was different.

And he was a sucker for redheads.

"Would you trust me with my help beyond that doorway?" he asked, observing the daring sideways movement of the two remaining rogues. He knew he'd be unable to take care of them here, with so many mortals around.

"You have got to be kidding." She sucked in her cheeks. Her chest rose and fell with each staggered breath, so that her breasts were close enough to touch. Only inches away.

"I've never been more serious," St. John said as his heart fell in sync with hers, virtually stealing her rhythm and adapting it as his own—a trick that happened with all vampires and their superior immortal counterparts when confronting a victim or an enemy. They tuned in, sensing every move, beat and thought.

The bloodsuckers closing in on Madison would know how frightened she had become and would be anticipating her departure with their fangs gnashing.

Following his gaze, she glanced to the exit. "Do you know something I don't?"

"The answer to that would take time that you don't have, I'm afraid."

She threw a second glance to the doorway, visibly shaking now. Her little silver sequins made tinkling sounds that only he could hear.

All that femme-fatale bravado on the dance floor had indeed been a show, St. John realized. Her expression had changed. The scent of her fear was stronger.

Maybe the dancing act had been for him, or merely to satisfy her own private needs, but getting Madison away from Space would not only save her life, but possibly also the lives of countless others in and out of the club. Newly turned blood drinkers were mean, fast and exceptionally hungry. When thwarted, *bloodbath* described the results perfectly. These rogues were barely hanging on.

When he held out his hand to her, Madison winced. Nevertheless, it was necessary for him to touch her. His scent would disguise hers, up to a point, until they were out of sight.

"There's a back way out," he confided.

"So, you really are going to be my Protector?" Her voice wavered.

He turned his palm up insistently. "In this case, you just might be right."

She wasn't going to touch him, no matter what, even after soliciting his help. Her anxiousness tangibly thrummed in the air, part real and part false, the falseness signaling to him that she wasn't completely dissatisfied with his offer.

Time was pressing. St. John took her hand, thinking to speed things up. Immediately, with the first feel of her fingers in his, he became immersed in an inferno-like flood of heat, shockingly molten and similar to getting too close to the sun. The onslaught of sensation hit so powerfully, so unexpectedly, he briefly closed his eyes.

It had been years since he'd touched a mortal for any reason, and centuries since he'd been one of them, yet in that instant, as their hands met and she looked into his eyes with what he knew was the fearful fire of both intrigue and disgust, St. John sensed that there was much more of this story to come. In order for him to find out about that story, he'd see to it that Madison Chase stayed out of the hands of London's monsters and stayed alive.

His job description of Protector, meant originally not for guarding people, but the special blood in his veins, had been changing lately, and had just morphed again to include Madison.

She might hate interruptions in her agenda and fear forward strangers, but the sparks crackling between them said it all. Underneath her fear, she reached out to him. She wanted to know more about him, and was drawn to him. Whether she actually believed him to be a vampire, or not, would remain to be seen.

As for himself…for whatever reason, he had made an instantaneous connection to her from afar, outside, on that street, in a way that defied description.

He was equally aware of fact that the Ancients, called the *Hundred* because they had all lived past that milestone in time, would get wind of this small indiscretion—his willingness to help a human, and in particular this one, tonight—while allowing rogues to get away with murder on the streets. They would know about this breach of protocol before he left the building.

Every action had risks.

This one might be worth it.

Tugging Madison to him before she had time to register his move, St. John gathered her body to his. He ran his hands over every glorious angle she possessed, exploring her with his eyes and senses wide open, looking for the secret to this unusual attraction.

The Ancients present who were observing this might assume he merely desired the kind of steamy sexual encounter a mortal like this one could provide. Taking a woman or man to bed wasn't completely forbidden by this fanged community. Biting them for anything other than pleasure was.

He laid the flat of his palm against the smooth bareness of her back in an intimate touch that moved him way down deep in memory and made Madison shut her eyes.

Daring to slide his fingers downward, beneath the loose silver fabric and over each bone of her naked vertebrae, one at a time, toward the curve of her buttocks, he heard her sharp intake of breath.

"You bastard. What the hell are you doing?"

She had meant to say *monster.* He heard this as if she had actually shouted the word.

He didn't stop touching her, feeling her, caressing her. It was imperative his flesh touched hers, skin to skin, and equally as important for him to scare her out of her crazy solo reverie.

With a gentle lightness, his hands retraced their way over every inch of her anatomy, floating briefly over off-limits sensitive spots in what would seem to her a ghastly transgression. He did this, not because he wanted to distress her further or pleasure himself at her expense, but because it really was necessary on so many levels.

"I have to make them believe you're mine," he told her, leaving her most vulnerable spot for last. Nothing could be left out of this scent transfer. Not one part of her.

With his knee between her legs, as if they were merely engaging in a slow dance of lovers, and with his mouth next to her ear, he lightly stroked the V between her thighs that was covered by damp, lacy lingerie. Touching her there seemed to alarm her. Hell, it shook him up more than he had anticipated.

In a flash as ephemeral as a dream, he imagined easing that lace aside and slipping another part of himself in. Amid the crowded frenzy of the dance floor, if he held Madison tightly enough, close enough, possibly no one would notice the rise of her dress, and how easy it would be for him to claim that hottest and holiest of spots between her slender, silky thighs.

What then, Red?

She gasped with a sound that suggested she might want the same thing, and that this torrid fantasy had been one of her creation, all along. She had admitted she'd been dancing to lure him to the floor. To her.

So, was he helping her for her sake, the public's sake, or merely indulging himself?

Stopping his exploration of her body, St. John rode out a series of aftershocks rolling through Madison that echoed his own. In tandem, their pulses soared. Their heated breath mingled in the steamy air.

She wasn't completely against his actions. When his exploration had been completed, neither of them moved. The seconds ticking by were unexpectedly rich, and roughly textured by doubt. Two strangers were pinned together for whatever reason had drawn them together, and sharing an incomprehensible desire for more.

Sadly, seconds were all the time they had. They were the wrong kind of strangers, opposites in every way, from the true rhythm of her heartbeat to the name she had called him and what it meant. *Protector.*

Riding the crest of the temporary time stall, and reveling in the enormity of the pleasure this awkward intimacy gave him, St. John waited to see what she'd do next. Which of them might finally break the spell.

With her chest against his, the beat of life within her seemed strong and slightly intimidating, coming from an organ that monitored itself and needed no reminder to function. He had forgotten how loud a mortal heart could sound. The noise filled his ears.

The heat she radiated was the best thing of all. Soaking it up as though he had never been privy to such warmth before, and as though he'd never get enough, St. John whispered, "What I'm not telling you may come back to bite us both. You will be marked now, from this day forward, as mine. Because of your request for help, and because this is the only way to accomplish that, you will forever crave this touch as much as I will."

His sigh stirred her fine, baby-soft hair. One lustrous strand tickled his face.

"There is payment due for every action, you see," he went on. "This closeness is mine."

With his mouth in her hair, he heard the blood rushing through her veins, beneath her ivory skin, sing a song that called to him as seductively as her body had. That blood meant life. Living, breathing, life. Fragile. Heated. Special. Mortal.

Take me...Madison's blood sang.

Drink me.

But those were the rogue vampires' thoughts, not his own. He was tapping into their desires, too, which only somewhat paralleled his. Distance had to be encouraged from the delicate arteries just centimeters from his lips. He wasn't one of *them,* and never had been. Christopher St. John had never bitten anyone...for sport.

With that protest live in him, St. John reluctantly and with the greatest effort allowed Madison to tear herself away from his embrace. Once free, she raised her hand and slapped him hard across his face, as he'd known she would. For all the world, he wouldn't have stopped her.

"Ready?" he asked.

Smiling grimly, and without waiting for a reply, he took a handful of silver spandex and backed up, pulling her overheated, angry, extremely luscious body through the oblivious crowd.

Chapter 4

The suddenness of finding herself fleeing from the dance floor came as a surprise, and meant that the arrogant bastard beside her might actually be keeping his word about getting her to safety.

After all the touchy-feely personal exploration that she'd had no ability to stop, and may even have helped along in a moment of complete mental lapse, Madison didn't know what to make of any of this. She refused to look closely at the guy holding on to her, afraid of actually believing her brother, and that gorgeous British males could potentially be vampires.

Surely this guy had put a goddamn spell on her?

She had always believed Stewart, one hundred percent, in the past. So, what if vampires were real? Conversely, what if Stewart's research amounted to a pile of nonsense, which was much more likely the case?

As this guy whisked her through the crowd, Madison kept unuttered cuss words to herself. Shouting obscenities in a night club would be a very bad idea. Any incident centered on her might make the headlines.

Every nerve in her body twanged from the illicit touch of the man who had hold of her. In the case of a quick exit, though, he appeared to be helpful.

At least they were moving.

The fact that her pulse raced was an annoyance. This gorgeous guy leading her might have wanted to help her for dubious reasons, but in his brief embrace she had nearly forgotten about everything else—all the bad things, all the work she had to do.

This was a grim reflection on her present state of mind. She wasn't often fooled by offers and false ardor from people who wanted something from her, either because of her job or merely to score points by bedding a minor celebrity.

Probably, this guy wanted one of those things.

The arrogant male hadn't introduced himself. He hadn't rejected the vampire foreplay, or shunned the title of Protector, a term her brother's notes had listed as being the vampires' liaison to the rest of the world's population.

Of course, this guy could simply have been playing the game she'd started, toying with her by making spooky small talk. She had brought the whole monster thing up. Without that freaky conversation, their meeting might have gone in a different direction, despite her former resolve.

Protector and *predator* were probably interchangeable terms in swanky nightclubs.

"This is far enough," she said after passing through some of the club's back rooms.

"Not nearly far enough," he countered in that deep masculine voice of his, speaking over one impressively broad shoulder.

They moved on.

He'd said there was a back door somewhere.

The club was aptly named, and much larger than it appeared from the outside. Striding through dim corridors, dodging people doing all sorts of activities that shouldn't have been open for public viewing, Madison began to breathe in the dank, stale smells of the original portion of the old building. Eventually, the hallways narrowed and the people disappeared.

They were moving quickly through a dark area. She had voluntarily trod the fine line between remaining safe and tiptoeing toward trouble by going out alone tonight, and by asking this stranger to help her. Whatever happened next, she was responsible.

Damn though, he seemed to have the eyes of an owl. A twinge of concern surfaced over that, because she couldn't see a thing.

Maybe he had vampire eyes?

Wanting to kick herself for the cynicism, she quickly replaced that thought with another.

Her strange bodyguard was rescuing her from a bunch of idiots bent on trouble, but he could just as easily be taking her from the club for nefarious purposes of his own. He, or someone like him, could have taken all four Yale girls away in a similar manner, pretending to take charge of their safety. Those girls had just dropped off the face of the earth.

Finally, her strange guide led her through an unlocked back door. They emerged into an alley. Hit by a blast of cold night air that seemed extreme after the closeness of the club, Madison sighed with relief. This guy had done what he said he would, but her nerves remained jumpy. Her skin felt red-hot where his hand fastened to her wrist.

He didn't stop in the alley, or show signs of slowing. Rounding the corner of the club's exterior, Madison dug in her heels, sliding on a filthy stretch of pavement.

"It's quite possible this won't be far enough," he said with a tug that effectively got her moving again.

"Wait a minute. Stop." Madison swallowed gulps of the chilled night air. "You're saying those idiots watching me might follow us all the way out here?"

"Yes," he replied.

"Pursuing you, or me?"

This earned her a lingering look.

"Okay. So, why me?" she asked, deciphering his look. "They recognized me?"

"You're beautiful, exotic," he said. "In that outfit, you look like a piece of some distant constellation, and yet you feel like the sun. Who wouldn't want to be close to that?"

"Even taken as a compliment, is that supposed to make sense?"

"It does if you know what your pursuers are, and what drives them," he said.

Before she could address that, he pulled her off balance, tipping her sideways onto the hood of a conveniently parked car. She landed in a compromising position with her skirt hiked up and her bare legs dangling over an icy metal fender. No blaring car alarm went off to warn anybody within hearing range. There was no one around to respond to a shout.

Primed to fight, Madison struggled to get up. "You can't tell me this position helps in a getaway."

"Yet it demonstrates how easily you might be over-powered by someone stronger than yourself."

She was held down by her companion's hands as he arched over her. His outrageously angular face came close enough to see each shadow that outlined his face in the faint illumination of a nearby streetlight.

"Okay. I get that," she said.

Light eyes searched hers intently. She avoided the scrutiny by glancing away. Adrenaline spiked through her in a sharp, nasty flood. Usually she thrived on this kind of scrambled energy.

"I need you to listen, and to pay attention," he said. "You requested my help, and I am helping. At least I'm trying to, because danger is close behind. Can't you sense it, smell it? Aren't journalists supposed to have a nose for danger?"

"My reactions to everything so far have danger written all over them," she said pointedly, referring to her current position on her back. "What I'm smelling is bad, and way too close to me right now."

The comment hadn't been lost on the man hovering above her. He had the audacity to crack a smile, and said ominously, "Do you want to continue to argue, discuss the mysteries of the world, or get away from what could turn out to be your worst nightmare? *They* are coming."

"Then it might be a good idea to let me up and dial whatever the hell the emergency number is in England."

"What will you do then? Run? How far do you think you'd get on your own, not knowing the city?"

"Farther than this."

Her next intake of air drove this guy's scent deep into her lungs. The masculine odors, topped by the faint-est trace of musk, had nothing artificial or perfumed in them. No hint of aftershave, because it was highly possible, she again thought cynically, that vampires, being the walking undead, couldn't grow a five-o'clock shadow.

"Just who is the danger here, anyway?" she demanded.

When he turned his head to listen to a sound she didn't hear, another round of apprehension struck her. He sniffed the air, in the manner of an animal detecting its prey.

"What the hell?" She resumed her struggle to rise. He held her easily—this mystery man who possessed a graceful, threatening, controlled elegance that made him more than a little frightening and at the same time disarmingly seductive. Sort of like a big, sleek panther decked out in a really expensive, perfectly tailored suit.

His eyes might have been blue. She upheld her refusal to check them out. Every horror movie she'd ever seen proposed that it would be suicidal to meet a vampire's gaze, though the same should be said for all predators.

She figured that looking into the eyes of any incredibly chic bastard would be the equivalent of handing him her hotel key. On her back like this, underdressed and on a side street, she wasn't going to take that chance.

Screw the heat beating at the air between them. Getting away was urgent. This man was too darn sexy for anyone's good, and pushed all her buttons, some of which shouldn't have been up for debate.

Kicking out with her legs, she managed to sit up.

She froze.

"Oh, shit," she said, the sound of her pounding heart nearly drowning out everything in the surroundings. "You weren't kidding, were you? I think I hear them."

Her companion nodded. "They're young and persistent. They've found the scent."

"What scent?"

"Yours," he said.

That reply, made so casually, brought on a quick stab of real fear. "Let me go," she demanded.

He obliged.

St. John let Madison slip off the car, regretting the necessity. Emotions, long ago buried along with his mortality, had no place here.

He was helping her, not completely for personal reasons, but in favor of keeping bloodsuckers away from the unsuspecting crowds. At the same time, he was preventing another international incident.

The oncoming gang of young vampires demanded action. Their imminent approach needled his skin like tiny pricks from the point of an annoyingly icy blade. He needed them to follow, and had allowed them to play catch-up.

But something else nagged at his conscience: Madison Chase's heartbeat. When he had pinned her to the hood of the car, their hearts—the beats, rhythm and pulse—had shared an intimate moment on a subconscious level of awareness, as if they'd met like this before.

He didn't fully understand this new sensation, and found it disturbing.

"Go now," he said, and she rocked back on her heels as though unsure of how to respond to her sudden freedom.

"What will you do?" she asked tentatively, brushing fiery strands of silky hair back from her face.

"Wait for them."

St. John wanted to touch those flaming strands, and press them close to his face. He wanted his hands back on her.

"By yourself?" she asked. "You'll wait for them by yourself?"

"Go," he repeated. "I recommend that you start right this minute."

She turned, and started walking. Then she stopped as though halted by a hidden roadblock, and just stood there.

St. John found himself wondering why she'd blow her chance to get away from him, as well as the others, if she was scared. He wasn't holding her there physically. He hadn't imposed his will.

For a fleeting, perhaps untrustworthy moment, it seemed possible that she had hesitated, not because of the bond he'd set in place between them on the dance floor, but because she was contemplating the same strange attraction to him that he was experiencing with her.

There was no ignoring the heat of having her so close. He fisted his hands to keep from reaching for her.

"What part of *right this minute* don't you get?" he said.

"The part you're leaving out."

"The devil is in the details, Madison, and he's not very attractive."

"I'm familiar with the devil."

"Somehow," St. John said, "I don't believe that's true."

His shoulders ached as the metaphorical knife pricks got deeper, warning that the time for discourse with Madison was over. He felt a pang of remorse over that. She was beautiful, radiant and alive, but it was nearly too late to keep the identity of the approaching vampires from her. One look at those rogues, up close, and Madison would know for sure that their vampire foreplay on the dance floor hadn't been a game at all.

His interest in her had to wait. All five of the misbehaving misfits were rounding the corner. The sight of the group caused Madison to stumble backward.

"Do this for me, if not for yourself," he said to her. "Run."

"Not without you." Her voice quivered.

"You're afraid of me," he pointed out, using up precious time they didn't have.

"But more afraid of them," she admitted.

Bloody hell! The woman was interfering with the unnatural order of things by sticking her pert little nose where it didn't belong. She couldn't be privy to his dealings with these creeps, and not facing them, not dealing with them in the manner they deserved—the manner necessary for maintaining his community's anonymity—was already weighing heavily on him.

He wasn't used to distractions or abandoning one cause for another. This went against his grain, an impressively nonhuman grain. The purest form of immortality animated his body, forging within him a direct link to the source of all immortal blood on earth. Only six other beings in the world could claim this, if in fact they still existed.

They had been the special Seven. Seven men chosen for the gift of life everlasting, and all that came with this gift. A fraternity of souls designed for an endless quest.

He had lived through numerous crusades, continent expansions and too damn many world wars. Given all that, what would be the cost of the possible loss of one woman, met at random, in comparison? Why risk anything for her?

When her eyes met his, perhaps accidentally and perhaps because he had unknowingly wished for it, the impact of the connection struck him like a fresh wound to his chest. He knew that losing Madison, if she were to be harmed, or if she ran off into the night, would be not only a shame, it would be unbearable.

He craved the fire. Her fire. He craved her heat, and the beautiful body radiating so much of it. He tried to get a handle on this as he held her gaze.

Her blue eyes, large, round and wary, hinted at depths that contrasted her scandalous state of undress. In those seconds, with their eyes meeting, St. John confirmed that Madison Chase was indeed much more than she seemed on the surface. More than heat and sparkle and a partially naked display.

She was a fighter, strong-willed, confident and maybe even slightly mad. These were characteristics she shared with her brother, and the very traits that also made her a threat.

Did she want to be like her brother, pursuing vampires? Had she come to London for the same reasons that Stewart Chase had come here for, using the missing girls as a ruse to further their own agenda?

The uncertainty obviously fueling her visible tremors hadn't budged her. Five vampires heading her way didn't have her running. For all her wariness and his warnings, when faced with the unknown, Madison Chase was concerned for him.

The Protector was being aided by the damsel in distress.

You really are going to be a pain, Red.

Smelling death's fetid breath, feeling its presence surf across his senses, St. John whirled. Fighting for control of his automatic reactions that would have made him walk toward that oncoming darkness and confront what was hidden within it, he instead took Madison's hand.

She had kicked off her shoes. They lay at her feet, looking on the black asphalt like spiky bits of fallen silver stars. He found himself smiling joyfully, in spite of everything. After enduring years of an empty, benign lack of emotion, he had experienced several in the last half hour. With her.

Holding out against a surge of possessiveness so strong it threatened to take him over, St. John said to her, "Just this once," and started to run.

Chapter 5

Shudders rolled over every inch of Madison's body, stemming from the electrical charge that came with this man's skin meeting hers.

Again, she found herself sprinting through parts of London with a stranger. She may have made a stupid mistake by trusting in him in the first place. It wasn't like her to take this many chances.

They were sprinting through a maze of narrow side streets. Her bare feet were taking the brunt of both the pace and the debris littering the ground. She vowed to complain if things got weirder.

No sound came from behind. Only the rush of blood echoing inside her head filled the silence. Her companion's legs were twice as long as her own. His shoes, striking the streets, seemed to be working in mute mode. He wasn't laboring, wasn't breathing hard. He was definitely the one in better shape.

With all the twists and turns they'd made, she lost all sense of direction. Since they hadn't slowed, it became obvious that her companion knew the area well. The hour was late, well after midnight. The side streets were quiet. They hadn't passed anyone since leaving the trendy West End. If she shouted for him to stop now, or asked where they were going, would the idiots behind them hear?

If they were still following.

Around the next bend, a set of steep concrete steps loomed, looking in the dark like a stairway from hell to whatever lay above. Madison tackled those stairs in her guide's wake. His hold on her hand never loosened. Tiny bursts of electrical charges continued to pass from his fingers to hers, his skin to hers, each surge bringing up more questions and fresh rounds of anxiety.

She was harboring lusty, ridiculous thoughts about one-night stands with strangers. With no idea who her companion might be, or where they were, the drama and the obvious electricity between them turned her on, despite the situation.

They reached the top of the steps with her heart working near to full capacity. She sucked air through her mouth without the ability to catch up or stabilize her breathing. Her bare feet were sliced up pretty badly, and probably bleeding, leaving a blood trail for vampires to follow, if, as in Stewart's world, blood was their drink of choice.

If she got out of here, she might not be able to wear shoes for a week.

When her guide suddenly slowed, she wanted to cheer, until she sensed movement from their left. A subtle shifting of shadows in the distance produced a new layer of gray on black that her companion noted with a sigh.

She heard voices, laughter. Her heart careened wildly.

With a smooth tug of his arm, her compelling stranger shoved her against an old stone wall. What air Madison had left in her lungs whooshed out as he pressed himself close, as though he would shield her from whatever was out there by grinding his body tight up against hers.

His body was hard, taut, and her reaction to him was swift. Her legs and arms began to shake with expectation. Her breasts strained against his chest.

"Damn you," she whispered.

The fabric of his pants felt soft against her bare thighs. His breath warmed the side of her face. This sensual stranger felt solid, human and exactly like a man in every way that counted. In spite of that, her breath suspended, because there was something about him she couldn't mentally digest. Her instincts warned that something wasn't quite right.

What was it?

Before she could think about it further, he brushed his lips over hers so softly that Madison wondered if she'd made those warning signals up.

A flush of heat rose from her chest to her neck, and into her face. Her thighs began to simmer, despite the chill of the London night.

"So," she said breathlessly. "You think I owe you just because you saved my ass?"

His hands were on the wall behind her. Madison felt him looking at her, sensed those big eyes continuing their careful observation in the same darkness that wouldn't allow her to reciprocate.

"I have never forced myself on anyone," he said.

The pressure of his body against hers was erotic. Way down deep, she shook with a series of internal quakes.

An insistent drumming beat out a warning that had the words *no good* attached to it.

This closeness was wrong, somehow. At the very least, it was distracting, when she had to keep focus. For the sake of her sanity and self-respect, she had to get away from this man who might brag about an intimate liaison with a TV celebrity, or post illicit photos on the internet.

She had to escape this predicament in spite of the fact that the hips tight up with hers fit in all the right places, setting those places on fire.

This was too freaking unbelievable.

Her reactions were unsound. They were in some god-forsaken alley, and part of her didn't care. Part of her wanted this, and him. She just couldn't resist his magnetism and graceful animal allure. Against the onslaught of physical reactions, she stood little chance of thinking straight. Her last one-nighter had been a very long time ago.

"This isn't like me. I'm not this person." The words stuck in her throat. As a rule, she didn't lose her wits. Couldn't afford to. Yet the urge overtaking her at the moment wasn't to run away, but to lock her mouth to his mouth, so hot and close and beckoning. The impulse was to tear at his clothes with both hands in order to maximize a crazy, all-consuming and insatiable hunger for him.

When her exotic companion spoke in the gravelly, velvet-clad tone of a man unfulfilled, she knew he was experiencing the same thing.

"Madison," was all that he said, but the word caused her body's deep throb to intensify. She was certain this man knew it. He had to be feeling each beat.

His lips danced across hers lightly, without lasting

pressure. His face moved to the crook of her neck in a slow slide of his smooth, cool cheek over hers. She felt his lips touch a spot beneath her right ear before he moved on to place a soft, almost tender kiss on her shoulder.

She was getting hotter, hornier.

"All right." Her lips formed those words against his lips. "Damn it, all right."

He didn't react or respond until her hands crawled up his back. Then he made a faint sound of startled acceptance. After that, the night became a hungry, mindless blur.

His hands were back on her. In a replay of the naughty touch on the dance floor, they slid between her legs with a dangerous spontaneity.

The hem of her silver mini rose. His fingers moved under it, drifting over her lace-covered mound.

When her thong began a feathery, downward descent, Madison wanted to shout at the time this was taking. Spontaneity didn't mix well with taking the time to consider the possibility of mistakes. She wanted him now, inside her, hard and fast. She wanted to get this over with, because it was insane and unavoidable, and too late to do anything about.

He lifted her up. Her back hit the stone in a scrape of sequins. The lace panties fell silently to her ankles, and then to the ground. She was naked from the waist down, and his fingers flowed over her sensitive places like some kind of molten liquid. Confidently. Possessively.

He urged her to wrap one leg around his hips with a slight motion of those hips, and her bare, moist, sensitive parts met with his swollen groin as cool palms danced over her thighs.

Madison loosened her grip on his tensely muscled

back just enough to make room for a second brush of friction; his fingers on her folds without the thin, almost indecent barrier of lace.

The subtle external caress, accompanied by the silky seduction of his golden hair sweeping across her face, kicked up a rolling internal rumble that rushed toward this personal touch. Each breath she fought for was shallow. She could not have opened her eyes, no matter what.

The guy dealing out this exquisite level of pleasure hadn't yet even fully participated, and she was already on the verge of a climax.

But the deep-seated evidence of his seduction also seemed to carry something else in its wake. A dark shadow rode this seduction like an unwanted hitchhiker.

Something was wrong.

Madison whispered a throaty, "Stop!"

The hand pleasuring her stilled upon her command.

The inner chaos of her approaching orgasm hovered some time more before eventually starting to recede. Her insides ached for its loss. Her mind whirled.

He hadn't reached that place she'd so badly wanted him to reach. His hand remained on her quivering slit, and she couldn't allow him to move.

She had no idea where the protest had come from, or what that darkness was that she'd felt so extremely. Yet as the orgasm she hadn't quite reached disappeared, the dark haze lifted from her sight, leaving her and this stranger motionless, and glued together in a compromising position.

It was a truly awkward moment.

He moved first. Her would-be lover set her on her feet, and backed up a step, forcing her to overcome the weakness in her knees.

"We will meet again," he said in an unsteady tone, and gently pushed her toward the concrete stairway, where she was again out in the open without her shoes, without her panties, unsatisfied, alone and exposed.

The transition from being in his arms one minute, to being on her own the next, was too quick.

Was it possible that this hunk of a man might give her to the creeps who had chased them, turning her over to them after having his fun? He and that gang couldn't be some kind of kinky, faux-vampiric tag-team, out to separate tourists from the crowds?

She supposed that anything was possible. She had been uncharacteristically gullible, but at least they hadn't had sex; no penetration and going all the way. She was lucky that her companion had let her get away with this protest, and had stopped when she'd asked him to.

Would he have done so if this was part of some scam?

Hearing laughter echo off the buildings, Madison spun to face it. This was men's laughter, loud and unrestrained.

Were they laughing at her expense?

She gazed into the dark, to the wall she had been pressed to, no longer able see the man she'd been with. Panic shot through her as she pressed her dress down, and glanced at the steps.

Someone shouted at her, too close for comfort.

Rigidity overtook her. It was too late for retreat.

The laughter became a roar in her ears.

Balling her hands into fists, Madison turned as another shout came. Two more shouts followed, sounding like…greetings. Sounding, in the vast stretch of foggy, foreign darkness surrounding her, vaguely familiar.

Nerves revved, skin tingling with fear, Madison felt a scream claw its way up from her chest. On wobbling legs, she processed the familiar lilt of a voice, unable to confront the rush of relief she began to feel.

"Hey, Madison! Is that you?" Theodore "Teddy" Jones, her network cameraman, called. "What are you doing out here?"

Collapsing with relief was not an option.

St. John watched the four mortal males surround Madison. In a swirl of his own shadow, he silently leaped onto the wall at the edge of the alley. Walking quickly along the top, he backtracked along the same route he and Madison had taken.

The rogues were heading this way.

His sexual escapade with Madison would have been short, if allowed to continue. But he had been up close and personal with the American media anchor twice, enough to ensure that some of her scent had rubbed off on him, as well as the other way around. Smelling like her, he would lure the rogues away from where he'd left Madison, and lead them to a more secluded area.

Fledgling vampires tended to squeal like teenaged girls at a party when taken down. If it weren't for Madison's scent, saturating his pants and jacket and hands, the murderous villains wouldn't even see him coming.

On the downside, her lingering fragrance was as enticing as it was delicious, and a heady distraction from his usual routine of avoiding mortals whenever possible. His coat smelled like an orchard of trees basking in Florida sunlight. His fingers, having dipped inside her glorious heat, smelled like…heaven.

He stopped midstride as if pulled to attention.

Something wasn't quite right about either scent. In the heat of the moment, he had missed that.

He wanted to turn around, find her again, and to hell with the Americans he'd left her with at the steps, as well as the bloodsuckers on Madison's trail. He wanted to know what had just happened, what this new scent was and why she had been the one to step on the brakes.

Madison had been willing. He hadn't imagined this. The spike of electrified current he'd experienced with her, with every touch, in every breath, had also caught her up. She had been soft and supple. And yet she had only gone so far.

Had she heard the others approaching, with inferior mortal ears, or had she merely had second thoughts about a sexual liaison in a dark alley?

She hadn't pulled away or raised a hand to slap him a second time. Her sensational body had ached to give in to the bond he'd set in place in the club, just as his ached.

But he had begun to detect the anomalies in her as soon as his mouth had met with hers. Although it had taken him a while to process the information, he'd tasted the thin layer of darkness that Madison kept tucked away, hidden.

That's what the unusual scent also had to be. Darkness. She may have hair the color of flames, and lips like heaven…but all of that was tinged with a subtle layering of shadow.

He had sensed a similar darkness hovering about her brother on the one occasion they'd met.

This gave him pause.

Nevertheless, he couldn't afford to reason things out at the moment, with his responsibilities here only half over. He'd gotten Madison to safety, and although her safety was important, his initial task remained.

Taking off again, St. John jumped from the wall and

landed soundlessly. The nearness of the young vampires ruffled his nerves beneath Madison's darkened, woodsy fragrance.

"Job to do," he said aloud, with determination.

With Madison's scent in their noses, the fledglings searching for her like cats after a rat would never give up. After one whiff, these vampires would follow her until they found her, however long it took.

They had to be stopped before they did, stopped before they encountered other people on the streets tonight who got in their way. Fledglings didn't know how to curb their appetites. These upstarts had outlived their welcome in the West End. Madison was far too intriguing to wind up as pulp on a damp sidewalk.

Miss Chase had to be around for a while longer, so that he could see her again.

He intended to learn how much she knew about her brother's research, and what part she played in it. But the truth was there were more personal reasons for keeping her safe that had little to do with whistle-blowers, hidden inner darkness and her capricious, lacy lingerie. He just wasn't sure he wanted to accept those reasons.

As St. John kicked up his speed to a pace that made him little more than a blur to any onlooker, he admitted to himself that it was entirely possible that, darkness aside, Madison smelled nothing like a Florida orchard. Since he'd never been to Florida, he might be wrong about that.

One more alley...

He paused in an open-legged stance, listened, waited. When the five savage youngsters, probably no more than a week or two old as vampires, full of themselves and finding comfort in their numbers, stopped on the opposite side of the lane, sneering at him with their fangs exposed, St. John shook his head.

"Now that," he said, "just makes it easier all the way around."

Then he waited for the stupid bastards, who knew no better, and knew nothing about him, to attack.

Chapter 6

Sleeping had been tough before. Trying to keep her eyes shut now amounted to torture.

In her unair-conditioned hotel room, located a short hop away from Buckingham Palace, Madison tossed and fretted on the mattress, struggling to relax, finding it impossible.

Fresh air might have helped, but there was no way she could open the window when the man who had rescued her from those thugs had freaked her out about who might be out there. Hell, he had sent her imagination into overdrive. Possibly, that damn loose screw was at that very moment turning inside her head.

She didn't even know that man's name.

She had stood in the shower until the hot water turned lukewarm, and scrubbed her skin raw with a washcloth, and she still smelled *him* on her skin. Wool and musk and that other more elusive undercurrent that permeated the air around him as he'd taken her for a midnight run were still there.

Her hotel room smelled like him. So did her sheets. Her oversize white T-shirt had picked up the smell. It had been impossible to rid her freshly washed hair of this lingering fragrance of seduction and mystery.

She didn't know why he had initially played along with Stewart's vampire games. Admittedly, though, the guy she'd been groin to groin with was too special to be a mere mortal, any way she looked at it. And way too sexually exciting. From the start, it had been obvious that something had clicked into place between them. Lust at first sight was a powerful incentive for tossing inhibitions aside.

That stuff about *them* following might have been a ploy for him to get her alone. *Them,* as in what, London's version of a low-life street gang? Certainly he didn't mean the monsters her brother would have her believe frequented London's crowded places. That had just been a game. Strange foreplay.

"Vampires. Jesus." She made a face.

The man she'd been tight up against hadn't been some ephemeral bit of mythological mist. He had been solid, and interesting in all the right places.

"No mistake about that."

If she hadn't come to her senses, she'd be even sorrier now about the whole ordeal.

Madison smacked the mattress with her open hand. She had placed herself in a bad situation, and luckily had come out of it reasonably well. But she had also been distracted, big-time, from the after-hours search for her brother. Distractions she couldn't afford.

"So why does this hotel room lack a minibar, as well as an all-night pharmacy in the lobby that could cough up an aspirin or sleeping pill?"

Her nerves were shot, she couldn't breathe properly and there was no way she'd open that window, a crack, even if she didn't really believe there were vampires or some other *things* out there.

Flipping over on the bed, she knocked over the half-full box of Band-Aids that Teddy Jones, now holed up down the hall with another member of the television crew, had graciously provided after seeing her safely back to the hotel. She waggled her toes, lacerated with superficial cuts and fairly sore, though she'd been fortunate enough to have avoided broken glass.

Losing her expensive shoes was a drag. She had discarded the designer Choos somewhere near the club and would have to replace them with a cheaper pair. The silver stilettos had been a rare twenty-fifth birthday splurge last year.

"Shall I send you a bill for the shoes?" she asked.

If she met the handsome maniac at the club again, she'd register a complaint in person. Going beyond that, she might also press charges for scaring the wits out of her. Again, she glanced to the window to make sure it was closed.

"Sucker," she said.

In the morning, in the daylight, and prior to her crew's meeting for updates on the Yale Four case, she would hit a department store for some forgiving footwear. She'd already done ten interviews with the families of those girls, as well as some potential witnesses. The morning broadcast cameras wouldn't need to include any shot below her knees.

She'd also need to use extra makeup to cover the dark circles that would no doubt appear from a lack of sleep, and perfume to mask the scent haunting her.

Tugging on the edge of the rumpled sheet, Madison looked to the window for the twentieth time.

"Feeling claustrophobic," she muttered.

In Miami, in her modern high-rise condo, the windows were always open at night. No one in their right mind would attempt to climb up the outside of a twenty-four-story building to bother her, unless they were related to Spider-Man. No one would probably bother her here, either, in this busy hotel, in her cubbyhole on the sixth floor, unless the invader happened to be one of Stewart's vampires. A Protector, maybe.

She blinked slowly, in disgust, and said, "Don't even start."

On the desk were stacks of files pertaining to her assignment. She had a few more interviews to do. If she had stayed in tonight to work on those files, none of this would have happened. No chiseled, fake vampire. Nothing embarrassing.

Then again, hindsight wasn't worth much these days. The four young women who had vanished while vacationing in a civilized country didn't have the option for a do-over.

She hoped to God those girls were alive. After tonight, she could see how one false move might have been the key to their downfall. If her crew hadn't shown up when they did, there might have been a chance she wouldn't have made it back in one piece.

Next to those case files on the desk sat her laptop, loaded with her brother's files on monsters. She'd had to work hard to crack his password.

"Absurd," she said, her gaze straying to the window. No one could actually be out there. Her memory pulled up something. A warning, or a threat, issued by a blond stranger that she hadn't registered at the time.

"You will be marked now, from this day forward, as mine."

"Frigging nonsense," she snapped.

Nevertheless, she found herself at the window, searching the street below.

She saw nothing out of the ordinary. A few people meandered toward the palace and Green Park. Other than a handful of cabs and cars, London had gone quiet.

Leaning against the wall, Madison smoothed her hair back from her face. The movement caused the masculine scent she'd tried so hard to get rid of to waft over her. Coughing once, she lunged for the bed.

On her back, with the blanket pulled up to her chin, she traced small visible cracks in the ornate, slightly luminous white ceiling plaster, hoping counting cracks would be better than counting sheep. Hoping to avoid erotic fantasies about strange men...with fangs...

Even though her hand had already slid under the elastic band of her underwear, to the same spot *he* had touched.

St. John felt Madison sink beneath the surface of consciousness. Cautiously, he climbed over the window's iron railing and entered her room.

He was trespassing, but the need to see her was great. Dark had a tendency to draw dark, which was a viable reason for him being here, and maybe why the fledglings had been drawn to Madison as well.

There was something about her.

She lay curled up on the bed, with her knees to her chest. A thin, well-worn white T-shirt replaced what had earlier passed for a dress, and was equally as sexy.

Her lithe body took on softer aspects in sleep, when she didn't expect surprises, though her position told him she wasn't comfortable. Faint sounds came from her each time she moved—noises so very inviting to a hungry soul.

"I'm far too interested in you," he said, watching Madison's eyelids flutter as if she might sense him beside her.

"For the first time in a long while, I hunger for a mortal. I am a man, you know. Not in the way other mortals might define the term, but my desire remains the same."

A twitch in Madison's right cheek made him want to touch her, but he didn't dare.

He was aware, even now, of the darkness she harbored. It sat beneath her taut, ivory skin. She and her brother had come here under the auspices of following the case of the missing American girls, yet her brother had already shown his true hand. Stewart Chase had ulterior motives for arriving in London, and look, St. John wanted to tell Madison, where that had gotten her brother.

"Are you like him? Do you share your twin's need to find creatures that aren't mortal? Do you also hunger for the supernatural?"

There were so many kinds of vampires, he thought. Those who drank blood, and those who soaked up the very essence of others in a different way, by taking away their freedom.

Mortal souls thrived on freedom. Madison's soul needed more freedom than others, he supposed, which is why she took chances. Madison Chase, the gutsy newscaster, went to any lengths to unearth a story. This is what made her dangerous to his cause. Exposing the immortals in this city would be a stupid move.

"I wanted to look at you when you aren't looking back or looking away," he said to her. "Few women turn the heads of beings like me. Few cause us to look beyond ourselves and our long pasts."

She wasn't awake, or listening. Her fingers moved restlessly on the pillow.

"A moment more. Only that, Madison."

St. John leaned over the bed.

Breath. Touch. Skin. Scent...

He ached for the woman on those sheets. His fangs were extended, and throbbing. She had made him hard. She had made him laugh, severing the bottomless world of melancholy from which he never completely escaped. Madison Chase had lightened his world for a few brief moments, and then she had left him wanting.

Her fine crimson hair spread out over the white pillow in coronas of radiant sunfire. Transparent skin stretched beautifully over the planes of her delicate face. Staring at her made St. John wonder if he might find some kind of salvation in his nearness to her, if only for a while.

There was no real future here. They weren't alike. Though his body and hers would fit together perfectly, her life's spark was what separated them.

"Can you blame me for wanting what you have to offer? I can feel your heart and your heat from here."

If allotted the time to get to know her better, Madison still would have been hard to handle and out of bounds. If there were to be a replay of their intimate moments in the alley, he might actually learn to care for someone like her, when his agenda couldn't strain that far.

Madison was a television darling, but she hadn't dealt with the likes of the Hundred, who ruled this city and what went on there. For them, and the ring of immortals surrounding the Hundred, there could be no long-lasting peace if they were discovered. The world wasn't ready for what they represented.

A low murmur escaped from Madison, as if she had heard that thought. St. John didn't step back. He was experiencing longings formulated from centuries of ignored, pent-up emotion.

He had to know everything about Madison, and he had to stay away from her. He wanted to settle himself between her long legs, and could not do so. It was essential for him to find out how much she knew about Protectors and vampires, when even this small closeness brought pain.

"You must not find your brother," he whispered to her, observing how his breath stirred one glossy strand of her hair. "You won't like what you'd see."

His hungry gaze traveled down the length of one pale arm to find the imprint of a breast, outlined behind the thin fabric of her shirt. His body pulsed with the effort of his restraint. He snapped his fangs angrily.

He had to get away, quickly. The turn of her head had exposed more flawless skin, and his attraction to that bit of naked flesh was disconcerting.

"I'll leave you now."

Turning from the bed, he tucked in his fangs. A weaker being would have acted on the cravings, but he had never been weak. He had, in fact, been chosen for his strength and honor. The gift of immortality had been bestowed upon him because his Makers had known he would uphold that honor at all cost.

At the window, St. John spoke again. "You have never

come across the likes of the Hundred, and must keep off their radar, Madison."

Filled with regret so tangible that he could taste it, St. John left his sleeping beauty, refusing to look back, turn back or change his mind…already hating the necessary separation.

Chapter 7

The knocking sound seemed to come from a long way off. Annoyed, Madison rolled over.

The sound came again.

This time, she came fully awake and glared at the door in the haze of the early-morning light coming through the window.

"Chase, you in there?" Teddy called from the hallway. "Open up."

A surge of adrenaline propelled her into alertness. Grabbing the blanket off the bed to cover up with, she padded to the door and yanked it open.

"Ted? What's up?"

"Why didn't you answer your cell?" Teddy's voice was tinged with wary excitement.

"It didn't ring." Madison looked to the bureau, where she usually put her phone. "Great. I must have left it somewhere."

"Well, that's bloody inconvenient," Teddy said. "Get dressed and be out here in five."

"Why?"

"I'll tell you then. It's something you'll want to hear."

Knowing better than to prolong the five minutes Teddy had asked for by demanding more details, Madison closed the door. There was no time to worry about the dreams, or that damn window. The dimensions of the room were small enough to prove that she was alone in it.

She knew the routine. Her makeup case sat in her bag by the desk, ready in case of emergencies. Clothes were on hangers and easy to grab. Shoes... Hell, her feet hurt just standing on the carpet.

She wiggled into jeans, pulled a loose black sweater over her head and slipped her aching feet into a pair of worn athletic shoes. With everything she'd need to be camera-ready in hand, she stepped into the hall in just three minutes flat.

Every member of her crew was there, crowded into the narrow hall and looking rumpled. Madison tossed her things to the assistant in charge of details, and tore an elastic band off her wrist to tie back her unruly hair.

"Dish," she said.

"There's news," Teddy explained as they headed for the stairs. "The police have found something they think might be important."

"Pertaining to the girls' case?"

"In lieu of you not answering your cell, I got the wake-up call to get our butts in gear and get over there to find out."

"There's a hotel phone in my room," Madison pointed out.

"Have you heard how loud that thing is? It would have

woken the entire hotel and scared the pants off everyone, including you."

"Yeah, and a rap at the door wouldn't do that."

"It was a gentle rap," Teddy said.

Madison threw him a sideways glance. Teddy appeared to be more rumpled than the rest of the guys. That call for action he'd mentioned must have just happened. Then again, Teddy always appeared to have just gotten out of bed. His short dark hair stuck up at odd angles. He hadn't shaved. His blue shirt was partially unbuttoned, and untucked. It appeared that Teddy had also had a sleepless night.

"Where are we going?" she asked, racing with him and the other crew members down five flights of steps, hearing the bump of the equipment bags they carried striking the walls.

"The London Eye," Jerry, the new assistant, said.

"That's the big Ferris wheel thing," Teddy clarified. "By the Thames."

"What do we know?" Madison brushed through the lobby toward the revolving glass doors that showed a white van with its door wide open waiting curb-side. The crew had gotten the rented vehicle here quickly.

The others began storing the equipment inside. After they'd jumped in, the metal door slammed behind her, and they took off.

"Okay. What?" she said, looking to Teddy.

"Clothes," he said. "They found some clothes."

"Belonging to the girls?"

"No."

The fine little hairs on the back of her neck lifted.

"Whose clothes?" she asked.

"There's a whisper about a possibility they might belong to your brother."

Although Madison tried to take this news in, she had a hard time digesting it.

"Stewart?" she managed to say.

Teddy nodded. "The network told me that the authorities are hoping you might be able to identify the items. I said we'd be there shortly, before the morning newscast, and that we didn't want the police coming to get you."

"Thanks."

It was a miracle she'd gotten that one word out. No further conversation seemed possible. Someone had found what they believed might be her brother's clothes? Clothes he wasn't wearing?

Her empty stomach turned over.

The ride was short at that early hour. As the sun rose in the east, the London Eye appeared above a sparkling glint off the Thames—a humongous, permanent carnival ride perched on the bank in front of a block of centuries-old buildings. She had always wanted to go up on the Eye, in one of the glassed-in baskets that provided a bird's-eye view of the rooftops of London. Now, the contraption was still, and slightly ominous in its silence.

"Are you going to be okay?" Teddy asked.

She nodded. "When were these articles discovered?"

"Either sometime last night, or early this morning. That's all I know."

The van stopped in front of a line of yellow crime tape. The sight of that tape rendered Madison speechless.

A male uniformed officer met the van, but Madison hardly took in the guy's features. She was out of the van in seconds, with Teddy showing his press badge behind her.

She rushed toward the three men in suits standing near the ticket booth for the Eye. Suits were always the guys to see in situations like this.

Situations. Hell, what have they found?

"You're expecting me," she said to them without taking her attention from the Eye itself.

Where were the clothes she was to identify? How had they been found? Who had found them and why did these cops assume that whatever had turned up might belong to Stewart?

Most of all, she wanted to know how they knew Stewart was her brother, and where to find her.

She thought about asking all of those things before any of the men had offered a greeting. She was on the other end of the crime spectrum here, not only reporting on missing cases, but involved on a personal level. She had to keep it together, somehow. As a representative of her network, she had to stay grounded.

"I'm Madison Chase," she added for clarification.

One of the men turned to her. Six feet in height, with close-shorn brown hair, dark eyes and an age she gauged to be approaching forty, he said solemnly, "Sorry to get you up so early. I'm D.I. Crane. Thanks for coming, Miss Chase."

She nodded at the detective inspector. "You have something for me to see?" There was no time for any "cut to the Chase" jokes that had become so prevalent in her job. This detective wore a serious expression.

"We do. Can you step this way, please?" he said.

He moved away, and then stopped to wait for her. Swallowing her fear, and knowing she would have to look at whatever they had found, no matter how sick she felt, Madison followed him, passing several other uniforms until she and the detective had reached the entrance to the Eye itself.

She looked up at the mechanical beast with trepidation.

"We won't be going up," D.I. Crane said.

"You think you might have found something of my brother's here, on this thing?"

Crane gestured for her to step toward the open door of one of the Eye's baskets. "The supervisor stumbled upon this when he got to work this morning."

Madison was starting to feel really panicky.

D.I. Crane seemed to understand. "Right here," he said. "Can you take a look? Are you up to it?"

"There's no body or anything?"

"Nothing like that. Just this." He carefully lifted up something dark that had been stuck behind a pole.

Madison recognized what it was immediately. Though her whole body tightened, she kept the reactions in check with a stern warning that this was just a coat. A black leather jacket, to be exact, with worn patches on the sleeves.

The coat was very similar to the one Stewart often wore in his off time, though reasoning suggested that there wasn't only one leather jacket in the world, and that this one could belong to anybody. There was just one way to find out if this one belonged to her brother.

"Can I touch it?" she asked D.I. Crane.

He shook his head. "We'll take it to the lab for processing."

"Can I smell it?"

That question earned her a raised eyebrow from the detective inspector.

Madison leaned close to the jacket, and inhaled. *Stewart, is that you?*

What came to her was a shocking nightmare of images. Stewart, running. Being chased. Hurt. Limping to this spot. Removing his coat to see whatever damage he'd been dealt. Leaving in a hurry.

Oh, no. Stewart...

She kept her eyes shut for what seemed like forever as her heart pounded with a fury suggesting it would never slow down again. She feared that if she opened her eyes, she'd scream, and that if the scream came out, she'd lose consciousness.

"Miss Chase," D.I. Crane said.

Just a minute more, she wanted to say. *Please.*

Stewart had been hurt. She had seen that, or so she thought. Their connection ran deep, but she had never felt as though she was inside his skin. She felt like that now.

But Stewart had been alive here, and alive when he left that morning. She didn't want to believe that any lingering aura of death stuck to his jacket, discovered only that day. There was no trace of blood on it that she could see. If there had been blood, the investigators wouldn't have allowed her to get so near to it.

So there was hope. God, yes, a chink of light had opened up after a long dark spell. She felt her brother's presence here.

"Miss Chase?" D.I. Crane repeated, resting a hand on her arm.

"It's his," she said. "The jacket belongs to my brother, Stewart Chase."

To the detective's credit, he didn't ask how she knew this by smelling the coat. Maybe he was saving the hard questions for later.

"It's his scent," she said to gain some credence with the trained detective. "The only scent he wears. Have you looked in the pockets? What made you believe it might belong to my brother?"

D.I. Crane said, "We found your brother's business card in the pocket. Since he has been reported as missing by both you and his law firm, your ability to identify the jacket could help our investigation."

He held up a plastic evidence bag. "What about this? Do you know what this is?"

Madison gaped at the item in that bag with a disbelief that bordered on horror. The bag contained a pointed wooden stake.

"That's an odd item to be carrying around," D.I. Crane remarked. "Don't you think so, Miss Chase?"

She couldn't possibly answer. Having just gotten the word *vampire* out of her mind, she found that the word again began to blink with the vibrancy of a Vegas neon sign.

St. John felt the chill that riddled Madison's body and knew she was thinking of him. How easily he read her. This was the way the connection he'd set into place between them worked, and the result of helping her out of last night's mess.

Glad of the tip about this meeting at the Eye, he stared down at Madison from his penthouse above the Thames. He saw her sway in reaction to the sight of a weapon made for piercing the chest of a vampire.

He didn't like this.

Hell, he didn't like anything about this.

With his enhanced senses and superior vision, he watched Madison's features go from shock to relief, eventually settling into an expression of defiance. Already, she was putting two and two together, rerunning their interesting vampire foreplay of the night before.

Stewart Chase had been a fool to leave such a thing behind. Finding that stake in her brother's jacket had just upped the ante of not only his strained relationship to Madison, but also endangered her safety.

Each minute she remained in London, now that she and the detectives had viewed an example of her brother's strange obsession, the degree of risk to Madison's security would escalate. Cameras were everywhere. Eyes other than those belonging to law enforcement were watching. If she set her agenda to causing more trouble over this, she'd become a liability.

Two Chases in a row.

That ungainly adjective, *tenacious,* blinked in St. John's mind. Madison was in a state of wary suspension right now, but when the initial surprise wore off, she'd be bolstered by what the detectives had found and driven forward by it.

She'd assume she had discovered a clue to her brother being alive, and tonight she would double her efforts to find him, whether her twin was dead, alive or occupying the space in between.

She would start by going back to the club where Christopher St. John hadn't laughed at her vampire game, and had, in fact, played along. She might demand answers about her brother's research. She might wield a similar weapon to gauge his response.

"Don't you be foolish, too," he whispered to her, his throat tightening due to the knowledge of how dangerous her next appearance at Space could prove to be.

"Take your time and think this through. If you don't

believe in vampires, there must be another explanation for that wooden stake."

The way she was staring at that stake made him frown. The way her hand opened and closed, as if she wanted to wrap her fingers around it, left him uneasy.

An icy chill crept up his spine.

He narrowed his gaze.

Madison looked different.

He thought…

But couldn't be sure…

Had some kind of alternate reasoning been awakened in her just by seeing a damn sliver of wood? Was this a reason for the darkness trailing her?

It was possible, and terrible. St. John leaned against the window frame as if those few inches could get him closer to her.

"Are you like your brother, then?"

Anxiously, he tossed the cell phone she had dropped in the alley from one of his hands to the other. Madison would be missing her phone, but for the time being, it was the only piece of her accessible to him. It was another link, if he chose to use it.

Restless, St. John shifted on his feet, forced to think ahead. It didn't take a master to predict how the Hundred's thoughts would go. Getting rid of Madison would be necessary if she showed her face again at Space waving sharpened sticks and muttering the word *monster*.

If she, as a media insider, came sniffing around, an edict would be issued that she had to be dealt with, from the same beings trying so hard to blend in with society.

Hell, it was not only dangerous for him to see her again, but crazy to do so. This was an untimely distraction that threatened his agenda, when he had spent several years shoring up his own well-cultivated place in the vampire community in order to flesh out the identity of the one traitor that had infiltrated the Hundred.

If Madison were to come nosing around, he'd be faced with a choice. Find that traitor, and let fate have Madison, or forget all the time and effort spent on finding that traitor and his degenerate vampire cult, in order to protect innocent mortals, and ultimately the secrets of his kind.

The situation was grim. Even so, he had to choose one of those options. He knew Madison well enough to guess she wouldn't back down on the issue of her brother.

St. John stiffened suddenly. His skin grew colder as his gaze moved to the detective who had placed a hand on Madison's arm. The man had stepped closer to her, offering comfort of sorts in a way that he, himself, could not do.

His fangs flashed. He gritted them in distaste.

And he knew why.

Christopher St. John, one of the seven Blood Knights fashioned for the task of protecting the sacred blood of the immortals, was experiencing a pang of jealousy that nearly choked him.

The little cell phone case snapped in his grip. An old curse left his lips.

A woman like Madison could no doubt have any man she wanted. But she was so much more than a *mere* woman. So much more than a beautiful face. Madison Chase was intrigue in a delicate package. She was light tinged with dark, a challenge and an enigma. She was the keeper of her own secrets, and the temptation of the damned.

And that hellish weapon taken from her brother's coat had made her awareness prickle, as it had his. It had opened her up to taking a second look at her brother's obsession.

Oh, yes. It was necessary for him to meet her again, if only to discover why his bond with her, his snare, so carefully set into place on that dance floor, had worked the other way around…ensnaring him.

His purpose for being in London had hit a fork in the road, a five-foot-six, redheaded fork in the road.

"Tonight," he said, his attention riveted to Madison. "Tonight, if you are going to be foolish about this, I will be waiting for you. Be glad it's me, Madison."

Chapter 8

"I will be waiting for you."

Had she heard that? *Couldn't have.*

"Do you know what this is?" D.I. Crane asked, but she tuned out his voice in favor of the distraction that had come in the form of a disturbing mental touch; a whispered voice that struck like quick, exploring fingers, leaving her feeling violated, and vulnerable.

Trying to locate the origin of the voice that no one else seemed to have heard, Madison looked around, then up at the Eye. When the detective beside her removed his hand from her sleeve, she reluctantly returned her attention to him.

D.I. Crane gestured for Teddy to join them.

"We won't need you for anything else at the moment," he told her as Teddy approached. "Why don't you get some breakfast." To Teddy he said, "Where are you staying?"

"The Doncaster," Teddy replied.

"Can you see that Miss Chase gets back there, and remain in the area in case we need something further?" the detective asked.

"No can do," Teddy said. "We're off to work right now."

"Ah, yes." The detective glanced to the van and the crew standing beside it. "I forgot about the press call."

When Madison glanced down, there was no awful pointed stake or leather jacket in the detective's hands. Another detective had taken them away, saving her from the unwanted scrutiny of her crew, if not the rest of the cops present.

"I'll be around," Madison said. "There's more than one case to be solved here."

"There usually is," the detective concurred. "But we'll have questions, such as what your brother might have been doing here at the Eye, and when he left the jacket. I suppose you'd have no idea about that?"

Madison shook her head.

"Well, I'll be in touch, Miss Chase," D.I. Crane said before walking off in the direction of the other officers.

"That was your brother's jacket in the detective's hand?" Teddy asked.

"Yes."

"If they found it this morning, then your brother must have left it here."

"Him, or someone else."

"Are you okay with that, Madison?"

Stewart running. Being chased. Hurt. Limping here. Removing his coat to see whatever damage he'd been dealt. Leaving in a hurry...

Those flashes replayed in her mind, over and over in a continual loop. There was no way to be okay with that if the images were real. But were they real?

"I'm fine," she said. "If it means my brother is alive, I can't begin to tell you how happy I am."

But as she headed toward the van, Madison had to shake off a spooky chill of acknowledgment that the voice in her mind had just issued a warning for her to be careful.

"Are you like your brother, then? Don't be foolish...."

She could have sworn she heard those words, and tried to shake off the notion that there was one too many sets of eyes on her back.

"There are press teams here from all over the world," Madison said on camera, holding a microphone in both hands and trying to keep herself together after the shock she'd had.

"It's a good start on the Yale Four case. With all this coverage, surely someone will come forward with a tip, a break."

She held up a piece of paper and moved it closer to the lens.

"We've just learned that the reward for the missing girls has been bumped up to a million dollars, and that the prime minister will formally announce this in a live interview this morning. That interview will take place in less than one hour. We will be covering his speech, keeping you informed and updated on all the efforts to find those girls. *Our* girls. For now, this is Madison Chase for CRTS Television."

Teddy gave her a nod as the camera lowered. "Good sentimental call at the end there with the *our girls.* It's possible the prime minister might mention your brother eventually."

Now that the camera had been turned off, Madison's insides were churning. Stewart might have been alive that very morning. He might be hurt. She needed to find him, do something, and was stuck here for a few more hours.

"We have time for breakfast if we can find a restaurant close by," Teddy said. "I've been more or less ordered by that detective to make sure you eat. I think he liked you."

Madison shook her head. "You go. Take the guys. I feel like walking."

Both of them turned as noise broke out above the din of several other crews talking things over. In the span of seconds, the area around them fell silent, and a whole bunch of interested faces focused on the ruckus going on in front of the Parliament building.

Teddy grabbed and hoisted the camera, already focusing as he strode that way.

Madison took a step, stalled, whirled back, drawn by the strangest sensation of being called.

She saw him. Her mysterious stranger from the club stood in the shadow of an open doorway, looking as tall and chic and intimidating as he had the night before. Maybe more so, because of her nocturnal fantasies about him.

The arch over the doorway kept his features hidden. If he saw her, he made no move to indicate recognition. But she knew him without the necessity of a close-up. Her nerves had begun to vibrate with a low-pitched hum. Her heartbeat ramped up to a tempo she didn't like and sure as hell didn't appreciate when the guy's scent still clung to strands of her hair.

"Teddy."

Her cameraman pivoted back with a nimble camera-balancing act.

"Can you get the front of that pub on tape?" she asked.

Teddy did so, then took off with the others.

"Got you for posterity," she said, swinging around to find that the man of her secret nighttime desires had already gone.

Running after him as fast as her wounded feet would carry her, Madison stumbled into the crowded pub, where at eight in the morning news crews from all over the world were killing time until the prime minister's speech.

New and familiar faces were swapping anecdotes, information and jokes. In spite of the seriousness of the press call, these seasoned veterans of the information highway knew how to relax when time allowed—a necessity to their health and well-being in a job that detailed loss and sadness on a daily basis.

Lots of faces glanced her way, none of them the one she sought. The mystery man had given her the slip. Yet if he wanted to avoid her after the alley escapade, why had he been here?

Leaning against a portion of the long, gleaming, mahogany bar, Madison looked around for a back exit. He liked those.

Conversations ceased abruptly as someone else entered the pub. Her attention strayed to the front door, where a man had stopped. His gaze found hers. He headed toward her.

"Miss Chase," D.I. Crane said in a lowered tone.

"Detective," Madison acknowledged with another unwelcome jump of nerves.

"Would you please come with me?" he said.

Everyone on the room listened with the uncanny instinct all newscasters and journalists possessed for a potential story in the making.

Madison frowned. "Have you found something else?"

"Please," he said. "Step outside for a minute."

She preceded him to the door, then to the sidewalk, where two other officers waited.

"What is it?" she asked, really antsy now.

D.I. Crane pulled an item from another ziplocked plastic evidence bag he was handed.

Good Lord, had they found something else?

When the item in the detective's hand appeared, Madison was so taken aback with relief, she almost laughed. He was holding up one of the silver shoes she had lost.

"Yours?" he asked, addressing, she assumed, the surprise written all over her face.

"Yes. Where did you find it?"

"Where did you lose it?"

"Somewhere between a club called Space and the street beside it."

He nodded. "You're sure this is your shoe."

Madison looked to his other empty hand. "Hell, do you only have one of them?"

"Only one." He held it higher for her inspection.

"It's mine. Would you like me to try it on, like Cinderella, to prove it?"

"Would you do that?"

She was glad he grinned. Until that moment, she hadn't been sure folks in the law-enforcement profession were capable of humor.

"I kicked the shoes off so that I could run faster," she explained.

The detective's right eyebrow went up quizzically.

"The hour was late. I had to get back to my hotel and couldn't find a cab."

This, she realized, was known as withholding information from the police. Private, personal information about her hunt for her brother, and the man she'd found instead in the club her brother believed housed creatures that went bump in the night. All these things were best left out of any conversation with the authorities.

"You just left your shoes behind?" D.I. Crane asked.

"After three drinks, let's just say I lost them, and leave it at that," Madison said.

Crane's grin thinned out. "We thought the shoe might belong to one of the missing girls until one of your roaming cameramen identified it. I wonder how he would know what you wear?"

"A lot of people have seen me in those shoes, on more than one occasion."

"That's what the guy from your crew confirmed when he saw the shoe arrive at the Eye."

"I'm sorry it doesn't help on the Yale case. We would all like to come up with a clue as to their whereabouts. After finding my brother's coat, I understand why you jumped on this."

The detective shrugged. "Is the shoe expensive?"

"You have no idea."

"In that case, we'll keep a lookout for the other one." He handed her the silver stiletto.

"I'll offer a reward if you do," Madison said.

D.I. Crane made to turn without quite getting all the way around. "May I offer some advice, Miss Chase?"

"I'm all ears, Detective."

"That club, Space, isn't the best place for tourists."

"Has there been trouble?"

"Lately, it seems there has been trouble everywhere."

The detective dug into his pocket for something, and handed her a business card. "You can reach me at this number, day or night, if you want to talk about your brother. We are looking for him, Miss Chase."

"I'm glad to hear it," Madison said.

He had more to say and wasn't shy about getting to it. "I'd prefer you heed my advice about that nightclub and the others around it. And if you lose more shoes, please let me know before we get our hopes up."

"I'll do that."

Wearing a good rendition of the perfect cop face, the detective said, "It's getting to be a habit…finding bits of your family's clothing lying about."

"At least I'm not missing."

"Not yet, at any rate."

The detective left her with that cryptic remark. Yet it wasn't his warning that tugged at her senses; it was the feeling that the mysterious stranger was somewhere nearby, and that she hadn't been entirely out of his sight since they'd met.

Her sigh was one of exasperation. A handsome, brazen stranger and a cryptic cop? What the hell was going on in London?

She should have been more concerned about the cops actually helping to find her brother than wondering about that stranger, and the fact that the words she heard in her head had become like the melody of a subliminal song.

"Don't be foolish…"

"Yes, well, I'll try not to disappoint you," she said aloud, earning a wary smile from an innocent passerby. "And I'll raise you one pointed stake."

Chapter 9

St. John stood on the rooftop of Space, looking down at the dark street, waiting. Would Madison's rebellious streak get the better of her? Would she show up when she had been warned to stay away?

He was dressed in black, his usual choice, not only as a metaphor for the loss of his soul, but because black was perfect camouflage for slipping in and out of darker places.

He and his brethren, called the *Seven*, had chosen ebony for the background of their crest, highlighted by a golden cup centered between two parallel stripes of crimson. One red stripe to represent the blood of the mortality they had left behind, and one for the first drink of the new blood that changed them so radically and forever.

They had painted this design on their shields with fluid from their veins, and etched the same design into the skin of their upper backs with the tip of a heated knife.

The tattoos were there now, between his shoulder blades; an ever-present reminder of what he had become and the goal he served—all of those things so much bigger than anyone knew.

He remembered, as he stared down at the crowd gathered by the club's entrance, how people had once flocked to him and his brethren for aid. And how, over time, those same people had run from the sight of the fated knights who never aged.

Times had changed, but his goals hadn't. Presently, he was more or less in disguise as just another immortal amid the world of London's immortals, playing a part, acting less than he was after a long, self-imposed exile.

He would break the very heart of the Hundred if necessary to find the being responsible for the creation of so many fanged monsters rummaging around in this city. His vow, taken so long ago, dictated that he find and eliminate the beast whose habit of biting and turning innocent people into bloodthirsty vampires created havoc on the streets.

His job was to guard the innocent, and protect them from the spread of vampirism, though the Seven had long ago all but given up on stemming the bloodred tide taking over the shadows. As the population of mortals exploded, so did that of the beasts. The Seven now had to settle for doing their best.

The wind whipped through his hair and St. John briefly shut his eyes. No one alive or dead, except for his six lost brothers in blood who were scattered around the globe, was privy to the reality of what his function in the world was. No one else knew that his quest continued to this day. Now, with rogues and Shades turning up all over the place, one woman threatened to challenge his goals by getting in the way.

And here she was.

"I didn't want to believe this," he whispered as Madison's fragrant scent filled him.

She stepped from a cab with her body cloaked in a black sheath and her hair glowing like urban wildfire. Stunning, contained, leggy and luscious, she had arrived tonight with a personal army in tow. Four of the men he'd seen around her that morning flanked her.

"You assume this might help, Madison?" he said.

She was tight, tense. Her presence ruffled across his nerve endings, urging him to move. She had ignored his warnings, but carried no questionable weapons.

"At least you had the sense for that," he said, sadly.

St. John braced himself, accepting the implosion of willpower that removed evidence of his superior strength by sucking some of his power inward and away from his outer shell of muscle, skin and bone. He left only enough of that power visible on the surface to firmly set his most recent, well-moderated, practiced persona.

Although the tattooed sigils stretching between his shoulder blades protested the loss of power with a warning sting, he shrugged it off.

"Just another run-of-the-mill immortal at the moment, attempting to ward off disaster," he muttered, taking the quickest way down.

This time, Madison had come prepared.

Arriving at Space armed with her crew, she hoped the four guys in her entourage would amount to testosterone camouflage.

The day had been disappointing. The prime minister's speech hadn't lived up to its expectations of offering anything new on the Yale Four, except for raising the reward. Since there were no new clues about the girls themselves, there had been plenty of media chatter and a lot of standing around after the necessary interviews.

Tired beyond belief, and emotionally drained from thinking about her brother's jacket and what the cops had found inside it, Madison kept a sharp eye out for any sign of hoodlums on a bender. She had mixed feelings about a rematch with the one man she figured might be here, because after finding that wooden stake, the vampire game they'd played seemed particularly dirty.

She had gone through her brother's research again after the incident at the Eye. Space remained the club of choice for finding vampires, Stewart had written. That chiseled stake only served to press home the fact of how serious her brother's quest was to find the fanged gang.

She had to take this equally as seriously if she were to find Stewart.

"Open your mind," she said. But embarrassment made her hope she'd make it through this night without meeting the fair-haired hunk who had nearly had his way with her in a cold, dark alley.

No such luck.

Two steps inside the club, she sensed him, possibly in the same way some animals sensed an oncoming storm system. The acknowledgment made her waver on her new black pumps.

"What'll it be, Madison?" Teddy shouted over the blaring music. "First one's on me."

"Virgin something. Thanks. I'll get the next round."

Jittery inside, Madison slowly raised her gaze. *He*

was there, all right, on the balcony in a languid echo of his pose from the night before. No doubt about it, he was looking back.

"So," she said, wondering if Tall, Fair and Distracting could read lips. "Now you show yourself?"

She ran a hand over her body-skimming black dress to rid herself of the sensation that his hands were on her, and braced for a meeting that seemed inevitable.

"Here." The sudden coolness of an icy glass pressed to her elbow made her jump.

"The BBC is at the bar," Teddy shouted over the music, handing her a neon-hued drink. "Want to hobnob?"

She nodded and shouted back. "Be there in a minute."

Raising his glass in salute, Teddy left her. Being alone in this club hadn't really been the plan. Madison looked up again to find that the man she had straddled in that alley was gone from his perch.

Resigned to getting back to her crew, for now, she started for the bar. "I suppose the only way to handle you is with a good dose of truth serum," she said over her shoulder.

Cool fingers closed over hers, stopping her motion, virtually stapling her in place. A sighed breath, close to her ear, stirred a few wisps of her hair.

There was no need to turn around. Only one man had the ability to affect her this way. His fingers on her wrist sent waves of explosive charges up her arms, made her heart flutter. She didn't appreciate the feeling that told her, in spite of her resolve, and against her better judgment, that she still had the hots for this guy.

"Truth serum wouldn't be my drink of choice," he

said in a tone as rich as she'd remembered, and twice as suggestive.

He let go of her hand. Madison lowered her glass to keep from dropping it.

"There isn't actually any drink called O Positive?" she finally said.

"Which is why I usually stick to a good malt whiskey."

Madison faced him, compelled to do so with what amounted to a very bad craving.

"You're here again," he said. "I don't suppose you were looking for me?"

"What would make you think that?"

"Just a wild guess."

She raised her glass. "Actually, you seem to turn up everywhere."

"London is a small place when there's a lot going on," he said.

"Yes. You were out there today. Do you work in the media?"

"I don't, though I have a vested interest in those who do."

"Really? How so?" she asked.

He really was quite something: smooth, elegant and not actually cocky, but way too confident. Her body was responding to those traits, as well as whatever other kind of magic he possessed. Rationalization seemed to have no say in the matter.

"I prefer quieter times," he confessed.

Even in her three-inch heels, she found that he towered over her. He also wore black, in the form of a soft coat and slacks. His black silk shirt was open at the neck. His brilliant mass of blond hair was long enough to cover his ears and, from memory, as sleek as the shirt.

The guy looked like an archangel gone over to the dark side, and Madison's body was appreciative of the results. She felt a flicker of excitement. Last night in bed, the mere thought of him had gifted her with an easy orgasm.

"Quieter times will help us all if things return to normal as quickly as possible," he said. "It's important for London."

"You do realize that people are missing. Maybe they're lost, or dead," she remarked.

"I hope they are alive, just as you do."

Despite her inner warnings, Madison looked up. "So, if not a member of the media, who are you?"

His eyes were a smoky sky-blue, and flecked with gold.

"I thought you knew," he replied.

"Let's stop with the games, okay? The time for them is over."

He conceded with a nod and the slightest hint of a grin. "My name is Christopher St. John."

"Yes, well, I'd be willing to bet you're no saint," Madison said.

"Most assuredly not a saint," he agreed.

"So, what do you want with me? Insider information? Are you with a London rag, or some other newspaper? For the record, I don't have any new information on those girls, and I regularly engage in sexual escapades with strangers in foreign cities, so doing so with you wasn't special."

His grin widened, suggesting that he knew she was full of crap. She saw a flash of white teeth behind the lips that had greedily trespassed on hers, but no sign of fangs.

He didn't move to press back the hair curtaining the

sharpness of his cheekbones. Nor did he show any sign of the smug expression she'd been expecting. He was, in fact, acting more or less like a gentleman.

She took a sip of her drink before setting the glass on the table beside her. Although she was used to men being attracted to her, and adept at shaking them off, she wasn't dislodging the focus of this one. She hadn't meant to dodge his attention, really, because she had questions

But his eyes sought hers now in the same way that his mouth had sought her mouth the night before. He had only touched her hand for a few seconds tonight, and that touch was a heady reminder of how far they could get on lust alone.

More to the point, she wanted a replay of the last night's events right now. He was so damn…*something*.

"I'm afraid I'm busy tonight," she said. "I'm with my crew. Rain check, maybe?"

His grin remained fixed. "Are the gentlemen at the bar here to protect you from me, I wonder, or protect you from yourself?"

Madison blinked slowly to avoid his gaze. If this bastard was going to push every single one of her buttons without letting up, she'd have to take back that stuff about thinking him gallant.

"I'm here looking for someone else," she said. "Maybe you know him? Stewart Chase?"

"Husband?" he said.

"Brother."

"What leads you to believe I might know about your brother?"

"A weapon the police found in his jacket made me think so."

There was a tap on her shoulder. Teddy had returned.

Damn. She had been asking crucial questions, and starting to get somewhere…while also contemplating what Christopher St. John's chest would feel like beneath that black shirt—a wicked thought that was totally out of place and at odds with her agenda.

She wasn't here for a replay. She was here for Stewart. Coveting Christopher St. John, in this circumstance, was an unforgivable sin.

Their game of the night before, that stake in Stewart's possession, St. John's remarks about *them* chasing her, had to be addressed. St. John and everything about this ridiculous club seemed to circle back to vampires.

Of course, she couldn't explore any of this in front of her cameraman.

"Yeah, Teddy?" she yelled.

Teddy made a comical dancing motion with his arms and feet.

Madison looked to St. John, thinking that the man across from her actually did look too good to be mortal. She hadn't been wrong about that. Or blind.

However, there was no way his voice had been inside her head that day. She had just imagined it.

"Ah. Then I'll leave you to your friends," St. John politely conceded with a nod of his head to Teddy. "We will run into each other again soon enough, I'm sure, Miss Chase."

"I suppose I can count on it," Madison agreed.

But when Teddy took her hand, she felt as though she had just made an error she might soon regret. She had a crazy notion that Christopher St. John did know more about the creatures her brother had been seeking than he let on. Call it intuition. Hell, call it whatever…but their meetings were so strange.

At the very least, he had to know about Stewart's suspicions about vampire presence in London, if he had played along the night before. Besides, Stewart had been to this club often enough to list it in his notes.

A vague disturbance seemed to hang in the air as St. John's eyes met hers one final time. Neither of them took a breath. Her heart raced.

Teddy had to lead her away. Madison turned to look back, struck by a strange feeling that each step away from St. John made the air between them thicker, and that the crowded room had begun to revolve, as if it would take her back to him.

St. John wasn't smiling.

She walked through the crowd with Teddy, without getting far. A brief flare of insight slammed into her like a dire warning alarm.

Whirling toward the direction of whatever had dragged at her attention, Madison watched a shadow cross the stairs to the balcony. As that shadow passed beneath a high-tech wall sconce, a pale, proud face became visible for a fraction of a second.

She was startled. Her body jerked. Tearing herself from Teddy's casual grip, she ran toward the stairs, pushing people out of her way, sprinting after the man she would have known anywhere.

Her brother.

Chapter 10

St. John was watching Madison when her expression grew stricken, as if she'd seen a ghost.

He caught her at the exit with a firm hand on her elbow. Stopping her momentum, he swung Madison around and encircled her with his arms.

"That wasn't who you think it was," he said as she wriggled to get free. "Trust me on this, you do not want to follow that man."

"Let me go!"

Releasing her wasn't a possibility, though they were making a scene by the door and people were eyeing them with concern. Beyond that crowd, St. John scented another immortal heading their way.

"Not for you," he said to Madison. "Do you hear me? What you saw is not for you."

When she refused to settle down and listen, he picked

her up in his arms and headed outside so fast, her glossy scarlet lips parted speechlessly. Even there they weren't alone. The queue for the club was long. The picture he presented by holding her in his arms attracted attention. To get out of this, he'd have to improvise.

He pressed his mouth to hers, absorbing her rising shouts, blowing gentle breaths into her that were the equivalent of an instant dose of Valium.

Her struggles ceased.

"That's it," he encouraged. "Good."

Although her body relaxed slightly, Madison's lips trembled beneath his as if she'd fight this directive if she could get any words of argument out. Those vibrations, so very alluringly feminine, forced St. John to take stock of his balance.

She felt light in his arms. He felt the sleekness of her long, bare legs through his clothes.

Her lipstick tasted like cherries.

The physical desire he had developed for this mortal was beyond his comprehension. Each ragged breath she fought for was sweet, stirring in him memories best forgotten.

But Madison had seen the shadows. Stewart had been moving fast, with a speed few human eyes should have perceived, and yet she had seen him. The truth was that Madison possessed at least some extraspecial senses, just as her brother did. She was showing signs of becoming exactly like her twin.

St. John's arms tensed. His mouth stopped moving over hers.

It was possible, even probable, he thought, that Madison shared her brother's tweaked genetics, and this was the source of the darkness he had detected. But two vampire hunters in one family was unheard of.

He tasted that darkness now, with his lips on hers and her breath in his lungs. If Madison didn't know about the darkness, it meant that her genes had to be latent. However, like her brother, she was seemingly driven toward vampires, instead of away from them.

Bloody hell. It was entirely possible that the Chase twins had shared more than a womb, and had been sprung from a family of Slayers.

As he continued to hold Madison, with his lips resting on hers, St. John's mind raced on.

The attraction between Slayers and vampires was legendary. Vampire hunters had some special cocktail added to their DNA sequencing that didn't dilute or disappear as generations of them lived and died. This was a symbiotic relationship meant to keep the balance between mortals and the monsters that preyed on them. A negative relationship, really, since in the end both Slayer and monster became victims of the very drives that pushed them toward each other.

Was this it? Had he found the key to Madison? The blood in their veins recognized each other?

Or…perhaps he had merely lived too long, and his mind played tricks by offering a respite from the trials of his past in the form of an insatiable attraction to a beautiful woman.

His guess, the one that felt right, was that Madison wasn't completely human, and didn't know that the traits hidden inside her were the same ones that hadn't made things turn out well for her brother.

That morning, he'd made it his task to find out everything about Madison Chase.

The family that had produced the twins had been taken from them prematurely. Madison and her brother were raised by a foster family that they had left as soon as they were able to, due to some kind of trouble there.

Overcoming the trials of their upbringing, the twins were both successful, bright and glamorous. But the loss of her one remaining family member might be the final straw for Madison. Without her brother, her twin, she was alone in the world.

It was entirely possible, he thought now, that Madison had no idea how special she actually might be, if his intuition was right. Slayers were rare enough. Two in one family was a complete anomaly. As his mouth moved over hers, St. John tasted pain. He knew the cost and the toll pain took, but couldn't afford to overthink how Madison's might have affected her.

For everyone's sake, you must leave this city before others take your life from you. He silently sent messages to her. *Maybe then you'll have a chance.*

They were, after all, allies in the war against vampires. His vow as an immortal had been to protect the purity of the original few immortals, and see that their blood didn't get spread around. No one despised the fanged hordes creating chaos on the fringes of mortal society more than he did.

And Madison...

What would make her leave London?

He didn't want to see her hurt. Being a Slayer-in-the-making would do more harm than good, with no skill set to back it up. Fledglings would continue to scent her.

If she refused to leave without her brother, she'd have to be forced to go by removing the one hope she clung to, that of finding Stewart, even if doing so broke her.

If she was going to be a Slayer once her inner and outer awareness merged, she'd be needed in the world. Eventually, she would help to keep the balance. They were in accord about this.

As for her recognition of him…

She couldn't know about his true identity or purpose. No one could be allowed to find the Seven. He'd have to distance himself before she found out. He'd have to prove to her that he was no gentleman at all, and send her sprinting away. He'd play the bastard, and watch her run.

The persistent ache in St. John's chest told him he'd do this. He would do it to save her.

Damn though… The back of his neck prickled with a physical warning that the ancient entity in the club who had seen them together had reached the door.

Not only could he *not* distance himself from Madison at the moment, he had to make this moment count, and make it look good.

"No time like the present for a show," he said to Madison, drawing back slowly, meeting her dazed, questioning gaze. "Everyone loves lovers."

He crushed her mouth with his in a sudden, deep, drowning kiss, fighting to make himself believe this didn't actually matter.

He worked to keep his fangs from her as Madison began to spiral upward from numbness, waiting to see what she'd do next, telling himself that she would forgive him if she understood the problems at hand.

What happened was the biggest surprise yet.

She didn't put up a fight, or slap his face. She didn't go on about her brother. She sighed through parted lips. Likely those lips hadn't opened for him in order to participate in the kiss, and only to protest such treatment, but an explosion of searing passion caught St. John up in a whirling vortex, all the same.

His nerves fired. The blood of the blessed immortals surged in his veins. He kept kissing her, deeply, seriously, as if his life truly depended on this meeting of their mouths, not wanting to confront the disturbing thought that fate might be offering him a final test regarding his vow, after all this time.

He held a being that immortals called a *Recumbent* in his arms: a sleeping Slayer who hadn't yet come into her own. And he could not stop kissing her, or wanting to possess her.

Madison's slick, lush lips opened for him like the folding petals of a night-blooming flower. Their tongues met, darted away, came back in a dance of tension and need that erased the boundaries of enemies in transition.

Enslaved by her mouth, St. John pressed on, unable to help himself, physically enforcing a connection that now catapulted them to an arena where pure sensation ruled. He seemed to be drowning. After centuries, time finally came to a standstill.

His fangs were extended. His cock was erect and aching for her. All the while, his heart thundered in time to hers, as if every inch of their bodies called out to the other for a unification that would have been dangerous in any circumstance, and at the same time sublime.

Levels of awareness peeled back, hurtling him and Madison toward something forbidden, and wondrous. They were nearly there. Not long now, and their souls would find each other through a porthole that defied the rules of life and death. A space reserved for like minds and thirsty souls, no matter what housed those souls.

Dangerous.

Scandalous.

Deadly.

And bloody poor timing.

Meeting Madison in that luminous place where the sun paled by comparison meant that the only thing left would be to take her soul in his hands and twist it out of recognition. Doing so would be the end of her, and a swift exit from his vow.

Noise faded in from the periphery.

Exulted by the open display of mouth-to-mouth sex on the sidewalk, the crowd beside them clapped their hands, laughed and jeered. "Get a room!"

Stop kissing her. Pull away, St. John's mind warned.

Madison was limp in his arms, and not from any loss of spirit. She seemed to be waiting for him to devour her completely. Expecting it. She wanted to lose herself in the strength of his passion. He sensed this in her.

In the end, he had done nothing to help her. He had, in nearly every way that counted, made the situation worse.

Her bare arms clung to his neck, capturing him as surely as if she'd slipped a silver chain around his heart.

Her skin scalded him. Her mouth was an inferno. St. John raked the points of his fangs across her lower lip, leaving a lipstickless line there, a line in the sand of sorts, and a warning of the impossibility of actually crossing a final boundary.

He wondered how bliss like this could end, when he had searched for such a thing for so long without knowing it. When he hadn't been moved in this way for more years than he cared to count, if ever.

But the enormity of his pleasure came with its own shadow, in the form of an interruption.

A fresh, looming darkness stretched across the promise of the light resting in his arms. As the crowd beside them trudged toward the club's door, the etchings between St. John's shoulder blades began to burn as if someone had tripped the tattooed sigils carved into his skin.

Tearing his mouth from the lips clinging to his, he raised his head to meet the gaze of the immortal who stood in the club's open doorway.

A blast of frosty air ripped through the surroundings with a desire-wilting chill. This was a stern warning from the other entity, a pronouncement of that Ancient's disapproval.

St. John didn't want to heed that warning. The bittersweet torment of having Madison in his arms was too great. Her heat spread through him like a violent, raging fire, warming him from the inside out. Until now, he hadn't realized how cold he had been.

The surrounding chill met that heat with a soft hiss. His shoulder blades pinched with a new discomfort as the stripes fused to his skin with the blood of the seven Blood Knights writhed like living things.

This kind of alarm he could not ignore.

How he wanted, against all his principles and the approach of a powerful ancient entity, to throw Madison against a wall and take her in every physical way possible, front to back, teeth to groin. Right there. Right now. He wanted her that badly. He had all but decided.

Yet he could not possibly want her badly enough to ruin what he'd so carefully set in place. Or badly enough to leave so many others vulnerable to the network of evil that had ensnared one of the Hundred, and made one privileged Ancient a traitor to his kind.

By listening to the song of his own longings, St. John might lose sight of the beast he had been after.

With a last brief return to Madison's lips, he pulled back. Madison should have been running by now. He wasn't holding her so very tightly.

A nonphysical touch pierced his mind. Coldness invaded, quickly overwhelming and replacing Madison's marvelous heat. This cold was far more lethal than his ambitious liaison with Madison. This cold would eat the woman in his arms alive if it touched her.

He set Madison down and stepped in front of her to deflect the chill. Although it was imperative that he keep hold of her, and hide her latent abilities from the others, it was equally as important to maintain his disguise. So much depended on that disguise.

Madison moved at last. Sidestepping him, she looked to the immortal in the doorway, then back to St. John.

She was a sight, with her dress creased and her hair in disarray. Her smeared lipstick gave the impression of a chin covered in blood. She looked wild, and so very lovely.

Beneath wide, uncertain eyes, her swollen lips opened. Steadying herself with a bracing breath, she tried to take a step. Satisfied that she could walk, she took another step, then another, her heels making tapping noises on the concrete as she headed for the club's entrance.

There, as she made to brush past the two-hundred-year-old vampire who kept St. John in his sights, she paused, as though some part of her recognized that the entity in the doorway might be dangerous.

Good God...had his kiss made that possible?

Had his good intentions been wasted?

St. John felt the shiver that ran through Madison. He watched her last step wobble. *Do not let him know,* he wanted to shout. *Do not meet that creature's eyes.*

Had she heard? She left the entity in the doorway alone, and said over her shoulder with a vehemence of tone that didn't quite ring true, "Damn you, and the fantasy you rode in on, St. John. If you try anything like that again, I'll sue."

Then she was gone.

Reluctantly, agonizingly, St. John transferred his attention to the immortal gazing questioningly after Madison, not realizing he had just interfered in a life-altering moment, and that nothing from here on out, for any of them, would ever be the same.

Madison made it through the front door of the club before collapsing against a wall. Her hands were shaking. Her entire body shook along with the hands.

Her brother had been here, hadn't he?

Christopher St. John and the old creep in the doorway blocked her from finding out, and now it was probably too late.

What had St. John whispered to her this time?

"What you saw is not for you."

The earlier anxiousness came tumbling back. If Stewart had been in this club, the fact that she had missed him was hurtful, unthinkable. Whichever way it had gone down, the man with the name of a saint and a mouth like fire had a hand in that. He had kept her from going after her brother.

After regaining her balance, Madison found herself surrounded by Teddy and the other guys, a circle of males that wasn't quite as comforting as it should have been, because as it turned out, she had needed protection from herself. From her attraction to a monster, whether St. John was human or not.

"Ready to go?" Teddy shouted over the music.

Madison nodded. She had to get out of there. Alongside these guys, no one would dare to stop her exit.

She'd made a fool of herself in public two nights in a row and needed some thinking time. She felt confused, frightened. Not one real answer had been found here, unless it was a question of Stewart's possible, momentary whereabouts, and the realization of her own character flaws.

That was something, right?

Teddy handed her a napkin, and pointed to her face. Madison wiped at her mouth, removing the smeared lipstick, feeling stupid. Her walk to the door garnered smiles from people she passed.

"Yeah, I know," she said. "Quite the show."

Although she had a good grip on herself at the moment, she dreaded going outside. Taking a firm hold on Teddy's arm, she sighed with relief when there were no tall, fair strangers on the sidewalk, and no gray-haired creep in the doorway who actually looked like a vampire.

Climbing into a cab at the curb, she couldn't begin to comprehend the pang of regret running through her— not only about the possibility of Christopher St. John keeping her from going after a man that may have been her brother, but because St. John's kiss had so easily disrupted her sense of purpose.

And something else about the night nagged at her consciousness.

Wait a minute.

Madison snapped herself straight on the seat and blinked slowly to pull up a memory.

She and St. John had been having a conversation near the dance floor, and neither of them had been shouting.

With the music blaring, she had heard every word he'd said, when that was impossible.

Goose bumps appeared on every available surface of her body. She rubbed her arms, pretty damn sure she actually was going mad. But no, everyone else had been shouting in order to be heard.

She stopped rubbing.

How could she have heard St. John? Surely not by any normal means, unless she had suddenly become adept at reading lips, and he had the same ability.

And if not?

If she took those oddities into Stewart's world, of which that damn club was supposedly a part...did those things insinuate that Christopher St. John might be one of the creatures Stewart had been after?

Could a vampire mesmerize her into wanting and giving in to that kiss?

Laughable.

What about the sex they'd nearly had on a side street?

No, she was looking for an out, and setting all blame on Christopher St. John.

All the same, her nerves spiked annoyingly as she looked at her hand, picturing a sharpened stake in it. Her beloved brother's stake. A thing that belonged to Stewart, her twin, who seemed to believe wholeheartedly in his research. Not a hobby. Nothing like that. Who the hell else, other than a true believer, carried a weapon like that around?

Absurd? Well...yes.

Besides, what reason would Christopher St. John, as a man or as some other creature, have for thwarting her plans, when those plans were as simple as finding her brother, and reporting on those missing girls? What would he gain by distracting her?

A more reasonable explanation was that Christopher St. John might just have been the right guy at the right time to tempt her, and it turned out that lust was blind to everything else going on.

Still, once the ridiculous thoughts had taken root, Madison couldn't dislodge them.

In the backseat of the black London cab, sandwiched between the guys in her crew, and trying not to shake hard enough to draw attention to herself, Madison laid her head back, and closed her eyes.

"She saw her brother," St. John said to Simon Monteforte on the street bordering Space. "My distraction worked, but what was he doing here? How did he get inside?"

Simon Monteforte, a formidable creature, looked the part of the ancient vampire. He was as tall as St. John, and deceptively lean. Under his coat were several layers of steel.

Stone-gray hair, worn straight and long, splayed out over the shoulders of a forest-green velvet tunic as dark as the night itself. Black form-fitting jeans covered all but the tips of expensive polished black boots. Born of French aristocracy, Monteforte retained his original patrician bearing and airs. He had never lost his accent. His love of luxury showed.

He also owned half the block around Space.

Because Monteforte had been around a long time, St. John continued to rein himself in—no easy feat when his heart was in that cab with Madison.

He wanted to look at the street, and didn't dare. Immortals as old as Monteforte could easily smell trouble. They scented lies and deceit like those things were simply new fragrances wafting in the air.

St. John had centuries on Monteforte, and a strength that had once been the stuff of tales. There was no one amid the Hundred, here or anywhere else, for a Blood Knight to truly fear if he exposed his true nature. But he could not blow his cover.

"Besides," he said to Monteforte, "who are we to stop her brother? Stewart Chase killed two young rogues last night."

"So, my friend, did you." Monteforte tilted his head in mock thought. "Or was it five fledglings you took down? I lose count these days when I'm not concentrating."

St. John smiled at the wily immortal's obvious lie. The creature across from him, like himself, probably remembered everything he'd ever done and every idea he'd had. This was both a curse and a blessing for those who had lived so long, depending on the immortal's outlook.

Often, if he didn't watch himself, St. John still heard the voices of the people in his own past, as well as the screams of those he had killed in battle, in the name of honor and the golden quest. After years of this kind of haunting, he had grown used to the whispers inside his head.

At the moment though, those distant voices were silent. His heartbeat continued to echo Madison's. His tattoos burned with cold blue fire.

He willed himself to stay in the moment, knowing Madison was thinking about him, desiring him in a way she didn't understand.

Twitching his shoulders to ease the discomfort centered between them, St. John eyed the creature beside him. As he allowed his gaze to roam over Monteforte's sullen face, the burn on his back became barely tolerable.

Is it you, then, Simon? Is it possible that you're the traitor? My marks think this might be so.

"I suppose you can find her brother quite easily," Monteforte said.

"Why call him out when he does us a service?" St. John asked.

"For the time being, that may be true. There are indeed too many unauthorized, random turnings lately. However, we wouldn't want these kills to go to Stewart's head, so that he desires bigger and better fare."

As Monteforte spoke those words, he stroked the sleeve of his velvet coat with a slender white hand, as if the sleeve were part of a lover's limb.

"It was wise to remove the fledglings from the club last night," Monteforte continued. "Yet you took the woman with you."

St. John nodded. "As bait to get them out in the open."

The white hand stopped stroking the sleeve. "Did she see them?"

"*Thugs* was the term she used, likely thinking they were after her purse. Since they were trained on her, getting her out of the club and out of the way seemed crucial."

So is this deception. What might you be hiding, Simon? Do I see something in your eyes?

"Thugs." Monteforte pulled a face. "A rather brutish American word, *n'est ce pas?* She doesn't hold to the beliefs of her brother, then?"

"She does not." St. John knew he had to be careful now, when standing close to Simon Monteforte. He had to be sure the pain streaking across his shoulders was in honor of this ancient French immortal.

"Nor does she know what you are?" Monteforte asked.

"It's doubtful that anyone knows."

More caution was necessary here, St. John realized after making that remark.

He had tasted the edge of the secret buried inside Madison Chase. Last night had been a fantastic game to her, when thugs and vampires inherently were no part of her reality. But as a newscaster, she'd latch on to any oddities tossed her way. And as a Slayer, fully awakened to her skills, no vampire would be off her radar.

If Madison believed she had seen her brother tonight, she would hunker down and pursue the issue with talons of steel. Simon Monteforte, the creature across from him, would see her again and perhaps glean her secrets as well.

Another piercing stab between his shoulder blades brought St. John up from thought.

Monteforte said, "You do realize that Miss Chase may become a liability?"

"Any minute now," St. John agreed, hating the need for such deceptions, but noting that the burning chill of his tattoos definitely seemed to be tied to the being across from him.

He took a step closer to Monteforte, just to be sure.

The tattoos screamed with distress.

"You will take care of this?" Monteforte asked point-edly. "Take care of her?"

"Of course," St. John said, watching the old vampire carefully.

"Then I'll bid you *adieu,*" Monteforte concluded, and disappeared back into the club like the shadow he was.

"Adieu," St. John echoed, not to the immortal that had

just tripped his alarms as a possible traitor to his kind, but to the street where Madison's cab had taken her from him in the nick of time.

One more moment in that heady embrace, out of the trillions of them he had endured since his death and rebirth as what he now was, and he wouldn't have been responsible for his actions.

His fangs thrummed. His skin hurt. The sigils on his back were cold enough to frost the night. He was anxious for more of what the dazzling redhead had to offer, and couldn't be allowed to trip her latent Slayer switches.

Amid all that, he had to look into the fact that Monteforte had become a viable candidate for the term *monster maker*.

Anxiety made him turn.

The taillights of Madison's cab were gone.

He had to deal with Monteforte. That was his job, and he would do it. First, though, he'd make sure that Madison got back to her hotel safely.

"Safe from everyone, other than myself, that is," he said aloud as he took off at a run.

Chapter 11

She was bone-tired, flustered, and a detective was waiting for her in the lobby.

Madison didn't bother to hide her displeasure, and wondered why she couldn't cut a break.

D.I. Crane addressed her crew with a brief nod, and then turned to her. "Can I have a minute, Miss Chase?"

"She's been through a lot today," Teddy said.

"I understand that." Crane took a handkerchief from his pocket and handed it to her.

Madison glanced to Teddy, who shrugged, then nodded for her to use it.

The white handkerchief she used to wipe her face and mouth with came back as red as the napkin at the club had. The detective's white hankie was ruined.

"It's important," Crane said. "Has to do with what we found today."

Sweet Lord, Madison thought. Had it only been that

morning they had discovered Stewart's leather jacket and what he'd hidden inside it? That awful weapon that seemed to haunt her?

She smiled stiffly at Teddy. "I'll be up in five."

"Better make it ten," the detective said, earning a glare from her crew as they headed for the stairs.

"I don't think they like me," he said.

"Does anyone truly like cops?"

"I find that unusual, since we're the good guys."

"You bring bad news. People don't like bad news. I'm assuming that's the case here?"

The detective shrugged. "We've stumbled upon something else I'd like you to take a look at."

"I'm not sure I can take more surprises."

"Oh, I'm fairly certain you're able to stand a lot, Miss Chase. More than most."

Madison wondered what D.I. Crane would do if she asked him if he believed in vampires, and decided to let the question sit, since he was openly staring at the red marks on the handkerchief.

"What is it you want to show me, Detective?"

He removed an article from an evidence bag. It was her other silver shoe.

"We needed to be alone for this unveiling?" Madison asked.

"It's more a case of where we found this shoe, than the shoe itself, that's important."

"Where did you find it?"

"Near an abandoned building by the water."

Madison raised an eyebrow.

"Next to a pile of ashes," the detective said.

"Someone tried to burn my shoe?"

"If that was their intention, they failed. No, Miss Chase, I'm afraid it was a person that burned up."

"What?" Madison's chills returned. The knot in her stomach that she hadn't been able to get to dissolve since landing in London twisted. "What do you mean?"

"The ash we analyzed appears at first glance to be the remains of a person." He let that sink in for a minute. "The question I now have is why your shoe was found next to him?"

"Him?"

"Figure of speech," D.I. Crane said. "It could just as easily be female."

Madison had a bad feeling about this. She had kicked off her shoes last night in order to ditch some lowlifes. True, the silver stilettos were expensive, but what would a bunch of hoodlums want with only one of them? Why hadn't they picked up both while they were at it, since the detectives had found the other one right where she'd left it?

The immediate reply she heard inside her head was totally insane, but the first answer that came to mind. Maybe that gang had used her discarded shoe to somehow aid their search for her.

But the only instance in which a shoe could have helped in a chase, unless it had a directional chip in it, was if…

Was if those young asses had been vampires, and had used the scent of her shoe to track her.

Which would also mean that Christopher St. John had been right in his inferences about *them*.

"Is something wrong?" D.I. Crane asked.

Madison widened her stance as far as the hem of her

tight skirt would allow in order to remain upright. What she was thinking was nightmarish and unutterable.

"I don't know how my shoe ended up anywhere but where I lost it," she heard herself say. "I left them near the club called Space, as I explained earlier, when you gave me the first one. I don't know anything about ashes, or a body."

She couldn't go on. A paragraph in her brother's notes had mentioned what happened to vampires when they suffered a final death. They were reduced to ash.

Ash.

Suddenly, she wanted to sit down.

She dropped the handkerchief to the floor.

"Miss Chase, were you alone last night?" the detective asked.

"Do I need an alibi?"

She'd have given anything to ask about the length of the teeth they'd found in that pile, but the detective was studying her intently. Being labeled loony by law enforcement wouldn't help anyone here. She could not speak of vampires, and of chasing through the night, away from a pack of them.

"I'd appreciate it if you'd answer the question," the detective said.

"No. I wasn't alone."

"You were with your news crew?"

Madison shook her head.

"A friend?" the detective pressed.

"I met a man at the club."

"His name?"

"St. John. Christopher St. John."

D.I. Crane gave her an odd, unreadable look, then he

nodded and let the subject drop, as if St. John's name was some kind of magic password.

"All right." He glanced at the handkerchief on the floor by Madison's feet. "I'll have to keep this shoe."

"Fine."

The truth was that she didn't want anything to do with that shoe. Maybe a vampire had touched it, and maybe it had just appeared at the scene of a homicide. She supposed there was no way that vampire ash could be checked for DNA, or if the police could track down someone who had died twice.

She looked at the floor. *To hell with you, Stewart, for that grisly thought.*

The detective continued to stare at the red-stained handkerchief. If he was wondering about that wooden stake in Stewart's jacket, he might also be pondering if the Chase twins were homicidal maniacs.

"A few years ago there were cases of homeless people being torched on the streets," she said, needing to come up with an alternate explanation for the one ludicrously taking over her mind. Because if that pile of ash had been a vampire, the world as she and every other human on the planet had always imagined it was a fake.

She put a hand to her forehead.

"Yes," the detective said. "That could be the case here as well. This kind of burn, however, would have required a flamethrower."

Or a wooden stake through the heart.

Madison pressed her hair behind her ears with shaky hands. "Flamethrower," she said. "God, I hope not."

The detective bent over to retrieve his handkerchief. "Well, you're tired," he said. "So, I'll leave you with more advice. It might be a good idea if you keep your crew with you tomorrow."

"You mean in case I might need another alibi?"

Crane tucked the handkerchief into his pocket. She wondered if he was going to check it for DNA.

"Shall I walk you upstairs?" he asked.

"I can manage."

"I'll see you tomorrow, Miss Chase."

"Hopefully not," Madison muttered as he walked away.

Somehow, she made it to the elevator, and heard the ping of its arrival. Before stepping in, she spun back. "Detective?"

He stopped at the door.

"Do you know Christopher St. John?"

"Not personally," he said.

"Is he a credible alibi for last night?"

"Most people around here would think so."

"Do you?"

"What I think doesn't matter. St. John is…highly regarded in important circles."

Trained to pick up on the importance of hesitant nuances, Madison said, "What circles would those be?"

"Just about every one that counts these days," the detective replied.

"I really can't figure out how my shoe got to where you found it," she said.

"I believe you."

With a polite wave of his hand, D.I. Crane exited the lobby, leaving Madison alone with all of the injustices of the world pressing in on her. A world that was shouting for her to consider the possibility that it might be populated by fanged dead men, even though she wanted to think she knew better.

Pressing the button to her floor was a chore.

The elevator, empty, small and ancient, seemed crowded with the thoughts plaguing her.

But Stewart was alive.

And she would find him, if she could keep herself on track.

When she got upstairs she found Teddy sitting on the floor outside her door. He got to his feet. "Everything okay?"

"The good detective found one of my shoes," Madison said.

"He needed to see you in private to talk about a shoe?"

She shrugged. "It's mind-boggling."

"Well, I'll say good night, then. I'm beat." Teddy yawned. "I still have to go over some video footage."

"Do you want some help?"

"No, but thanks for the offer."

"'Night, Teddy," Madison said. "Thanks."

"For what?"

"Being there." Madison pointed to the spot on the floor where he'd been sitting.

Teddy smiled. "You're entirely welcome."

Madison waited with her hand on the doorknob until Teddy had disappeared, almost afraid to go into her room. The tingling sensations at the back of her neck had started up again. Her nerves were humming, leaving her jumpy and on edge. If this was a premonition of something about to happen, it was a doozy.

Shaking off the idea of calling Teddy back, she entered the room with her senses on full alert, and sank against the closed door without taking another step or reaching for the light switch. Her eyes didn't have to adjust to the dark for her to know that the room had been disturbed.

Her gaze moved to the window that stood wide open.

Her pulse pounded against her throat, inhibiting speech.

This was the same reaction she'd had from the beginning. Always the racing heart. Always the almost visceral need to step closer to a gathering storm.

The man causing this was here. No mistake. But if the police knew him, and thought him a good enough alibi, Christopher St. John couldn't be part of any alien, otherworldly species. As for her earlier concerns, she had merely read St. John's lips at the club. There was no second-guessing the laws of such a fierce, animal attraction.

What she should be doing was returning to the streets. Anyone with real strength of conviction would return to the West End to look for further clues as to Stewart's whereabouts, in case it had been him she'd seen tonight.

A whiff of the scent of musk hit her.

She blanched, said, "I know you're here."

Christopher St. John's closeness was like a brush of black velvet on her overworked senses. The surface of the door felt hard and unforgiving against her tense back muscles, but there was no way she'd leave it. She couldn't have moved if she'd tried.

"If you used that window to get in here, I don't know how you managed it without actually being Spider-Man," she said.

The telling flutter deep inside her was taking over her interior. Waiting for St. John to speak, Madison perceived every other noise, from her own raspy breathing to the sounds on the street outside, but St. John, the trespasser, didn't say a word.

"Vampire got your tongue?" she said.

With an unbelievable speed, St. John was beside her, crushing to the door in a replay of their closeness that first night in the secluded alley. His body was close enough for her to feel every exquisite inch.

"How dare you show up like this," she said, fending off a medley of signals that were the exact opposite of the stern chastisement she'd meant to issue. The sheer, almost mystical power of St. John's masculinity had the ability to make the choicest arguments fade. He was potent, and live with a virile form of raw sexuality. God help her, she was a sucker for those things. She could not turn away.

"Why are you here?" she demanded.

"You may be in danger."

Her voice cracked. "There was a detective here not five minutes ago, and probably still within shouting distance."

"Do you imagine that if I was the danger, that detective could stop me from taking what I want?"

Madison shook her head. "I don't imagine anyone could stop you from doing anything."

Whatever she'd said made him close his eyes. Although she couldn't see that in the dark, she knew he had, because she had shut hers.

She was pinned to the door, and the intensity of whatever was going on between her and this man was not only insane, it grew stronger by the second. As crazy as it seemed, she wanted to tear his clothes off and feel his hardness firsthand. She wanted to finish what they had started the night before.

None of it was logical, but did it have to be? So many emotions were running rampant.

"Come away from here, with me," St. John said.

"Where?"

"Does it matter?"

"Of course it matters. I've got a job to do."

His cheek, cool and smooth against hers, made Madison's pulse sky-rocket with beats that filled the room.

The bed was a few feet away. She wondered if St. John would take her there and fire up this ongoing, raging desire once and for all, so that she could move beyond it. So that she could think straight, and get this guy out of her system.

When his lips rested lightly on her temple, she sucked in air as if starved for oxygen. He stayed there for a while before angling his mouth toward her chin in an agonizing trail of heat and tempered passion that was all the more seductive because of its soft, ethereal nature.

Nothing bad could be this good, surely? She was a hormonal explosion waiting to go off, and thankful she couldn't fill in his outline. She was glad the darkness hid her face from him. Her lips were quaking with the need for him to find them. The rush of damp heat between her thighs signaled that her body was willing to take this as far as it would go, for better or worse.

In no way could she stop this tumultuous longing now, in spite of the fact that she and St. John were strangers, really, and despite the former, ridiculous suppositions that he might not be human.

She gave the desk a sideways glance. On it sat her computer, containing a hundred files on vampires. The detective had just told her someone had been turned to ash, near her shoe. The shoe she had been wearing when she was with Christopher St. John.

Was it possible that St. John knew anything about this? St. John, who could very well fit the bill of being an immortal, according to her brother. Hadn't she, minutes before, been considering that very thing, because of the intensity of her insatiable lust for him, as well as her ability to think she heard him, and her inability to avoid him?

God...

St. John's lips were on hers now, again. They drifted over her mouth in a flaming reminder of the former make-out session that had tripped every fail-safe switch she possessed.

"What do you want from me?" she asked breathlessly.

"Everything," he said.

Okay. They would do this. Get it over with.

He wore no coat now, making it easier for her fingers to clench the fabric of his black silk shirt. His muscles tensed when she touched him, almost as if the gorgeous, overtly sexual St. John wasn't used to being handled in return.

Tugged free of his waistband, his shirt bunched in her hands. He groaned when she pressed her fingertips into the bare flesh of his lower back. His roving lips paused, poised against her neck, beneath her right ear, above her thundering pulse.

The energy building between them was wild, and whining for release. Emotion? Hell, this was so far beyond emotion as to be laughable. What she needed right that minute was to join St. John on the floor if necessary, to resolve this. All of their scrambled heat needed an outlet.

Possibly it wasn't even this illicit meeting that was causing the emotional arc, but instead, the pain of the last few weeks needing to be replaced by something mind-blowing and special.

"Come with me," he repeated hoarsely. "Away from here."

"So that you can protect me from the bogeyman?"

"Yes." He lowered his voice. "The man you saw outside the club tonight has focused his attention on you, and your search for your brother. He is dangerous. You must take care."

"He knew who I was?"

"Oh, yes."

"Is he a vampire?" Madison stumbled over the term. Though she'd used it partially in jest, there was nothing funny about her need to understand her brother's obsession with fanged creatures, and her own growing belief that things weren't as they seemed. She had felt that old man's strangeness when she passed him in that doorway. For a second, maybe two, she had believed him to actually be one of her brother's creatures of the night.

"Why would that man care what I do?" she asked, feeling his teeth graze her very sensitive neck.

"You bring notoriety to private concerns," St. John said. "Space is close to those interests."

"Some Protector you are, then. Will you issue a warning, and then offer a kiss to make it all better? Will you keep returning to me as if I were your own personal plaything?"

The sound he made in response to that remark was as silky as his shirt, and wickedly delicious. "Yes," he whispered.

He seemed to be anticipating something. A green light

for a momentous sexual escapade? One thing was certain. This guy was all male, all man; no bit of ephemeral mist topped off with fangs. Who could step away from him, or this, when her feelings for him were so insanely intense?

His needs matched hers, washing over Madison in relentless waves. The air heating up between them was new and exhilarating. She'd never felt anything like it, like this, like him, and didn't want this moment to end.

"Are you doing this to me? Making me susceptible to your finer points?" she demanded.

"You're admitting I have some finer points?"

"This close, I'm fully aware of them."

He drew back and smiled. "You knew I'd come."

"I should be questioning how I knew."

St. John's hands reached up into her hair. He held her face so that he could gaze at her in a way she couldn't return in the dark. She felt his attention, though, just as she'd been aware of his smile. Her body knew what was coming.

Her lips parted for him with no further thought. When his mouth claimed hers with an intimacy that was so much more than lips and tongues, it felt to Madison like a continuation of the ravenous mingling of two hungry souls.

When his hands drifted possessively over her hips, and down the length of her thighs, nothing else mattered except the relief of finally getting to the core of her cravings.

She had to get this unwieldy attraction out of the way, and giving in to that attraction was the only way to do so.

In a slick repeat performance of their time in the alley, his fingers found the hem of her dress. As the material rose over her thighs in an agonizingly slow ascent, time seemed suspended. St. John's fingers were pure sensory bliss. The promise behind the rise of her dress had the impact of a shout.

Cool air on her skin told her that only the thinnest of lace barriers kept him from her now. She'd worn black lace tonight, in his honor. His interest in her partially naked body clearly showed.

Strong hands cupped her bare buttocks, freeing her from the door. With a flex of his arms, St. John lifted her slightly, settling her over him as if they were already fully unclothed, and getting down to it.

Dissatisfied with that, he slipped one hand between her legs, in search of the place that if he were to reach again tonight, skin to skin, would lead him to her sexual soul, if not her actual one.

Her head hit the wall, hard, and Madison didn't care. The flames licking at her were coming fast. She was going down in those flames, and this time, she wouldn't stop them. She had no intention of calling this off. She was completely under his spell.

The movement of his talented hands—over her mound, under the edge of her black thong—hinted at what pleasures were to follow. To ensure that those pleasures did follow, Madison separated her legs and uttered the sultry sigh bubbling up from inside her.

His lips came back to hers with a hunger that rocked her. Her body melted into him. Her hands crawled up the curve of his spine, expecting perfection, relishing in the feel of his bare skin.

She hesitated, surprised when she discovered several raised lines of what had to be scar tissue. The man kissing her had incurred injuries in the past, serious ones to leave such marks. Had someone hurt him badly? Was the cause of these marks an accident, or war wounds?

She knew nothing about him, her mind warned, and yet she desired to kiss those marks away, taste them with her tongue, trace them in the light. She hardly noticed when the pressure between her thighs increased, and how she willingly accepted this.

Then she was on the floor. Not the bed. Urgency demanded that they couldn't get that far.

St. John's weight eased on top of her. He was propped on his elbows, with his face above hers. He still wore his clothes. She wore most of hers. There had been no time to draw this out.

Before her final shudder of expectation, he had pulled her underwear over her ankles. The action, and the knowledge of what it was going to lead up to, was as rich as it was dangerous.

"I—" she sputtered, cut off when he entered her with a slick, partial thrust.

Startled by the sheer pleasure of this, she cried out. St. John made a similar sound, his gasp of surprise threatening to bring her to a peak way too soon.

It seemed to her that his breathy response wasn't indicative of a man's victory over a woman, but of one closer to a verbal manifestation of pain.

She couldn't hold on to any thought for long. St. John was well-endowed and talented. His next thrust, so deep and exactly right, filled her completely, bringing spasms of internal pleasure in what turned out to be only the warm-up. The introduction.

She wanted more. Wanted it all. Was nearly out of her mind with need.

He knew when to back off and make her writhe. He

understood how to prolong her obscene craving for him.
Holding himself motionless for seconds at a time, he
then sent his hips forward, dipping into her slowly, almost maddeningly gracefully, while she clutched at his
hips and his back.

She wanted him closer yet, deeper, and opened her
mouth to demand satisfaction. But he had foreseen this.
His next thrust was harder, slicker. Straight, true, this
one stretched her to her limits, demanding full access
to what she kept back.

She wrapped herself around him, used her muscles
to encourage their connection. She dug at his back and
shoulders with her nails, tearing at the silk shirt that remained the only cool sensation in a world on fire, wanting him to share in this crazy, sublime form of torture.

If he felt the pain of her talons, it only drove him on.

A rhythm built between them until their bodies
slammed together with a damp, explosive heat. Madison gripped him hard. She beat at him with her fists, in
need of something she couldn't yet define.

In the dimness, the eyes above hers, once so blue, appeared a solid midnight-black in his pale face. St. John's
fair hair shone like moonlight. Her talented lover brought
her to the edge of that peak of satisfaction over and over
again, carefully monitoring how long she'd stay there,
suspended on the verge of an orgasm. He left her panting, gasping, needing more.

Not one piece of her was left out of this taking. Arms,
legs, breasts, thighs, as well as every nerve and cell she
possessed, burned for him. The only thing left was to
let him have it all, sure that no one could survive much
more of this.

Relaxing her insides took effort. When St. John felt

that last release, and the internal shudder accompanying it, he took full advantage. Pushing himself into uncharted depths, able to get past the last of her reservations, he stroked the sweet spot she had been saving.

The world dropped away as the intensity of this final action brought down a rain of feeling, emotion, fire and wonder. Madison screamed, not recognizing her voice, and with no idea that she was saying, "Vampire. God-damn vampire."

St. John's mouth absorbed those curses, and the sob that followed. With his cock still buried inside her, his mouth scorched hers insatiably.

Madison's muscles seized when the orgasm arrived, volcanic, exotic and vicious in intensity. St. John kept her in that shivering, shuddering place where essences mingled and the mind took a holiday. He held her there, sheathed to his hips inside her, and he didn't move or ease up.

Madison rode this cresting wave of outrageous plea-sure that made her vision go haywire. Behind closed eyelids, colors revolved, moving rapidly from black to gray to light, like the turning of a mental kaleidoscope, before landing on red. A vibrant, shimmering crimson overlay that overpowered all the rest.

Suddenly, she was no longer soaking up this pleasure, but was out from beneath him.

With lightning-fast reflexes, she rolled Christopher St. John onto his back, and straddled him, on her knees. Her hands, on his shoulders, pinned him down. A strange sound escaped her that was exactly like a growl.

Horrified, and reeling from the brilliance of her cli-max, Madison launched herself sideways. She opened her eyes, and said in a voice as shaky as the rest of her, "What the hell was that?"

Her lover was quiet for several beats. When he spoke, his tone was husky, his words drawn out. "So," St. John said. "I guess we now know about you."

Madison sat back on her heels, more confused than ever as she pondered what he had said. *Know about her?*

"Bastard," she said. "Do you mean that I've proved to be an easy conquest?"

"I didn't mean anything of the kind," he replied. "It's you who stopped the pleasure."

Had she? The lingering rumble of her orgasm was fading into the distance like an earthquake blowing through. Breathing was tough. The rest of what had happened was a blur.

Yes. She had stopped this.

Was her reflexive disengagement from St. John her body's way of rebelling against such incredible intimacy? Was she trying to protect herself from what would happen next, when Christopher St. John would smile and then leave, having successfully impaled the media sweetheart?

Could she be as vulnerable as that?

The room had gone dark again, but the fright of the red stain behind her eyes wouldn't leave her. Instead of going back to St. John, on the floor, she got up on unsteady legs and backed away. This had been so very good. The best. A first. Jesus, this round of sex had made her hallucinate.

When St. John stood, her eyes remained riveted to him. Having adjusted to the dark, she saw the expression of concern on his face.

He was silhouetted by the light from outside the window. His shirt was open, and torn, revealing the phenomenally bare muscularity of his chest. Crossing his flesh, and easy to see in the dimness, were the scores of scratches she had made while trying to get at him. Each of them had drawn a thin line of blood. Dark blood, of a color approaching maroon.

She couldn't look anywhere but at those scratches, when the awful truth was that she wanted to be in his arms again, and couldn't figure out how to get there.

Sex hadn't resolved anything. What they had between them hadn't even begun to burn itself out. She had to speak. Someone had to.

"I'm sorry." She pointed to his welts with trembling fingers. "For that."

"It's nothing," he said.

"Someone has hurt you before. Those raised lines on your back."

He didn't acknowledge that comment, or explain.

"Did you come here tonight, to do this?" Her gaze dropped to the floor.

"No," he said.

"That's right. You came to warn me to be careful. Did you expect this, though? That this might happen between us?"

"Yes," he replied. "But I came here for another purpose, to warn that you've become an easy target for trouble, whether or not you realize it, and that until you leave England, that won't change."

"I'm used to the spotlight, but the word you used was *danger*. You've insinuated that the man in the doorway of the club is the danger," Madison said. "Why?"

"You are prying into private business."

"I haven't even begun to pry," she said. "And I have

no idea what you're talking about. I'm here to report on the missing girls. How could the interviews I've done in regard to that case get me in trouble?"

"It brought you to the club, Madison, twice."

"Lots of people go there."

"None of them looking for Stewart Chase."

The mention of her brother's name was like a slap in the face.

"What has my brother got to do with any of this?"

"I can't tell you that, and suggest that you don't return to Space in your search for answers. I'd ask you not to be alone right now, and that you keep your crew nearby for the rest of your stay."

"Are you in league with that damn detective? I'm not sure what right either of you have to suggest anything like that," Madison said. "If you can't tell me what's behind those cautions, how do you expect me to give them credence?"

"I'm asking you to believe me," he said soberly, "because I actually have your best interest and safety in mind."

Madison's hand went to her forehead, to the ache between her eyes that had made her world color and shine. "How do you know about my brother?"

"I know that he also has disappeared."

"Why would my going to the club in search of him be dangerous?"

"Because of his beliefs."

Madison blinked slowly, and repeated, "His beliefs?" She added softly, "You know about that?"

"I know about it."

Madison had a hard time taking this in. "I'm not sure how many more surprises or warnings I can take at the moment, to be honest," she said. "You, and what we just did, seem to be the biggest surprise of all."

It was a confession of her scrambled feelings. She knew this, and so did the man across from her. What they had just shared was different, special, mind-blowing and possibly even scary as hell. But their intimacy, and what he had to say afterward, left her more confused than ever.

Christopher St. John said he knew about her brother's obsession. But she hadn't known about it until recently. So, how did St. John know?

"Tell me," she said. "Tell me how you know about Stewart."

She waited for him to answer, but his nearness was creating more questions than that. Grinding their bodies together on the floor of her hotel room had left her with a desire for him that went far beyond any normal man-woman attraction. She was on fire, even now, with so much up in the air.

"Take a minute," he said without moving closer to her. "Then meet me downstairs."

Things might have been different if he had touched her, or if she had gone to him, and they had comforted each other, held each other. Maybe the questions wouldn't have mattered so much if she had someone to share them with. But they were acting almost as if nothing had happened, when she…God, when she wanted more than anything for it to happen again.

Why couldn't she chalk this up to the one-night stand, and move on, when she so desperately needed to do that?

How could one little spark derail something as important as finding Stewart?

St. John finally moved. He took an item from his

pocket, which he set on the sill. "Meet me in the lobby, Madison," he said. "As soon as you can."

"I'm not going anywhere else tonight."

"You asked for my help. I think you'll want to hear what I have to say when we've both had a few seconds of breathing time. Meet me downstairs. It may not be in your best interest to do so, but you will value the importance of what I'm going to show you."

"You will answer my questions? Why not do so first, and I'll decide what to do next."

He looked at her for a long time. "I've had a tip about those missing girls," he said.

Madison leaned on her hands to hide how badly they quaked. She used the wall to keep upright.

"Why didn't you mention this before?"

"We needed to get something else out of the way first."

The sex. Yes, they had needed to indulge in the thing that was gumming up the works. The problem was that it was obvious, by the tension between them, that it had only made the cravings worse.

Priorities? Hell. Her brother and the Yale girls were at the top of the list, and the urge to straddle St. John had been powerful enough to make her almost forget that.

Smoothing her dress over her hips took self-control. As she shoved the tangle of tousled hair back from her face, Madison's gaze snapped to the window while she called up her courage and her wits.

She stared beyond what was out there, at a city drenched in mystery and intrigue, all those things tainted in one way or another by her brother's horrid files, because Stewart's research haunted her, even now, in these moments with St. John, in a way that defied explanation. Stewart's research just would not go away.

Her feelings of being on the verge of an important discovery, right here, this minute, wasn't only due to St. John's knowledge of Stewart. It was more than that. It *meant* more than that.

She heard St. John's heart beating from a distance of two feet. She perceived his anxiousness as if it were her own. His voice sang in her mind with phrases she shouldn't have been able to hear, and yet she had heard him whispering from the start.

That wasn't all.

The blood rushing through her veins felt unnaturally hot. Her muscles twitched and danced across her bones. The room smelled like wool and musk and forbidden liaisons, and it tasted like sex—sweet and sultry on her tongue.

Beyond those things lay the unmistakable metallic odor of blood. St. John's blood, pooling on the scratches she'd made with her nails, though she could no longer see those marks because of the way he was standing.

Then, there was the red haze that had cloaked the dark.

Frowning, Madison glanced to her left, where the light on her laptop was a niggling form of harassment, telling her to beware of strangers and their intentions, telling her that not everything was always as it seemed, at least in her brother's world.

And Christopher St. John stood there, among all those uncanny perceptions, looking not like a lover, but like some kind of dark, angelic avenger.

"How archaic death by staking seems," she said, voicing a thought instigated by her awareness of the computer. "Unlike using a gun, and firing a bullet, using a wooden stake for a weapon, with the intention of piercing a victim's heart, would necessitate being close enough to look an opponent in the eyes."

St. John eyes met hers. She felt his rapt attention.

"If there were such a thing as vampires, would I be able to kill one, if necessary?" she said. "Would I be able to take you out, if you proved to be a monster in disguise?"

"That's a funny thought," St. John said. "What made you say it?"

"Obsession." Madison struggled for a breath that eluded her. "The tendency must run in my family. My brother was obsessed with London. I appear to be obsessed with you."

More time passed, uncomfortably, after that pronouncement.

"If you won't tell me about Stewart, what kind of tip do you have about the girls? Give me something. Anything," Madison finally said.

"The girls were seen at a hotel near here. I'll take you there."

"Now?"

"It's not public information, Madison. This is for your ears only. The hotel is private."

"Who told you about this?"

"I can't say. You understand about protecting sources."

Madison set her shoulders. "Sex was the payment for that information? With sex out of the way, you'll assist me in the job I've come here to do, in regard to those missing girls?"

"You don't really believe that what we did has anything to do with anything other than what's happening between us on a personal level," he said. "Why even go there."

"I don't know what to believe."

Madison eyed the laptop and the blinking light that haunted her so mercilessly. "You just cautioned me about roaming around. You said going to the club in search of my brother was dangerous, without saying why."

"That warning still stands. More, I cannot say."

She knew that his tip had to be followed up on, no matter what she did or didn't feel about the man who had given it to her, and how cryptic he could be. Other lives were at stake.

"I'll meet you. Give me that minute," she said.

"I'll be waiting."

Those simple words startled her in a way she couldn't explain. She had heard them in her mind all day. It suddenly seemed that St. John used them here to prove that he truly had been inside her mind telepathically, first conquering that, and then her body.

Christopher St. John appeared to be the bigger danger here, and Madison wondered how she'd move her feet, let alone face him in any kind of light. If he was so perceptive, how could he not know that she was suddenly afraid to leave her room, and that he was partly the cause of this fear?

"I'll bring Teddy," she said.

"I'm not the bad guy here, Madison. Not tonight, anyway. No Teddy. I'll have a car standing by if that will make you feel better."

"You can't carry me?"

She was sorry for the sarcasm, but didn't know what else to say. She longed for his touch as if truly addicted, and sorely needed time away from him in order to recuperate.

When St. John stepped up to her, and again slipped

his hands into her hair, she withheld what would have been a telling whimper.

He let several strands of her hair slide through his fingers. He was close enough to kiss her and yet he didn't. He wasn't making this easy at all.

Madison had to move away from the door, away from him, to get a grip on her flailing feelings. She watched him pull his shirt around his bare chest, and reach for the knob beside her.

She stopped him with a question.

"Do you believe in vampires, St. John?"

"Really, Madison. I wonder why you'd mention death by wooden stake, and then ask such a question."

"As much as I wonder why you singled me out in that club and led me to believe…"

"Believe what?" he prompted.

"That you know about vampires."

"Isn't it true that a small percentage of most populations believe in the supernatural?" he said.

"Are you one of them?"

"You're asking if I believe in such things?"

"I'm asking if you're one of them. If you are a vampire."

Madison was sure she saw him wince.

"Not a vampire," he said. "Not in the way you mean."

"Is there another way?"

"Anyone who preys on others, in any way, is a vampire, don't you think?"

"Yes," she agreed. "I suppose you're right. But that doesn't answer my question."

"I'm not one of them," he said. "Not one of those."

"You aren't lying?"

"I don't lie, Madison. I never lie."

"Everyone lies."

"There would be consequences if I did, none of them very pleasant."

"Now you actually believe you're a saint?" she said.

"I have already confessed to having no aspirations in that direction."

"Then why don't you just tell me what you've found out about the hotel and those girls, and save us a trip. That would be saintly enough."

"Because you'll go there alone, without me, and that wouldn't be a good thing," he said. "No story is worth that."

"It would be dangerous to go there without you?"

"You have no idea how much." Christopher St. John left the room, taking his disarming, addictive presence with him, and leaving Madison, half-naked, completely unenlightened and hungering for him in a way that was too crazy to be tolerated, staring after him.

It was becoming a habit.

A very bad habit.

Chapter 12

Small licks of leftover desire inhibited every step St. John took as he left Madison. Delicious heat. Monstrous heat.

He could have stayed inside her forever. He hadn't wanted the moment to end. But something had happened on that floor. Madison, he believed, had glimpsed her destiny.

Through the closed door, he heard her sigh of relief, and longed to feel that breath on his face. He wanted to see her skin glisten with anticipation, and watch her cheeks flush pink, when going back to her, getting close to her again, wasn't right, or to be condoned.

He hadn't meant to do this. Take her. Indulge. He had known he'd have to stay away from her for this very reason. In the heat of passion, with her body wrapped around an immortal, she had revealed her true colors. What might have been a fleeting glimpse for her of what lay ahead, was devastatingly real for him.

And yet it truly had only been a glimpse for you, Madison.

She had asked about vampires without realizing her special connection to them. In their lovemaking, she had perceived his Otherness without fully recognizing it.

He had to soak this in, and see his next move. But he didn't like it. How could he? In order to address this with her, he'd have to explain about himself.

It seems that your brother has kept one particular secret to himself.

That secret pertained to what the Chase twins actually were. When Madison had moved from beneath him, it was because her instincts for survival had inadvertently kicked in. Her latent genes had gone into action. Their intimacy had made her see him with half-closed perception.

Madison. Hell. What now?

This was an untimely mess. With repeated proximity to vampires, Madison was beginning to use her senses in a different, predetermined way. Taking that further, if a single dose of Other could awaken her, what might repeated sexual encounters with a centuries-old immortal instigate?

Their blood was calling to each other. There was no doubt about this. Chemistry was sealing the deal. Created to be opposite, he had confused her because he truly wasn't one of the vampires a Slayer could identify clearly.

They were on the same side in the fight against vampires. Again, though, explanations for this would be necessary if she found out about her calling and mistook him for something dangerous.

Why don't you know what you are?

Slayers were usually fully honed by the time they entered puberty. Madison was in her twenties. Her brother had also only recently stumbled on the new image of his future.

Maybe being a twin has stifled some of your ingrained perceptions, overwhelming those perceptions with others.

The dilemma was excruciating.

If he were to remain close to Madison, in any way, there was a chance her nature might take her over completely. She'd be unable to resist following her instincts about going after vampires. It's what they all feared. And what Simon Monteforte had warned him of. Notoriety. Secrets getting out.

In a city teeming with freshly bitten, mindless fledglings and fanged rogues, and ruled by a hundred elegant immortals, how could she keep her identity safe from the Hundred? She'd be driven, compelled to find them, once she woke up. Whatever particles swam in her genetic makeup would demand that she did so. And there were more monsters in London than anywhere else on earth.

Slayer.

St. John shut his eyes to block out the image of Madison with a wooden stake in her hand.

He had done this. In getting as close to her as a man could get with a woman, he had encouraged that dark thing inside her to blossom.

Not only that, he was going to take her to an establishment that reeked of immortality and unedited extravagance, where women willingly came to bleed for the creatures who kept them in the lap of luxury, and who catered to their keepers' monstrous whims.

He'd told her he had a tip, and hated to think what that kind of atmosphere might do to a Slayer who was awakening. But if she got her story, she'd leave the city and be safe from those who preyed on the Slayers who threatened to prey on them.

She had scented his blood. He'd seen this in her. If Madison happened to see a drop on the carpet of that hotel, would that further hurtle her toward her future? Toward the very thing her brother had come here for, before it all went bad?

He had to be careful. He smelled that Otherness in her now, on him, in her lingering scent—the addicting peppery flavor that heralded the reason he'd been drawn to her.

The fact was…he should have known from the beginning. It was a grave oversight. A rueful one. He didn't make mistakes often.

Stewart Chase had come to look for vampires, and had been bitten by the vampires he chased. To ensure that Madison got out of London before becoming a full-fledged Slayer, causing more trouble, hurting herself, he had to leave his attraction to her behind.

Christ, the thought hurt.

Nevertheless, it had to be done.

After all the time he'd spent alone, the woman he'd bonded with wasn't truly mortal at all. Not completely. She was a vampire's natural-born enemy, and would soon have the strength to prove it.

And he couldn't tell her about his own task, or how important it was for him to maintain his disguise, allowing the Hundred to trust him. To her, he'd be one of the monsters. She'd never know the whole story.

As he got off the elevator, St. John glared at its open door. He'd be willing to bet that if any of his brethren had ever run across a Slayer, none of them had dared to bed one.

He should leave now. If he didn't wait for Madison, she might go back to her room. She might be safe for a while, on her own.

"You might never know what you are."

His voice was hushed, almost angry. "Yet I told you about the hotel around the corner, and that the missing American girls had been there. What media-savvy newscaster would let that tip go unheeded?"

Damn...this...dilemma!

In no way could he actually afford to explain that her brother had been right about London, and that due to Stewart Chase's beliefs, her twin had become monstrous in his own right.

He dared not tell her that by aiding her here, in London, with Simon Monteforte and the rest of the Hundred looking on, more harm would come to her than good, and that because of her brother, her death warrant may already have been signed.

Death warrant.

Simon Monteforte had become a prime suspect in St. John's search for the hidden traitor to the Hundred, and if Monteforte was creating scores of rogue vampires for some sinister purpose, the old immortal could easily send the monsters Madison's way.

Damn and blast. He was stuck. Damned if he helped Madison, and damned if he didn't. His longing for her was so viciously palpable, even now, he wanted to pry the elevator doors open with his teeth, and get back to her.

"And when you find out that vampires helped to kill the humanity in your brother, what then?" he said.

Yes, what then?

Ignoring the pressures building inside him, St. John paced in the lobby. It was too late to do anything but await his lover, who was not only in serious danger, but ultimately the enemy of every nonmortal creature, anywhere.

It was too damn bad there were so many of them.

When she could breathe normally, Madison went to the window. The item St. John had left on the sill was her cell phone. There was no use in wondering how he had gotten it.

She jumped when the phone buzzed, and pulled up a text message from Teddy. You might want to take a look at the video footage. Something strange about it.

Who in the world, she wanted to shout, had time for more strangeness?

Although St. John wasn't in the room, she felt his nearness. St. John's vibe was subtly sexual, like a kiss of moonlight on sun-warmed flesh. Like swallowing parts of the night, and perilously close to metaphysical intercourse. Her senses were blaring, shouting, warning, that he was waiting for her.

In order to get the information he possessed, she had to see him. If she could help to solve this case, and find her brother, they could all go home.

From the neckline of her dress, Madison retrieved D.I. Crane's business card. She looked at it for some time, hearing those whispers in her head again, this time clearly in St. John's voice. *"Your only chance is to accept what help I can give."*

Palming her phone in one hand and the detective's card in the other, Madison weighed her options.

Then she noticed the blood on her fingers.

She ran her fingers across her mouth, and found another trace of blood. Their lovemaking had been rough. Her mouth hurt.

But there were girls to be found. A brother to be found.

She picked up her shoes and said to St. John, in case he somehow was actually listening with that spooky telepathic connection, "Just so you know, I told Detective Crane I was with you last night. You're the first place he will look if anything happens to me."

Inwardly cursing her ability to place herself in danger in situations where information was at stake, Madison added one more thing.

"It's for them this time. Those girls. Not for you, or because I need to see you again."

She showered off quickly, and stepped past the dress on the floor that still smelled like her lover. She exited the room quietly. Four girls and one man were already missing. Odds were against her possessing the personal magic necessary to keep out of that count if she continually placed herself in the path of danger.

She'd had trouble keeping on track lately, but would have to gear up for the game. Maybe, just maybe, Christopher St. John really was a good guy, besides being phenomenally good in the sack.

"Yeah, well, I never said I wasn't stupid," she muttered, tucking herself into the corner of the elevator as the contraption began its descent. "If I had, I'd be lying."

Chapter 13

She was not prepared for the breathtaking sight of Christopher St. John in the hotel's ambient light. She had to speak to keep from beating at him with her fists over the chaos he was causing with her resolve.

"I have a funny feeling that your voice speaks to me inside my head," she said.

"The voice of good conscience, I hope," he returned.

"If this leads to those girls, I'll be the first to let you know."

He nodded. "My car is waiting, as promised."

"If the place we're going is around the corner, I'd rather walk." She really needed a blast of chilly London air to cool her off.

Acquiescing, St. John moved aside without touching her, though she was sure he'd thought about it. Worse yet, she had. He had donned a fresh shirt and a black leather jacket, brought to him by the chauffeur of his car, no doubt.

"I hope there aren't any gangs roaming around tonight." Her tone was harsher than she would have liked. Self-defense, she guessed. St. John was staring at her mouth, at the blood she tasted on it.

She wiped her lips with the back of her hand.

"I can assure you those same monsters won't be here," he said.

She felt a stir of air on the side of her face when he waved off his driver. The car he'd alluded to was a black Mercedes. St. John, himself, was a streamlined Ferrari.

He wore expensive clothes and had a chauffeur, and had never actually mentioned what he did for a living. She hadn't thought to ask. Big reminder: she knew nothing about him, and her skills as a journalist were sadly lacking whenever he was around.

Taking a quick visual sweep of the street turned up an uncomfortable lack of people. The incident in her room remained a silent undercurrent between herself and the man beside her as they walked.

"Where are we going?" she asked.

"The hotel is called Germand."

The deepness of St. John's voice was similar to a smooth caress between her thighs. Her mouth wasn't the only body part feeling bruised as she pulled those thighs together.

"Inside, there's a private area where local businessmen and dignitaries often go," he explained.

"Dignitaries? What would four college girls be doing in a place like that?"

"They would have to be invited."

Madison stopped walking. "College girls? That doesn't sound right."

There wasn't any point in explaining about her instincts and how they worked, especially since her initial instincts hadn't been wrong about him. But she knew something. The place St. John was taking her to was *off*. Just hearing the name of that hotel gave her shivers. The Germand wasn't right, somehow.

"Do you go there?" she asked.

"Never."

Somehow, that made her feel better. When St. John walked on, Madison followed.

"I take it someone saw the girls there?" she said.

"They stayed at the hotel for a couple of nights."

Madison stopped again, perplexed. "Are you kidding? Why hasn't that come out?"

St. John turned around to face her. "Maybe they were broke, flattered, and it was an offer too good to refuse. Maybe their parents never told them about the possible perils of accepting attention from strangers."

"The people working there didn't come forward to talk about it, or provide what may be an important detail in the case?"

"The staff at that hotel are notoriously discreet."

"They're also withholding information from an investigation."

"You know sometimes things aren't completely black or white, Madison. However, they did tell me, when pressed."

When he brushed up against her, meaning to urge her forward, unexpected jolts of electricity shot through Madison. Although she kept walking, she gave St. John a sideways glance.

Did he also feel the heat burning between them?

Planning to say something about that, she stopped abruptly, as if someone had yanked on her arm. Scanning the dark street, she was caught off guard by a distant voice. Not St. John's voice this time, but a thin voice, sounding tired, and strained.

Madison forgot to breathe. She felt her face drain of color. She recognized that voice.

"Stewart?" she whispered. "Is that you?"

Seeing Madison spin, St. John dropped all semblance of calm and reached for her. Pulling her with him, he backed toward the building.

"It's my brother," she said. Her face was as white as paper. Her eyes had taken on a haunted cast.

Stewart Chase, damn the beast, had found his sister.

And his own decision not to get close to her again had just blown to pieces.

"It's Stewart," Madison insisted. "He's here."

The new vibration ruffled across St. John's skin with a recognizable chill. It was her brother, all right, but again, not the same one she was expecting, and Stewart had the fangs to prove it.

This new turn of events was a fine mess. Finding her brother would seal the lid on Madison's coffin. She'd know for sure about vampires and Others, and was in a convenient position to expose them, if she didn't attempt to take matters into her own hands first.

Ninety-nine of the immortals comprising the Hundred weren't killers, but they would act to protect their own, if it came to that. Only one of them was a cold-blooded murderer. He wanted to find that one. Especially now, before that killer found the next Slayer.

He tightened his hold on Madison to keep Stewart Chase's presence away from the woman who wanted it most, surprised that her twin had been able to locate her so quickly, when Stewart had only recently been turned.

He hoped that Stewart wasn't so far gone yet that he'd harm his sister, though he'd harm her enough just by showing himself.

Go from here. He sent a silent message to Stewart. *You will hurt her more if you stay.*

"He called to me. He's here." Madison was twisting in his grip. "Where is he? Why doesn't he come out?"

"You may have only thought you heard him."

"Bullshit. I can *feel* him."

"Come on." St. John led her quickly to the sidewalk. "The hotel is just there."

Shaking her head spread crimson curls that were now a blatant contrast to her colorless face. "Help me," she said. "Help me, St. John. Christopher. Please."

Maybe the *please* did it. Possibly it was the stricken look on her lovely face, and the way his heartbeat entwined with hers. He was one of the most powerful creatures on the earth, but in that moment, as Madison's eyes met his, he felt powerless to resist her.

"If it is your brother, he can follow," he said, fisting his hands to keep from taking what he wanted. Madison's mouth. Her body. Her innocence about the existence of monsters.

Due to what he had become such a long time ago, he also selfishly wanted her soul. Because only with her soul surrendered, could he truly have her, truly protect her.

"One thing at a time, Madison. Possibly that one thing will lead to another."

He could almost guarantee that it would.

The Germand's doorman eyed them solemnly, then bowed his head and stepped aside. St. John took one more look over his shoulder, at the street, where Stewart's vibration was like broken glass along his neural pathways. The man had been changed, bitten by the wrong sort of vampire. The Ancients hadn't cared overmuch about the aggressive young American attorney knocking at their door, or what he might have had to say about bartering for their help with the missing girls.

Stewart Chase, in his current incarnation, was a wild card, an anomaly, and still killing vamps. At least for the present.

"I don't like this place," Madison said, balking just past the door.

St. John hardly heard her. It wasn't her brother now who had drawn his attention.

He sniffed the air, and swore beneath his breath. Outside, nearby, more visitors were coming, the likes of which St. John hadn't sensed for quite some time. Monsters he instantly knew the feel and taste of. The atmosphere stank of their imminent journey here. The fabric of the night was shifting to accommodate them.

Surprised, St. John looked from the street to Madison, with real concern. Blood Hunters were on the prowl. Fanged invaders were on their way. *Nosferatu,* an ugly name that made most immortals cringe.

Along with the scent, a full picture appeared in his mind, and the image was damnable. This new plague wasn't coming to London for the sport of killing humans. Not if there wasn't an army of them.

Another spike along his nerves told him these monsters had to be coming for him, personally. There was no other reason for letting a few select Nosferatu loose in a city, other than having a target of consequence. Outside of his search for the traitor among the Hundred, and more and more vampire kills, there was nothing out of the ordinary going on.

The thought stopped him cold. His cover had to have been blown. His commitment here had been compromised.

Having found the whereabouts of a Blood Knight, someone had sent Nosferatu to find him. Creatures notorious for prying secrets from other vampires in the most gruesome of ways would hope to peel back the pieces of his golden vow in order to reveal that vow's source.

Grotesque in the extreme, warrior Nosferatu were strong, mean and driven. They were the minions of a strong master, their Prime, and were vampiric hit men of the worst kind. Soulless hellhounds, bent on destruction. Though a small number of them couldn't take him down, the damage they would inflict on London streets while trying to find him could bring long-hidden secrets into the open. Innocent people might be slaughtered by the dozens. Mortals could finally find out what else walked among them.

Who had done this?

Whoever it was knew about him, and also knew him well enough to figure that he might barter to keep the lives of the people in this city safe. They might assume he'd trade information on his origins, in return for saving the city from a bloodbath.

With an uncharacteristic uneasiness, St. John focused on Madison. Her back was rigid. She fought to maintain an outward appearance of calm when that calm had been stripped from her.

He hoped to God she wasn't picking up on his own

tenseness with her up-and-coming Slayer sensitivities. He had pledged to protect her from the darkness, but the presence of these particular monsters, sent for him and spiraling closer, was about to change everything…if he didn't find them first.

In order to save the woman at his side, the only way for him to help her, and so many others now, would be to get clear of all of them and, when the freaks arrived, go after the abominations coming after him.

Someone else would have to watch over Madison in his place.

A nosy detective, maybe.

Madison had pleaded for his help, and he couldn't oblige. He couldn't allow her, or any other innocent, to get in the crossfire of an old feud.

A shock of cold pain between his shoulder blades made him turn. He scanned the room. Apart from the oncoming wave of fanged creatures, this hotel had also been compromised. A noticeable heaviness lay on the air. Shadows hid in the corners. Something sinister had just occurred here.

"I'm sorry," he said to Madison. "We have to go. I shouldn't have brought you here. It's no longer safe."

The stricken expression on the face of the woman with whom his soul had braided told him she awaited an explanation that she would never get. He had to remain here, and face what lay in this hotel's shadows before doing anything else. It took a monster to fight a monster, with any hope of success, if that's what the atmosphere of the Germand indicated.

Anxiously, he grabbed hold of the clerk behind the desk and hauled the poor man onto the shiny oak surface. Peering into that man's worried face, he said, "Get her back to her hotel. Now. Safely."

As the man emphatically gestured for Madison to follow him, another presence filled the room—a green velvet haze that looked for all the world like a patch of lush, verdant grass with the promise of a snake hiding in it.

"No need to scare the pants off the poor devil," Simon Monteforte said in a voice rivaling the night's chill as he fastidiously wiped a drop of crimson liquid from his mouth. "I will see to Miss Chase, personally."

"The hell you will," St. John replied.

Chapter 14

"*Run!*"

The silent command beat at Madison's ears, compelling her to obey. She had never been so frightened.

Looking back and forth from Christopher St. John to the gaunt, sober-featured face of the man she had earlier brushed past in the doorway of Space, she immediately picked up on the strain in the room.

Without waiting for what might happen next, knowing only that she had to get away from that ghastly hotel and the scary apparition in green, Madison turned and sprinted through the open doorway.

No one stopped her.

She ran as if her life depended on it, pretty sure that it did. The quickly covered-up grimace of distaste that St. John hadn't been able to hide from her as he faced the gray-haired man provided the impetus for a fast getaway. Instead of answers to the questions she'd started out with, new craziness had piled up.

That man in the hotel had blood on his chin.

At the end of the short block, where a sharp turn led to her hotel, she realized she was no longer alone. Static pulled her fine hairs to attention. Goose bumps arrived in droves.

Her legs faltered, feeling unnaturally heavy and weak. Without hearing anyone coming, she knew someone was there. The hotel clerk? Another gang of creeps bent on harassing tourists near the long line of popular hotels?

The word *run* replayed over and over like an echo in her overworked mind, in St. John's voice, forcing her to put one foot in front of the other. The entrance to her hotel was only a few yards away, but she ran as if the sidewalk were composed of ankle-deep mud, each step labored and hard-won. Not enough air got into her lungs to make breathing count.

Tired of this crap, disgusted with weakness, she made herself move, and skidded on a damp section of concrete. She broke her fall by bashing the building's wall with her right shoulder, and she cried out. A hand covered her mouth. An arm wrapped around her waist.

Her fear multiplied, though she hadn't lost her wits this time. Using her teeth to try to free herself, Madison bit the palm of the hand covering her mouth, hard, hoping to do damage.

The acrid taste of blood, hot, thick, made her gag, but it also gave her more anxious energy. She kicked out behind her with nearly useless legs, and felt one kick connect.

Take that, prick!

Whoever held on to her didn't seem to notice the kind

of injury a well-placed high heel could inflict. Her attacker made no sound and no other move, other than to try to suppress her maniacal energy with one strong arm around her and the hand that kept her from shouting.

Madison refused to give up. Though each struggle required more effort than the one before, she gave it all she had. But it had been a very long day, and she was running out of steam.

An image of four college girls filled her mind, each of them caught in an iron grip on a dark street far from their home. Had their lives ended like this, in fear and useless struggle? She'd be damned if she'd become one of them.

With one last concentrated effort, she again bit the hand covering her mouth. As the blood from that bite ran down her chin, the last remnants of her energy finally failed. She could no longer lift an arm or a foot, open her mouth or fight back.

"Stop fighting, mad one," a whispered voice commanded.

Flailing, Madison felt herself slip, felt the darkness of her surroundings close in...until she became one with the night.

"Ah, my dear St. John," Simon Monteforte said in a voice as dark as the paneled walls. "You'd prefer she takes to the streets alone, without my assistance?"

"Out there, she stands a chance," St. John replied, wanting to follow Madison, and having to carefully hide those feelings.

"You think so?" Monteforte remarked.

St. John didn't bother to nod. He wasn't sure how he could maintain his camouflage with any of the Ancients if he were to test Simon Monteforte's fealty here, among so many of them.

The sound of Madison's heels on the sidewalk had grown faint. He found it strange that nothing else seemed to matter to him at that moment, except getting to her.

"Hurting her would make a mess of things," he said to Monteforte. "There's no reason to do so."

"Yet you brought her here, a place off-limits to most mortals."

"For information about those girls."

"Ah, yes. The missing girls," Monteforte said.

"We can't afford to have another one go missing, Simon. All eyes are on this city already. Haven't you noticed?"

"The other Americans may turn up yet, and then they can all go home and leave us to our own…pleasures," Monteforte said.

"Madison Chase must be with them when they go."

"I suppose you'll see to that, in spite of your earlier pledge?"

"My allegiance lies with maintaining our society and its secrets. Madison might be a nuisance, but is no threat. Getting rid of her won't help any cause."

"Your tune has changed, I see. I find that most interesting, St. John."

"My tune hasn't wavered since I first arrived in London," St. John corrected. "When our goal was to exist alongside the mortals in peace."

"In that, I believe we have fared well."

"Until now, when too many missing people are stirring up public sentiment against those in charge of this city."

St. John took his time with the final question. "Where are those girls now, Simon?"

Monteforte grinned, showing crimson-stained fangs. "You think I know?"

"I believe you might."

"You give me far too much credit, St. John."

"Or else not nearly enough."

In that moment, as the comment left his lips, St. John realized fully that Simon Monteforte was the one he sought. The reek of the immortal's indiscretions sat in this place like another layer of haze. Without the crowd and scent of hundreds of mortals in the club to mask it, Monteforte's foulness was readily apparent.

St. John stared at the Ancient, who had to have known his secret identity for some time. Monteforte had unleashed the hellhounds. Did Monteforte imagine those hounds could take a Blood Knight down?

Something else drew his attention.

A prickle of fear twitched the thread tying him and Madison together. It was Madison's fear.

Monteforte was formidable, and needed tending to, but St. John knew he was needed elsewhere. Something had happened to Madison. He had to go to her.

He spun for the door, not bothering to stop when Monteforte called out, "You feel the new darkness on the wind, St. John? Does it whisper your name?"

Free of the weighty Ancient's presence, and out of the building at last, St. John opened his senses. Sniffing the air, he grunted a curse. That new trouble Monteforte had mentioned now tore at his senses as if it had been magnified by the Ancient's recognition of it.

The trouble in the wind hadn't yet arrived, though it was too close for comfort when his strength was needed elsewhere.

The people of London would be lucky if they stayed off the streets in the hours to come.

Facing the direction of the odor of the Nosferatu in the distance, St. John bared his fangs. The unearthly sigils carved and seared into his back were speaking to him in whispers and undulations that confirmed the rightness of the direction of his thinking. Under all of their noses, Simon Monteforte had become a servant of the Dark.

But that wasn't all, certainly not the worst of things. He could no longer sense Madison. She must have lost consciousness. The thread had gone lax, even as his sigils rippled.

Madison opened her eyes, blinked, but saw nothing. She was on her back, on a cold floor.

Sheer fright made her sit up. With darkness enveloping her, and a loss of all direction, a wave of dizziness made her stomach heave.

Flipping onto her hands and knees, she strained for a couple of clear breaths. What she sucked in wasn't pleasant. The air was filled with particles of dust, decay and the awful smell of something rancid.

Crawling on all fours, she tested out her surroundings, afraid of what she'd find. She rotated in a full circle, unhindered. That was good. A start.

The floor wasn't concrete, so it couldn't be a sidewalk. The ground beneath her had the coolness of slick ceramic tile, with grooves in regular intervals. She counted four large tiles by crawling forward and backward and feeling with her fingers, and more tiles to her right and left. She was indoors, then, on a floor. Her attacker had left her, without bothering to tie her up.

"Stupid bastard."

Her searching fingers found something soft that gave her a start. She backed up, sliding over the hard floor on bare, throbbing knees. Nothing happened. No one pulled her back.

Inching forward again, she reached out, closed her fingers over the soft object. No bad consequences presented themselves.

Sitting back on her heels, Madison pulled the object through both of her hands. A sweater? *Yes.* Long-sleeved, loosely woven and smelling faintly of perfume.

Her heart gave a gigantic thump. Waiting in silence, she half expected her attacker to laugh, and sighed with relief when no laughter rang out.

Crawling farther, the silence creating pressure in her ears, Madison found another item that felt like a canvas bag. Fumbling, she wrenched the bag open and moved her hands over more fabric. Another sweater, and a pair of jeans, easy to identify because of the unique smell of the denim. With further scrutiny, she concluded that whoever owned these clothes was small-boned, thin.

Excitement made her heart lurch. Clothes meant that either she'd been tossed onto the floor of someone's residence, or someone had been here recently. *A young woman.*

Her mind spliced that information together, driving Madison to her feet. Again, she waited for danger to strike and said in astonishment and relief when it didn't, "Okay."

Since she was free to move about, she might also have the freedom to leave this place.

With the sweater grasped tightly in one hand, and the other hand held out in front of her, Madison shuffled forward. She found a wall, and next to it the arm of a chair.

The smell of decay grew stronger. Gagging, Madison felt around, paused, recoiled when breathing became difficult. The object in the chair was large, stiff, cold and unmoving.

It was a body.

Swallowing a scream, she backpedaled with her pulse exploding, then she dived forward again, refusing to lose the wall. Maybe there was a door or a window in that wall.

Hand over hand, with the sweater dangling from her fingers and the blood pounding in her ears, Madison felt her way across the room until she found a crack. Tracing the crack, she discovered a doorknob that turned in her hand.

Breathless, frightened, she took a cautious step forward and felt the chill of fresher air on her face.

St. John strode through the night, alert, determined.

Stopping on the side street bordering Madison's hotel, he glanced once at his surroundings, then looked upward. Gripping the building's brick exterior with both hands, he began to climb.

Madison's window was open. Knowing immediately that she wasn't in that room, he hauled himself in, landing agilely on both feet. As the skin prickle of warning washed over him, he closed his eyes to process any new scent that might overlap hers, and snapped his fangs in frustration over not finding any.

The room was just as he'd last seen it. Some of Madison's things were spread out on the bureau, personal things he wanted to touch.

The doorknob to the hallway rattled. St. John turned his head, and gathered to spring.

The door opened slowly, but no monster stood there. On the threshold was one of the men from Madison's network, wearing a startled expression and a wrinkled shirt.

"Who the hell are you?" that man demanded.

"I might ask you the same thing," St. John replied, unfisting his hands.

Chapter 15

Madison didn't bother to wonder why no one kept her from leaving the dark room. She was absorbed in getting away as fast as possible.

She ran down a dim corridor punctuated by other open doors until she found stairs heading down. There was only one wall next to the staircase. The other side showed a gaping hole of nothing, open to the night. The meager illumination of distant streetlights helped in her race for freedom.

After descending four floors, she hit flat ground. Only then did she stop to take stock of her surroundings, because she had to. She'd need to find this awful place again.

She made quick mental notes. *Shabby building. Deserted. Derelict. Big dark holes where windows should have been.* Due to the unsoundness of the structure, the whole thing may have been slated for destruction. What was left of it sagged on its foundation; just the kind of place for keeping a kidnap victim, or hiding a body, though her kidnapper had been inexperienced enough to have forgotten to lock the door.

What about the body?

Glad she hadn't had to see it, she knew help would be needed for those details. Police.

Madison took precious seconds more to look herself over and get her trembling under control. Everything seemed fine, which under the circumstances was a blessing. She still wore her dress, and both shoes. Her knees were bruised, her fingernails were chipped, but if she had been able to get away so easily, what had the guy gained by accosting her on the street in the first place? She hadn't carried a purse or wallet. She didn't own any jewelry.

"Not a robbery, then."

Her fingers were cramping from holding tightly to the sweater she'd found. Her mind raced. One thing was crystal clear. Detective Crane had been right in that pieces of clothing were turning up all over the place. At least, thankfully, this sweater didn't belong to anyone in the Chase family.

What if that body turned out to be one of the Yale girls?

She had to get help, when the biggest problem facing her now was having no idea where she might be.

"Damn it to hell and back!"

The curses she uttered followed her through the dark as ran down the street in search of a car to flag down.

St. John was too worried about Madison to consider the mortal in the doorway anything more than a hindrance.

"I'm looking for Madison," he said, already moving toward the window.

"How did you get in?" the man demanded.

"How did you get in?" St. John countered.

The man held up a key. "It was under my door. Madison must have put it there."

St. John had no time for explanations or hiding his next move. He sat for a moment on the sill before swinging his long legs outside, said, "Tell her I came by," and jumped.

He landed on the sidewalk in a crouch, with one hand touching the ground and his chin lifted. The malignant odor of the rogues was stronger, though they weren't advancing as fast as he had anticipated, and were still outside of the city.

What good was hurrying, he supposed, when they and their counterparts had been after him, unsuccessfully, for centuries. When animals like these had plagued the Seven for an eternity.

As he straightened, he wondered how Simon Monteforte been able to fool the rest of the Hundred about his position within the community. Monteforte had hidden his darkness from the other creatures, when fooling the Hundred wasn't easy. Nearly impossible, in fact. Yet the old monster would now call attention to the beings who actually ruled most of London, and quite probably cause a rain of bloody terror to fall upon the innocent bystanders who got in their way.

No doubt Monteforte pined for the Grail, like so many others before him. He would shake the foundation of the Hundred to gain the knowledge St. John possessed. Thinking to bargain with the lives of the people in London, he would demand to know the resting place of the most holy of religious relics, sought for centuries and protected by the Seven Blood Knights bound to it.

Monteforte desired the magic that went with the chalice of Christ. No doubt he believed that with the Grail in his possession, Monteforte would have power beyond belief, and command the Seven.

Mason LanVal, the last of the knights to be added to the Seven, had been entrusted with the task of hiding the Grail, and was its keeper still, as far as St. John knew. Had Nosferatu been sent after LanVal, as well? Perhaps monsters were emerging all over Europe, hoping to track down his reclusive brethren.

Monteforte. Traitor.

Very bad news, indeed.

He had found what he'd been seeking, but was torn. Tonight, he had made a promise to keep a special mortal safe. His vow, meant for protecting the masses, or as many of them as he could manage, had truly enlarged in scope.

"Where are you?" he called to Madison, sending his senses outward. "I know you're near."

He looked down at his feet. She had been here, on this spot. He saw her in his mind's eye as a shimmering outline of pale gray mist.

"I can smell you, little Slayer."

Her fragrance lingered, hanging on the damp night air like a cloud partially tainted with the iron odor of fright, and blood.

Icy knife pricks of discomfort returned.

He had told Madison to run, and she had done so, blindly. Instead of sprinting to what she would think of as safety, however, she had met someone else along the way. Some*thing* else, smelling not quite so sweet.

He instantly recognized the image forming next to hers in his mind. Stewart Chase. The twins had indeed found each other here, not long ago. And all because St. John had left her alone for what was, in his world, an insignificant amount of time, but was in hers direly significant, the difference between life and death and another type of existence after real breath was gone.

St. John tried to appease the gnawing marks on his back that continued to pain him. Even without Nosferatu on the way, his dealings with the Hundred, and among them a traitor of the worst kind, this particular meeting between Madison and what was left of her brother could have bad consequences for everyone.

Monteforte would know this, too, and that in splitting his allegiances, St. John would become weaker in regard to any one of them.

The screech of sirens roused St. John from thought. The sirens were close, slicing shrilly through the heaviness of the otherwise deceptively quiet London night. Intermittent with those sirens, he heard the approach of a car.

He spun, slamming his stinging back against the side of the building, and waited for the arrival of the woman he felt with every sense in his body. The flame-haired object of his soul's desire was coming back to him. Stewart, bless that damn hybrid, hadn't harmed his sister.

When the car pulled up, he saw Madison through the window. He couldn't rush out there and tear the door from its hinges. What he could do, though, was offer up a prayer of thanks for her return, even though his prayers were seldom, if ever, answered.

As the detective's car came to a stop in front of her hotel, Madison shivered. Her inner radar told her that St. John hovered just out of sight.

She wasn't sure she could withstand another encounter with him just now. Yet she couldn't wait for it.

He had warned her to run because he believed the creature in the Germand hotel lobby had been extremely dangerous. She knew he'd been right. Just the sight of that hotel had caused a flare of unease in her. And there had been still more danger on the surrounding streets.

"You'll need to come back to the department with me to make a statement," Crane said, cutting the engine. "You have time for a quick shower and a change, that's all."

Probably sensing the distressing way he had put that, he hurried on, more gently. "You look like you need that shower, as well as a good, stiff drink."

Madison searched the dark. "They'll find out who's in that place, and who the sweater belongs to?"

"We'll do our best."

The detective got out of the car, crossed to her side and helped her out. She hated the fact that she needed his arm in order to stand.

"I'll take you up," he said in a tone that let her know he'd accept no argument.

"I can shower by myself, Detective."

"Of course you can, so I'll wait in the hall."

He wasn't smiling when Madison looked. His forehead showed deep furrows as he said, "You saw St. John again? Could the blood on your hands be his?"

"No. Not his."

She didn't dare address the reason why the detective had been spying on her, and instead thought about the Germand hotel, and how wrong it had felt leaving St. John there. Had it only been hours ago that he'd held her in his arms?

"Is something wrong?" the detective asked.

"Funny question, isn't it, given the circumstances," she said.

She realized as they passed through the lobby that she'd begun to hate this place, and every hotel like it.

"There's a hospital a few blocks away. It might be a good idea to stop there," D.I. Crane said in a tone of honest concern.

"Thanks, but I really do need that shower."

Her stomach was queasy, but Madison couldn't recall the last time it hadn't been. As for the weak-kneed condition currently crimping her style, well, that had to go. She was smarter than this, stronger than this. She was alive. She hadn't been hurt by whoever had abducted her. In fact, she had gotten away without much fuss at all, as bizarre as that was.

Her journalistic side wanted to know why she had been allowed to leave the scene of a possible homicide, and why her abductor had let her walk when he had to figure she'd go straight to the police. The detective beside her had probably asked himself those same questions.

Would he also consider that whoever had taken her to that apartment might have done so for a very specific reason? So she would find the body in it?

The clock over the lobby desk told her she'd been gone an hour. One freaking hour, when it felt like twenty.

She eyed the detective as they approached the elevator, finding it interesting that he'd give her a pass to return to the hotel for a quick cleanup, when that kind of leniency surely had to go against police policy in any country. She had been part of a crime scene. Even after they'd taken samples from under her nails, she remained the bearer of important details, and a credible witness.

Contrary to Teddy's analysis, British D.I.s weren't stupid or notorious for fits of lovesickness. Nevertheless, too damn many things were popping up that any skilled journalist would have gone after with lights and cameras blazing…which was exactly what she intended to do.

As she and the detective stepped into the elevator, the smell of the blood on her hand made her stare at her fingers. She'd bitten some guy, acting like one of Stewart's vampires. She had tasted the awful stuff twice tonight, and wondered how vampires could like it.

However, the dried blood on her hands seemed to signify something of real consequence. And damn if that didn't always bring her back to Stewart, and the way his insane explanation for the events of the past two days would go down.

Vampires. In London.

As the elevator started up, Madison delved into her memory of her brother's files, unable to help herself. Because there had been, she was sure, blood on the old man's lips at the Germand.

Blood that may not have been his.

Stewart had written that there were two Londons, one for the living and one for the dead, and that the two worlds had collided in the worst possible of ways. He had suggested that innocent people were suffering the consequences of the secrets known only to a few savvy souls.

What if there were actually such things as vampires, and everything she'd been through was tied in to that?

What if what she had seen on the old man's face at the Germand had been blood, as in he'd been drinking some?

What if vampire existence somehow explained the disappearance of the four Yale girls who had been seen at that hideous hotel, and Stewart knew it and that's why he'd come here?

Vampires, in London.

For real.

Screw the shaky stuff. She had a job to do and by God, she would do it. Finding that body tonight only served to up the ante.

"I remembered something," she said to D. I. Crane. "I'm sorry I can't recall where the information came from, but it was to check out a hotel around the corner called the Germand. Do you know it?"

The detective nodded. "Fancy place for fancy people."

Again, she thought of the image of the old man in green.

"Can you send someone there to investigate whether the girls might have been there recently?" she asked. "Right away?"

"I can, and will," he said, eyeing her quizzically. "It was a good tip? Trustworthy?"

"As good as it gets."

She was shivering again, and positive that Christopher St. John waited for her. He felt close enough to touch.

Who was St. John, really?

He had rubbed his hands over her on a dance floor, and had taken her, body and soul, in a hotel room. He had stepped in front of her on the street, and in that awful hotel, in an attempt to protect her.

Protector. Beings who were liaisons between immortals and humans. This was the term she had bandied about the night she'd met him. And just after he'd offered his assistance with this case.

St. John. With his easy access to all sorts of clubs and private hotels, was there any doubt that he might also be socially well placed enough to be able to pull the strings necessary to get her a shower and her current chaperone?

Had the Protector, in lieu of not being able to do his job, recruited someone else to do it for him?

She gave the detective a covert glance before her gaze strayed to the bloodstains on her hands.

The dried blood was the same color as the blood that had pooled on St. John's scratches. Not the faded hue of dried blood, but much darker, older.

Her stomach tightened. A flash of white heat seared across her neck. This meant something, surely?

It certainly didn't have to be proof that Christopher St. John had lied about not being mortal. Or that the old man in green in the Germand's lobby had been unearthly.

So, how could she prove these things once and for all?

"Proof," she whispered, earning her a second raised eyebrow from the detective beside her. "I have one stop to make," she said when the elevator stopped at her floor.

"No time for that," Crane said.

"I just have to let my crew know I'm okay. It'll take a second."

Crane didn't actually nod, though he didn't look happy about this.

Passing her door, continuing down the corridor, Madison stopped, lifted a hand and knocked. In spite of the ungodly hour, the door opened and Teddy stood there, looking not worried, but excited.

"There was something on the tape you wanted to show me," she said. "You sent a text about finding something strange in the footage you shot yesterday?"

If Teddy replied, she didn't hear it. Her heart rate was escalating. St. John had entered the building. Her body knew it and was already heating up.

She had to see that footage. She had to see it so that she could put Stewart's obsessions behind her, and get on with her own.

She knew exactly what she'd be looking for on that tape: a man in the doorway of a pub. A man who would show up on that tape because he was mortal, not some idiotic version of her brother's wicked imagination. That was the vampire deal, right? No captured image for the undead?

D.I. Crane grunted his displeasure over allowing her to stretch the leeway he'd allowed her. As his hand closed on her elbow with a subtle pressure, Teddy switched on the monitor.

The picture came on the screen. Madison zeroed in, ready to laugh, feeling relieved.

She watched other newscasters scrambling to get to the scuffle going on in the distance, and paid attention as the camera turned in Teddy's capable hands.

"What the—?"

She stared in disbelief at the doorway as the camera swept past it. She wanted to shout for Teddy to rewind.

Empty.

Christopher St. John was not in that doorway.

But St. John had been there. She had seen him. Possibly Teddy had taken too long to focus the lens.

"Did you see that?" Teddy asked excitedly.

Her cameraman rewound the tape, and pointed at the screen.

Dazed, trying to rally, Madison saw the face in the crowd that Teddy was alluding to. So did the detective beside her.

"That's Janis Blake," Teddy said, rewinding again. He looked to Madison for confirmation. "Isn't that one of the missing girls?"

"Damn well looks like her," Crane replied, loosening his grip on Madison.

The two men in the room would assume she was as stunned as they were to see a familiar face in the crowd— the face of the youngest of the missing Yale Four. They might even have been right if this had happened two days ago.

Unfortunately, she was stuck in the loop of video footage preceding that flash of the missing girl's face, seeing the pub's doorway over and over in her mind and picturing Christopher St. John standing in it.

The room went unnaturally quiet. Madison observed the scene around her as if it, too, was being played back on a machine in slow motion.

The detective studied the screen, with one hand on his phone. Teddy beamed, realizing he had made an important discovery. The room, for her, had gone hazy. Her ears filled with static. In that scratchy noise swam a memory, a message meant only for her, and for times like this.

"You will crave this touch as much as I will."

And there was something else, another voice overlapping St. John's.

"Mad one," the voice tonight, on the street, had whispered. She remembered that only now.

"Stop fighting, mad one," that voice had directed.

Fending off a rising panic, Madison swallowed a cry. Only one person in the world used that nickname for her. *Mad one.*

She flashed back to the hand on her mouth and the fact that the abductor hadn't really harmed her. Blacking out had nothing to do with him hurting her; she just hadn't been able to hang on.

She'd been so scared.

But she hadn't been tied up in that awful place where she'd been left. Escape had been easy. The abductor hadn't meant to hurt her. He meant for her to find that body.

Her abductor hadn't been just anyone, reason now told her. It had, in fact, been her brother. Her twin. Stewart. No one else on the planet knew his nickname for her.

The wall felt hard and unyielding against her injured shoulder. She was shaking, had been shaking nonstop for what seemed like hours, from distress and fatigue and so damn many loose ends. Now, there was light.

No!

Hell...

She had provided the police with a blood sample from her attacker, and it might have been Stewart's DNA they would discover. She might have bitten her brother's hand.

Locking her jaw to keep the shouts trapped inside, Madison reached for the doorknob. She had to see St. John. She had to confront him. No matter what he was, if he had connections, she'd ask him to use them to get her brother back.

The detective's voice stopped her from leaving. Slowly, and with her heart revved by a new kind of panic, she turned to face him.

Chapter 16

A foul wind, impossible to ignore, reached St. John as he stood beneath Madison's window. The Nosferatu hadn't yet breached the city proper.

They had been sent to find the royal blood in his veins and in the veins of the other Knights offered immortality, exactly as his Makers had long ago predicted.

Evil, it seemed, never gave up or gave in. The thirst for greed never waned.

Peeling himself from the wall, St. John rolled his aching shoulder blades. What was happening in London, and about to get worse, went so far beyond the concept of right and wrong, as well as the most basic, normal perceptions most people had of the world, as to be unrecognizable fragments of those ideas.

Ruthless monsters were coming, due to the fact that a traitor had infiltrated the Hundred, desiring to upgrade his personal stockpile of power.

With his etched skin searing, St. John searched the street, setting mental boundaries for the battle to come.

In his mind, the haunting refrain of a question issued through moist, parted lips plagued him.

"Are you a vampire?"

After all this time, St. John wondered if he might be losing his mind.

"Can you skip that shower?" D.I. Crane asked Madison as she went to leave Teddy's room. He turned to her cameraman and said, "I'll need that tape."

Madison's hand was frozen on the door. He hadn't mentioned anything about St. John. When he looked at her again, she said, "I need my purse and my credentials. I'll skip the shower but I need a quick cleanup. I've got blood on my hands and knees."

Crane nodded as he opened the door. "We've got to get back to the station with this information."

"Back?" Teddy sounded confused.

"I'll have to go with the detective," Madison said. She didn't sound like herself, and wondered if anyone noticed.

"At this time of night?" Teddy said.

Madison shrugged, hoping she looked nonchalant, feeling like hell. Now wasn't the time to go into what had occurred. Explanations would take time she didn't have.

The news world would be rocked by what was on this tape. This network exclusive would advance the careers of everyone on their crew, but at this moment, she couldn't have cared less about her job. St. John was near. Her brother was near. Answers as to what the heck was going on were required from both.

"There's something I was supposed to tell you," Teddy said, as if just remembering. "A man stopped by."

Madison looked to the detective to make sure he didn't sense her sudden stiffness, and found him making another call.

"What man?" she asked.

"Don't know," Teddy said. "I wasn't paying attention. I only remember that I'm supposed to tell you that he came by. I must have been groggy, or too excited about the tape. Sorry. I think he knocked at my door."

Madison controlled her reply. "It must not have been important."

"Want me to go along, wherever it is you're going?"

"I'll have her back before breakfast," Crane said.

Teddy made a point of looking at his watch. "That's about an hour from now."

"Is it?" The detective seemed surprised. Probably his night had also been long.

"We have another briefing in the morning," Teddy reminded her. "You look like hell." He turned to the detective. "We're going to air the tape. It'll be a gut-busting exclusive for us, and Madison has to be there to present it."

"I'll be there," Madison promised.

Teddy handed her the key to her room. "You must have dropped this by my door."

The preoccupied detective was checking and rechecking his messages, adept at texting while walking as they headed for her room.

"Five minutes?" Madison said to him, when they reached it.

"Four," the detective countered, leaning a shoulder against the wall, and continuing to fiddle with his phone.

Madison closed the door behind her, drew in a long breath and said to Christopher St. John, "I know you're here, and I know what you are."

Chapter 17

"Do you know?" St. John countered from the shadows of her hotel room.

Madison feared that her heart might jump right out of her chest, it was beating so fast.

"Show me, or prove me wrong," she said.

"It would hurt me to see the disappointment on your face, either way."

"More than everything else has hurt me?"

"What do you think you know?" he asked.

"A question for a question is a clever parry, St. John, but won't work. What I want is a confession."

Madison stared at the figure in front of her, and blocked out the soft rap at the door.

"Miss Chase," Crane called from the hallway. "Only four minutes."

"You found Stewart," St. John said.

"He was out there. I was right."

The silence following her remark eventually filled with his whisper. "He didn't harm you, then?"

"Why would you think he'd harm me?"

St. John didn't answer the question. He said, with relief in his tone, "For that one thing alone I owe him."

He stepped forward. "Are you afraid of me, Madison?"

"Scared out of my mind. And I now think you know more about my brother than you're letting on. I believe you might have purposefully kept me from going after him at the club, and also on the street tonight."

St. John's voice was like sifted gravel. "It would have been in your best interest."

"Did you know that Stewart was there?"

"Yes."

Feeling faint, Madison stood her ground. "Why would you keep me from him for any reason? Something is wrong with Stewart. I get that. But he is my brother."

"Your brother came here after creatures he was sure hid in the shadows."

"You think I don't know that? I've thought of nothing else since I arrived in this city. So, are you admitting that he was right to do so?"

"He was right," St. John conceded. "You would have found this out soon enough on your own, but the knowledge places you in more danger."

Madison shook her head. "Stop it. You're freaking me out, and I'm freaked enough already."

"You said you know about Stewart." St. John's voice was tender, which made things infinitely worse. "Do you also understand what he has become?"

"I know that he's possibly gone off the deep end, and that he is hiding."

"Is that all?"

"Isn't that enough?"

The protest she'd been about to use stuck in her throat. A chill rippled across the back of her neck. Gathering her courage, Madison raised her hand, and placed her fingertips against St. John's mouth, sure she had heard what he'd said, and that he hadn't moved his lips.

"Isn't that enough?" she repeated.

"Not by far."

Beneath her fingers, she felt the shape of something she envisioned in her nightmares, but had never expected. She swayed as if she'd been struck, and reached for the light switch.

The room flooded with light that was blinding in intensity after the darkness she had endured. What that light showed her was alarming.

The chiseled face across from her wore a pained expression. The eyes looking into hers were part blue, and also midnight-dark. Too dark to be human.

God help her, Christopher St. John was a vampire.

"Show me." Her tone was sharp with despair. "I need to see."

He smiled sadly, and there they were. Between the lips that had kissed her gently, and savagely, and torturously, were two long, white, lethal-looking points. Fangs.

"You lied," she charged weakly.

"No," he said. "You asked the wrong question."

This time when he leaned forward, she twitched with anger and fear and frustration. She had nowhere to go to get away from him, and from the pain of this.

"Tell me they're fake," she said, knowing this was a last-ditch effort to make sense of what she was confronting.

"I wish I could," he said. "You have no idea how much."

The door handle beside them jiggled with an interruption of metal and wood. D.I. Crane's voice rose in pitch. "Miss Chase? Madison?"

Her fingers untangled from the jacket she had inadvertently clung to as that jacket was dragged from her grasp. Cold invaded the room as St. John backed away from her.

Christopher St. John had teased, tempted, shown his true nature and left her. In the blink of an eye, he had gone, leaving her room the same way he'd gotten in. That damn window. She hadn't seen a thing after the fangs. Her eyes had been closed.

"Stewart..." she sobbed. "I've found one of them. Damn you, brother, I've...found one."

She had gotten close to the embodiment of danger, had been physically intimate with a creature of the night. A real one. No trick of the light. No fantasy. Not her imagination.

Stewart had been right, all along.

Madison stared after St. John. He had fangs. Possibly he wasn't alive at all...and yet the throb deep inside her, the one connecting her to him, was more insistent than ever.

Impossibly, she wanted those fangs on her. She wanted him inside her. How did a person reason with insanity?

They weren't *people*. This wasn't just any frenetic love affair between strangers. In some rule book, somewhere, a liaison like this one had to be forbidden.

St. John was a vampire.

And he was magnificent.

If there were vampires all over London who could mesmerize with a look and a kiss...heaven help everyone.

"Heaven help me."

She remembered again the wooden stake hidden in her

brother's jacket, and how it had shocked her. She remembered believing that she saw, in her mind, Stewart limp to the London Eye, possibly wounded, to hide that stake.

Her brother had come here to chase vampires, and there seemed to be plenty of them around.

St. John was a vampire. And her brother was alive.

"Miss Chase? Time to go."

She'd nearly forgotten Crane in the hallway, and wasn't sure about opening the door, or what the detective would see when he looked at her. She wasn't sure if she could stand up straight, or if her face held telltale signs of her inner struggle.

Was it possible to look relatively normal when the earth had tilted off its axis?

There were vampires in London, and she had seen them firsthand. She had, in fact, gone a lot further than that.

She swallowed back the urge to shout St. John's name. She had to internalize the fear, and she could do so. She would handle this. She'd have to. It wasn't over.

It was far from over.

There were vampires in London, and one of them had her name on his lips.

Had her brother been showing her a body, she now wanted to know, or trying to get her away from Christopher St. John?

She had stopped shaking. That, too, seemed odd.

The truth didn't actually set one free, as the saying went. Truth could be terrible, unbelievable, earth-shattering.

"Forgive me, brother," she whispered, with a last glance to the window.

A final thought came to her as she watched the curtain blow, perhaps out of a need for just one minute of normality in a world that had gone insane and was pulling her down with it.

Teddy had been wrong about there being an hour until breakfast. A gray English morning was set to dawn.

"So, now you know."

St. John looked up at Madison's window. "You know about me."

Daylight was minutes away. He had to start walking, and couldn't make his legs work.

No one knew why vampires and other monsters needed the night to animate them. He had never heard one plausible explanation for the phenomenon, other than that death had always been equated with darkness. Though he was old enough and strong enough to tolerate some light, it was inconvenient as hell.

He turned with a concerted effort that strained his ligaments, and raised his face. In the small wedge of time when darkness slipped into submission and the horizon grew colorful, he usually felt the most alive, and almost normal. Almost mortal.

While humans began to stir in their beds and the monsters went to ground until the return of night, he walked and breathed and thought things over as if he were still an integral part of the human landscape.

Today was different. Because Madison knew, and he'd left her with that.

At least she would be safe for a few more hours.

Often, he had yearned for simpler times. Lately he'd been thinking about going back to where it all started—to Castle Brocéliande, in Brittany—in search of a respite from the world. The castle where he had traded his old life for immortality might still be there. He had never gone back to see. He had been unwilling to face the place of his death, and the site of his rebirth into what he had become.

"I have sipped from the Holy Grail," he wanted to tell Madison. "The blood that chalice contained was a mixture of my Maker's and another's blood that once stained the famous cup."

He didn't tell her this in a way she would hear. She couldn't know that the golden chalice had been passed through time by careful hands until it eventually wound up in the possession of the three special creatures at Castle Brocéliande. And that the beings there had chosen St. John and his brethren for a special task that saw them killed and resurrected—bringing them back from death with their souls turned inside out and their bodies strengthened for a new purpose.

He wanted to tell Madison that he had experienced life as a mortal, with its pain and hopes and death, and that he remembered parts of his former life, his last breath and what had come after.

He needed to explain to her that he would never forget his first sight of the five men who had preceded him as Blood Knights, and how much they meant to him.

"Seven new beings of molded muscle, sinew, cold flesh and purpose became the servants of both the Grail and the holy blood in our veins," he whispered to the dawn mist, and to Madison over their unique connection. "We rode forth from Castle Brocéliande's gates on black steeds that matched our emblazoned shields. Seven men, who were no longer men, but something more, bound to each other and hungering in ways no one else could imagine. Immortals."

Lance Van Baaren. Mason LanVal. Alexander Kent. He was often left hurting for the companionship of the creatures most like himself who also had traded their mortal souls for immortality.

"Who else but they knew what I need, and what I feel? The regrets, the desires."

His building lay ahead with the promise of refuge. In a perfect world, he would have brought Madison here and loved her within an inch of her life, saving that last inch for the decision she'd have to make in order to join him. He had actually considered going that far. Not offering just his heart, but immortality, and a love that would last forever.

"And danger rains down from all directions."

With Nosferatu coming, and Simon Monteforte uncovered as the traitor, all he wanted to think about was *her*. Madison. The radiant woman with the shrewd blue eyes that fate had tossed in his path as if offering a bone to a ravenous beast.

He had to settle things with her before the Nosferatu arrived. A dark hand had disturbed the fabric of London, and threatened to distort it further, but she had to understand that Stewart's ravings about vampires had been correct, though his warning had fallen on the wrong ears.

St. John would not barter with Monteforte, a heinous example of a modern-day terrorist. Monteforte might assume to know how his mind worked, but that assumption would be a mistake. Nosferatu could not kill a Blood Knight. There was only one way to end his existence forever, one unique key to a final death for each of the Seven, and neither sword nor fangs came close to being his.

He dared not involve the rest of the Hundred in this

situation. He couldn't afford to show his true self to them, or anyone else. Although his goal here in London had been achieved, and the traitor among them exposed, the situation remained fragile.

In the meantime, the detective outside Madison's door should be able to protect her. For a while, anyway.

Luckily, the sun was about to rise. Simon Monteforte would be going to ground, locked away somewhere until that sun went down.

Madison, can you hear me?

Her face appeared all around him as he walked.

"My strength is not endless," he said. "Still, I will honor my promise to help you."

Come to me tonight, he sent to her, using their bond.

By nightfall you must find me, Madison. Hurry. Do not delay.

He knew the second she received this final message, and that its arrival stunned her. As he lifted his face to the pink brilliance of the rising sun, thinking of Madison's warm, lush body and worrying that she might never come, now that she knew about the fangs…the sun, like so many other things in his age-old existence, finally began to betray him.

Chapter 18

For the tenth time in as many minutes, Madison pressed a hand to her neck, searching for possible puncture marks that might explain her ability to hear Christopher St. John as clearly as if he sat next to her.

Looking out the window of D.I. Crane's car that hadn't yet left the curb, she said, "Have you gone to the Germand?"

"Officers are there now," the detective said.

"Have you found out anything about that apartment where my abductor took me?"

"You mean in the four minutes you were in your room?"

Madison filed away the detective's cynicism. She had no idea how long she'd actually been in that room with St. John, or where he had gone after he'd jumped out her window. She strained to see the faces passing on the street at this early hour, searching for St. John and Stewart among them.

"I'm afraid so," Crane said, cutting his eyes to her.

Madison faced him directly. "What did they find, Detective? I can take it. Trust me."

He took a minute to think that over, appearing not too sure. As the sun began to rise between the buildings, he said, "It was a girl, as yet unidentified."

"Not one of those—"

"No. Presumably not one of the missing American girls. Another young one, though. We can't get an ID until more tests are done. I'm telling you this because you were there last night, and I'm asking for this information to go no further. This is off the record. Is that clear?"

Madison nodded. "What happened to her?"

"It seems," Crane said, "that there was a wooden stake sticking out of her chest."

Madison sat very still, trying not to scream. Then she said, "Not through her heart, then. The stake would have to pierce her heart if she were one of them. She wasn't. That's why she could be found, and why she wasn't reduced to a pile of ash."

Horrified that she'd said those things aloud, she stiffened. "I'm sorry," she said. "I didn't realize…" D.I. Crane nodded warily.

"So," the detective finally said. "You did know what that weapon in your brother's pocket was, and what it potentially could be used for."

"My brother didn't do that," she said. "In case that's what you're thinking, Stewart would never hurt anyone."

Would he harm a vampire, though? she wondered.

The detective seemed to be waiting for her to come up with a better excuse for why such an odd weapon had been in Stewart's possession, now that a similar weapon had been found at a crime scene.

"I can't explain that to you," she said before he could even ask his question. What she didn't add was the idea that Stewart, after all his research, would know better than to miss the heart if the victim had been a vampire, and if killing a vampire had been his objective.

A wooden stake through the heart was supposed to explode a vampire, turning them to ash, to dust. There would be little left to identify, like the ashes the cops said they had found near her lost shoe.

That's how the story went. Stake through the heart, and gone, baby, gone. Yet the girl in that apartment hadn't gone. And Stewart had taken his sister there why? To find that girl, and make Madison wonder what the heck was going on.

News flash. I know they exist.

God, yes, she knew they did.

And she knew that her brother was no homicidal maniac, so he couldn't have been the stake wielder. Someone else had killed that girl.

"I can't go to your department," she said. "My head is splitting. I need to lie down. Please, Detective, give me just a little more time." She glanced at the detective's wristwatch. "I have a job to do in thirty minutes."

She needed to figure out how she could clear her brother's name. A clear head was necessary for that.

She wanted to believe that vampires were killing people, and making it look as if Stewart had a part in that. To frame him? To stop him from going after them?

She had to help. She would hunt the vampires down in the only way she knew how. The media. She would shine the light of camera exposure on London's vampires by regaling them with unwanted attention.

D.I. Crane spoke. "The time of death was estimated as

the night before last. The same night you lost your shoe. That's a strange coincidence, I believe."

"Come to me tonight..."

The unspoken invitation came with the jolt of a charge that streaked through Madison's body like a lightning bolt. She uttered a gasp of alarm.

"It's been too much," Crane said. "Take a deep breath."

Deep breaths weren't going to do it. Madison recognized the thrum in her body and knew its source.

"By nightfall you must find me, Madison. Hurry. Do not delay."

There was no doubt whatsoever about whose voice this was, and how freaked she was, hearing it.

Crane continued to study her, as if waiting to see if she'd faint. But he didn't know her, or what caused her shakes. He didn't know what she was capable of when cornered. Hell, maybe she didn't even know.

She had to stop herself from running to her vampire lover, and the effort that took was rough.

A girl with a stake in her chest, she sent back to St. John. *What would you know about that?*

"All right," Crane said. "I'll see what I can do to let you off. I'll be at the announcement this morning. One missing girl is alive and walking around London, and that's a good thing. Janis Blake is out there. Let's focus on that."

Madison said, "I have a feeling the Hotel Germand may turn up something."

The detective seemed about to reply, then didn't. Maybe he had some intuition of his own as to when to let things go.

And to hell with you, St. John, she added inwardly. *I'm nobody's mind slave or future blood supply.*

As she went back inside the hotel, the concentric rings

of madness seemed to close in. The dead had risen up in this city, and how many people knew?

She wished to God that she didn't.

It was a new night.

The undercurrent of darkness running beneath the streets of London angered St. John. The grooves in his skin burned as he waited for the pack of Nosferatu to hit the city.

They had already infiltrated the outskirts. Other things were following in their wake, stuck to the darkness like barnacles on a whale's back. Shades and vermin usually relegated to their own spaces were feeling the terrible presence of the Hunters and experiencing their own kind of perverse glee for the desecration ahead.

True night was about to befall London if he didn't find those monsters first, and take care of them.

In the distance, he heard Madison's voice. The television set behind him replayed that morning's newscast. The world had been stunned by the footage of Janis Blake in the crowd the day before. Madison's network had celebrated a coup, yet he knew that Madison wasn't joining in that celebration.

He knew also that she wasn't coming to him. He didn't blame her. He had allowed her to see the truth, and by doing so he had hurt her.

"I understand," he said, tugging lightly on the invisible thread stretched tightly between them.

The walls of his lair were several feet thick and heavily reinforced with silver-coated steel. Silver was a decent vampire deterrent that he had been reborn with the ability to tolerate. If he could get Madison here, she would be safe.

He had little time now to do what was necessary, when

time had always been the enemy. He had to kill Nosferatu and round up Simon Monteforte, the pompous,
velvet-clad, ancient French deformity who had set those
Hunters upon him.

And Madison?

"Don't you see that I can't rest until what's between
us is settled?"

He was, in fact, already heading for the door.

Madison had grown sicker as the day wore on. Though
London and the rest of the world buzzed with the news
about the Janis Blake sighting, and things were moving in
the right direction for one of the Yale Four, she couldn't
concentrate on that. Secrets were eating away at her.

Ignoring St. John's call had become nearly impossible. She wanted to scream, shout, if that would make
him stop.

He couldn't get to her. A detective stood in the hotel
hall, at her door, and another cop lounged downstairs.
Like a shadow, Crane had been in the crowd all day, following her around when she did her interviews. He hadn't
said a word about the Germand.

Resting a hand on the window frame and her forehead
on the glass, Madison gazed out. Night had fallen. A full
moon hung in the sky, visible between a long block of
buildings and a bank of navy-blue clouds. Seeing that
moon brought on another violent attack of anxiety. Light
from the big silver disc seemed to amplify St. John's
voice. *"I understand."*

"Nonsense," she whispered back. "Leave me alone."

She wasn't sure of the exact moment the hair on her
arms began to rise. After noticing it, she found herself
standing near the head of the bed with her right hand
gripping the crudely carved bedpost. She couldn't recall
how she had gotten there.

She didn't want to go to bed.

Truly, her mind was slipping.

Back at the window, she threw a wary glance to the street below. She saw a shadow, and shook off the feeling it could be anything other than a shadow.

Then she saw another.

A filmy gray when seen against the pools of moonlight, the shadow moved from the street to the corner of her building, where it disappeared.

"Stewart? Is that you?"

He couldn't get in to see her with cops all over the place, knowing they were probably looking for him. She had to see him, talk to him.

Without weighing the consequences of her actions, Madison sat on the window sill, waiting for the rush of blood beating at her veins to subside. Then she swiveled her body around and climbed out onto the ledge six stories high.

Chapter 19

There were police on the street next to Madison's hotel, and more inside. The detectives were on guard.

From the shadows lent by the moon in its full phase, St. John watched the officers on the street round the building. Looking up, expecting to climb, he sobered when he saw the figure on the railing outside Madison's window.

"My brave, foolish love," he said. "Pity the poor bastards who'd try to keep you in line."

Swinging up the brick, hand over hand, and from floor to floor by way of the ornamental railings and the ledges beneath them, he reached Madison before she had turned around far enough to search for a firm place to put her foot.

Perched on the railing, he said, "If it's a quick fall to your death you're after, you're well on your way."

She turned her head. "Go to hell."

"Actually, I've been there, and wouldn't want to go back."

"Then just go away."

He pictured Madison shimmying up and down the trees of those Florida orchards she smelled like. "You're six stories up," he said.

"It's none of your business," she snapped.

"I beg to differ. A lot rides on your ability to stay alive, my own feelings among them."

"What feelings would those be?"

"Oh, I have them," he said. "Never doubt that."

"What I doubt is anything you say. You lied to me. I wonder how many times."

"I never lie, Madison. I told you that."

"So you said, but have you looked in a mirror lately?"

St. John grinned. She had scored with a vampire slam dunk, or so she thought. If the situation with the Nosferatu wasn't so dire…if he was free to expand his relationship with her, at least for a while…he would help her to comprehend what each of them soon had to face.

"That's a myth, you know," he explained quietly, so as not to scare her further or make her loosen her hold on the railing. "That we can't see ourselves in shiny surfaces."

"Damn it, why can't you leave me alone?"

"We're connected. Haven't you figured that out? I hear your thoughts almost as easily as I hear my own."

"Yeah? Well, tell that story to the video equipment that didn't pick up your image in the doorway of the pub."

"You didn't get me on film because I saw your cameraman coming."

He saw her think that over, then shake her head, dismissing his excuse.

"Stewart and I are connected," she corrected. "You and I are…"

"Lovers," he said. "Possibly even closer than that."

She winced. "I wasn't coming to you tonight."

"Then why are you hanging from the side of a building in the middle of the night? What are you planning to do when the officers below stop you?"

"Shit," she said. "Are they down there, too?"

"Several of them, any one of which might look up at any moment."

"I thought Stewart…"

She didn't complete that sentence, and didn't have to. He also felt Stewart Chase's nearness, as well as the closeness of two filthy Shades.

Madison could not go down there, whether her brother was close, or not.

He looked at her. She wore the same clothes she'd worn for the camera that day. All black, not in honor of the girl who had been seen alive in the crowd, but for the few still missing. Flared skirt. Soft sweater. None of it prime climbing attire.

Her bare left leg, stretching downward in search of a ledge, was hindered by the fabric of the skirt presently trapped by the railing. The Shades in the alley would sniff that bareness out, and hope the vampire killer in their midst would bring them some dinner to make up for missing a live mortal.

As she reached the stone ledge with the tip of her shoe, Madison let her hands slide down the wrought iron until her foot had a firm placement. She suspended there between two hotel floors without completely letting go of the upper railing, naked from the tops of her shoes to the tops of her thighs.

St. John took stock of his reaction to this before speaking.

"You're hurting, seeking," he said. "By coming with me tonight, you'll hear some of what you want to know, and I'll be sure you're safe."

"I think I'll pass."

"Don't be foolish, Madison. You're wondering why all this has happened and I can help to clear some of the puzzle up."

"You're not human. You look human, and act like one, but you're not. My brother came here after you, and those like you, and I…I didn't believe him."

Her voice faded. Her eyes glittered. St. John thought he saw dampness beneath her lashes.

"I can yell, and the cops you say are down there will come running," she said.

"They won't find me. I can't let them, or I'll be late for an engagement."

"Don't let me keep you. And besides, I'm almost certain the fly-like-a-bat thing is a joke. Possibly the only joke regarding vampires," she said, looking at him. "Isn't it?"

"What will you do if you get by those on guard?"

"Find my brother."

"I see. You know where he is, then?"

After a hesitation, she said, "Somewhere close."

"London is a big city, and you are not free of its dangers. If you assume vampires are the only hindrances in the dark, you'd be gravely mistaken."

"I'll take my chances."

"And if that detective finds you out here, he'll lock you up in a padded cell."

"He'd see you, too, barring the bat thing."

By the time she'd said those words, he spoke to her from the floor above her. "No flying. Just fast."

"Go to hell." She had whispered this, and was looking paler.

"I need some time, and your trust," he said. "I need to make sure you're safe while I take care of something. Please humor me. It might be all right if I have your trust."

She said nothing.

"Forces are about to be unleashed that will have innocent people caught in the crossfire of an age-old struggle for power if I don't get to them first."

Madison didn't move, or respond.

"If those forces get through, London may become the first of many cities to fall before the darkness," he explained.

"I know," she said.

"How do you know?" He studied her face, sculpted by moon shadows.

"There's an undercurrent," she said. "I feel it."

"What's this undercurrent like?"

"Like a dark river running beneath the city, under my feet, that's flowing in the wrong direction."

"How is it affecting you?"

"It scares me, almost more than you do."

Her explanation startled him. He saw that it also alarmed her to have confessed such a thing. Madison's eyes were wide and fearful, though she looked every inch the Slayer, with her muscles tense and straining for a hold on the railing, and her face as white as the moon's.

Her explanation about what she felt was stunningly similar to how he perceived the oncoming movement of the Nosferatu. There was only one way for Madison to perceive monsters in the distance. She was catching up to her destiny, on a fast track.

"Bloody brilliant," he said.

Madison's face, when she looked up at him, told him that she maintained hope of there being a viable explanation for what she had been sensing, and that she expected the truth from him, no matter how much he might have lied to her before.

She had bitten her lip hard enough to draw a few drops of blood. Seeing that, St. John's hunger raged. Not for the blood, but for the hides of every outside force that would try to take him from her.

"Tell me," she said. "Why am I feeling this? Feeling wrong. Feeling things? Hearing you inside my head?"

"Because you were born to do so," he replied. "You and your brother."

"How?" She closed her eyes as if what he'd said pained her. "Why?"

"You are vampire hunters," he said. "Just as someone in your family had to be, before you. Our word for what you are is *Slayer.*"

She seemed to listen. Nevertheless, as he moved to catch hold of her arm when her grip on the railing loosened, Madison made good on her threat to scream.

Chapter 20

Madison found herself in someone else's room when she was finally able to draw a breath. A strange suitcase sat open on the bed. The bureau drawers were open.

St. John was beside her, looking every bit the supernatural creature he was. His fair, wind-blown hair served to highlight his serious expression. His eyes glowed with a blue-black fire.

They stood there, staring at each other, hungering for each other. She was sure he'd hear her heart racing, and that St. John would see the fear in her eyes.

When the muffled noise of big men on running feet on the street caught her attention, St. John took hold of her wrist, and pulled her to the door.

"I wish you could trust me," he said.

Before she could think of anything to say, his lips were on hers, softly, gently, in what felt to her like goodbye.

And God help her, her own lips softened beneath his, independent of her will to get away.

She felt him stiffen. Then his body gave in, as hers had. His mouth ravished her, kissing her savagely and almost cruelly. For a few brief seconds, Madison felt as if she were drowning in the sensual, seductive shadows surrounding St. John that she had feared to find.

He didn't give her time to finish a single thought. Parting from her, yet remaining just inches away, he said hoarsely, "Wake up, Madison. It's the only way I can leave you. Wake up. Find your strength. It's there, waiting for you, hiding near the surface. Call it up. Call it now, and watch the dark."

Reaching around her, he yanked open the door. She let him push her into the hallway corridor, and then raised her face to him.

"If I'm what you say I am, you'd be on my list."

"Someday," he said sadly, "maybe I can explain. I'm sorry that it can't be tonight."

"How can I trust you?" she asked in frustration.

He smiled, and ran a finger over her cheek. Then he called out, "Here! Up here."

When the door to the stairway slammed open and Crane stepped out, St. John said to the detective in a low, barely audible voice, and with the force of a command that rang in Madison's ears, "I'm counting on you. Don't let me down."

And St. John—vampire, saint, Other, Protector, lover—disappeared.

"What the hell were you thinking!" the angry detective demanded, catching hold of her.

He smelled faintly of cologne, hair gel and wool, scents that stood out as recognizable, now that she'd noticed. The hallway smelled like carpet and dust and paint and peeling paper somewhere close. Over everything lay St. John's unique scent. A vampire's scent.

The detective hadn't once looked St. John's way.

Madison didn't answer his question. Didn't even try. What she was thinking would get her booked into an asylum if it were to be vocalized. St. John had known this. He had used his mesmerizing voice to direct the detective beside her, and it was possible that Crane didn't even know.

As for herself…

Slayer?

Vampire hunter?

Instead of freaking out, her thoughts were for Stewart. Did he chase vampires because he had to? Because he was born to chase them?

She stood here now in one piece, having been up close and personal with a vampire. And yet Christopher St. John had done nothing to harm her, unless having sex with him amounted to some kind of abuse. On the contrary, he acted like a bodyguard. He seemed to always have her back.

Peculiar behavior for a bloodsucker?

Could St. John truly be the Protector in Stewart's notes?

"Madison," the detective began. "How did you get up here to another floor when I had a man outside your door? What was that scream?"

The explanation was so unbelievable, she couldn't use it.

I'm here because of an undercurrent that feels filthy and like the end of the world is coming. And, by the way, Christopher St. John says I'm a vampire hunter.

By allowing those words to take shape in the real world, they began to make some kind of sense. But could she afford to lose her sense of normalcy? Forever?

"You're feeling this because you were born to do so," St. John had said. *"Wake up."*

Well, she was wide-awake. Her head hurt. She felt sick. That red haze had appeared behind her eyes again, as if she were bleeding bad thoughts internally.

"Let's get you back to your room," Crane said.

She was so damn scared, she couldn't speak.

"Are you okay?" he persisted.

Madison shook her head. Her throat felt tight. The floor, and the carpet covering it, were absorbing some of that terribly dark undercurrent. Whatever was coming had gotten closer. The dampness of that metaphorical river soaked through the soles of her shoes.

Her senses were on overload. The darkness. Vampires being real. The lingering imprint of St. John's lips on hers. Her scream had been a manifestation of all those things.

"Maybe you were sleepwalking?" Crane suggested rather wryly, his patience starting to wear thin.

"Yes," Madison said, paying little attention. The red haze was coloring everything now, from the walls to the detective's tanned face. An odd flutter began in the pit of her stomach, and spread to her limbs. She began to sense a new awareness of each muscle in her body, and to feel how tense those muscles were.

"Please," she said. "Get me out of here. I need to find my brother."

"We have people out looking for him," Crane said. "Is that what you were doing outside your window? Attempting to get out, and get to him?"

"Yes."

"I would have taken you anywhere you wanted to go, in my car."

"You would have frightened him off, or taken him in."

The detective cleared his throat. "You could have fallen from pretty high up," he said. "It was a stupid thing to do."

It was the only way to escape you all, Madison wanted to shout, wondering why she was keeping St. John's secret. Wondering how St. John could have cloaked himself from the detective, like he was the invisible man.

The detective's expression was one of puzzlement. He would be thinking he'd just witnessed a sample of the madness plaguing her, and he'd be right. He'd be supposing it was possible that he and others had made a mistake by trusting her to help them. About that, too, he'd be correct.

Vampires had gotten in the way.

Vampires had been in the way from the start.

"I'll take you to the hospital," he said. "You may be in shock."

Madison nodded, resigned that she'd have to ride this out while she decided what to do next.

Crane punched the elevator button, and looked her over once more. "Whoever told you about that Germand hotel had good information," he said. "The girls were there, at that hotel. Whoever gave you that tip deserves a reward. If I had my way, we'd close the godforsaken place down."

The girls…had been found.

The American girls.

"All of them?" she asked.

"Every one."

She had lost all sense of color now, as if she looked out through scarlet-tinted lenses. Her legs felt weak. But she could do this. She was determined to get outside, and then to someplace where someone could help her. Even if that meant finding Christopher St. John.

Intuition now told her that if she didn't find him, the nightmare might never end.

"I can almost guarantee you're not asleep," Crane said, his appraisal as steady as his grip. "Though you do look dazed."

She couldn't look at the detective. The dark undercurrent beneath her had grown stronger and was shaking the ceiling, and the walls. Somehow, she understood that monsters were coming, and that's where St. John would soon go. He was going to face them.

The detective didn't notice the quaking surroundings. When she stumbled, he said, "We'll get you looked at. Maybe a sedative will help."

He had noticed how badly she was twitching, though. He wrapped one arm around her waist.

Trying to calm herself down and stop the convulsions was useless. The harder Madison worked at it, the more the shakes took her over. She'd been trapped by her own outrageous behavior, and was going to pay the price. What could she do now? Push the detective out of the way and run? Run where?

"Truth serum would also be nice," Crane said. "I'd give an eyetooth for some of that stuff in my job. Right about now, my gut says you might not have been telling me the truth, or all you knew about this missing girls case, from day one. And though you helped work miracles with that Germand tip, the rest is downright frustrating."

All Madison could do to maintain her slipping sanity was to grit her teeth and act meek, when her energy was beginning to buzz and soar, and the red haze covering her vision was the color of Christopher St. John's blood.

The darkness outside the building was a relief. The chill was necessary to her ability to breathe. In the dark of the night, the redness tinting her vision faded.

The hospital Crane took her to looked like a big beige box, sterile, benign. The heavy odors of alcohol and antiseptic blocked out any trace of her connection to St. John's lingering scent.

No vampires here, Madison told herself, wondering how she knew that, and how she was going to ditch the detective after making it plain that she was ailing, and not a lunatic.

She'd be safe here at the hospital, she supposed. But if she couldn't perceive St. John, maybe he wouldn't be able to find her, either. And what good would hiding do, in the end, when nothing could be gained that way? Could a doctor, or the detective, explain to her what the dark under her feet meant?

D.I. Crane, her self-appointed bodyguard, leaned against a bookshelf, looking as fatigued as she felt. The lines on his face had deepened. He hadn't smiled one time.

The honeymoon was over.

"Don't you have business to attend to?" she finally asked as they awaited the doctor on call.

"You're it," Crane replied.

"I can take it from here."

"I'll just make sure that's true."

He observed her a bit too carefully, she decided.

"I'm here of my own free will, Detective."

"So am I," Crane said.

Not the truth, she wanted to tell him. A vampire had issued a demand for her safety with the mental voodoo in his repertoire, and Crane had unknowingly become St. John's puppet.

If St. John could command the cops, would nothing prevent him from doing whatever the hell he wanted to?

A few minutes more, she decided, and then she'd be out of here. Someone would tell her where St. John lived. He'd tell her what the darkness was, and what she was supposed to do.

When the doctor arrived, he first glanced to her, then to the detective. She saw something unsaid pass between them.

"Possible shock. Possible sleepwalker," Crane explained.

"Another one?" the doctor asked.

Crane shrugged.

"There appears to be an epidemic of sleepwalking every time we have a full moon," the doctor, whose shirt was embroidered with the name D. Dillon, remarked.

"Why would that be the case?" Madison asked.

"It's as good an alibi as anything else for unusual behavior," Crane said.

Madison listened for sarcasm in this odd pronouncement, and came up short. The detective had been serious.

"Of course," he continued, with another glance to the doctor pressing a stethoscope to her chest, "if you'd care to elaborate on what you were doing crawling out of a sixth-story window, we can probably forego the meds."

"I told you. I was tired and trying to get away from the scrutiny of cops at my door."

"Actually, you told me you were going out to look for your brother. So which is it, sleep deprivation messing with your actions, or slipping out to find your twin?"

To the doctor, Crane added, "Can you just give her something so she can sleep, and a secure room she can do that in?"

"I think I can manage that," the doctor agreed.

"Screw the meds," Madison snapped. "I'm all right now."

"That's a matter of opinion." Crane showed her a text message on his cell from someone at his department that read, Keep her there.

"Besides," Crane went on as she tried to get to her feet. "What do you have in mind in terms of a destination, if you were to leave?"

"I need to find Christopher St. John's house," she said.

"Sorry," Crane said. "That's just not an option."

When Madison glanced down, a needle was heading for her arm.

She felt a sharp prick, tasted something funny in her mouth, and the walls went slack.

St. John spun to face the west.

The first Hunter had arrived in London proper, and was nosing around. Its feel was slimy, and oiled up the air.

He cursed in the old English language, out of a habit too ingrained to break. Leaving Madison in the detective's hands was the only way to track this new burden. He had put all of his considerable weight behind the request to keep her safe and out of the way. But he felt Madison stirring. He felt her growing rebelliousness.

Theirs was a preordained attraction—the mesmerizing relationship of one kind of hunter to the species she was designed to hunt. A female to male pairing was how the vampire versus Slayer thing usually manifested, creating a unique bond between opposites that was so deep-seated as to be sexual in nature.

Definitely sexual in nature.

Each time he closed his eyes, he felt her sultry heat.

Madison couldn't have sidelined this attraction any more than he could have. The draw of a Slayer to her target, and vice versa, went back in history nearly as far as vampires had been in existence.

The origins of the enticement for a vampire and a Slayer to find each other were ingrained needs set in place for that purpose. Cells calling to cells. One kind of life calling to another kind. A signal from one genetic mutant to another that had evolved over time.

Slayers were the second universal check against one of this world's many anomalies. Protectors like himself had been the first line of defense in maintaining balance in the world between species.

Although the tale of how the first Slayer had been born and activated wasn't information he possessed, the goals and objectives driving Madison, once she realized who she was, would be similar. Rid the world of the plague of vampirism. She had to be made to realize this.

Her brother had been the true anomaly here. Stewart had been a male Slayer with no roots to any of his opposites, carrying the Slayer building blocks only because he had shared a womb with his twin. Stewart therefore hadn't been as strong as Madison would ultimately be. He had the urge to find vampires, without the internal backup necessary to perform the task.

Still, Christopher St. John wasn't a vampire, and explanations for what he really was couldn't be forthcoming to a Slayer or anyone else, whether he wanted her or not. He was different. Not a vampire, but a chosen immortal. His life was to be kept secret.

The thought of losing Madison sickened him. His tie to a vow that separated him from all others sickened him. And yet he would go endlessly on. Alone, if he had to. If Madison refused to use their connection to further their bond.

He sniffed the air and looked up at the sky.

It was possible that the detective could handle a Slayer coming into her own for a while, though the arrival of a full moon wasn't going to help. A full moon brought out all sorts of Others. Vampires, Madison truly would be sorry to find, weren't the only species trolling the streets.

Traitors like Simon Monteforte also walked among the shadows. Stewart Chase's bane. The ancient entity that Stewart had found in London had changed everything.

Recognizing Stewart as a Slayer and a potential problem to his own plans, Monteforte must have sent his dogs after Madison's brother. Something as simple as one word to the wrong monster had removed one Slayer, and now threatened another.

The haze was starting to lift. Pieces on the game board were already shifting. Yet St. John couldn't be in two places at once, no matter how fast he was.

He would take care of the Nosferatu, and teach Monteforte a lesson. He prayed that Simon would be waiting when he returned from sparring with the monsters, and that he could get his hands on the Frenchman's pasty neck.

The tattoos carved into his back undulated in anticipation of the events to come, reminding him that through those sigils there was one other possibility of help open to him for aid, should he need or decide to take it.

Using the power of those sigils, a call could be made to those of his own brethren still able to heed the signal they themselves had created for such a purpose.

Who among the other Blood Knights, he wondered, resided within calling range? He had no idea what direction their existence had taken them.

And he wanted Simon Monteforte for himself.

Contracting his muscles to savor the thought of seeing even one of the Seven again, St. John again sniffed the air.

"Stewart?" he said. "Come out."

The infected Slayer, so close St. John could reach out and touch him, didn't oblige.

"I would never hurt her, Stewart. Not ever. This I swear," he said. "Just as I never would have harmed you. We fight for the same things."

No reply.

"Monteforte," St. John said. "He's the one who found you?"

"Monteforte," came the echo from the shadows. And then Madison's brother's scent faded rapidly between the buildings, as if it had just wafted away.

Confirmation. Damnation.

St. John smelled the air again, turned his head and let out a low growl of displeasure.

It wasn't Nosferatu that captured his attention at the moment, though, or vampire hunters. It was *her*. Madison was going to slip D.I. Crane's net and get into trouble. Her intentions surfed his skin like a bad sunburn.

Can't have that, my love.

Not even if it meant postponing his meeting with the

monsters for a while longer. Letting those creatures get closer.

Spinning, he said to the fetid odor in the distance that was the Nosferatu's unique calling card, "Not long now, I promise."

Then he raced for the hospital where Madison Chase, and his heart, lay.

Chapter 21

Madison's limbs felt heavy. Her throat was dry. But she was awake.

She kept her eyes closed.

"She's been out for ten minutes," a voice said.

"Can we lock the door?" asked another.

"Sorry. It is a hospital, when all is said and done. Don't worry. She'll be out for two hours, at least. Have you gotten any rest, Crane?"

"You saw the news?"

"You've found one of those four girls."

"We've found them all."

"What?"

"They're in pretty bad shape. We had a tip that led to finding them. This woman on the bed gave us that tip. I can't go into it any more than that. All four girls are on their way here right now."

"Well, thank heavens for that. I have a large stash of sedatives here if you need a little something for the stress."

"You know I can't do that, and that I appreciate the offer."

"Actually, I wouldn't have offered if I'd assumed you'd accept."

"You didn't have to tell me that, Doc. I thought maybe you were being nice for once."

Sensing someone's approach by the sound of rubber-soled shoes on a linoleum floor, Madison kept still and squeezed her eyes tighter.

Under the sheet covering her, she fisted her fingers, grasping for an object out of reach: a sliver of the bedpost in her hotel room; a wooden weapon like the one tucked inside her brother's leather jacket. It was true that she knew what those things could be used for. She wondered if something as simple as a stake could be used against whatever was heading their way, and if St. John would be able to stop its progress.

"She's moving," a voice noted.

"She isn't comatose, Crane, just sedated."

"Can I leave her in your care for an hour, at most, while I check on those girls, and make sure their parents are with them?"

"Of course. Miss Chase will be fine here."

"She won't get out?"

"Crane, if she gets out after what I've given her, she's not human."

Guessing I'm not completely human, then, Madison concluded, waiting for the opportunity to get to her feet.

The first Blood Hunter had reached Wimbledon, heading in a straight line for the city. Its presence was vague because it had used the Underground tunnels en route to its destination.

This monster's master had trained it well.

He would soon find out how well.

But first, a detour.

London's Central Hospital rose before him. As was usual on a weekend night, the place bustled. St. John went in. He headed for the E.R., tracing Madison's scent on the ceiling, the walls and the floor.

The detective had been wise to bring her here, where her sweet scent could be partially masked for most of the creatures looking for it. No doubt Monteforte would be salivating for the taste of another budding Slayer, now that he'd seen her.

Foregoing the elevator, he opted for the stairs. His skin continued its pattern of twitches and undulations under his black sweater as he strode to a room where Madison's scent was the strongest.

She wasn't there. The bed was still warm.

"Madison, you little fool," he whispered.

He went through the adjoining door, and into the next room, which was also empty. Then he started back down the hallway, driven by a vicious need to find her.

He came face-to-face with the one man he didn't particularly want to see at the moment. "You've lost her," he said cuttingly to the detective, who had stopped to return his stare.

Crane anxiously looked past St. John. "Hell. She's gone? That's not supposed to be possible."

"You were to watch her," St. John said.

"Do you give the orders in this hospital now, too?"

"Isn't it common sense, Detective, to keep her out of

trouble while searching for her brother? At least, I'd have thought so."

"Not that it's any of your business," Crane said.

Arguing wouldn't get him anywhere. St. John passed the detective in a hurry, nearly brushing shoulders with him in the narrow hospital hallway. Two steps beyond the cop, he paused with the hair at the nape of his neck bristling. Turning his head, he gave the detective a last glance, and grimaced.

"What?" Detective Crane snapped, anger creasing his features.

St. John kept walking.

Back on the street, he dialed up more of his senses. Picking up the faint trace of the fragrance of orange blossoms nearby, he started in that direction.

Madison continued at a sluggish pace up the street, slowed by drugged limbs and feeling as if she were dreaming.

The night seemed darker than usual and saturated with smells. The old bricks of the building facades she passed gave off odors of weak, trapped sunlight eating away at rampant, aged mildew. The sidewalk stank of the thousands of feet that had used it that day.

Without her cell phone and wallet, hailing a cab was useless. Though her hotel wasn't far, she had no intention of returning there. The guys would be celebrating their video coup. Their work would pick up again in the morning. Joining them probably would be expected, but was also the first place D.I. Crane would look for her after discovering she'd escaped.

She needed a breath of fresh, untainted air, and wasn't finding it. Unsure of where to go, what to do or how to deal with the truth about the existence of vampires, she found London doubly ominous now.

Before seeing St. John's fangs, she had vowed to pressure the monsters in the media. That idea had fallen away, with no viable way to resurrect it. By shining light on monsters, she'd be placing her entire crew in danger, and maybe a good section of London's human population.

"Where are you, St. John?"

Did vampires prefer the lower floors of buildings? Basement apartments? Coffins? London was huge. The odds of finding him without outside help were slim, and she'd left the detective and his resources behind.

What she could do was test her own version of speaking to him via their strange internal connection. It was only fair for communication to work both ways.

Nothing to lose.

Waiting for a break in the line of people on the street, she looked up and spoke loudly. "Okay, St. John. You're all I have. Bring it on. I'm here, and I'm listening."

"Good," he said clearly, in a voice that definitely hadn't come from inside her head.

Madison had appeared before him like a desert mirage, spreading flickers of familiar fire throughout his body that he now knew were meant to be warnings, but what the hell.

She leaned against a building with her eyes raised skyward. Her face and lips were bloodless. Dampness gathered on her forehead. The cloying odor of drugs hung in the air.

His heart lurched when she met his gaze.

"It worked," she said, just as she had on the dance

floor the first night he'd seen her in person. "Imagine that," she added.

The desire to hold her beat at him as fiercely as if they were normal people finding something special in each other in a normal world, when nothing could have been further from the truth.

St. John held himself back.

"They gave me a sedative." Her words slurred. "I'm probably helpless if your intention is to harm me."

"Harming you never entered the picture," he said. "I'd have thought you had figured that out by now."

"Your nature is to…" She left that remark unfinished, took a rattling breath and started over. "Can you get me off this street? My legs aren't working properly. People are staring, and will recognize me. I haven't the money for a cab."

"Will you trust me now?" he asked her.

"Do I have a choice?"

Her eyes held to his as if she'd seek the truth there and know it when she saw it. If she had any intuitive knowledge of how this meeting affected him, she gave no indication.

"I give you my word that your safety is foremost in my mind," he said. "You know that I'm not the only one looking for you."

"The detective is a good enough guy." She lowered her gaze. "It's just that he can't fill in the blanks. Only you can do that, and you'll have to if you help me now."

"Can you walk?"

"Made it this far, didn't I?"

"You're less than a block from the hospital," he said. "I can see it from here."

Her eyes rose to his again, briefly and unfocused. "Am I to believe what you say because you never lie?"

"Quibbling over semantics seems silly when there's so much at stake," he countered. "In any case, you asked for my help, when being near to me at the moment is an added danger."

"Is that some kind of disclaimer?"

St. John smiled. "I suppose it is."

"That old man in that hotel lobby has it out for you," she said, surprising him again with her insight and her candor. "Am I right?"

"I believe so."

"He is a vampire?"

He nodded. "A very old one."

Madison blinked slowly. "I knew it without knowing how I knew it. So, where will you take me?"

"To my home."

"No. Not there. It's too intimate. Too private and personal. I was going to find it. But now that I see you, I…"

"You'll be safe there," he said. "Only there."

"Safe from who?"

He knew what she meant, and that she was thinking of a kiss and a hardwood floor and the potential hazard of his fangs.

"Protector," she muttered weakly, though St. John perceived her strength and wits recovering with an astounding swiftness that only someone with her kind of secrets had the power to pull off.

The bit of darkness he had discovered when he had first observed her now lay like a fine film over her skin, changing her skin's tone. Some of that darkness curled upward, foglike, over her spinal column.

In addition, his scrutiny turned up something else.

In the center of Madison, a new skill set was building,

even as she drunkenly staggered. Her body was uploading a program that was her birthright to possess.

That tiny illumination inside her would soon get brighter. Already she'd find strengths to tap into if she figured out how to access them. She'd made it here through the meds.

When he roused from thought, he found her attentive.

"I have to know," she said, "what that look was about. What our strange relationship means, if it isn't supposed to be."

"There's so little time left, Madison." He offered her his hand, assuming she'd back away, as she had done the first time he had wanted to touch her.

Then again, he had to acknowledge how far they had come since that original meeting, where she'd been nothing more than Stewart Chase's sister, a potential media pain in the backside, and he hadn't shown her his teeth.

Clearly, and in spite of everything since that first meeting, Madison's hunger remained, relayed to him by the soft gleam in her eyes.

Yet also inside those big blues of hers lay another clue about her oncoming evolution. Sparks of liquid silver swam there, as if a ghost were sharing her vision. The ghost of what she was to become, not long from now, if he kept her with him much longer.

She knew about the dark river coming their way. She was maturing before his eyes, with no way for him to turn back time, or start over. By remaining close to her, he would have no way to stop her transformation, and transformation might be her only way to cope with what lay ahead.

He just didn't care about any of that. He no longer wanted to take one single breath, real or otherwise, that didn't contain the scent of orange blossoms.

Madison was special. She was, in essence, a fighting machine with a nose for the supernatural, and the enemy of all those who had begun their new lives by drinking the blood of another. She was halfway to her heritage already, and sparring with the learning curve.

"So very little time," he repeated as she voluntarily placed her fingers on his upturned palm. "I will explain as much as I can before then."

She had touched him because she wanted to, had chosen to, and the pleasure this gave him was extreme. Hers was the first touch he had allowed, in any manner, in a few hundred years.

His heart beat faster, keeping time with hers. Without thinking of an action that possibly harked back to the days when chivalry ruled the land as the foremost rule of behavior, he brought her knuckles to his lips.

"Too easy," she said breathlessly. "Need answers."

"You won't like what you hear," he warned. "You might not remember what came before those answers. I'll regret that, Madison. I'll regret it deeply, I swear."

No longer hindered by having to keep some of his identity hidden from the woman beside him, St. John swept Madison into his arms. Not because she needed to be carried, or even would allow it, but because it might truly be the last closeness offered them, and he wanted to take full advantage of the minutes left.

Turning on his heels, gripping her tightly, he and the Slayer he had bonded with, for good or ill, became one more shadow in an already troublesome night.

Chapter 22

Wind whipped through Madison's hair. Buildings moved past as if they were made of rubber. Streetlights left thin streams of luminous thread suspended in the air.

The surroundings passed by at a fantastical pace as she and St. John rushed through it, seemingly shredding all known theories of time and space.

St. John hadn't lied about being exceptionally fast. He was also stronger than anything she had imagined. She hoped that her trust in him was warranted, but a debilitating fear of vampires hadn't entered the picture. Her stomach hadn't turned over.

Cohesive thought patterns were returning. She no longer felt heavy with fatigue. The reason she allowed St. John to carry her was that he was so much faster than she. And because he still had a fight ahead.

Her plan had always been to be self-sufficient, and

most people perceived her to be. Madison Chase, they thought, was strong, independent and forthright. Her very private fear was that by giving in to St. John, or anyone who got close enough to mine the gaps in her plan, she'd lose some crucial part of herself. That was a feeble thought, she admitted now, when a vampire had hold of her and she had delved her fingers into his thick blond hair for no other reason than she liked the feel of him.

This special being carrying her had helped her that first night to escape the rogue vampire gang who'd had her in their sights. He had checked to make sure she was all right, she now felt sure, using her hotel window when she was at her most vulnerable, unconscious, asleep, without disturbing her.

St. John had provided the information about the Yale girls being at the other hotel and had taken her there, intending to help her find them. Because of that, the girls had been found, Crane had said. The girls were safe.

Jesus, they were safe.

St. John and his tip about the Germand hotel had proved that he had a tender side. He had proved this over and over, as a matter of fact.

He had come to her after her ordeal in the abandoned apartment, keyed up and worried about what she had been through. His features had registered pain and guilt and sorrow over having left her open to that awful event.

They had kissed, screwed their brains out and shown evidence of their feelings for each other in one way or another each time they met. A quickly formed kinship had taken the place of fear and wonder. In spite of what St. John was, and what he'd told her she was, they always found each other.

Finally, most importantly, St. John had allowed her to

see him, sharing a confidence that could turn out to be harmful to him in the long run. He didn't have to let her know his secret, or view his fangs. He had trusted her.

In all their time together, and through all those things, he had not harmed her in any way, or shown an inkling of an intent to harm her.

The truth was…she had feelings for him. Deep feelings. For a vampire.

Vampires, he had told her, had been people once upon a time. Some of them could and did adhere to the path of virtue. Not all of them were evil bloodsuckers.

Bigger, stronger, twice the presence of anyone else. That had been her first impression of the man on the club balcony. This remained as obvious to her now as it had then. It was indeed a special kind of being that held her.

"God help me," she whispered. "I think I'm falling in love with you."

When she again looked up, they were exiting an antiquated elevator, the kind historical warehouses used, made of an open-weave iron mesh with visible cables.

Time regained its foothold after having brakes applied to its wheels, dumping them into a lofty open space filled, not with dungeonlike darkness, but brilliant wood floors and long spans of floor-to-ceiling glass.

Bewildered, Madison stared at St. John's refuge as her head cleared away the last remnants of the sedative.

"No one has seen this place," he said, setting her on her feet. "Except you."

Madison faced him. He still had a stabilizing hand on her elbow. "What are you, really?" she asked.

"First. Can you repeat what you just said?"

"I said I think I'm falling in love with you."

She watched him close his eyes.

"So, now that I have admitted that, what are you really?" she pressed.

"Immortal," he said.

"Another term for vampire."

He shook his head, corrected her gently, his voice little more than a sigh. "Not a vampire, Madison. The source from which vampires spring."

"You…make them? Make vampires?"

Another shake of his head tossed his golden hair away from his cheekbones. She would have touched his face, had they been real lovers having a reunion. As real lovers, human lovers, she would have remained in his arms.

"I do not make them. I fight against those who do, as you soon will," he said.

"You've got that wrong. It's my brother who carries a stake."

Without pausing, she spoke again. "You are older than the vampires on the street, and in the club, right?"

His affirmation was a nod.

"You are different," she pressed.

"Yes."

"There is a distinction, then, between the term you used, *immortal,* and vampires? A real difference?"

"A vast one."

"I have to know if there are others like you. Not vampires. Immortals."

"Only a few."

"In London?"

"There are immortals in London. Old vampires we call Ancients."

"Not like you, though. Not exactly like you."

"No. Not like me."

"Stewart wrote that the club, Space, along with half

of London, is owned by vampires." She gestured to the stunning room around her. "This is yours?"

"Not material gain by way of tyranny or theft," he said. "Only a long succession of careful acquisitions."

She nodded, feeling the pressure of time's passage, and St. John's need to confront what lay beyond those windows.

"The creature in Germand's lobby is a vampire, you said. An old one."

"Vampires are what most Ancients originally were before they learned to control their appetites."

Madison waited out a beat of silence before continuing. "If they don't feed on mortals, how do they sustain themselves?"

"As a vampire ages, it loses the necessity for sustenance."

"Does that mean they live on air? Regular food?"

"They must take in blood now and then, when necessary, but only if it's offered freely. That's the way it's supposed to go, anyway."

"Except when they feel like biting somebody for fun, like in the good old days?"

St. John remained patient, his voice quiet. "The Ancients in this city are supposed to forego their beginnings and their pasts. They've evolved."

"All of them?"

He frowned. "They have taken vows to, if not fit in with the mortals surrounding them, come close to doing so. They stay away from people and are lucky to have made it this far without being hunted and killed. They are well provided for with stocks of blood, kept stored for needs that arise and willing donors who are well paid for their services."

Though Madison winced at the *donor* part, she took all this in ravenously.

"They have formed their own community here," St. John continued. "They do more good than harm, for the most part."

"How many? How many of the old ones are there?" she asked.

"I can't tell you that for reasons which will soon be made clear."

"Can an Ancient die? Again? Can you?" She didn't wait for his reply. "Just how ancient are you?"

"Older than you. Older than the rest."

"Are there females among these Ancients?"

This was a selfish question. The thought of females like him, tall and elegant and hurtfully beautiful, brought on a wave of jealousy she could barely contain.

St. John read this, and smiled. "None. No females."

"Why not? If you mention the words *weaker sex,* I'll stake you myself."

Something she had said caused him to smile again. Madison sensed a fresh round of heat beating at the air between them.

"Actually, I'm not sure why," he finally replied.

"You've never asked?"

"It never mattered."

His answer took some time to absorb. She'd been correct, then, when she had touched his bare back and thought his reaction odd. He hadn't been handled by a female for years.

How many years?

She wanted to be the only one to ever touch him, and ever get near to him. She felt an icy blast of jealousy for this creature beside her that was so very much the male she wanted.

"If you're not like the others, why are you here?" she asked.

"I have a task to do, and have been building up to it."

"Where does the term *Protector* come in?"

"I serve the Hundred in a guiding capacity, when I choose to. I help them to deal with mortals and keep their secrets, a job that suits us all, for now."

"Mortals like me," Madison said.

She held up a hand, as if asking him to hold off on answering her. "Why would they believe you'd serve them in any capacity, if I can see the flaw in that in about two seconds, and that you're so much more than they probably are?"

Did he smile again? She thought he did, though the darkness outside the glass wall now hid all but the outline of the contours of his face.

She was aware of the line of his shoulders. Aware of the fall of his hair and the lean hardness of his hands. She tried desperately to erect a barrier against the notice of those things, hoping to section off her feelings. It was more than the masculine attributes of this figure beside her she craved, though the exact meaning of what she needed from him still remained out of reach.

"They don't know everything about me," he said. "And serving them serves my purpose."

"Now I sense a change in you, St. John," Madison said.

"That purpose has almost been satisfied, after a very long time."

Madison watched him, soaking up every detail.

"I believe that my brother came to London to find all

of you, for a reason I can't comprehend," she said. "Not to kill you. Not as a vampire hunter. Stewart used the case he was working on as an excuse to get here, where he had something else in mind."

"Yes," he said. "It is possible that your brother had other motives."

Excited, Madison pressed on, desperate to know everything.

"Possible, or probable?"

She placed her hands against St. John's chest, ready to shove the answers out of him if necessary. Finally, they were getting somewhere. Half the questions had answers. Surely he sensed her frustration over him withholding the rest.

Against her palms, she felt the hardness of muscle and bone beneath his sweater. She felt a beat, and wanted to damn this creature whose heart worked much in the way a mortal man's would, each stroke strong and sure and as fast as her own. Each stroke seeming to bring her closer to him.

Beside her stood a being whose pulse was a mockery of life. The forces invigorating him should have disappeared, fading to nothing on the day he had died.

God, yes. St. John had died.

Did the remembrance of that death pain him, as it pained her to think of it? Was that the source of his dark demeanor?

She knew in that moment that she did truly love him, in spite of all that. In spite of knowing about him.

The acknowledgment of her emotions wasn't a shock. It was depressing. St. John was a special being, even within the tiers of special beings. He had a job to do that might soon take him from her. And though he'd said she was special, she was still mortal, and would eventually, after finding her brother, go home.

Twisting the fine weave of his sweater between her fingers, Madison felt the steady throb of his heartbeat reverberate in her forearms, shoulders, chest and the pit of her stomach. She had always tuned in to Christopher St. John as if they were fatefully connected. This made them closer than normal, and incessantly intimate.

"If Stewart wanted to chase vampires, he could have done so anywhere. But he came here, Christopher," she said.

It was the first time she had used his given name. Madison observed how his expression softened.

"Your brother came here to find himself," he said, his velvet voice husky. "He tried to distance himself from you, having to leave you behind in order to find answers."

Her grasp on his sweater tightened. She didn't have time to think about ruining the expensive cashmere, or the fact that St. John was already facing the door.

"His wasn't a completely selfish action," he said. "Your brother also came here to find those girls, hoping to pick up their trail, meaning to ask for direction from those who could find out what had happened to them."

"The Ancients," she said.

"Yes."

"You knew who he was?"

"I saw him once. By that time, it was too late to help."

"Too late? What do you mean?"

The immortal male she clung to remained silent for a short time. Then, as if he had considered what he was about to say from all angles, he said, "Stewart killed a vampire when eyes were watching. No one could have saved him from what came after."

Hearing this, Madison wanted to change her plea. She wasn't ready for this. How could anyone be ready, no matter how desperate they were for facts?

"What did Stewart want to find out about himself?" she demanded.

St. John's hands covered her own, inflicting a level of pleasure and support that by all rights should have been torture. Madison allowed the sparks flickering between them to fuel her depleted energy.

Her voice emerged strongly. "I love my brother. I deserve to know what happened to him. You must see that."

Yes, she was feeling stronger now. She felt ready.

"The police believe I'm withholding evidence and hiding Stewart's whereabouts," she said. "They assume I'm purposefully hampering their investigation, and will charge me eventually unless I give them something. I don't have anything to offer them. I don't know where Stewart is, or what he is doing."

"Maybe that's a blessing in disguise," St. John suggested.

"Not a blessing. I think you know that. I think you understand. They think he might have killed a girl."

"Yes," he said so softly that Madison wasn't sure she heard him at all. "You deserve to know more, though not from me."

"From you," she argued. "I want to hear it from you. Who will tell me if you don't?"

She planted her legs apart in case the information he might eventually provide turned out to be as outrageous as everything else so far. She decided not to let him go until she had something more, and planned to block his exit if he tried to get away.

"Stewart can tell you. He should tell you," he said.

"If he could be found."

St. John nodded, and hesitated again, as if considering what she'd said. "Your brother was bitten," he finally said.

"Bitten?" Madison repeated.

"Stewart was what you are. A Slayer. He thought his strength might help when facing the Ancients. The problem was that he wasn't strong enough to actually find them. The old one he did discover was the wrong one. I know this now. Stewart didn't have a chance to get the information on the girls that he sought. Fledglings found him, sent by a bigger monster. Too many of them. I'm sorry, Madison."

Madison tried to make sense of this explanation, without success. "Bitten," she said, reeling from the idea. "Are you saying that my brother is one of them now? He is a vampire?"

"Not one of them, exactly."

"Then Stewart is alive? He's okay?"

When St. John didn't immediately reply, Madison knew that more bad news was coming. She snapped her body straight. As if to steady her, St. John pressed his chest tightly to hers.

Her ears filled with the sizzling buzz of a lightning streak, and the sound hadn't come from outside the wall of windows, where the moon shone brightly. The charge had originated right there, from St. John's touch. He continued to affect her this way.

But instincts about what he might say next were warning her to beware, pay attention, run away, suggesting that she actually was unprepared for the explanations to come.

She hung on, filled with dread.

"Madison," he began, using her name like a lover's caress. "Your brother is killing vampires. He is staking vampires because he has to. Stewart is killing them because that is his destiny, even though he has become something like those he chases."

Madison saw in the smooth planes of St. John's hard, proud face that he had told the truth. He had given her what she had asked for. It was up to her to connect the dots.

Stewart was a Slayer *and* a vampire.

Was that even possible?

What kind of special monster did that sort of mixture make?

St. John broke away from her. He moved toward the windows and looked out. His face, his expression, his demeanor had changed again when he glanced back at her.

With trepidation, he said, "You'll have to let the rest ride for now, my love. Time is up. The first of the Nosferatu has arrived."

Madison had no idea what Nosferatu meant, though the word was more terrible than anything she had heard so far, and struck fear into her bones.

St. John was going to face some dreadful beast. Maybe more than one. He seemed calm enough about the upcoming engagement, when a dark river was carrying monsters closer.

Christopher St. John's expression was gentle when he looked at her, showing his worry and his concern for her. Monsters had arrived, and his thought wasn't for himself.

Looking to the window, and the red-tinted night outside it, Madison felt like screaming.

Chapter 23

"If you stay here, you'll be safe."

St. John said this from the doorway, and in a way that made Madison want to weep.

"I've taken great care to keep this place hidden," he said. "Possibly for just such a night as this one."

Madison moved toward him, willfully making her feet move.

"I have to go," he said quietly, his voice the draw for her that it always had been. "So much depends on what happens now."

"Who is going to help you? Does the detective know?" she asked.

St. John shook his head. "Stay here, Madison. I'd have you safe, you know. Always."

"My brother is still out there."

"I couldn't stop them from biting him. I didn't know

until it was too late. You must believe that I would have tried to stop it."

She nodded. "He helped me. Stewart didn't hurt me. He isn't a monster."

"I don't know what he is now," St. John confessed. "No one really knows."

St. John pulled her hands from his sweater, and held them clasped in his for a few seconds longer. "Wait for me here, my love," he said. "Please."

"Not knowing what will happen to you out there?"

"For now," he said. "Just for now."

"What if I do love you?" Her voice was faint. "What happens then?"

"It would make everything I have ever done worthwhile," St. John said.

His voice echoed in the wide expanse of space he had called his refuge. It echoed inside Madison.

She had told him the thing she had barely admitted to herself. Love, she had said. What if she loved him.

It was a fascinating word to describe the complex emotions that had somehow entangled them both. There was no explanation for how it had arrived between two beings that had spent so little time together. But what was time, after all?

Did caring for another person, really caring about them and what happened to them, constitute being in love? Did the fact that she ached for St. John prove the truth of her feelings?

When she opened her eyes, she was alone.

Her immortal lover had gone.

"It would make everything I have ever done worthwhile," St. John had said, if she loved him. She didn't know how she would cope if he didn't return.

Her brother had come here to help those missing girls, and that had gone wrong. She had come here to find Stewart, and how would she categorize what had happened to her since?

Although she had felt strong the moment before, the room began to revolve around her as St. John's presence faded. She seemed to feel those enemies closing in.

However, this wasn't about enemies. The spinning sensation had been caused by the recognition of a title that she was afraid now defined her. A title that could keep her from St. John forever, if it were true.

That word lit up her mind, lit up St. John's apartment, reflecting off the windows, hitting her eyes with an uncomfortable glare.

Slayer.

She was what her brother was, St. John had told her, and it had been Stewart's downfall.

It wasn't a choice or an option, St. John had led her to believe. Genetics determined who would be a vampire hunter. *Born to it,* was the way this went.

Her parents had produced a set of Slayers without letting their children know. Their silence, before their deaths, had resulted in Stewart being nearly killed because he wasn't strong enough to hold his own when he came here.

Nearly killed.

She clung to that. St. John had said her brother had been bitten. Not killed. He hadn't used that awful death word.

There was hope. In a world threatened by darkness, there was some light, and she was starved for light.

"I believe you," she whispered to St. John. "I trust you."

She had to confess everything.

"If what you say is true, I see the horror of the future. I will be the one running through the shadows with a wooden weapon in my hand. I will be seeking fanged creatures that will know how to fight back. I will do so in your honor."

When the flash of rightness came, streaking past her vision in prisms of multicolored light, Madison realized it was a sign of her soul opening up to what had been hidden there.

Slayer.

She held tight on legs that no longer wanted to support her. It all seemed too much.

After taking a step, she crumpled to the floor, refusing to give in to the waiting void that offered a temporary respite from the world, its secrets and what part she would play in it after this, if she chose.

How could she make it work, when she loved an immortal soul that she had been born to fight?

Love...

Opposites...

St. John had gone to confront a wave of unspeakable terror taking shape. *Them. Nosferatu.* But he had seen to her safety first. He cared for her that much.

Using the window for support, Madison picked herself up. Pushing back her fear, she sent her senses inward, in search of the thing St. John said had long lain dormant inside her.

What she found instead was Stewart's voice, calling. "Maddie. Mad one...."

It was a voice she had to find.

St. John emerged from the Tube station through a blocked-off exit used by underground workers. He soon found what he was seeking. The creature was grotesque in the simplicity of its design, a tall, slender beast with the bone-pale face of the dead.

Nosferatu. Eternally damned, savage vampires with the bite of a bear trap and no remembrance of a soul. Creatures with no thoughts of their own, and no heart-beat.

At first sight, its features were human enough, save for the mouth and eyes. With its dead-white skin, its lips glowed red, as if it had been snacking on some poor soul on its way here.

Its eye sockets were black, bottomless holes, sur-rounded by circles of more blackness. Sparse, stringy hair, as white as its face, covered only the bottom por-tion of its head, curtaining large pointed ears.

The rank odor of death trailed behind this Hunter like a kite. Moldy earth, fetid flesh, death trapped in a body. Once free of the exit, the monster moved with a gliding motion, as if on skates, never seeming to actu-ally touch the ground.

Its long, threadbare coat kicked up dust and debris as its arms swung menacingly at the air. This ungodly en-tity, not of the earth or what lay below, had been created to mock both places as a mindless beast on the rampage.

St. John observed it from the rooftop above, standing half hidden behind a sign made of the same kind of steel beams that reinforced his apartment, though these beams weren't silver-coated. Vampires couldn't detect anything through exposed metal. Metal, like sunlight, could hurt them, become the true end of them if coated. If silver pierced unholy flesh in the right place, they were dust.

In this day and age, a silver bullet through the head or through the empty cavity that had once held a heart was the quickest way to take down a monster like this one. A quick, final death that could be issued from a distance.

But that was too easy.

Since his own new existence had begun with drinking from a golden cup, he was exempt from the problems of metal. He had exposed himself to all kinds after that, and had for long years carried both shield and sword.

This hideous Nosferatu had caught a scent. Lifting its chin to sniff the air, it then swung around, searching for the source of the smell, failing to look up, perhaps sensing and disliking the heavy tonnage of beams.

The game of the moment had become hide-and-seek.

Unable to trace what it had scented, the beast's narrow head cocked once before its body went completely motionless, like a statue carved from a block of flawed marble. It didn't blink because it didn't have to, didn't breathe because it had no need for air, and never had to fake breath in order to fit in with any other kind of society.

Not even its long coat moved.

St. John heard its thoughts, and they weren't pretty. The mantra was a cycle of hatred, disgust and bloodlust looped together. He felt its venom and the chaos holding the white carcass together.

This sucker was a forerunner, the first trickle of a nightmarish stream of monsters on their way. It was also alone at the moment.

St. John's tattoos became a barely tolerable ball of fire, calling up the strength of his background, urging him to action. For the sake of the people of London, who might get in the way at any moment, and for the sake of everything he'd given up in his own past in order to prevent such a circumstance as this one from happening, he had to deal with this crazy sucker and the flood of others behind it, quickly.

Walking to the edge of the rooftop, he braced himself. With the wind on his face and his power rising swiftly to the surface of his skin, he began, measure by measure, to shed his disguise.

Chapter 24

Madison's heart hammered. Restlessness returned.

"Stewart?" she said.

She pressed her forehead to the glass.

The street below St. John's apartment was dark. A big moon rode the sky behind a bank of black clouds.

St. John was out there somewhere, chasing demons. Her brother was out there, too, waiting for her.

The glass felt cool against her fingertips. The night beyond the glass resonated with indistinguishable shapes, and movement. Even St. John's refuge wasn't immune from the pressure of those things.

She didn't know how to help St. John. If she tried, she might distract him. She could go after her brother, though. One of those shadows on the street below might be Stewart. In finding Stewart, she'd find herself.

As she turned for the door, rage began to build inside

her for whoever had hurt her brother. She didn't feel particularly brave or courageous. The thought of having to go outside, for any reason, made her stomach roil.

Damn it, though, she had to go out there, ignoring St. John's *"Please."*

Unable to stand the suspense, and with her missing courage overruled by sheer determination, Madison headed for the door.

"I'm sorry," she said to the ghost of Christopher St. John. "You, of all…people, should understand."

"You're looking for me?" St. John called out to the monster on the sidewalk, landing quietly beside it.

The thing had no tongue, making a reply impossible. Nor did it possess a functioning brain able to process surprise or fear. Nosferatu were terrors designed only for one purpose—to hunt their prey. They were ghosts of the worst parts of the human psyche. Animals, really, with one-track desires.

They wouldn't notice St. John's glowing white skin that had burned through his clothes, or the ripples of extraordinary muscle fueled by a mythical resurrection. They wouldn't be afraid of the halo of golden hair radiating outward as if he were a dark angel, or the reddened gleam of his Maker's blood tinting his eyes.

The beast's black sockets trained on St. John. He felt a shudder of satisfaction run through it.

St. John smiled. This one wasn't so very old, and therefore inexperienced.

"They sent only one of you?" he remarked as the creature moved first one arm, then the other, as though thawing from a deep freeze. "You do know what I am?"

The creature lunged so fast, it became a colorless

smear. St. John, with equal speed, sidestepped the thrust of a specially made knife, pulled from the monster's pocket. He had only seconds to study that weapon, forged of both gold and silver, one of those ingredients the same as the chalice that had changed him.

Someone had their facts straight about the Grail, too. But most facts having to do with the Seven who drank from that holy cup were erroneous.

The Nosferatu spun in place and lunged again, catching the edge of St. John's sweater where only traces of it remained, clinging to his waistband. In a burst of extraordinary speed, St. John raised his arms, spreading the blooded sigils carved into him—the sigils that responded to the Nosferatu with an almost audible whine.

Cool London mist clung to his bareness as he widened his stance. The scars crisscrossing his body became livid reminders of past battles, each one of them scalding the cooler skin around them.

His tattoos burned hotter than the depths of the hell the monster beside him had sprung from. Not a cold burn this time. Powerfully hot.

His power focused.

He felt himself growing further into the terrible entity he had been created to be. The one he had to be in order to best the worst of the villains.

More muscle was there for the asking. His shoulders stretched, pulling at his bones. He heard his spine crackle with a live energy conceived of centuries of righteousness, after having being born in the dark. The two worlds met in his body, throwing sparks and shadow that were divinely beautiful and fiendishly terrible.

The Hunter came on, fast, strong, determined. Before it had moved too far, he had the thing by its throat and its weapon in his hand. As the Hunter's eyes locked with his, St. John sunk the knife deeply into the creature's gaunt chest.

"Are you an example of what I can expect?" he said to the monster. "Because that would be nice."

There was an explosion of body parts, and a rain of mottled gray ash. St. John watched the ash fall, thinking that killing this beast had been alarmingly simple for a Blood Knight in pursuit of peace. There had been no fight to speak of. Not this time. This had been a warning. Merely a hint of what was to follow.

More monsters were coming. Two of them had entered London from another direction. Another slithered in their wake in the old tunnels beneath the city.

Their approach filled St. John with rage.

With the weapon grasped tightly in his hand, he paused. Raising his eyes to the sky, he was struck by a new pain. Madison had left the safety of his refuge. Her voice reached him along the thread tying them together.

"I'm sorry. You, of all...people, should understand."

Muttering a sharp *"No!"* across the link connecting him to her, St. John sucked in a lungful of the crackling power that was his immortal birthright, and turned back toward the city.

Madison crept from the safety of St. John's building with her nerves on fire.

Stepping to the street, she waited, listening for footsteps, finding some and thinking that vampires probably moved soundlessly, and that footsteps meant the two figures she'd seen from the window had to be people. Humans. Mortals.

If she possessed the special genetics of a vampire

Slayer, shouldn't she have been able to tell the difference between men and monsters?

Other than the footsteps retreating into the distance, the night was eerily silent. Long shadows, cast by the moon, made the street look seriously *noir*. She sensed nothing. Not one special trait kicked in to help her.

Setting her shoulders, gritting her teeth, she stepped off the curb. She walked to the center of the narrow street. There were no passing cabs or cars. The moon shone from straight up in the sky.

Ears straining, she felt the slow seep of a rising panic, not knowing which way to go, or what to do.

She ventured a call. "Stewart?"

Movement behind her spun her around. She hadn't heard this coming....

That was her last thought before a black-eyed monster, its appearance unimaginable even in nightmares, threw her to the pavement with a simple flick of its wrist.

The arrival of the Nosferatu sat like a bad taste in St. John's mouth. The fear of them meeting Madison, if that were to happen, fueled his outrage.

He twitched the thread connecting her to him as he sprinted street by street toward his apartment, and found that thread unreasonably taut. Across it, he heard Madison's scream.

Utilizing every bit of the power he had so carefully hidden, he raced on, fearful for the first time he could recall, and calculating how long it would take him to get to her.

Turning one last corner, his speed too fast to raise dust or debris, he slammed to a halt in front of two of the monsters he had sensed.

One of them leaned over Madison, who was stretched out on the ground.

"At last," Simon Monteforte said. "We see the Protector in action."

St. John flicked his eyes to Madison. Her breathing came in gasps, but her heart beat strongly. The Nosferatu hadn't harmed her because she wasn't on his radar.

"What is it you want, Simon?" he asked, his tone deadly serious.

"Look at you," Monteforte said. "You're some kind of freakish angel, not one of us. You've never been one of us, and the others are too self-absorbed to see it. You glow from within, special, pale and pretty. You have the blood of angels in you, as well as your Maker's. Due to this, you have hidden yourself well from the Ancients. But you haven't fooled me. I want to be like you. I want you to tell me how to make that possible."

"What is it you want, Simon?"

"The thing you've kept hidden from us. From me."

"Name that thing you'd do all of this for," St. John said.

"Power."

"I'd have thought you had enough power. You are one of the Hundred."

Monteforte waved that suggestion away with a subtle twist of his fingers. "That's ninety-nine vampires too many."

St. John stood his ground, his bare chest reflecting the moonlight, his arms tense at his sides.

"What you want isn't possible," he said. "You know it."

"I will have the Grail, St. John."

"The Grail is a legend."

"As are you, supposedly, and yet your light blinds me. Which one of the Seven Blood Knights are you? The first? The last? I've paid a lot of people, some of them immortal, some not, to find out about you. And here you were, in our midst, the whole time."

St. John observed the ancient traitor closely. Monteforte stank of this selfish greed. With Nosferatu by his side, under his spell, and Madison at his feet, Monteforte posed a real threat. He'd hurt Madison if given the opportunity, in order to hurt St. John.

However, St. John's expanded senses perceived another visitor in the shadows of the overhang of the building to his right. Someone not on the Nosferatu's radar, either, since the monster hadn't turned to look. Oddly enough, neither had Simon Monteforte, whose attention remained locked to St. John as if the old vampire's greed had indeed blinded him to anything other than getting his way.

St. John's sigils pulsed, the danger in them building until his back was crawling with movement indicating the promise of what he could do to the old vampire in seconds if Madison hadn't been involved.

It was a strange time to discover just how much he loved her, and to realize the extent of the agony he'd suffer if he were to lose her, or leave her behind.

"What would you do with the power you seek?" he asked Monteforte to gain time.

"Rule the world, as you and the others of your kind could, if you chose. Surely you've considered doing so?"

Monteforte gave a signal that amounted to little more than a slight raising of his hand, and the black-eyed monster took a gliding step forward.

Something else moved, as well. The shadow lurk-

ing near the building came on fast, and St. John heard
Madison's intake of breath when she, too, identified who
it was.

By then it was too late for Monteforte to ignore his
surroundings. Casually, as if facing a conspirator, the old
vampire glanced sideways. He said to Madison's brother,
"I thought we took care of you, Stewart. Pity you didn't
stay down."

When confronted with so many monsters, hell had no
option but to break loose.

Chapter 25

The horrid, twisted creature holding her had let go. Scrambling sideways, Madison knew better than to run to any of the beings here for assistance. There wasn't a mortal among them.

"Stewart," she said.

Her brother didn't respond, or look her way. Stewart's face, free of the shadows that had hidden it, told her all she needed to know.

Stewart was parchment-pale, and gaunt to the point of starvation. His face was sharp, cold and soberly intent. He wore a dark shirt, partially tattered, and an old pair of jeans, torn at the knees. His hair was disheveled, with long streaks of gray running through the red-auburn color.

He didn't look strong, or completely alive. Yet Stewart had again arrived when needed, as though he had been keeping watch over her all this time.

With a snap of her head, she swept her gaze to St. John, who had also become someone else. Some*thing* else. Bigger. Painfully beautiful. Altered both in shape and content, he radiated power that was visible as it crossed his skin, as if power were waves of moving muscle.

He was the personification of the knights of old, and radiated with the glory of angels. A human made more than human. A being apart from the rules governing reality.

Madison could hardly look at him, and yet couldn't make herself look away. She had heard the conversation between him and Monteforte, and the old vampire's accusations: something about St. John being able to rule the world if he wanted to.

His half-naked body gleamed with the luster of a south-sea pearl as he met the wiry, black-eyed monster rushing at him. The dichotomy of the twisted flesh of the monster meeting with St. John's fierce, deadly light, was breathtaking.

The impact of their bodies hitting was loud in the quiet of the night. The monster moved with incredible speed, but it was clear from the start that the beast had no chance against its superior counterpart.

St. John reeked of power. The air had become electrified with it.

And he had purposefully left the gray-haired vampire he had called Monteforte for Stewart to deal with—which suggested to Madison that Stewart had met the velvet-clad monster before.

This was the Ancient that St. John had said was the wrong one for Stewart to have found, and was the creep in the Germand's lobby. Simon Monteforte was the beast who had betrayed her twin's confidence.

Madison didn't know where to look, or what to do. The fighting had started in two places, and her attention remained glued to her lover.

On his back, covering an expansive space from shoulder blade to shoulder blade, a fiery design burned in the night as if it were a live flame. The tattoos looked like a blaze of wings about to unfurl. Unearthly. Beautiful. Angry. Unlike anything else in existence.

He had told her there was no other like him.

Shaking off her stupor, Madison finally tore her gaze from him to see that her brother had circled the old gray-haired vampire. In Stewart's gloved hand a knife glinted wickedly in the moonlight. Silver. Metal for killing vampires, if the aim was true.

The vampire St. John had addressed as Monteforte wore a feral expression of sly cunning. Her brother's face remained dangerously expressionless, as if emotion had been stripped from him, along with parts of his former life.

Monteforte was wild, and frightening. He seemed to her a deadly foe in the sheer length of his existence alone. Still, her twin moved as though that didn't matter. Sustained by vampire blood passed to him through the savage bites of Monteforte's vampires, and therefore maybe even Monteforte himself, her twin, because of his heritage and his destiny, had beat the odds of death's two-fisted knock.

It was too damn incredible an event to go unnoticed on a public street. Alerted to movement in the shadows, Madison jumped sideways to meet it. Through their bond, she shared St. John's awareness of another monster, not too distant, on its way.

She didn't have time to confront that oncoming shadow. Another shadow beside it pushed her out of the way and stood in her place.

Madison held her breath.

If this was another Nosferatu, the good guys here, no matter how strong they were, would be outnumbered.

Uncertain now as to where to look, fearing for her brother, wanting to watch St. John, she felt her chest begin to ache from the riotous beating of her heart.

She had to do something.

Madison flung herself at Simon Monteforte, ramming into him with every ounce of strength she possessed. Monteforte tilted sideways. Recovering quickly, he rounded back to Stewart.

Her brother had been prepared. He swung himself off-balance as Monteforte struck with both hands, and righted himself with a graceful lunge. Stewart's arm came down in an arc, slashing at shadows, his silver knife coming up red with the old vampire's blood. But the knife hadn't hit its mark. It had been impossible to see, let alone find Monteforte's chest, in his flurry of seemingly effortless moves.

Nevertheless, Monteforte had been struck. And that one thing created a lucky gap in the fight.

Scenting the blood, St. John's ravenous Nosferatu made a sharp turn. An error in judgment that allowed St. John's strong fingers to find its throat.

With the force of a whirlwind, St. John yanked the beast backward. The monster fell back, writhing against its capture, too energetic and focused on the scent of blood in the air to be held for long.

But St. John hung on to it, his muscles corded, and a look of defiance on his face. It was a terrible dance of power. And it gave Madison the courage she needed.

She lunged again at the monster keeping pace with her brother, and who was flinging blood from his wounds in all directions.

Tossing herself at the old vampire a second time, she knocked him into her brother. Stewart moved with a practiced precision, whirling in place, raising the knife, bringing it down.

More blood tinted the blade of his knife, but the old vampire continued to move.

God, how she hated vampires!

Stewart didn't register the slightest bit of fear. Madison was terrified. Across her overworked, inflamed nerve fibers, she sensed the imminent approach of the newcomer. Not only one newcomer, she sensed, but two.

Fueled by fear and a surge of adrenaline that shot through her, she hurled herself at Monteforte, who appeared suddenly to her right. Instead of connecting with anything solid, two strong hands caught her and flung her aside.

Rebounding from the wall, ready to go at it again, Madison hesitated when she recognized one of the newcomers on the scene. He stood on the outskirts of the area of fighting wearing an expression of disgust on his lined, familiar face.

That newcomer was D.I. Crane.

St. John threw the Nosferatu to the ground, aware of the bloodlust that had overcome its instructions to take a Blood Knight down.

The scent of its own master's blood was driving the

creature mad. If he let the Nosferatu loose, it would go after the source of that blood, potentially helping to solve everyone's immediate problems. But his thought was for Madison, who didn't need to witness what a frenzied vampire could do. Or what he, himself, would have to do to stop the monster.

With the beast trapped between his foot and the pavement, he threw a calm look over his shoulder at the tall figure that had come late to the party. *That damned detective.*

Too late now for excuses or disguises. The cat was very obviously out of the bag. And though he didn't need help, Stewart Chase might. He had given Stewart a chance to take his own revenge out on Monteforte, but a second pair of hands when dealing with an aged entity like Monteforte was probably always welcome.

Especially when Detective Inspector Ellis Crane was so much more than a second pair of hands.

St. John glanced up at the moon, then down at Crane, who stood beneath the overhang of the buildings.

"Wrong party for you," he said to the detective.

"Every party in this city is my party," the detective snarled in reply.

St. John shrugged, and nodded to the detective. "Want to get your hands dirty?"

"I'd like nothing better," Crane said, tossing a revolver to Madison with the harsh directive, "Silver bullets," and "Watch your aim." Then Detective Inspector Crane began to let his own beast out.

The wet, flesh-morphing, bone-cracking sounds of a man shifting into another shape made Madison cringe. What was happening to the detective went flagrantly against nature.

The detective's shoulders widened. He grew taller, as if the moon overhead was stretching him closer to it. Muscle built upon muscle, as if someone had just poured more onto his frame.

His face lengthened. More bones cracked and heaved. He tipped forward from the waist, as if the whole process hurt him greatly. And when he stood up again, seconds later, a creature that was half man, half beast looked out of big black eyes from a feral-featured face above a body covered by a brown fur pelt.

It was official, Madison thought. She had entered another dimension.

The detective's gun felt cool in her hand, and heavier than she'd have expected. She knew what silver bullets were for. Killing monsters of all kinds.

The good detective was a goddamn werewolf, and had come prepared because of the full moon and the antics he'd said ran amok beneath it.

With trembling hands, Madison raised the gun, thinking she should fire on them all—all of London's monsters. Narrowing her focus, squeezing the trigger, she went for Monteforte, who was clinging to Stewart with fingers like talons.

Kicked back slightly by the force of the shot, she heard nothing from the old vampire. Seconds later, a great howl split the night. God, had she missed, and hit the werewolf instead?

No, not the detective. He growled deep in his throat with a sound that was scary as hell.

Madison spun in place in time to see him leap toward the shadows on the curb, where another impossibly frightening, twisted creature had appeared. Setting her stance, she again used both hands to hoist the gun. Aiming at the quick-moving Monteforte, she fired.

Her brother suddenly stopped wrestling. The shadows dancing with him coagulated, showing an angry Monteforte holding his chest.

St. John let loose of the monster he'd been holding down, and in a blurred instant was at Madison's side, taking the gun from her, pressing her out of the way, his wide shoulders hiding the view of creatures killing creatures in a last-second turnaround.

But anyone for miles could have heard the terrible noises these beasts were making, Madison thought. The night rang with gut-wrenching nightmarish sounds of flesh tearing and gluttonous beasts ravaging each other.

St. John, beside her, tried to disguise those terrible sounds. "Good shot, my lovely, beautiful Madison," he whispered to her. "It's almost over, my love."

An explosion rocked the area. Then another, followed by a third. Three explosions, after which a rain of thick gray ash began to fall, appearing like snow, smelling foul. The ash of the final death of three vampire abominations obliterated everything in the area, other than the moonlight.

A hand appeared on St. John's shoulder, pushing him aside. Stewart's face peered into hers, tense, white, skeletal.

"I'm sorry," she said to her twin. "I didn't know."

She started over, feeling sobs choke her throat.

"I'm sorry for ruining your revenge with that gun. And for what happened to you. And for what you are."

Throwing her arms around him, she hugged her brother tight. He didn't immediately respond. It took him a minute to hug her back. When he finally closed his arms around her, it felt as though she had found that missing piece of herself again. It felt like heaven. She had her brother back.

But Stewart pulled back and stepped away. Mutely, he turned to go.

"Wait! Stewart, wait!" she cried. "It's okay. I swear it's okay."

Could she blame him for being wary, though, when Stewart knew he had become another kind of demon?

"We're going to go home," she told him. "We're going to be together, no matter what. We'll both see to that, and whatever it takes."

She turned to the werewolf, who thankfully had changed back into a bare-chested detective glowing with sweat. She had to find her voice. "My brother didn't harm that girl. He will swear to that."

"Then I'm sure he will tell me everything he knows about it," Crane said, his voice gruff. "But I believe we have found the killers, thanks to your tip. St. John may have to do a bit of complying on his own, as to how to take care of that in a world where none of us are welcome. We'll have to spin the tale of that one girl's death into something believable—not to make light of it, you understand, but to protect the public."

"You went to the Germand?" St. John asked Crane.

Madison looked to her lover to find him St. John again. Merely that, on the surface, anyway, though his skin still seemed lit from within.

"The Germand. Disgusting place," Crane said. "No offense."

"You found the other girls?" St. John asked.

"All of them. Seems everyone wants to meet a vampire, and the girls were enticed by the prospect until they were actually faced with reality."

The detective paused for a grimace. "I don't get that. Blood is ugly. It tastes like hell. But we're lucky we found them. Janis Blake had escaped once, and they'd caught up with her. The girls were hysterical when we found them."

All eyes shifted to Stewart, who nodded. His voice emerged roughly, as though he hadn't used it lately.

"I found that dead girl," he said.

"Yes, well, your DNA, taken from your sister's hands, will be of no use, of course. The lab will cop to making a mistake, since the sample will be all messed up. The good news is that there is nothing to tie you to that murder. Nothing at all."

Crane turned to St. John. "The girls have fang marks on them. Some bastard bloodsucker had been snacking on them. Will this mean they also will be hungry eventually?"

"Did they drink, in return?" St. John asked.

"Not as far as I know. They were glad to be found, and have been taken to the hospital. Their parents have been notified, but if they're…"

"Give them a transfusion right away. Invent an excuse for that. If they didn't drink, or receive blood in return, they will likely be all right."

Loose screws…

Loose ends…

Madison's head hurt like a son of a gun.

She observed the scene in front of her, made up of St. John, in all his chiseled splendor, and Crane, looking mostly normal after his big, freaky surprise, and her brother, still there, whatever the hell Stewart had actually become…to find them all looking at her. Expecting her to what? Scream? Swoon?

"Yeah, right. Like that's going to happen," she said to them. "And it isn't as if I'm going to be able to tell anyone. Who the hell would believe it?"

"What about the Hundred?" Crane said.

"You mean the Ninety-Nine? You know about them, too?" St. John asked.

"No Lycan worth his salt can't tell a vampire from a hole in the ground," Crane said.

St. John grinned, looking very much like the St. John Madison was so uproariously in love with.

"I don't suppose they'll miss Monteforte," he said. "I'm not sure they ever knew about you," he added to Stewart. "Not for sure, anyway. I'm damned certain most of them didn't have any idea about what went on at the Germand. They can't afford to allow that kind of blasphemy against their rules."

His smile widened, showing two gleaming white fangs. "You will need to stop staking everything that moves, of course."

"Does the Hundred know about the detective here?" Madison threw Crane a look, still shaken up by that big, furry surprise.

Crane smiled back with a very wolfish expression that was in no way apologetic. "It's likely they do," he said.

"It's tough to hide the smell of a werewolf," St. John explained.

The detective grinned again. "That's what your look meant in the hospital hallway? You tagged me? Well, I wouldn't be so quick to call the kettle black, vampire. Most of you smell like burnt toast."

"And you," Madison whispered to Stewart. "What about you? Are you all right? Enough to come home?"

She directed a question to St. John. "Is that possible?"

He nodded. "Ocean liner. Darkened room. He can make it work if he wants to. He'll have to explain what the hell he is, and how that works, first."

Stewart's slump, Madison knew, was caused by the extremes of a relief he had no doubt lost sight and hope of. Though infused with vampire blood, enough of her twin remained in the mix, thanks, she supposed, to his Slayer base.

She wanted to cry with happiness over that one small thing. Her brother hadn't been taken from her forever. Hope shone in his eyes.

Although there was stuff to be cleared up, the Yale Four girls were alive. St. John was here. Stewart was here.

She doubted this kind of mess would happen again anytime soon in London. As St. John had said, a fringe community like those old vampires couldn't afford the attention.

So, what about her?

Where did she fit in?

Her network would be waiting for an update as soon as the story of finding the girls broke. She was going to break it. In spite of standing there in the moonlight with a vampire-hunter hybrid, an immortal she loved more than anything else on the earth, and a werewolf cop—all of those things part of London's dirty little secrets—she still had a job to do.

In spite of everything.

And because of everything.

She still had the energy to do it. Help clean this up. Put a shiny new spin on the news.

There were vampires in London, the biggest story of all, the story of a lifetime, and she couldn't tell that story. Her life, and the lives of many others, depended on her silence.

The world depended on it.

"Shall I take you back to your hotel?" the werewolf detective asked her.

She couldn't have taken a first step, if she had accepted that offer. The almost heart-rending expression of sadness on St. John's face kept her rooted in place.

That sadness told her she had one more thing left to do. She had to make peace with her own immortal obsession.

When he held out a hand, as if he had heard her thoughts, her brother stepped forward.

"It's okay," she said to Stewart. "He is the Protector, you know. My Protector. Can you go to my hotel, Stewart? Will you go, and wait for me there, please? I can't lose you again. We'll do everything possible to make you comfortable, I promise. The detective can let you in. Cops have ways to do that. This—" she gestured to St. John "—is important."

Crane and Stewart eyed each other warily. They were different species who had come together tonight for a common goal, but they didn't have to like it.

This was important.

She placed her hand in St. John's, feeling the familiar charge that hadn't lessened one bit. She wondered if this would be their last night together, and if he would move on now that his task had been accomplished.

He was one of Seven Blood Knights who could rule the world if they wanted to.

"One more night is not enough," St. John sent to her.

When she met his eyes, she said, "Not a Slayer. Nothing resembling a Slayer. There was some mistake. I was scared to death out here."

Before her next breath, and in a surge of motion that left her last remark trailing, they were running, together, toward shelter.

Chapter 26

St. John's bare body, perfectly proportioned and as powerful as poured steel, was a thing of beauty in whatever incarnation, and carved by a master artist's hand. A partly unsteady hand. Evidence of that artist's slip of the chisel showed in the long lines of ridged scar tissue that glowed whiter, grittier than the rest of his undisturbed flesh, and curved around the sides of his rib cage.

In what now seemed like ages ago, Madison had felt those ridges with her fingers and wondered who had dared to hurt him. She now knew that many of his enemies, mortals and vampires alike, would try to do the same if they understood what his presence among them meant. Christopher St. John was no friend to vampires or monstrosities of any kind, though he had been born one.

Supposedly, she was his enemy, though they didn't view things that way. Big lessons had been learned during these days and nights in London. Not everything that appeared as black and white had to be perceived as polar opposites, when a vast area of gray ran between. Although most people considered this gray area negatively, an awareness of how vast that area was had changed her.

Meeting Christopher St. John had changed her.

He'd been mortal once. His life had been taken from him, exchanged for another kind of existence. He lived in that gray zone as an elegant, honorable, noble immortal whose past remained a mystery and whose immediate future rose above her as she gazed up at him from the bed.

She also lived in that gray zone, because she loved St. John with every fiber of her being. Someone, somewhere, might damn her for this, she supposed, but Madison didn't care. She thanked the heavens that he so obviously felt the same way about her.

Many loose ends had been tied up at last in London, but this one dangling thread remained above some unanswered others.

Their future.

They were in his refuge. She didn't remember anything between being on the street and on her back, in his bed.

He was completely naked, pale, perfect and more beautiful than anything she had ever seen. It was the first time she had seen all of him.

Eyeing the fullness of his erection, her body reacted with a quiver of anticipation. The word *glorious* came to mind.

Would the sky fall in if two beings created to eradicate each other came together in this way, repeatedly?

She'd seen no evidence in herself of the traits her twin

possessed, except for the dangerous attraction to vampires. Particularly her attraction to this one.

Just now, with her breath coming in great gasps, she wanted a physical culmination of their feelings.

Just this one last time. At least.

The scent of his bare skin filled her with heat as he came closer, as he leaned over to place his hands on the pillow behind her head. As she looked at him, taking in the exquisite length of his magnificent body, a beating, soulful longing made her heart soar.

This was the same longing she'd felt from the first sighting of him on that balcony, in the monsters' club, magnified a thousand times and manifesting here, inside her chest, and between her legs. If this was to be the last time, with him, she didn't know how she would cope.

"So much to do," she said to him. "And you see only me."

"You imagine I could see anything else?"

His expression was tender, sober, provocative. His eyes captured hers with a glint of blue-black fire.

"Do immortals remember what to do in times like this, after a fight?" she asked.

"Why don't you be the judge."

The tickle of silky hair on her cheek made her reach for the wide shoulders she wanted crushed to hers. She sighed with pleasure when his long arms wrapped around her, lifting her from the mattress.

He sat down beside her, holding her inches away from him for an agonizing minute more.

"I don't think you do remember," she said. "It's not supposed to take this long."

"You're afraid you will change your mind?"

"Hell, no."

His laughter mingled with the sound of fabric tearing. Madison felt a chill of cooler air, realizing without looking that she'd been rendered as naked as he was, and that she had been the one to forget the details, such as clothes getting in the way.

Even then, St. John didn't immediately release her. His lips stroked across hers, sending jolt after jolt of red-hot current through her, each strike turning up the heat and causing moisture to rush to the place she wanted him the most.

The hungry, completely savage meeting of their mouths came like rapture. The slick dance of their tongues sent her heartbeat into overdrive and her breasts straining upward, hard and aching for the attention of his heat, hoping for just one touch.

He laid her back without breaking the contact of that kiss. Her arms encircled his neck, muscles contracting to pull him to her until she felt the smooth seduction of his chest against hers at last.

Skin to skin…

She had imagined this would be a vigorous taking— his hardness, her need. But his kiss became deeper, slower, producing a similar effect to having his hands slide down her body, covering every inch.

She arched her back, ran her hands over his shoulders, mindful of the fiery tattoos that had glowed like a bonfire, feverishly tracing the grooves she found between his blades.

More sound came from her throat when she found those muscled shoulders rippling, and feverish.

Touching him there seemed to strip from him his ability to restrain himself. He murmured something incomprehensible as his body slid onto hers, stretching them both out on the sheets.

As he breathed her name into her mouth, his erection found the home that would welcome him. He wasn't one of the Seven here. He was Christopher St. John, lover, giver.

He eased only the swollen tip of his cock against her, holding back, seeming to need this kind of restraint.

Madison's body opened to him without effort or resistance. Her legs separated to grant him full access. She was damp, anxious and waiting, wanting to see where this meeting would take them, when she had to go home to Florida soon after.

When her moan of invitation reached him, St. John drew his hips back. Slowly, he sank his cock inside her, one glorious inch at a time.

It wasn't enough. Not by far.

Clutching at him, wanting to shout with the pleasure of the sensation of having him inside her, Madison spoke into his mouth. "Prove how much you want this. Prove it now."

Her remark caused another motion of his hips. He pressed into her with a faster, livelier thrust that he followed with more, until he wrenched a series of cries from her lips, locked to his.

Each sound she made quickened his pace, and drove him deeper between her legs. Madison tried to hold off the pleasure by squeezing herself around him. She didn't want this to be quick, or over too soon. She didn't want it ever to be over.

Mindless of the old injuries he had sustained, she clawed at his back. Her need was endless. He seemed to be sharing every sensation, which was perhaps why he was in no hurry to reach the place inside her that wanted him so desperately.

When he backed off, she growled. When his fingers traced her collarbone, and dipped between her breasts, she uttered a breathy protest.

Nothing else mattered in that instant, not her straining breasts, or any other body part. She wanted this. She wanted him. Why wasn't he listening to her? How could he wait?

His fingertip was cool against the flush of her overheated skin as it circled the raised pink flesh of her breast. He gave her a devastating smile before lowering his mouth there.

With a slow lap, his tongue danced over her. In reaction, she clutched at his hair. The draw, as he suckled her, struck all the way to her bones, ending up in a deep place between her thighs, near where his cock waited to satisfy her.

Writhing on the mattress, she arched her back, liking what he was doing, lost in the sensation of his mouth on her.

He wasn't inside her now, but so damn close.

His hand glided over her stomach, and between her hip bones. At the same time, his talented tongue aided his next draw on the tip of her breast. Her insides began to ache. She felt each throb of her pulse, and couldn't tell which sensation mattered most: mouth, fingers, lips? She refused to give up or give in to the whole, not wanting to miss any part of this.

It was so very good.

It might be the last.

God, not the last!

His lips gave a last soft pull on her breast before his

face came close to hers. His eyes sought hers with an intensity that drove her mad with desire for the promise she saw there.

"Don't even presume to read my mind," she murmured.

His eyes were all black now. She heard the drop of his fangs.

It was as if their souls knew what came next.

His plunge struck hard, rocking the bed on its foundation, reaching her core. Her breath whooshed out. Emotion released, spiraling upward within her to meet with the largeness of her need, crashing into it, spilling the emptiness out, filling it with something altogether new.

The air on her face became a colorful burst of brilliant light. Electric blue. Pink. White. She became one with that light as it ripped through her, scattering her senses to pieces.

Her body rose upward in a violent jerk of intensity. The edge of her physical pleasure was joined by her mind, and soon after that, her soul. She and this special being were wrapped together, not just along some nebulous thread, but everywhere possible. In all ways possible.

One more slight move of his hips, and he had her completely. Swept along by the explosion that rocked her was the ultimate gratification of a need being beautifully fulfilled.

Her lover began to shine. His back began to burn white-hot, scorching her fingertips. Madison felt as if they were lifted from the bed, from the world, wrapped intimately together.

There was a sensation of wind, or maybe the air caused by the movement of wings, on her face. The place St. John took her to was brilliant, colorless and yet filled with light.

Images filled her mind.

Knights riding on black horses. Black shields emblazoned with crests of fire. Stern, pale faces of men fighting, then gliding through gardens of grass, red roses and gurgling, water-filled fountains. And in the center of that fountain sat a sparkling golden cup, its rim covered in blood.

Her cry of ecstasy went on and on, echoing in the room, mingling with the visions, as her orgasm merged with St. John's long, deep groan of satisfaction.

It felt like hours before the climax backed off, and faded. It felt like hours before she even began to come down to earth.

The room had gone quiet after their cries and shouts. In the new silence, neither of them moved...until that quiet was severed by the unmistakable crunch of splintering wood.

Madison opened her eyes to find herself not beneath St. John, but on top of her lover, straddling his naked body as she had done once before, but this time holding a narrow length of wood, its sharpest edge centered on St. John's chest, where his unearthly heart continued to thunder.

His hand surrounded hers, on that stake, the weapon she'd sworn never to possess, as if he'd stop her from using it. As if she might have used it.

Bewildered, dazed, Madison blinked and met his eyes.

"Instincts," he said.

A slow grin lifted his face, a damnable expression she immediately adored, and a sign of his new ease with her.

The tips of his fangs gleamed from between the fullness of his lips. And though she wasn't so sure how she felt about the fangs, she loved those lips, loved the way shadows caressed his angular face.

In a Slayer, this would have been a problem. She didn't want anyone to remove St. John from the equation, from her future, by using such a weapon—especially herself, due to hidden instincts she refused to accept.

But she hadn't shown any tendency toward being a vampire hunter. So how had she ended up with a stake in her hand?

"We'll probably have to invest in a furniture store until you learn to control those instincts," he said. "You just destroyed the bedpost."

"I'm no Slayer," Madison protested. But she had pointed a weapon at him before realizing she had moved, seconds after they had climaxed together.

"No Slayer," she repeated.

His grin remained fixed. His eyes were softening, showing a hint of blue in the center. His tender expression registered empathy, because he also had become something other than mortal, once upon a time.

"You said that you can make monsters," she said breathlessly. "Will you make me one?"

"Like me, you mean?" He removed the stake from her fingers.

"Can you do it? Make someone like you?"

"Yes."

"Have you ever?"

"It is forbidden."

"Will you do it to me, anyway?"

"No, Madison."

"Because I'm something else already?"

"Even if you hadn't held that stake in your hand, I'd refuse."

"How else can we be together?"

St. John's smile wavered. Madison saw on his face dueling emotions of satisfaction and suffering that made her chest tighten.

"Are you saying you might learn to love me, Slayer, as the monster you may think me, or that you merely want a rematch?" he asked. "For old times' sake."

In response, Madison again found the crude stake clutched in her fingers. Swore to God, she didn't remember moving. Finding the weapon a second time had been as automatic and mindless as the first time.

St. John, able to move much faster, didn't stop her when the point of the stake touched his skin. His expression didn't change from that gentle, sad, knowing smile.

"Do you want to bite me?" she asked him. "Not *will* you do it, but do you *want* to?"

"I want to," he admitted.

"Will you always want to?"

"Just as you will want to point that thing at me," he replied.

"I didn't want to point this at you."

"You are waking to your destiny. It takes work, effort and vigilance to tamp those instincts down and then learn to control them. We will learn to adapt."

He'd said *we*. A flutter resulted, close to the place he had just found and conquered.

"I want to go home. Take Stewart home," Madison said.

"There are vampires in the States," he pointed out.

"I don't care if there are. I don't want to care."

He nodded, and said in a manner that told her he had considered the question before, "I wonder if Florida really smells like oranges."

Gauging the meaning of this caused Madison to feel anxious for a very specific reason. Back to that term… *we*.

There should have been concern over this. Yet the marvelous being beneath her had proved trustworthy several times over in the brief time she had known him. He had helped to lead the authorities to the missing girls. He had reunited her with her brother.

Christopher St. John had rid the world of one set of very bad vampires, and in the process, had saved her ass a couple of times. And he was better than brilliant in bed.

Better than anything in bed.

Her immortal lover had well earned her trust. As strange as it seemed, he also filled the pockets of emptiness that she had long harbored.

He was smiling, damn him.

He'd read that in her mind, too.

"Some of Florida smells that way," she said, answering his question long after he'd asked it. "Do you have a sudden craving for fruit?"

"Ever since I met you," he said.

Madison smiled, widely, fully, expectantly. That simple reply was his way of telling her that he would go with her to America. He didn't seek permission because he knew what her answer would be. Communication along the thread binding them worked both ways.

They were going to be together. Their unique relationship, merely beginning, had a long way to go, but looked promising.

Understatement.

Madison's face flushed. Intelligence warned that she should be running in the other direction. St. John's task

in London had finished. She assumed he'd have another
He was, after all, the Protector.

Maybe that new task would be aimed at taming her
and her terrible new instincts. Maybe he was *her* Protector, after all, and had been meant for that particular
task, all along.

"In time, you'll tell me about my genetics?" she said

Maybe he'd tell her what his title actually meant, and
about his life before and after being granted immortality.
Maybe he would tell her about that image of the garden,
and the fountain she'd envisioned in it.

She'd given up trying to picture St. John the mortal, the man, but there were enough of the good parts to
make her realize with perfect certainty how badly she
wanted him with her, whether she accepted her own bizarre destiny, or not.

"Yes," he replied. "I can do that. I can tell you some
of what you want to know."

"Some?"

His smile met her.

And well, damn. She had no idea how to make this
work. More questions would arise. More answers would
come. In the meantime...

There were vampires in Florida.

And plenty of beds.

Florida. A state large enough that freaks like Stewart and St. John and herself might go unnoticed if they
behaved. With two Slayers and an immortal the likes of
Christopher St. John about to descend, Miami's rogue
vampires didn't stand a chance.

Mere centimeters above her lover's pale skin, Madison
moved the tip of the stake, drawing her name in the air.

Slayer.

She said, "If that's what I'm going to be, whether I want it or not, I'd better face facts."

When St. John smiled up at her in earnest, the light in his face eager and hopeful, the blue in his eyes again receding into a flat, liquid black, Madison knew what this meant. She knew it before acknowledging the feel of his erection.

Handing him the stake, and with his hints about *forever* in her mind, Madison tossed the hair out of her eyes, squeezed her legs tighter around his hips…and smiled back.

* * * * *

JUST CAN'T GET ENOUGH
ROMANCE
Looking for more?

Harlequin has everything from contemporary, passionate and heartwarming to suspenseful and inspirational stories.

Whatever your mood,
we have a romance just for you!

Connect with us to find your next great read,
special offers and more.

Facebook.com/HarlequinBooks
Twitter.com/HarlequinBooks
HarlequinBlog.com
Harlequin.com/Newsletters

www.Harlequin.com

SERIESHALOAD

SPECIAL EXCERPT FROM

H HARLEQUIN®

ROMANTIC suspense

Discovering he's a father of a newborn, rodeo cowboy
Theo Colton turns to his new cook, Ellie, to help out as
nanny. But when Ellie's past returns to haunt her,
Theo's determined to protect her and the baby…
but who will protect his heart?

Read on for a sneak peek at

A SECRET COLTON BABY

by Karen Whiddon, the first novel in
The Coltons: Return to Wyoming miniseries.

"A man," Ellie gasped, pointing past where he stood, his
broad-shouldered body filling the doorway. "Dressed in
black, wearing a ski mask. He was trying to hurt Amelia."

And then the trembling started. She couldn't help it, despite the tiny infant she clutched close to her chest. Somehow, Theo seemed to sense this, as he gently took her arm
and steered her toward her bed.

"Sit," he ordered, taking the baby from her.

Reluctantly releasing Amelia, Ellie covered her face with
her hands. It had been a strange day, ever since the baby's
mother—a beautiful, elegant woman named Mimi Rand—
had shown up that morning insisting Theo was the father
and then collapsing. Mimi had been taken to the Dead River
clinic with a high fever and flulike symptoms. Theo had Ellie
looking after Amelia until everything could be sorted out.

But Theo had no way of knowing about Ellie's past, or th danger that seemed to follow her like a malicious shadow. " need to leave," she told him. "Right now, for Amelia's sake.

Theo stared at her, holding Amelia to his shoulder and bouncing her gently, so that her sobs died away to whimpers and then silence. The sight of the big cowboy and the tiny baby struck a kernel of warmth in Ellie's frozen heart.

"Leave?" Theo asked. "You just started work here a week ago. If it's because I asked you to take care of this baby until her mama recovers, I'll double your pay."

"It's not about the money." Though she could certainly use every penny she could earn. "I…I thought I was safe here. Clearly, that's not the case."

He frowned. "I can assure you…" Stopping, he handed her back the baby, holding her as gingerly as fragile china. "How about I check everything out? Is anything missing?"

And then Theo went into her bathroom. He cursed, and she knew. Her stalker had somehow found her.

Don't miss
A SECRET COLTON BABY
by Karen Whiddon,
available October 2014.

Available wherever

HARLEQUIN®

ROMANTIC suspense

books and ebooks are sold.

Heart-racing romance, high-stakes suspense!

Copyright © 2014 by Karen Whiddon

HRSEXPO914

ROMANTIC suspense

THE AGENT'S SURRENDER
by **Kimberly Van Meter**

Rival agents uncover a monstrous conspiracy

From the moment they met, sparks had flown...and not
the good kind. Agent Jane Fallon would rather chew nails
than work with arrogant—and much too good-looking—
Holden Archangelo. But, convinced his brother was no
traitor, Holden had Jane's investigation reopened.
And now Jane is forced to partner with him.

As new leads come to light, Jane's certainty about the
case is shaken. But the assassin's bullet whizzing past
her head convinces her they are onto something. Jane's
determined to keep things professional, but as the danger
around them intensifies, so does the fierce attraction they
try so hard to deny....

Look for *THE AGENT'S SURRENDER*
by Kimberly Van Meter
in October 2014.

Available wherever books and ebooks are sold.

Heart-racing romance, high-stakes suspense!

www.Harlequin.com

HRS27891

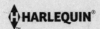

HARLEQUIN®

ROMANTIC suspense

Heart-racing romance, high-stakes suspense!

HIGH-STAKES BACHELOR
by Cindy Dees

More than hearts are at stake for a legendary Hollywood family in Cindy Dees' brand new miniseries, The Prescott Bachelors!

Wannabe stuntwoman Ana Izzolo can't believe she lands a starring role in actor-producer Jackson Prescott's new film. A plain-Jane nobody and a megastar? Their on-screen chemistry is electric, burning up the celluloid...but offscreen, Ana is stalked by danger.

Like a true Hollywood hero, Jackson whisks her to his oceanfront mansion, practicing love scenes while keeping her safe. But when their real-life relationship starts mirroring the movie's leading couple, the confirmed bachelor fears he may fall for the doe-eyed ingenue. If the stalker doesn't get her first....

Available **NOVEMBER 2014**

Wherever books and ebooks are sold

www.Harlequin.com

HRS78947

JUST CAN'T GET ENOUGH?

Join our social communities
and talk to us online.

You will have access to the latest
news on upcoming titles and special
promotions, but most importantly,
you can talk to other fans about your
favorite Harlequin reads.

Harlequin.com/Community

 Facebook.com/HarlequinBooks

Twitter.com/HarlequinBooks

Pinterest.com/HarlequinBooks

HSOCIAL

Love the Harlequin book you just read?

Your opinion matters.

Review this book on your favorite book site, review site, blog or your own social media properties and share your opinion with other readers!

Be sure to connect with us at:
Harlequin.com/Newsletters
Facebook.com/HarlequinBooks
Twitter.com/HarlequinBooks

HREVIEWS